NORTH STAR BRIDES

THREE-IN-ONE COLLECTION

ERICA VETSCH

BARBOUR
PUBLISHING

Print ISBN 978-1-62416-256-5

eBook Editions:
Adobe Digital Edition (.epub): 978-1-62416-441-5
Kindle and MobiPocket Edition (.prc): 978-1-62416-440-8

All scripture quotations, unless otherwise noted, are taken from the King James Version of the Bible.

This book is a work of fiction. Names, characters, places, and incidents are either products of the author's imagination or used fictitiously. Any similarity to actual people, organizations, and/or events is purely coincidental.

Cover image: Image Source

Published by Barbour Publishing, Inc., P.O. Box 719, Uhrichsville, Ohio 44683, www.barbourbooks.com

Our mission is to publish and distribute inspirational products offering exceptional value and biblical encouragement to the masses.

 Member of the
Evangelical Christian
Publishers Association

Printed in the United States of America.

Dear Readers,

I love stumbling upon a hitherto unknown-to-me bit of history and spinning a story around it. That's what happened when I first learned of an epic winter storm known as the Mataafa Blow that hit Lake Superior in 1905. And when I learned about the isolation and dedication of the lighthouse keepers on America's largest freshwater lake. And when I learned of the revolutionary changes made to Great Lakes ships to adapt them to their special task.

Each of these stories, The Bartered Bride, The Marriage Masquerade, and The Engineered Engagement, started out as a tiny spark of interest over an historical discovery. And because I love both history and romance, I can never resist combining the two. I hope you fall in love with the Kennebrae men and the women who come to love them, and that you'll discover a little about the remarkable history that has been made on and around the Great Lakes.

Many Blessings!
Erica Vetsch

THE BARTERED
BRIDE

Dedication

For Peter, Heather, and James Vetsch. All my love.

Chapter 1

The idea's preposterous, and I'll have nothing to do with it." Jonathan Kennebrae bolted from his chair and stalked across the office. "You won't manipulate me like this. And I doubt Noah or Eli will go along with the scheme either."

His grandfather, Abraham Kennebrae, sat ramrod straight behind the walnut desk. For a man confined to an invalid chair these past eight years, his voice still rang with authority and vigor. "I've spent a lifetime building up this family's fortune and power, and I want to die knowing it will continue. If not through you, then through your brothers. The best way to ensure this is to marry you boys off well. You act as if contracted marriage were something new. It's been going on for centuries."

Jonathan clasped his hands behind his back under his coattails and stared out the window of Grandfather's library. Two acres of emerald grass stretched below to the shoreline. Lake Superior spread before him, cobalt blue under an azure sky. The *Lady Genevieve,* the family yacht named for his grandmother, bobbed gently along the dock beside the boathouse. Her white hull gleamed; her mast pointed to the cloudless heavens. He wished he stood at her wheel, skimming over the waves, away from this incredible conversation.

"It's all arranged, Jonathan. Three weddings, three sound marriages, and the consolidation of four of the wealthiest families in Duluth. And not only that, but it brings together under one name all you need to control every aspect of this harbor: shipping, grain, ore, and lumber."

Jonathan turned and leaned against the windowsill. The morning sun fell through the stained glass of the upper windows, shattering rainbows on the Persian rug. He crossed his ankles, trying to appear casual. "All arranged? You and your cronies have everything mapped out? And Noah, Eli, and I have no say? Have you decided who is to marry whom, or were you just going to have us draw straws?"

His jaw ached, and the pain between his eyebrows increased. An image of Grandfather and his bewhiskered, cigar-smoking circle of friends bending over charts and arguing the relative merits of their offspring wavered before his eyes. "I have no intention of marrying an empty-headed showpiece chosen by you. Are your grandsons no more than pawns to be shuffled about at your command? Whose idea was this?" His throat ached with the desire to yell, but years of training and deference to the man before him kept his voice controlled.

"Now, lad"—Grandfather made a dismissing motion—"you make it sound worse than it is."

"I don't see how that's possible. I feel like a horse at auction. Did you sell us to the highest bidders?" Sarcasm dripped out, laced with exasperation.

Grandfather wagged a gnarled finger. "Don't take that tone with me. I'm still the head of this household. I made a sound business decision for this family. You'll accede to my wishes in this. You're nearly thirty. It's past time you were married and setting up your household. As a member of the aristocracy of this city and this state, you have an obligation to marry well."

"Shades of the Four Hundred." Jonathan jammed his hands into his pockets. "This is 1905, and your ideas are outdated. This isn't New York City. It's Duluth. I'm not marrying someone so I can be invited to better parties and promenade through Newport every afternoon during 'The Season.' And I'm certainly not interested in any female who wishes to marry for those reasons either."

"You couldn't be further from the truth. You aren't marrying into the salons of Fifth Avenue. You're marrying to gain control of the harbor." He waved his hand in a sweeping motion toward the lake. "Control that harbor, and you control millions of dollars. Control millions, and you control the politicians in St. Paul and Washington. Control St. Paul and Washington, and you control the power to make more millions. Don't you see it?"

"What if I don't want to control the harbor? What if I'm content with what I have: a solid business with an excellent reputation and a sound financial base?"

"Then you're a fool. You'll have wasted everything I've spent my life building up. Now is the time to strike. Of the four richest families in Duluth, I'm the only one with male heirs. Lawrence Brooke, Phillip Michaels, and Radcliffe Zahn have only daughters. And don't forget, a marriage to Lawrence Brooke's daughter brings not just the grain docks in the harbor but the railroad that hauls the grain from the Dakotas, too."

Jonathan ran his hand over his hair. "You still haven't convinced me. I don't even know these women. Why would I want to marry any of them?"

Grandfather thumped the blotter. "Stop being obtuse. I'll make it as plain as possible. You will court and marry the daughter of Lawrence Brooke, you will gain control of the grain docks in Duluth harbor, and you will do so before Christmas."

"Before Christmas? That's impossible. Christmas is less than three months away. Isn't that a bit quick?"

"Poppycock. I see no reason to wait. Waiting only increases the chances that something will go wrong. We must act now. You, as the eldest, will set an example for your brothers. The twins will fall in line. And it isn't as if the young women won't receive the benefits of a sound match. Wealth, status, security, influence. What more could a woman want?"

Jonathan snorted. "I'm no expert on the female mind. I have no idea what they want. But what happens if I don't do as you say? Or what if the woman won't have me?"

"I will disinherit you without so much as a blink." Grandfather regarded him with glittering eyes. "I will leave my fortune only to those grandsons who do my bidding. Those who will not, receive nothing. I've already rewritten my will to reflect the changes."

Anger replaced the exasperation and unbelief in Jonathan's chest. "You cannot be serious."

"I've never been more serious in my life." Grandfather narrowed his eyes and pursed his lips, causing his wiry side-whiskers to bristle out like a badger. "Do you care to challenge me? The will stands as long as the girl is legally free and morally acceptable for you to wed."

Jonathan's mind raced, and his muscles tensed. How dare that old reprobate? Kennebrae Shipping was his. He'd run the company, chaired the board, and overseen the day-to-day operations for the past eight years. He, not Grandfather, had expanded the fleet, brokered new contracts, enticed investors. The company was his life. He'd be dead before he'd let anyone take it from him.

A knock sounded on the library door. The butler entered, a silver tray in his hand. "This just arrived for you, sir." He extended the salver toward Grandfather.

The old man took an envelope from it and turned it in his hands.

"Will there be a reply, sir? The gentleman who delivered it is waiting."

Grandfather picked up his letter opener. He slit the heavy cream envelope and read, satisfaction spreading over his face. His fingers drummed the desktop.

Jonathan paced between the marble fireplace and the glass-front bookcases. Grandfather's words were no idle threat. He'd disinherit Jonathan without so much as a by-your-leave should Jonathan cross him. He had seen it in the old man's eyes. Galling, that's what it was. To have a bride chosen for him based upon her wealth and connections. And worse, to be chosen as a husband based on his.

Grandfather leaned forward and uncapped the silver inkwell. He dipped his ebony pen in the liquid and scratched a few words on the card. "McKay, give the gentleman this."

"Very good, sir."

The door had barely closed before Jonathan whirled from contemplating the oil painting over the mantel. "Do Noah and Eli know about this?"

"No, of course not. I'll tell Noah when he returns to the harbor, and I'll tell Eli when he returns from Virginia. Though why Eli can't learn shipbuilding right here in Duluth is beyond me."

"He wanted to learn from the best, and the best shipbuilders are on the East Coast." Jonathan rubbed his palm against the back of his neck. How could he get out of this? His strides measured the room.

"Will you stop pacing like a caged wolf? You'd think I was asking you to go to the gallows." Grandfather backed his chair and wheeled it around the edge of the desk. A blanket covered his stick-thin legs from hips to ankles.

Jonathan sagged onto the horsehair settee. "From what I can tell, marriage and hanging have a lot in common. The man ends up dangling from the end of a string either way."

Grandfather chuckled then shook his head. "Where'd you get an idea like that? Your grandmother, God rest her soul, was a fine woman."

"What about my parents? To hear you talk, they couldn't be in the same room without bloodshed. How they wound up with three sons is beyond me."

Sadness lined Grandfather's face. "Your parents were both high-strung. Always convinced the other was being a fool. But they loved each other, in their own way. I thought they'd settle down eventually. It's a shame you never got to know them. Your father couldn't live without her. The carriage accident was a mercy. He was never the same after your mother died. And neither were you, though you were only four at the time."

"I have no real memories of my parents, only their portraits in the drawing room."

"Those were your grandmother's idea. Had them painted from their engagement pictures. Thought it might be nice for you boys to have them."

Jonathan took note of the nostalgic look in Grandfather's eyes. If he could just keep him talking about old times, about Grandmother, perhaps he would forget this nonsense about marriage.

"She was a saint. And what she ever saw in an old boot like you, I'll never know."

"Hah! That's just what her parents said when I came courting. Never thought I'd amount to anything. But I showed them. Built up the biggest shipping line on the Great Lakes and built Kennebrae House for your grandmother, too. Nothing was too good for her."

"She deserved every one of the fifty-five rooms for putting up with you."

"Well, your new wife will, too."

Jonathan blew out a breath. So much for getting Grandfather off the subject. "I haven't agreed to this madness. Anyway, I think you're assuming a lot. I haven't even met this Miss Brooke. We might not suit one another at all."

"You're both young and rich. You'll suit one another just fine. How do you feel about music?"

"What?"

"I asked how you felt about music. An evening of music and fine food."

What kind of sidetrack was this? Jonathan put his guard firmly up.

The old man had a gleam in his eye, an unholy sparkle that boded no good.

"You mean one of those parties where the hostess shoves her daughter onstage, and the poor girl scrapes away at some writhing violin concerto or pounds out a tortured nocturne on the piano while the audience tries not to wince or die from boredom? And at dinner they make up compliments over dried-out chicken and pasty potatoes until they can make a graceful escape?"

"I hope it isn't as bad as you describe."

"What are you hatching?"

"The note that came earlier. It was an invitation to Castlebrooke. Mrs. Brooke is having an evening of music and refreshments tonight. I sent the reply that both of us would be delighted to attend. And you'll have ample time to study your bride-to-be. She'll be the one performing the tortured nocturnes."

Chapter 2

Melissa Brooke stared into her mirror and caught the reflection of her new evening gown hanging on the wardrobe behind her. A couture creation from the House of Worth in Paris, the gown was everything she'd dreamed it would be when she ordered it. Now if only her piano performance lived up to the dress. Should she attempt the Chopin or stay with the Mozart for the opening? Melissa bit the edge of her fingernail.

Sarah, her maid, ran a brush through Melissa's dark-brown hair and began the task of pinning the heavy curls up for the evening.

Mother swept into the room. "You'll ruin your manicure, Melissa, if you don't stop that dreadful habit." A tiny woman, Almina Brooke carried herself regally, appearing much taller. She paused before the wardrobe, tweaking the sleeves of Melissa's gown.

Melissa dropped her hand to her lap and made a face at her reflection.

"And stop that scowling. You'll get wrinkles." Mother, in her dressing gown but with her hair already styled, sat on the end of the powder-blue chaise longue. "The guests will arrive in a half hour or so. The servants have lit the gas lamps in the music room. I don't think this newfangled electricity burns as brightly. I told your father it was a fad when we built this place. But he wouldn't listen." She smoothed her yellow satin belt. "Are you nervous?"

"A little. How many people did you say would be attending?" Melissa winced as Sarah jerked at a snarl.

"Sorry, miss."

"Only a small soiree, dear—sixty people. Just right for the music room. Nothing too ostentatious. We want this gathering to be cozy and intimate. That's why you're the only musician tonight. I want you to be the centerpiece."

"You make me sound like a bowl of chrysanthemums." Melissa ignored the tiny wings flapping in her middle. "I think you and I have different ideas as to what constitutes small and intimate. Anyway, I thought this was more of a business evening for Father. He said he had associates attending."

"Actually, that's what I came to talk to you about. Tonight is a big night. Your father has invited two particularly important guests, and I'm counting on you to make a good impression, especially on one of them. Don't frown at me, young lady." She pointed a finger heavy with diamonds at Melissa. "It's time you were making wedding plans. You've had a debut to rival a

Vanderbilt's. If we lived in New York, you'd have had the cream of society calling on you, maybe even a titled European or two."

Melissa held hairpins up one at a time for Sarah. "I don't want all that. And I'm not ready to get married yet. I have so much I want to do before I think about marriage."

Mother sniffed down her nose. "Your so-called 'progressive' ideas. What you need is your own household to run and your own husband to look after so you'll forget this nonsense. Your father and I have worked very hard to find a suitable match for you, and you're not going to ruin it. You'll be polite, charming, and keep your radical ideas to yourself. You will impress your intended tonight with the fine manners I've gone to great lengths to instill in you."

Melissa put up a hand to still Sarah and looked at her mother in the mirror. "My intended?" Her hands fisted in her lap, the hairpins biting into her palm. "Just what does that mean?" A sick feeling of dread slithered through her middle.

"That means, young lady, that you have a responsibility as your father's only heir. We, your father and I, have been looking for a man capable of managing the fortune that will be yours. We have found such a man, and he will be in attendance tonight. He's of a good family and has an excellent head for business. It's a sound match. He'll manage your inheritance well."

"I should think an astute lawyer and a competent accountant could manage my funds quite well, and I wouldn't have to marry either of them." Heat tinged her cheeks. They'd found a husband for her? Based upon his financial prowess? "And what about my wants?"

"Nineteen is too young to know what you want. Trust me in this."

"Who is he? Do I know him?"

"No, I don't believe you've met him before. He's not much for social occasions. Doesn't go out much. And he's older than you, so he wouldn't have been in your social set. Your father has known him for years."

Older? How much older? Her thoughts galloped through a list of her father's friends. No one she would ever consider marrying came to mind. In fact, her father's business associates tended to be even older than he was. Visions of a rickety lecher danced between her and the mirror.

Mother checked the timepiece hanging from her lapel. "I don't have time to talk about it now. You'll meet him soon enough. Let Sarah finish your hair." Mother rose and pulled a velvet box from her dressing gown pocket. "I want you to wear this. It's perfect with your dress. And don't dawdle. You play at eight sharp."

"But, Mother—"

"Not another word on the subject, Melissa. Everything's already decided. The match is more than suitable, and your father will rest easy knowing an experienced businessman will be handling your inheritance. You should be thanking me. He'll be in the front row with your father, so play well." She swept out of the room, her words floating back over her shoulder.

Melissa stared at the door. A suitable match? To manage the business? And she was only so much baggage that went along with the handshake? She bit her fingernail again. How humiliating. Who was this man? No doubt some middle-aged, paunchy boardroom bore with fat fingers and a cashbox for a heart.

"There, miss. You look lovely." Sarah tucked one last curl up and stepped back.

Melissa turned her head to one side then the other. Three navy ostrich feathers curled airily from the back of her upswept hair. A diamond pin held them firm and sparkled in the light of the gas globes overhead.

"I'll help you with your dress." Sarah took down the evening gown, slipping it from the padded, satin hanger.

Melissa stood, her mind awhirl. How could she get out of this? Could she pretend to be sick? The way her stomach was pitching at the moment, there would be no need to pretend. With numb fingers she loosened her pink dressing gown and laid it on the bed.

She jumped when the veranda door blew open. Chills raced up her bare arms. The cool October breeze off the lake wafted in, billowing the lace sheers. More than anything, she wanted to escape to the water. Perhaps the scrape and gurgle of the waves on the rocky shoreline would afford her the peace she needed to see a way out of this.

"Miss?" Sarah unfastened the bodice in the back and held out the gown.

How long had they been planning this? How could they choose a husband for her without even asking her what she thought? And a man she'd never met. What had they promised him? Well, it didn't matter. She wasn't going to go along with this. She stepped into the dress and slid her arms through the sleeves.

Sarah finished hooking her up the back and turned Melissa to look in the full-length mirror in the corner. "Ah, miss, the gentlemen won't be able to look away from you tonight."

Melissa smoothed her hand down the bodice, the fabric slippery and cool under her palm. Yards of white satin gleamed in the lamplight. And over the bodice and skirt, a curly grillwork of appliquéd indigo velvet like a wrought-iron silhouette. The train curled around her feet. How happy she'd been when she'd chosen this dress. She adjusted the neckline and settled the short, white, puffed sleeves.

"Here's your gloves, miss. Do you want a fan tonight?" Sarah held out the blue gloves, so dark they were almost black.

Melissa shook her head. "I can't wear the gloves while I play. Fold them up and take them downstairs and have one of the footmen put them on one end of the piano bench. And no fan. I feel so awkward when I have one."

While Sarah hurried on her errand, Melissa paced her bedroom, her mind a muddle. How did Mother expect her to play tonight after tossing a bomb like this at her? At the moment, Melissa couldn't even remember the music she'd selected. Surely Mother wasn't serious. And yet, Almina Brooke never said anything she didn't mean.

Sarah hurried back into the room, her apron crackling with starch.

Melissa sat on the low dressing stool once more and opened the blue velvet case. Nested on a bed of white satin, sapphires and diamonds twinkled mysteriously. Melissa's shoulders drooped. The jewels were perfect with the gown. Mother had thought of everything, as if Melissa were no more than an objet d'art to be shown off and admired. And sold to the highest bidder.

Sarah gasped at the jewels. "Oh, miss, they're wonderful! You'll be the most beautiful lady at the party. If those don't give you confidence, nothing would. Your parents will be so pleased, especially your father. He takes such great pride in you." She clasped the glittering stones around Melissa's throat.

They rested against Melissa's skin as cold and heavy as her heart. Melissa attached the dangling earrings, teardrop sapphires surrounded by diamonds.

Father did take great pride in her. Not an easy man to get close to, he did share her love of music and took pleasure in hearing her play.

"Sarah, please lay out the things I will need for later."

"Oh, surely not tonight, miss? Not with the concert."

"Yes, tonight. It will be tricky, but I'll manage. And, Sarah, thank you. I couldn't do this without your help."

Melissa regarded her reflection once more. No moping. Her chin lifted. She was more than a trinket to be trotted out by her parents and shown off. She'd play their game for awhile tonight. And she would find a way out of this mess, or her name wasn't Melissa Diane Brooke.

Chapter 3

Skimming the waves in *The Lady Genevieve*. Riding his thoroughbred at a gallop over fences. Sealing the deal on a new shipping contract. Jonathan ran through a list of things he'd rather be doing at the moment. He stood to one side of the brightly lit foyer watching his grandfather, impeccable in black tie, greet their hostess.

"Ah, Almina, you look radiant." The old rogue took her hand and kissed the air over her diamond-dusted knuckles. "May I present my grandson, Jonathan Kennebrae?"

Jonathan took the matron's offered hand and bowed. "How do you do, Mrs. Brooke?" He refrained from saying it was a pleasure to meet her, not wanting to lie. He took the measure of the woman his grandfather planned to make his mother-in-law. Handsome enough, he supposed, with high cheekbones and intelligent eyes. But calculation lurked in her glance as well. He swallowed and released her hand. Now he knew how a fish in a bucket felt.

"Lawrence is in the music room already. I've saved seats for you in the front row. I do hope you enjoy the concert. Do you like piano music, Mr. Kennebrae?"

Grandfather waved a hand. "Oh, call him Jonathan, and he enjoys piano music. We were just talking this afternoon about his past experiences at musical evenings such as this one, weren't we, Jonathan?" Grandfather sent him a wicked grin. "It seems he's particularly fond of nocturnes."

Jonathan stepped behind the wheelchair and clenched his fists around the steering bar. "Let's get you settled, Grandfather. I'm sure the music will begin soon." He directed the chair through the central hall, following the stream of guests. He leaned down and whispered, "Behave yourself. And I'm telling you, if this girl plays "The Wedding March," I'm leaving so fast you won't see me for dust."

"Beautiful home, isn't it?" Grandfather ignored him, pointing to the staircase rising ahead and curving off to right and left galleries above. "Stunning architecture."

Jonathan barely glanced at the ornate stained glass, marble, and gilded woodwork. A trip to the firing squad had to be better than this. His collar tightened a notch. He wouldn't admit—even to himself—he was a tiny bit curious to see Miss Brooke.

Perhaps there was still a way out of this. But how? He'd done nothing but mull it over all afternoon. As Jonathan saw it, only one possible plan of escape might work. He had to find something in the girl's nature or background that made her unsuitable as a bride. While the idea of digging into a young woman's life for something unsavory didn't appeal to him, marrying her in order to keep Kennebrae Shipping appealed even less. And perhaps he wouldn't have to dig too deep. Everyone had a secret or two in his or her cargo hold.

The music room, with its golden parquet floor, Renaissance paintings, and high windows draped in heavy brocade, trumpeted wealth in every detail. Chairs had been set out in neat rows—there must have been at least fifty of them—and yet the room didn't seem crowded. Dominating the far end, a grand piano stood alone under a blazing crystal chandelier.

Jonathan scrutinized each young woman in the room, wondering which one was Miss Brooke.

Several business acquaintances stopped to speak with Grandfather. Michaels and Zahn, co-conspirators in this marriage scheme, both greeted Grandfather with smiles and knowing looks. Jonathan schooled his features and pretended not to listen to them.

Lawrence Brooke stood near the front row, beckoning them to join him.

Jonathan regarded Brooke with a cold eye. Prior to this evening they had met only as business acquaintances—and that rarely. Tall, barrel-chested, with the look of a tenacious bulldog, Lawrence Brooke was a formidable man. Kennebrae Shipping had long sought his business but to no avail. Brooke shipped—through a Kennebrae rival—thousands of tons of wheat every year from Duluth Harbor and owned the three largest grain elevators on the docks. Added to that were more than two thousand miles of railroad through Minnesota and the Dakotas, all leading to Duluth. Brooke just might be the wealthiest man in a town that boasted more millionaires per capita than any other city in America.

"Abraham, glad you could make it. Going to be a fine evening." Lawrence clasped Grandfather's hand. "Jonathan."

When it was Jonathan's turn to shake hands, Lawrence Brooke's eyes bored into him, challenging and assessing. Jonathan tightened his grip, not backing down. He had nothing to be ashamed of, and he didn't care how intimidating Brooke tried to be.

Brooke broke the stare first, stepping back. "Welcome to Castlebrooke. Have a seat here beside me. Melissa will be down soon."

Melissa. So that was her name. Pretty name.

Jonathan wheeled his grandfather to the space of honor provided in the center of the front row. A business acquaintance caught his eye. "Excuse me for a moment." He nodded to Brooke and eased into the aisle.

"Don't be gone long." Grandfather's eyes flashed a warning.

"I won't."

Guests filed into the rows. Jonathan shook hands with one of his favorite clients near the back of the room, trying to ignore the way Grandfather and Mr. Brooke had their heads together in the front row. Maybe he could find a seat in the back of the room.

Almina Brooke made her way to the front. "Good evening, friends. Lawrence and I are so glad you could join us." She smiled, her dark eyes gleaming. "Without further ado, may I present our daughter, Miss Melissa Brooke, who will play for us tonight."

Polite applause from the audience.

A side door opened, and she entered.

Beautiful was the first word that sprang to Jonathan's mind. The second was *tiny*. His chest tightened. *Steady, man, you've seen pretty girls before.*

She had feathers in her hair. And her waist looked impossibly small. Jewels sparkled around her slender neck. Her train swept the parquet.

She stopped beside the piano, rested her hand on the edge, and scanned the crowd. Her gaze lingered on her parents then shifted to Grandfather. How old was she? Eighteen, nineteen at the most? She stood stock-still, staring at the front row. She reminded Jonathan of a songbird he'd once held in his hands, the tiny heart beating, the panic in the bird's eyes.

Blue. Her eyes were blue and fringed with dark lashes. Stunning.

Was it his imagination, or did her skin lose all color, washing as pale as the alabaster statue in the alcove behind the piano? She wavered a moment, and he thought she might faint. Then she swallowed and lifted her chin. Her breath came in short gasps, the jewels at her throat catching the light and winking it back at him as they shifted on her collarbones. She cast one desperate glance toward the door, her eyes locking on his for a long moment, then took her seat at the instrument. She looked like she might be ill.

Was he so disagreeable in looks that she nearly fainted? He admitted he was no dandy, but no one had actually gotten sick catching sight of him before. He scowled and shifted, lowering his arms to his sides.

For long moments she sat still, her hands in her lap. Not a breath of air stirred the ostrich feathers.

The audience began to fidget.

Mrs. Brooke turned her head and frowned, motioning for Jonathan to come take his seat. Maybe that's what the girl was waiting for.

His collar tightened another notch, and his mouth went dry, feeling the audience's eyes on him as he slid into the chair next to his grandfather.

At last the girl lifted her fingers to the keys.

Beautiful and gifted. It took Jonathan less than a minute to reach that conclusion. She played with total concentration, evoking emotion through the music, breathing life into the piano with her own passion.

He didn't realize he'd been holding his breath until Grandfather elbowed him in the ribs and leaned close to whisper in his ear. "Might not be quite as bad as a hanging, huh?"

One glance at the man seated beside her father confirmed her worst fears. How could they? Her own parents. Why, it was monstrous. No one would blame her for refusing to obey in this instance. The man they had chosen as her husband was old! Old, gray, and in an invalid chair. It took every ounce of courage she possessed not to hike up the skirt of her couture gown and run from the room. Why, he was old enough to be her grandfather. Tears stung her eyes, and a hot coal burned the pit of her stomach.

Someone cleared his throat, startling her back to her surroundings. The concert. She must play. She raised her hands to the keys, noticed her fingers shaking, and forced them to be still.

Don't look over there again. You'll lose your nerve if you do.

Melissa pushed aside the panic and focused on the music. The melody took over, soothing, carrying her away from her troubles to a place that was beautiful and peaceful. Chopin always had that effect on her.

Each time she emerged from the music at the end of a piece, the audience applauded politely. Their approval sounded far away to Melissa, whose thoughts raced, fragments of worry scattering across her mind. Visions of false teeth and rheumatism medicines, watery eyes, and gnarled hands crowded in on her.

No, don't think about it. Think about the music. Lord, help me!

After the second encore, her mother rose and stood beside the piano. "Thank you, thank you." She accepted the applause as if she had performed every piece herself. "No, no more tonight. Please join us next door in the ballroom for refreshments."

Melissa picked up her gloves and put them on, smoothing the satin up over her elbows. There was no escape now. How was she going to get through the rest of the evening, and when would she be introduced to her "groom"?

Guests crowded around her, complimenting her, thanking her for her performance. She deliberately kept her attention directed away from her parents and their guest of honor.

Finally her mother's hand snaked through the crowd and grasped Melissa's elbow. "I'm sorry to take her away from you, but there is someone waiting to meet her. Please, all of you, come enjoy the punch and delicacies next door."

The iron grip told Melissa her mother wasn't fooling. Melissa plastered a pleasant smile on her face and accompanied her mother to the front row of seats.

"Ah, Melissa dear, splendid performance tonight. I particularly enjoyed the last piece." Her father leaned down and kissed her cheek. "Abraham, I'd like to introduce you to my daughter, Miss Melissa Brooke. Melissa, this is Abraham Kennebrae of Kennebrae Shipping. I believe your mother mentioned he would be in attendance tonight?" Father's stare pierced her, demanding she behave herself and do him proud.

Melissa's mouth went dry. Mr. Kennebrae took her hand and gave it a squeeze, his brown eyes twinkling. "A pleasure, my dear. It did my old heart good to hear such beautiful music so excellently played. But it's even better to make the acquaintance of such a lovely young woman."

The old roué. Melissa withdrew her hand. Up close he was even older than she'd feared, his skin papery thin, his bones prominent. A shiver of nausea passed over her at the thought of being his wife. "Mr. Kennebrae." She nodded and sent her mother an imploring look. "I believe I'll check on the refreshments, if you will excuse me?"

Her father frowned. "Now don't run off just yet." He turned to a young man who had his back to the group, speaking to another couple.

"Jonathan?" Father tapped the man on the shoulder. "Melissa, Jonathan came with Abraham this evening."

Melissa lifted her hand, her mind astir with extricating herself from Abraham Kennebrae.

The young man took her fingers in his.

Melissa's breath caught in her throat. She stared into a pair of velvety brown eyes fringed in heavy lashes. Dark hair touched his collar in the back. His cheeks and chin bore a hint of rough darkness indicating a heavy beard should he choose to grow one. A jolt sizzled up her arm as the heat of his hand penetrated her glove.

"Jonathan, may I introduce you to my daughter, Melissa? Melissa, Jonathan—"

A roar of laughter sounded from the ballroom.

"Oh, perhaps we should join them in the other room. We can continue our conversation over some refreshment."

The young man released her fingers, which still tingled strangely, and she lifted her hem to follow after her parents. He put his hands to the back of the chair to wheel Mr. Kennebrae to the reception. He must be her intended's caretaker. An invalid like Mr. Kennebrae would need someone to care for him.

"My dear, I do hope you'll sit beside me. We have so much to talk about." Mr. Kennebrae smiled up at her.

Though it chilled her to the bone to think of being his wife, she had to admit he had a certain charm. Like a favorite old uncle. She'd play the hostess for a while then find a way to escape. Tomorrow would be soon enough to confront her mother about this impossible situation. For tonight she'd be polite. "Of course, Mr. Kennebrae. I'd be delighted." She walked beside him into the brightly lit ballroom, but she couldn't resist glancing at the younger man.

Jonathan? Too bad he wasn't her parents' choice. She might have entertained the idea then.

Chapter 4

I would recommend you consider the Chicago property. Your docks in Detroit have paid off handsomely, not only in the fees you've saved on your own ships but also in revenue received from other companies who use the docks. Chicago should pay as handsomely in the long run."

Jonathan took the batch of papers from his attorney and tried to focus on the columns. Where was his head today? Why couldn't he concentrate?

He blamed Grandfather. Grandfather and the conniving Brookes who'd cooked up this whole charade. The entire evening had been like a bad dream, unsettling and unreal.

Jonathan tried to loosen his jaw muscles and ignore his thoughts. Grandfather. The old codger sure enjoyed himself, shooting sly glances and addlepated grins at Jonathan every few minutes last night.

And the girl—she danced attendance on Grandfather as if he held the secrets of the ages. Why, she'd hardly paid any attention to Jonathan. Astute of her to study the old man. She must've been in on the plan from the start. Only Jonathan had been left in the dark.

And what a plan. Everything from the silver trays of canapés and savories to the masses of flowers surrounding the crystal punch fountain, every detail had been laid on to impress. One would have thought the king of England was visiting. And hadn't Grandfather lapped it up? Well, not Jonathan. He wasn't going to be shoved into this farce. Neither the sums involved nor the temptingly beautiful Melissa Brooke would entice him to stick his neck in this custom-designed noose.

"Mr. Kennebrae?"

Jonathan looked up to see eight pairs of eyes staring at him. He looked from one board member to another, hoping for a clue as to what topic was under discussion. His lawyer inclined his head slightly toward the papers in Jonathan's hand. *Ah, thank you, Geoffrey.*

Jonathan pushed back from the table, his chair creaking. "Gentlemen," he said as he rose, "I apologize for my inattention. The decision on the Chicago property will require finesse. I agree that it would be a sound business investment. I wish I could go myself, but matters here require my presence." He turned to the director of finance. "Jacobson, you will travel to Chicago and talk to Summerton face-to-face. Tell him if we are to strike a deal, it must be done before the first of the year. I'll make decisions on the other two matters on the agenda and get back to you. That is all, gentlemen."

Jonathan turned his back and stared out the window at the street below and, beyond that, to the rock-strewn shore. "Geoffrey, I'd like you to stay."

Jonathan waited until the door closed before turning around. His lawyer and best friend lounged in his chair, rocking slightly, tapping his fingers on the padded arms.

"Geoff, I'm in an awful mess." Jonathan jammed his fingers through his hair.

"I wondered what had that normally razor-sharp brain of yours as dull as a lake stone. I felt like I was talking to a statue this morning." Geoffrey Fordham laced his fingers and rested his hands against his lean middle.

"Grandfather is the one who has dulled my wits. You wouldn't believe his latest scheme."

"It must be pretty bad to have you in such a lather. What's he doing? Getting married?"

Jonathan rubbed his palm across the back of his neck. "Hah, I wish. No, he's gone a step further. He's trying to maneuver *me* into matrimony."

Geoff blinked. "He's nagging you? Why should that bother you? He nags all the time."

"Not nagging, negotiating. He's negotiated my nuptials without even bothering to tell me. He finally saw fit to enlighten me yesterday before dragging me off to meet the bride."

Geoff burst out laughing.

Jonathan scowled. "It's not funny. I tell you, I was poleaxed."

"I'm sorry. I can see you're worked up, but I have to wonder why. It isn't as if your grandfather's holding a shotgun to your head. He can't force you to marry anyone."

Jonathan shoved his hands into his pockets and leaned against the table. "He doesn't need a shotgun. He's got something a lot more powerful."

"What?"

"If I don't marry to his wishes, he'll disinherit me. Everything I've sweated blood for over the last eight years will be yanked out of my hands. I don't know how to do anything else, nor have I ever wanted to. But if I don't do as Grandfather says, there's no Kennebrae Shipping, no property in Chicago, no Kennebrae House, nothing. It will all go to Noah and Eli, as long as they, too, marry according to the master plan. He's already rewritten his will."

Geoff's eyes stretched wide, and his hands fell slack in his lap. "That's ridiculous. Is he mad? I knew nothing of this. Who prepared the will? Did he show it to you?"

"He's not mad. He's determined. Fixated on the subject. He intends to create a conglomerate of the wealthiest families in Duluth through marriage. And no, I didn't see the will. Wasserman probably drew it up. This place is rife with lawyers. Grandfather thinks you're not seasoned enough to handle his personal affairs, you know." Jonathan shook his head. "He says the will stands unless there is some legal or moral reason why the lady should prove unacceptable. But he must've had her checked out pretty thoroughly, or he'd never have thrown down the gauntlet like that. And he's not bluffing. Last night we made a social call on the woman he intends me to marry."

"So who's the blushing bride?"

"Miss Melissa Brooke, only daughter and heir of Lawrence and Almina Brooke of Castlebrooke."

Geoff whistled low. "Brooke Grain and the Northstar Railroad? Ambitious of the old man. And you met her last night? Is she as beautiful as people say?"

"I'll let you decide. Grandfather and I are attending a party at Castlebrooke today. You can come along as my guest and meet her yourself. Then you can rack your brain for a way out of this mess."

∽

"Melissa!" Mother's sharp voice pierced a lovely dream. "It's well past time for you to be up. You need to get dressed."

Melissa rolled over and buried her head under the pillow. "Not yet, Mother." Quick hands yanked the pillow away, letting the brutal sunlight assault her eyes.

"Young lady, I do not understand your laziness. You'd sleep until noon every day if I let you. Now get up. Sarah's drawn a bath for you. I've invited a few friends for luncheon today. Including Mr. Kennebrae. It's been so unseasonably warm that I thought a terrace party would be nice."

Melissa groaned, yawning and stretching. Delightful. Another meeting with her fossilized groom. The lace cuffs of her nightgown flopped back as she lifted her arms over her head. "What time is it?"

"Past ten thirty. Now get moving. And wear the blue dress, the one with the matching parasol." Mother's shoes tapped on the glossy floor, and she swept out, closing the door with her customary bang.

At noon Melissa let herself out the back doors onto the terrace. The breeze ruffled the lace at her throat. She blinked in the bright sunshine glinting off the waves. Maybe she should go back in for her hat.

Too late. Mother advanced on her, grabbing her elbow and steering her toward the buffet table. "Melissa, come stand beside Mr. Kennebrae, and greet your guests."

What had Mother in such a flap? She was as jumpy as a frog with the hiccups, as their gardener would say. Her grip on Melissa tightened, and they all but ran to Mr. Kennebrae's chair. "No, no, not that side. Stand here."

Melissa found herself directed to stand between the wheelchair and. . . Jonathan. A curious tickle started under Melissa's heart and caused it to beat double-time. His eyes were as dark, his jaw as firm as she remembered. What was it about him that so appealed to her? She turned to greet Mr. Kennebrae. She swallowed hard. "Good afternoon, sir."

"My dear, so delightful to see you again. You're as pretty as a rose. As you should be on a day like today." He took her fingers between his gnarled palms and patted her hand, his dark eyes sparkling with life.

She forced a smile. This was getting beyond funny. If only she hadn't slept in, she could've confronted Mother about the absurdity of this situation. But the concert had lasted so long, and then she'd had to go—

Melissa intercepted a look from Mother who inclined her head toward Jonathan.

Melissa turned. "Good afternoon."

"Miss Brooke." His brows came down, his lips stiff. He looked like a thundercloud just before a squall. Perhaps his employer was giving him a bad time today. His animosity was clearly directed toward the man in the chair.

Again a pang of regret hit her middle. Such a waste, a handsome man like that, forced to be a body servant to an ambitious old man. Perhaps she would get a chance to talk to him later, make him feel more a part of the doings. But for now she must concentrate on being pleasant to Abraham Kennebrae so as not to embarrass her mother.

Knots of guests milled around the fountain and the gazebo and across the green lawns. How many people had Mother invited? The staff spread luncheon on a buffet table laden with flowers, silver, and Mother's best linens. She certainly was laying it on thick for a mere garden party. And why were there no young people? Melissa recognized many of the women as friends of her mother's.

She put her finger to her mouth to bite her nails before she remembered she was wearing gloves. What was the matter with her? Just get through the luncheon then confront Mother head-on about this proposed engagement. It wasn't too late to back out. No one knew of the arrangements. A little patience and it would all be over.

∽

"She's beautiful. Are you sure you wouldn't rather just go through with it?" Geoffrey held out his plate to the servant and accepted the walnut chicken salad he offered.

Jonathan shook his head. "No. I won't be pushed into this. And besides, she's hardly even glanced my way. All her time's been spent cozying up to my grandfather. Guess she knows which way the tide's running." He vowed for the tenth time since arriving to stop letting his eyes wander to the girl seated beside his grandfather at the head table. She sat, stiff, her back straight. The breeze teased tendrils of hair on her neck, drawing his gaze again to her rosy cheeks, her lively eyes, her slender throat. *Stop it.*

Geoffrey cast a glance back over his shoulder, studying Jonathan's face. "Are you jealous?" He raised an eyebrow. "I'd swear your eyes have gone from brown to bright green."

"Don't be a fool. Jealousy would imply I wanted the girl for myself. Which I don't." Jonathan stopped abruptly when he intercepted a quizzical frown on the young woman serving the lemonade. "Let's go sit down."

They wove through the guests to the head table. Grandfather sent Jonathan a sharp look when he would've taken the chair farthest from Miss Brooke. Stifling his irritation, Jonathan set his plate down beside her.

She smiled at him, and he chided his heart for beating faster. *You're an idiot to let her affect you like this. Get ahold of yourself.*

The food was surprisingly good. He had not expected to be hungry. Of course he hadn't been able to eat his breakfast, downing several cups of strong coffee instead. This whole situation had him unsettled and well out of his routine. The sooner it was sorted out, the better.

Almina Brooke beamed on her guests, looking much like a lake bird who'd landed a large fish.

Jonathan intended to be the fish that got away.

"Abraham, I'd love to show you the late-fall roses." Almina dabbed her lips and waved to masses of blooms in an arrangement near the fountain. "I love having the conservatory. It means fresh flowers all year round." She gave a pointed glance in Jonathan and Melissa's direction.

Jonathan almost groaned. Not subtle, pushing them to be together like this.

"And, Mr. Fordham, would you be so kind as to join us?"

Geoffrey dropped his fork, midbite, with a clatter onto his plate. He snatched his napkin and wiped his mouth. "My pleasure."

Jonathan frowned at his lawyer for deserting him so eagerly. Geoffrey shrugged, wide-eyed and innocent. "I'll be back."

Almina adjusted her skirts. "Oh no, Melissa, there's no need for you to come along. Stay here and keep Jonathan company."

Jonathan sat staring at their retreating backs. Geoffrey gave him one sheepish glance over his shoulder then scuttled away behind the wheelchair. *Traitor.*

Melissa cleared her throat gently and laid her cake fork aside. She appeared about to speak but subsided. What was there to say, after all?

Well, he couldn't just sit here like a ninny. But frankly he had little experience talking to girls and none whatsoever in talking to prospective brides.

"Kennebrae Shipping is doing well this quarter." *Oh, you idiot. Can't you think of anything better?*

"Is it? How nice." She gave him a puzzled glance then looked away in the direction Grandfather had gone.

"Four new Kennebrae ships will take to the lake this year. Business is booming." His mouth was like a leaky hatch cover. Words kept spewing out.

A small line formed between her dark arched brows, but she nodded politely. "I suppose you know a lot about what goes on at the shipping offices, being so close to Mr. Kennebrae?"

"Yes, I attend all the board meetings and help oversee the day-to-day running of the company." Surely the girl knew that. She didn't think he was some sort of dilettante, sponging off the family business and doing no work at all?

Miss Brooke laid aside her napkin and took her gloves from her lap, inserting her hands and tugging them on with quick jerks. "You don't have to try to sell Kennebrae Shipping to me, sir."

Such a dolt. Of course she didn't want to hear about the company.

"I apologize, Miss Brooke. It's just that I'm more than a little concerned about this marriage business. My entire future's at stake here. I'd like nothing more than to call a halt to the entire affair, but I feel powerless. And no one is more stubborn than Abraham Kennebrae."

"Unless it would be my mother." She clapped her hand to her mouth and looked about her guiltily. "I'm sorry. I shouldn't have said it."

"Why not? It's true. The entire idea is ridiculous, and the sooner it's squelched, the better. I had no idea anything like this was in the works."

"I couldn't agree more. I've been so distressed since Mother informed me. I don't think I slept a wink until nearly dawn." She lifted her glass for a sip of lemonade.

Relief flooded through him. If neither of them wanted the marriage, then surely there was some way to call it off without jeopardizing his inheritance. "I'm so glad you feel that way. And it isn't just myself I'm thinking about here. The time to act is now, before the engagement is announced. After that it will be too late. Your reputation would suffer if the engagement was called off after the formal announcement. I wouldn't want that to happen to you. Not with you being a pawn in this entire chess match." He smiled at her, his blood heating when she returned the smile. Geoffrey was right; she was a beautiful girl, and in other circumstances, perhaps. . .

"Do you think there is a way to dissuade them? I don't see Mother budging. She's so pleased with herself. And my father, he's the king of his empire, but he's putty in Mother's hands. She's got his heart set on the match and in such a way that he thinks the entire thing was his idea."

"Don't blame it all on your mother. The old man had a hand in it, too." Jonathan jerked his chin in his grandfather's direction. Geoffrey pushed the chair along the flagstone path.

"I'm so glad I'm not the only one who sees the absurdity of the situation. I don't know what my parents were thinking. It's clear the age difference is too great. Why, it's scandalous."

That stung. How old did she think he was anyway? They couldn't be more than a dozen years apart. He didn't know much about such things, but he'd guess that was an average age spread for a married couple these days.

His attention was drawn from her by someone tapping a spoon against a glass.

"Goodness." She put her hand on his arm. He wondered if she even realized it. "Father's home in the middle of the day."

Lawrence Brooke tapped a glass again, and all conversation died down. He raised the glass. "Ladies and gentlemen, thank you for joining us on such a momentous day for our family."

Melissa's grip tightened on Jonathan's arm. He looked down at her, her face pale to the lips, her eyes wide. "Oh no," she moaned.

"My wife and I"—Almina had joined Lawrence Brooke, tucking her arm into his elbow and beaming on the crowd, her gaze lingering longest on Jonathan and Melissa—"are pleased to announce the engagement of our daughter, Melissa, to Mr. Jonathan Kennebrae. Please join us in congratulating the happy couple." He lifted the glass in their direction.

A polite wave of applause welled up.

Melissa stood, knocking her chair over onto the grass. She put her hand to her mouth, turning her head wildly from Jonathan to her parents then back again.

Jonathan rose slowly, easing up on numb legs.

"Kennebrae?" She whispered so low he had to stoop to hear her. "Your name is Kennebrae?"

"Of course it is. What else would it be?"

She blinked, staring at him. "But I thought—" Her throat spasmed as she tried to swallow. "I thought. . ."

He caught her just before she hit the grass in a dead faint.

Chapter 5

Melissa slumped against him. Jonathan's arms reached around her, grabbing her to keep her from disappearing under the table. "Miss Brooke?"

When she didn't respond, he stooped, tucked his hand behind her knees, and lifted her in his arms. Her head fit into the crook of his shoulder, her breath dusting his neck. Jonathan looked around for a place to set her, but only the hard, white metal chairs met his eye.

Guests gaped, frozen in surprise. It had happened so fast that it seemed no one knew just what to do.

Except Almina Brooke. She advanced on him like a coming storm, eyebrows drawn down, mouth pinched in exasperation. "That foolish girl. Please accept my apologies, Mr. Kennebrae. Melissa, Melissa, stop playacting this minute."

Melissa didn't stir in his arms. He had a strange desire to clasp her tighter, turn his back, and shield her from her battleaxe of a mother.

People stared, leaning in, listening to every word.

"Mrs. Brooke, perhaps it would be best if we continued this discussion inside?"

Almina took a moment to realize her audience, plastered a concerned look on her face, and beckoned him. "Of course. Please bring her into the house."

Jonathan strode through the crowd, his anger, both at Almina Brooke and Grandfather, steaming through his veins. Of all the ridiculous positions.

A maid opened the terrace doors, her face crumpled in worry.

Jonathan nodded his thanks.

"Bring her through here, sir." The girl scurried ahead to a pair of double doors on the left.

His footsteps echoed on the hard floors as he followed her into a gold and blue parlor.

The maid plumped a cylindrical pillow, beribboned and tasseled.

Jonathan felt a strange reluctance to let go of the burden in his arms. The delicate scent of roses drifted up from her hair. Dark lashes rested on her pale cheeks. Her lips parted, and he found himself staring at them. So soft, so perfect.

Someone cleared his throat.

Jonathan shook himself, dragging his gaze away from Melissa.

"Don't you think you should put her down?" Geoffrey lifted an inquiring brow toward Jonathan. He'd wheeled Grandfather into the house, and Abraham sat, covering his mouth with the side of his finger, a twinkle in his eye.

Anger surged through Jonathan. He laid Melissa on the davenport, easing his arms from beneath her. How dare his grandfather laugh at this situation of his own making.

Almina pointed to the maid. "Anne, don't just stand there; get a blanket or some smelling salts. Abraham, I'm so sorry. Melissa, so help me, if you're faking this, you're going to be— Jonathan, I can't believe—" The woman seemed to be mixing up her carping and apologizing.

He stepped between Almina and the sofa. "I assure you, madam, the girl has fainted. Perhaps you should send for a doctor instead of sputtering at her when she clearly can't hear you."

Almina's mouth opened and closed a few times, her eyes wide at his upbraiding. "Of course." She lifted her chin and bustled out of the room.

Jonathan knelt beside Melissa and took her hand between his. "Miss Brooke." Her face, lily-white, alarmed him. He chafed her hand, so small and cold. "Miss Brooke, are you all right?"

Her lashes fluttered, and her hand stirred in his.

Relief flooded him. He found himself looking into a pair of hazy sapphire eyes.

She blinked as if trying to understand where she was and why. Her mouth fell open, and she sat bolt upright, almost knocking him in the nose. "I'm supposed to marry you?" Her voice must've carried clear to the third floor.

Jonathan rocked back on his heels. "I assure you, Miss Brooke—"

"But I thought—" She turned to look at Grandfather. "Nobody told me. How was I supposed to know? You never said. Nobody ever said. Mother said Mr. Kennebrae. And I thought—" She broke off. "How did I get here?"

"You fainted, Miss Brooke." Geoffrey stepped closer, around the back of the brocade davenport. "Right after your father announced your betrothal. Jonathan caught you and carried you inside. Your mother's gone for some aid."

Melissa darted a look from one man to the other, finally resting her startled eyes on Jonathan. She looked at him as if he were a complete stranger.

"What is it that shocked you so, miss?" Geoffrey leaned over her. "Didn't your parents tell you of the engagement plans?"

"Of course." She stared into Jonathan's eyes, confusion, relief, and. . . Was that hope in her expression? "But Mother only said Mr. Kennebrae, and no one introduced Jonathan by his last name. I thought he was a companion or caretaker for the man I was to marry. I thought I was to become Mrs. Abraham Kennebrae."

Jonathan could hardly think above the laughter barking from both Geoff and Grandfather. He'd like to knock their heads together. No wonder she'd talked of age differences and the impossibilities of the union. Though where she got such an outlandish notion—

She broke their gaze, her face suffusing with color and her chin dipping. A single tear tracked down her cheek.

Pity stabbed Jonathan. "Enough, you cackling baboons. Get out." He glared over his shoulder at Grandfather then shot Geoff a frown.

"Okay, okay." Geoff held up his hands in surrender. "We're going." He snickered and snorted, wheeling Grandfather from the room.

"Well," she whispered, gripping her hands in her lap, "it was an honest mistake. I'm so glad, though, that it's you instead of your grandfather. I mean, a fifty-year age difference. . ." She shuddered. "It would be enough to knock anyone into a faint."

Jonathan closed his eyes and rubbed his forehead with his fingertips. What a farce. At least she thought him a better catch than a seventy-year-old.

∽

How could she be so stupid? Melissa lay back against the cool linen pillows and stared at the plaster medallion on her bedroom ceiling. She flushed from her toes to the roots of her hair.

Well, who could blame her for misunderstanding? It wasn't as if anyone had given her the courtesy of a clear introduction. Anyone would've made the same mistake.

One bright spot shone out in all this mess. At least she wouldn't have to be Mrs. Abraham Kennebrae, a septuagenarian's wife.

The look on Jonathan's face though. Melissa groaned and slid down under the covers. What was the matter with her, babbling on like an idiot? She had no more brains than a trout.

A tap at the door.

Melissa peeked out. *Please don't be Mother again.*

She blew out a relieved breath as a tea tray emerged through the door. "Ah, Sarah, it's you."

"Yes, miss. How're you feeling?"

Melissa shrugged, sat up, and punched her pillows.

Sarah twitched the coverlet and set the tray down across Melissa's knees. "It was real romantic, him carrying you in like that. Don't you think so?"

Melissa flipped back her drooping cuffs and poured the hot, fragrant liquid. She sniffed the delicate aroma. Romantic? How romantic was it to drop into a dead faint in the arms of a man she had no idea she was engaged to?

"I'm sorry I couldn't be here when the doctor came. Mrs. Brooke set me to clearing up outside. There was lots to clean up after the guests finally left."

Melissa set the cup down, rattling it against the saucer. More sickening embarrassment swirled through her. She put her palms over her eyes and dragged her hands down her face.

"Don't fret, miss. I'm sure things will work out."

Melissa crumbled her scone on her plate. How could she look either of the Kennebraes in the eye ever again?

"It's almost ten o'clock. Do you want me to send word to Britten's that you won't be coming tonight?"

Melissa threw her arm up over her eyes. No one had ever told her that acute shame drained the strength from you like grain from a leaky railcar. She wanted nothing more than to pull the covers over her head and sleep, for at least a decade or two, until the whole thing blew over. "No, Sarah. It's not like I'm really sick. I'll go."

She threw back the covers and slid her feet to the floor. At least the darkness would hide her blush.

✍

Jonathan paced Grandfather's office. "This is all your fault, pulling strings like Machiavelli. You piled so much stress on the girl she fainted."

"Now, son, you can't blame me for this. Her mother should've been clearer. I had no idea that little girl would think. . . Well, I'm flattered—I really am—but it never entered my head she'd react like that. Frankly, if I was forty years younger, I'd give you a run for your money." The old rogue's eyes twinkled, his cheeks flushed with pleasure.

Jonathan stopped pacing. "Be serious, won't you? What possessed you to allow the Brookes to announce the engagement in front of all those people? I should've denied involvement in your schemes right there."

He resumed prowling the carpet, hands jammed in his pockets, anger boiling in his middle. When he thought of her pale face on his arm, bloodless lips parted, her hair falling out of its pins. . . The protective rush of feeling that sprang up inside him had startled him. That the feelings hadn't faded surprised him more.

"You wouldn't do that, Jonathan. Kennebrae Shipping means too much to you. I knew it would. I don't know why you're resisting this so much. She's a nice girl, beautiful and good. She'll make you a fine wife. You have nothing to complain about."

"Nothing to complain about? You don't get it, do you? I want to be free to choose my own bride. I want to marry someone I love and who loves me in return."

"Love? Love isn't necessary to a marriage. Common interests, background, and social standing make for a sound union. I didn't love your grandmother when I married her. That came later."

"I surely don't want to marry someone on the off chance that someday she will love me. But that's going to be more difficult now, isn't it? Everyone at the party heard the announcement. How am I going to get out of this now?"

"Not just everyone at the party." Grandfather chuckled, rubbing the cover of his pocket watch with his crepe fingers. "It will be in the *Duluth Daily News* and the *St. Paul Pioneer Press* tomorrow morning. I imagine engagement gifts will begin arriving at Castlebrooke shortly after that."

Jonathan gritted his teeth so hard that he feared they might crack. His jaw ached from the strain of not yelling. He was caught in a whirlpool, spiraling down to the moment when he'd say, "I do."

He turned to his grandfather, striving to modulate his voice. "Don't think this is the end of it." He stalked from the room, Grandfather's delighted cackle following him down the hall.

If only he could speak to Miss Brooke. . .Melissa. He supposed since they were now formally engaged, though without benefit of a proposal, he could call her "Melissa." Embarrassment heated his face. She'd thought him a servant, his grandfather's lackey. Though, truth be told, what else was he, getting backed into a situation like this?

Knowing she didn't want the engagement either pricked his pride. But why? He should be relieved. He shook his head and mounted the stairs to his rooms on the third floor. How foolish to be piqued by the rejection of a woman he didn't even want to marry.

He opened the door to his suite, familiarity and comfort wrapping around him. The rest of the house might be Grandfather's, but this was his domain. Gas lamps lit the walnut paneling. Dark-blue and burgundy rugs covered the polished floors. Watercolors of ships and the lake in gilded frames brightened the walls.

Jonathan dropped his keys and coins into a wooden bowl on the pie-crust table beside his favorite chair. The chair creaked a familiar welcome as he stretched his legs. The papers from this morning's board meeting lay in tidy piles on his desk in the corner, chiding him about his lack of attention to them. He had never gone to bed without finalizing meeting reports, but tonight he couldn't concentrate on anything.

A knock at the door. "Sir?"

"Yes, McKay?"

"Telegram, sir."

Jonathan took the envelope and tapped his thigh with it. When the door closed behind the butler, he slit the envelope and unfolded the stiff paper.

Great, Noah would be held up in Detroit. Just when Jonathan needed one of his brothers to talk to. Noah was clever and a problem solver, using light banter to hide his keen mind. If anyone could find a way out of this mire, Noah could. And in such a way that would preserve Melissa's reputation and allow Jonathan to keep control of Kennebrae Shipping.

He wadded the telegram and fired it at the hearth. No matter where he turned, he was alone, his back to the wall. Give up Kennebrae Shipping, or give in and marry Melissa Brooke.

What if she was the one who called off the wedding? He couldn't be blamed for that, could he?

Sitting here was getting him nowhere. He needed to talk to her.

A strip of light showed under Grandfather's second-floor bedroom door. Probably in there hatching up some new misery regarding Jonathan's firstborn.

McKay met him near the front door. The man had an uncanny sense of where everyone in the house was at all times.

"Shall I call the carriage, sir?"

"No. I'll walk. Don't wait up." Jonathan snatched his hat and topcoat from the hall tree. A quick look through the canes and umbrellas sorted out his favorite, silver-topped walking stick.

A brisk wind off the lake fluttered lapels and caused his pant legs to snap. He anchored his hat and set off up Superior Street.

An automobile puttered by, the streetlights gleaming off its shiny metal. Behind it, slower, a delivery wagon rattled up the road, horses' hooves clopping on the damp pavement.

He tossed a look over his shoulder, picking out the silhouette of the new canal bridge. The *Kennebrae Jericho* lay at anchor just outside the harbor awaiting morning to enter the port. A light burned from her pilothouse, casting a glow in the hazy night air.

Jonathan knew the location, cargo, and manifest of every one of the twenty-eight Kennebrae ships on the lake. He knew their histories, their captains, their capacities. When one went down in a storm, he mourned the loss of not only life and income but also the ship itself. Each was an individual, unique, a member of the Kennebrae Shipping family. He chose their captains with all the care of a protective parent. His standards were high, and a job with Kennebrae gave a man status in the community and on the lake.

He couldn't walk away. It would be like cutting out his heart.

I need an escape, Lord. I can't seem to find my way through. Legally Grandfather's got me tied to the mast. I've worked so hard to build the company up. You know how scared I was, how green, fresh out of college, with Grandfather lying in bed unable to speak a word. But I saw it in his eyes. Pleading with me to hold on to all he had worked for. And with Your help, I did it. You've blessed the business in so many ways. I can't find words to thank You.

Jonathan cut across a side street with swift strides, continuing up the tree-lined sidewalk. His prayers came as fast as his steps.

Surely You wouldn't have brought me this far, allowed me to be this successful, then take it all away? Help me find a way out of this. Change Grandfather's mind, or show me some way of escape.

Castlebrooke loomed ahead, its front porch illuminated by two carriage lamp sconces under the porte cochere. Strangely no lights shone from the windows on the front of the house.

Jonathan slipped his hand inside his overcoat and palmed his pocket watch. He flipped open the engraved gold lid and turned the timepiece toward the fuzzy glow of the gaslight on the corner. Well after ten o'clock. What a buffoon. Of course there were no lights in the house. Why hadn't he thought of the time before he left Kennebrae House?

He glanced around him and backed out of the light into the shadows of a high iron fence. If anyone saw him lingering out here, he'd look like some love-struck fool sighing his soul up to the boudoir of his beloved. Not a chance. He gripped his walking stick until his fingers ached, trying to ignore the flush of embarrassment creeping up his chest.

He tugged his hat down and drew his overcoat collar up to hide his face. He took one look over his shoulder to ensure no one had seen him then stepped onto the curb. He'd cross the street and circle the block heading west.

A click, a creak, and the soft glow of candlelight stopped him in his tracks.

"Be careful. The fog will be coming in afore you get back." A woman's voice.

"I will. Don't worry, Sarah. You don't have to wait up for me. I'll be very late."

Jonathan slid into the shadows once again and peered through the hedge inside the fence. The front door of Castlebrooke closed, the light disappearing with a sharp *snick*.

Tap, tap, tap. Shoes on the curved brick driveway. Whoever was coming would pass by him on his left. He eased farther into the leaves spreading over the sidewalk until his back pressed against the iron bars of the fence. Then he stopped. What would be more embarrassing? To be found on the sidewalk outside Melissa's home or to be discovered skulking in the bushes? Enough of this foolishness. If anyone saw him, he'd just explain. He was out for an evening stroll. That was all.

A trim figure hurried through the gate and turned away from him, not even glancing in his direction. She carried a valise and swept under the street lamp. At the corner she paused and looked up.

Melissa Brooke.

Now where would she be going at this hour? And alone?

35

Curiosity won out over possible embarrassment, and he followed her at a discreet distance.

She kept her head down, not looking around at all. Did she have no care for her own safety?

He hastened his steps to close the distance a bit more.

A block from her home, she drew up to the same delivery wagon Jonathan had seen earlier. Britten's Bakery. A bakery delivering at this hour? More puzzlement. Without the slightest hesitation she handed her valise up to the unseen driver and climbed aboard.

The wagon set off at a sedate pace that Jonathan found easy to match. A suitable explanation for her behavior eluded him, but his curiosity was aroused so he couldn't leave off trailing her. When they passed Kennebrae House, he gave it barely a glance before hurrying after the wagon.

They entered the deserted business district. The horse's hooves clopped in a damp, gritty cadence on the now slick streets, echoing off the stone and brick buildings on either side of the road. Jonathan had to meld into the shadows when the wagon pulled to a stop on the steep slope of Lake Avenue.

She stepped from the wagon with her bag and set off at a brisk pace down the sidewalk toward Minnesota Point.

Lights reflected in yellow ribbons on the black water. But for the sound of the wagon turning around and heading back up the street, Jonathan was sure he would be able to hear the sucking and slapping of the waves on the rocky shore.

What business would a respectable woman have at the harbor in the middle of the night? Was it something he could use to reason with Grandfather that she was an unsuitable bride?

On the corner of Lake Avenue and Buchanan Street, across the street from his own shipping offices, someone stepped out of the doorway of a three-story brick building. He couldn't tell at this distance if it was a man or a woman.

What was Melissa doing? She walked right up to the person, and the two embraced.

A pang nicked Jonathan's heart. He stopped. The light was too poor to make out the person's face. He refused to acknowledge the disappointment that his search for something questionable in her background had been so shockingly easy to find. Somehow she hadn't seemed the type to have a sordid secret. He chided himself for being taken in by a pair of wide blue eyes and an innocent expression.

Time to confront her. He took a fresh grip on his walking stick and lowered his collar.

Two steps and the world went black.

Chapter 6

Melissa turned at the sound of something heavy hitting the pavement behind her. What on earth? Two figures bent over something on the sidewalk. She knew them. "Wait here out of sight," she cautioned her companion. "Peter, Wilson, what is it?" She called out to the two boys who weren't yet out of their teens.

"I told ya there was someone following us. He trailed you all the way from your house. We made like we was turning around, but Wilson dropped off the back of the wagon and followed him. I parked up there and hustled down to help if he needed it." Peter wiped his nose with the base of his thumb. His forelock fell over his eyes.

"Yeah." Wilson stuck out his chest a bit. "Ma told us not to let anyone bother you. This fella was hiding in the bushes in front of your house."

Alarm fluttered in her middle. She grabbed the young men's arms. "Did you kill him? What have you done?"

"Naw," Peter scoffed. "We just banged him on the head with this. Show her, Wilson."

Wilson opened his hand to reveal a blackjack, sinister and shiny. "He'll have a wicked headache when he wakes up, that's all."

"Who is he?" She leaned over but couldn't see the man's face.

"Dunno, but he has on some swank clothes." Wilson squatted and turned the man over so he lay on his back.

Melissa clapped her gloved hand to her mouth to stifle a cry. "Oh no!" She looked up at the brothers. "Not him!"

Jonathan Kennebrae lay sprawled on the pavement, his hat knocked off, his coat twisted around him. A welt rose on his right temple.

"You know him?"

She nodded and blew out a breath. What were they going to do now?

"Who is he?"

Her mind whirled as she sought to come up with a suitable answer. Finally she decided on the straightforward truth. "He's my fiancé."

Peter snatched off his hat and whacked Wilson with it. "You nincompoop. I told you we shouldn't hit him on the head. You done knocked out the fella she's gonna marry."

"Well, how was I supposed to know, him following her like that? He looked like a pickpocket with his collar all turned up and his hat pulled down low."

Melissa looked up the street. Nothing moved; no lights shone in the buildings. She tugged on her fingers, twisting them inside her gloves.

"What do you want us to do with him? Should we wake him up?"

"No, don't do that. Let me think." How did Jonathan come to be following her anyway? What did he know?

She stood and smoothed her coat. "You must take him home. Peter, go get the wagon. Bring it here, and you and Wilson load him in and take him—" No, they couldn't take him all the way home. Not in the bakery wagon. Someone was sure to see it, and tongues would be wagging. She couldn't afford anyone wondering why Britten's Bakery made deliveries at midnight.

"Take him a couple blocks from his home—you know the place, Kennebrae House—and park where there are no streetlights. Carry him home from there. If anyone asks, just say your friend isn't feeling well. There's a veranda on the north side of the house. We saw it when we went by. There's bound to be some furniture there. Find a davenport or chair. Don't just dump him on the floor." Guilt and urgency made her voice waver.

"Can we go through his pockets first?"

"No! You've done enough already!"

Peter frowned and turned to go.

She caught him by the sleeve. "I'm sorry. I shouldn't snap at you. I do appreciate you looking out for me. But hurry. We must get him home. If he wakes up, he'll be full of questions I don't want to answer."

"We'll get him home. And we'll come see you back safe, too. Don't leave without us. Ma'd skin us if we let you walk home in the dark." He whirled and ran up the street.

"Help me move him, Wilson. He looks so uncomfortable." She put her hands to Jonathan's broad shoulders. Why hadn't she noticed before what a muscular man he was? The smell of shaving soap drifted up as she put her cheek near his face and lifted, easing him over. "Give me your jacket."

Wilson shrugged out of his coat and handed it to her.

She folded it and gently lifted Jonathan's head to pillow it on the bunched cloth. He looked pale to her, and the welt stood out in an angry red line.

Please, God, don't let him be seriously hurt. For his own sake and theirs. They were just trying to protect me. And don't let him wake up before they get him home. He wouldn't understand why I'm here, and he certainly wouldn't understand why the boys knocked him out.

"Miss Brooke, I think you should go. I'll wait here with him till Pete gets back with the wagon." Wilson waved her away.

Torn, she smoothed back Jonathan's hair and placed her hand on his chest. His heart beat slow and steady, and his chest rose and fell rhythmically.

Perhaps he would be all right.

Wisps of fog curled along the pavement. With the wind dying down, it would shroud the city in another half hour or so.

"Stay with him, Wilson."

"I will."

She stood once more and hurried up the street, looking back every few steps. Fog swirled about her feet, creeping up the street to envelop Wilson and her injured fiancé.

Had she done the right thing?

⁓

Jonathan stifled a groan as his shoulder hit the floor of the wagon. He kept his eyes closed. Rough hands shoved his legs inside while boots clambered over him. The conveyance lurched forward.

Couldn't even put him on a seat. Who were these hooligans? The faint smell of yeast floated over him. Jonathan gritted his teeth and fought swirling nausea.

"Dunno why we can't at least toss his pockets. It's not like he can't afford it."

Jonathan fought to maintain consciousness.

"We can't because she said so, that's why. You have rocks for brains? If we rob him, the police'd be after us. They might be anyway, thanks to you."

Police? No, he couldn't do that. Too embarrassing.

"Hey, you were the one who said we had to stop him. What else was I supposed to do?"

"I figured we'd just scare him a bit, you know, maybe throw a couple punches. Never figured he was Miss Brooke's intended."

Jonathan wanted to sit up and protest being called Melissa Brooke's intended, but he couldn't muster the energy. His limbs felt like sails with no wind.

"Dunno why he should be following her anyhow. Not in the middle of the night. You think he knows?"

Knows? Knows what? Blackness engulfed him.

Something jostled Jonathan awake. Hands grabbed his legs and arms and hauled him into the night air.

Jonathan opened one eye a crack. He was sitting on the pavement. Several sets of wagon wheels appeared, merged, and separated in his vision as he tried to focus.

"Come on, get him up." His arms were jerked up and slung over the shoulders of his captors. "And don't forget that fancy cane."

His feet dragged the pavement, his weight hanging from his shoulders. Why couldn't he walk properly?

"Let's put him down and get a better grip. He's too heavy to carry this way."

The men lowered Jonathan to the ground and shifted positions. One grabbed his feet; the other slid his hands under Jonathan's arms and laced them across Jonathan's chest.

"Next time, you get the shoulders. He weighs a ton."

Jonathan wanted to argue. He wasn't fat. His tongue wouldn't form the words.

"Stop your whining. We're almost there."

Almost where? Jonathan tried to ask, but the words came out in a jumble.

"Hurry up. He's coming around."

"She said the side veranda."

Shoes on pavers. A street lamp. Trees.

Thud. His body hit the floor hard.

"She said to put him on the bench."

"You wanna be here when he wakes up? Let's go. We gotta get back to Miss Brooke anyway, before she decides to walk home alone."

Their footfalls receded.

Jonathan opened one eye. The silver head of his walking stick lay inches from his nose. It was too much effort to move. He slid into the darkness again.

Just after daybreak Jonathan held an ice pack to his temple, wincing at the chilling sting.

McKay set a tray of coffee at his elbow and retreated to stir the fire in the grate.

Jonathan longed to go to bed, but the chorus of anvils in his head made sleep impossible. Sitting here thinking was difficult enough.

Steam wisped from the coffee cup. Two sugars, just as he liked it. Then he noticed the glass of water and two headache powders on the tray. McKay was a saint. Jonathan mixed the powers and downed the opaque liquid in three swallows. He eased his head back onto the antimacassar.

Weak light streamed through an opening in the drapes. Sunrise. What day was it? Sunday. He groaned. Soon he must make an effort to gather himself and get to church. He hadn't missed in years, and he wasn't going to now. The explanations would be too humiliating.

Cramped muscles protested every movement. The chilly night and hard flagstones had done him no favors. Well, one, he supposed. The swelling on his head was much reduced. A look in his shaving mirror had shown him a slightly discolored bump along his hairline but not the grotesquely bruised goose egg he'd feared.

Groggy impressions of rough hands, grunts, and clattering wheels on pavement flitted around his memory, tantalizing but encased in fog.

"Sir, is there anything else I can do for you? Shall I summon the police?" McKay refilled Jonathan's cup, his pale-blue eyes disturbed, his brow furrowed.

"Such a dreadful thing, to be robbed like that."

"It wasn't a robbery."

"Yes, sir." He bowed, too experienced with the Kennebraes to question further. Good man. Jonathan closed his eyes.

No, not a robbery. He still had his watch, his walking stick, and even his wallet inside his breast pocket. And no thief would've brought him home. Jonathan couldn't blame last night's doings on a crook.

No, he lay the blame squarely where it belonged. At the feet of the beautiful Melissa Brooke.

Chapter 7

McKay's powders barely put a dent in the pain. Jonathan pushed Grandfather up the center aisle of the sanctuary, grateful for the handle on the wheelchair to help prop himself up. Bright prisms of color from the stained glass windows danced in the air of the vaulted ceiling high overhead.

Jonathan wheeled the chair into the special nook Grandfather had commissioned when he knew he would be an invalid the rest of his life. Four rows from the front on the left side, where the Kennebraes had sat since the church was erected twenty years before. Jonathan stepped into the pew and sat down, biting back a groan. Perhaps if he kept his eyes closed, people would think he was praying.

Grandfather nudged Jonathan's elbow.

He opened his eyes.

"She's here. Stand up and be nice."

"Who's here?"

"Your bride, you imbecile. Almina and I thought it best that your bride's family attend church with us this morning."

With the organ music in the background and his jumbled thoughts in the foreground, Jonathan had a fleeing moment of panic. Then he laughed at himself. No, it wasn't the wedding yet.

Lawrence Brooke strode up the aisle, Almina on his arm, but Jonathan looked right past them. There she was. He sucked in a breath, hit afresh at her beauty.

She wore a gown the color of his beloved lake, trimmed in lace like white-caps. Her hair swept up from her neck, and a wide-brimmed hat trimmed with a single, white silk rose covered her head. Very ladylike.

Jonathan nodded to the Brookes, husband and wife.

Almina frowned when Melissa seated herself firmly at the far end of the pew and did not make eye contact with Jonathan.

It suited Jonathan just fine. Until he had his headache and his temper under control, she'd best stay out of his line of sight. He ignored the black looks Grandfather shot from under his bushy white eyebrows.

"Our text for this morning is found in Proverbs 21:1." The pastor opened his Bible and spread it on the podium.

Jonathan opened his own Bible to the passage, the familiar sound of thin papers rustling around him.

"The king's heart is in the hand of the Lord, as the rivers of water: he turneth it whithersoever he will."

Anytime now, Lord, if You could turn Grandfather's heart, I'd sure appreciate it. It's going to take an act of Yours because he's so stubborn. It would be easier to drink Lake Superior dry than change his mind once he's set on something.

Jonathan's thoughts multiplied even as his headache receded. What was she up to, down near the harbor bridge at night? She had met someone in the shadows, that much he remembered. Was it a man? But for what purpose? Romantic? Illegal? Certainly clandestine. He grimaced. Unsavory to say the least. But if true, it might be his escape.

Before he realized it, the sermon was over.

The congregation stood to sing the final hymn, and then the pastor gave the familiar benediction. "And before we depart this Lord's Day, I have an announcement for you all. Please give your best wishes to Jonathan Kennebrae and Melissa Brooke, who celebrated their engagement this week. I've been informed that the wedding will take place at Castlebrooke on December 16. Congratulations, Jonathan and Melissa!"

Jonathan closed his eyes, his hands gripping the pew ahead of him. Organ music welled up and out, crashing around him.

Grandfather nudged him in the knee.

His eyes flew open. "You set the wedding date?" He spoke through stiff lips, his body clammy and tense. "What else have you done? Arranged a honeymoon? Named our firstborn?"

Grandfather's chuckle infuriated him. "No, son, but I wouldn't be hurt if you named him after me."

"It's too much. You've gone too far."

Grandfather sat back, looking up at him with dark, glittering eyes. "Take it like a man. Folks are coming to greet you. Think of Melissa. If you cause a scene here, it will ruin her."

Melissa. He'd completely forgotten her in his anger. Where was she? Had she escaped? He looked over the heads for a blue hat with a white rose.

Almina had Melissa by the elbow, urging her to stand beside Jonathan in what became a sort of informal receiving line.

Melissa looked so pale that Jonathan feared she might faint again. People crowded around, shaking their hands, clapping him on the shoulder, wishing them well. What a farce.

Almina stood, beaming, on the far side of Melissa, and Grandfather sat at Jonathan's side accepting congratulations, hemming them in and preventing either of them from bolting. Very clever.

But most disconcerting was Lawrence Brooke, who stood behind them both. Jonathan's imagination conjured up a shotgun held neatly to his back.

The wedding was on.

∽

"What do you think of her?"

Melissa jerked her chin up. It took a moment to realize Father wasn't talking about her. He waved his arm wide over the deck of the *Almina Joy,* his newest yacht.

Jonathan stood at his side, face to the breeze, staring out over the lake. His legs braced apart with the roll of the waves.

Sunday luncheon with guests on the family yacht had always been an enjoyable ritual for Melissa. Until today. The movement of the boat on the water only enhanced the uneasy feeling under her heart. And every time she caught sight of the discoloration on Jonathan's temple, her guilt grew.

How much did he know? Why had he followed her? What would he do now? Did he know who had hit him? She gripped her coat tight at the throat.

"Tell me more about him. He's so handsome." Zylphia Montrose clutched Melissa's arm as they strolled the deck. She leaned in conspiratorially. "Tell me everything."

"There's nothing to tell, really. I'd rather hear about your trip to New York."

Zylphia's eyes lit up. "Oh it was a wonderful time! We stayed at the Chelsea and dined at Delmonico's. We even saw Mark Twain there." She squeezed Melissa's arm harder. "He was in the bar, and Mother and I only got a peek, but I'm sure it was him. When I asked the waiter, he got all sly and secretive and said it was against policy for the staff to discuss the guests."

Melissa smiled and nodded, glancing over her shoulder at Father and Jonathan. What were they discussing? Surely he wouldn't ask Father about her late-night excursions, would he? Panic fluttered up.

"I'd better go to Jonathan, Zyl. I wouldn't want him to think I'd abandoned him. Besides, you'll be wanting to work on your next conquest. Mother's invited some very nice, eligible men today."

"None as eligible as the one you snagged." Zylphia gave her a grin. "If he were mine, I don't think I'd stray too far either."

Melissa buttoned her long coat with chilly fingers. This could likely be the last afternoon sail of the season. Indian summer had lasted through mid-October, but the nice weather wouldn't stay much longer. The *Almina Joy* would be dry-docked in the boathouse, wrapped tight to wait until ice-out in the spring.

Jonathan gave her barely a glance when she came to stand beside him. Her father, however, beamed broadly. She breathed a sigh of relief. Jonathan couldn't have mentioned last night. At least not yet.

Father tucked his fingers into his vest pockets. "You look a picture today, Melissa. You've always been a good sailor." He turned to Jonathan. "Loves the water. That's a good thing, eh? I hear sailing is one of your interests. You and Melissa will have to spend more time together. I'm sure you have lots of other things in common." He clapped Jonathan on the back.

Melissa caught the slight wince that passed over Jonathan's face at the impact. His head must still be hurting him.

"Yes, we have a lot to talk about." Jonathan held out his arm to Melissa. "Perhaps you'd fancy a stroll on deck?"

Perfect. She could get him away from Father. She tucked her hand into his elbow, surprised at the play of muscles under her fingertips and the warmth that radiated through his coat to her chilled fingers. "Let's walk to the bow. I like to be near the front whenever I can."

He led her up the starboard side, past the forward sail hatch, to the prow. A deckhand nodded to them and finished winding a rope. He touched his cap and backed away. Father claimed to love being on the lake, but he did none of the sailing himself. A captain and crew of six manned the *Almina Joy*.

"As your father said, we have much to discuss, don't we, Melissa?"

It was the first time she could recall his using her given name. The way he said it didn't sound too friendly. More like a warning shot across her bow.

She released his arm and stepped to the rail, turning her back on him. "Father says you enjoy sailing. Do you have a vessel?"

"Yes, the *Lady Genevieve*, a seventy-four footer. She's tied up at the dock at the house. But I didn't bring you up here to talk about boats. Let's stop pretending, shall we?"

"Pretending?" Melissa looked at him over her shoulder. Her heart picked up the pace. She turned to face him.

"Yes, stop acting like you don't know about last night. You owe me an explanation, and I intend to get one." He loomed over her, arms crossed on his chest, the wind ruffling his dark hair.

"Mr. Kennebrae, I don't owe you anything." She backed up until the rail embraced her waist.

He stepped forward, trapping her neatly. "Yes, you do. For the moment, I'm your fiancé. That entitles me to some answers." His eyes trapped hers as easily as his body hemmed her in. He put a hand to the rail on either side of her and leaned forward.

She eased back and tried to see over his shoulder. Where had everyone gone? "This engagement is a farce, and you know it. You said yourself you were looking for a way out of it."

"And I may have just found it. You've handed it to me on a platter." He looked grim, not like she thought he should at such wonderful news.

"How have I done that?" His eyes mesmerized her, and the words came out breathlessly.

He lowered his head to whisper in her ear. His breath tickled her cheek, warming it to tingling. "One word from me and the engagement will be off. I only need to mention the fact that you are in the habit of traipsing down to the harbor at night to meet a man and"—he snapped his fingers—"no more wedding."

She blinked, her mouth dropping open. "Is that what you think? That I—"

"What else am I supposed to think? It was obvious from your bodyguards' conversation when they took me home last night that this wasn't the first time you took yourself down there. And who was that in the shadows? I may not be in favor of this engagement, but I will not be made a fool of for its duration."

Relief crashed over her like a wave against a pier. He was off base. So far from the truth as to be laughable. But she still sailed dangerous waters. "How much did you hear?"

"Enough to know you're in trouble right up to your pretty little neck."

His patronizing manner infuriated her. She narrowed her eyes and put her hands on her hips. "Mr. Kennebrae, I can assure you, my late-night jaunts have nothing to do with meeting a lover. That you jumped to that conclusion does you no favor in my eyes."

His hands moved from the rail to her arms. "It was not a far leap. Can you deny that I found you in the presence of more than one man in the middle of the night on Lake Avenue? What were you doing down there if not an assignation? Aside from your minders, who was the person you embraced in the shadows?"

"None of your business. Now unhand me, you ungallant oaf."

His grip tightened for a moment, his eyes angry and hot. Then his hands dropped to his sides, and he stepped back. "Very well, you give me no choice. I shall have to discuss this with your father. I'll get out of the engagement in such a way that my grandfather cannot object, and you'll find your night ramblings put to an end."

To his credit there was no triumph in his look. . .only sadness and disappointment. Had he really been hurt thinking she was seeing someone else?

But if Father found out, it would be disastrous. Time for a little diplomacy. "Please, don't tell Father. Won't you accept my word that I'm not seeing another man?" She smiled up at him, tilting her head and giving him an entreating look.

"I cannot. If for no other reason than your safety. Those two delinquents you use as bodyguards, while effective last night, aren't to be counted on in real trouble. Something far worse might happen to you wandering in that part of town at that hour. Then there is your family to consider. If someone finds out, your reputation will be in tatters—and not only yours but, as your fiancé, mine as well. I'll be a laughingstock. And I can't imagine what your mother would say. She's a social dragon as it is." He took her hands in his, all anger wiped away. "Come clean, Melissa. If it isn't another man, then what is it?"

"I can't tell you. You wouldn't understand."

"Try me. You must tell me if for no other reason than to clear your name."

She twisted her hands, staring at the shore slipping by, the waves lapping on the rocky beach. He'd do it. She could see it in his eyes. His way out of the engagement. But would he hold his tongue if he knew her secret? Perhaps, once he understood. . . She'd have to risk it.

She drew in a ragged breath. "I can't tell you, but I can show you. Tomorrow night."

Chapter 8

Melissa slipped out the door, waggling her fingers back at Sarah. "I've got my key. Don't wait up for me."

"You know I have to. I never rest easy until you're back, miss. And I'm worried, you taking *him*. What if he blows the whistle?"

"If I don't take him, he says he'll tell Father I'm meeting a man at night. I have no choice. Now, I must go. He's waiting."

She closed the door and stood still to allow her eyes to adjust to the darkness. An ever-present damp smell off the lake surrounded her.

Please, Lord, let him understand. I don't want to take him, but I don't know what else to do. If he does tell, help me to bear it. Help me to stand up to Father and Jonathan.

Her shoes crunched on the path. She slipped through the iron gate, latching it with a *click* that sounded like a gunshot to her ears. Melissa sucked in her bottom lip and melted into the hedge. No lights appeared in the upstairs windows.

He was waiting for her—but not alone.

"What is this?"

"A carriage. Surely you've heard of them? I'm sorry I don't have an automobile. I've one ordered, but it hasn't arrived yet."

"We can't have this standing in the street while we're inside. The Kennebrae crest on the door would be a dead giveaway."

She couldn't see his eyes under the brim of his hat, but his hand on her arm closed tight. "Use common sense for once. You'll ride in my carriage, or you won't go. Where do I tell the driver to take us?"

The obstinate man needed a kick in the shin. He was ruining everything, and he didn't even seem to care.

"The Cassell Building." With bad grace she climbed into the carriage and plopped onto the seat.

He ducked inside and eased down on the seat opposite her. He put his gray-gloved hands atop his walking stick and stared at her. "Are you sure you just can't tell me what this is all about? I'd much rather be home in my own bed right now than traipsing about the harbor at this hour."

She lifted her chin and gave him a haughty stare in the light of the carriage lamps. "You can always let me out and go home. No one invited you. You're here of your own stubborn free will."

He laughed but not a friendly one. "Don't speak to me of stubborn willfulness. You epitomize the term. I can only imagine our destination. You say it isn't a clandestine meeting with a man, so I can only surmise the truth. A gambling den? Is that it? Are you squandering your inheritance on the turn of a card or the roll of a die? I've heard there are a few such establishments in the harbor area, though I confess I've never been to one."

"Don't be ridiculous. I'm not gambling. I wouldn't begin to know how."

He grunted. The sound grated on Melissa like sour notes on the piano.

The carriage clattered to a stop. Jonathan opened the door and hopped out, and then he held up his hand to help her alight.

Her feet had barely hit the pavement when she turned to him. "Please, won't you at least send the carriage away? No one could mistake it in this town, and it would cause talk. Please?"

"I don't intend to be here that long. The carriage stays. People will think I'm working late, as we're right across the street from my own building."

She wanted to whack him with her handbag. Stubborn oaf. If only Peter and Wilson were here. He needed another crack on the head.

Tears of frustration stung her eyes. Before she completely embarrassed herself, she lifted her hem and headed around to the side of the multi-storied brick building.

Narrow strips of light seeped around the edges of the basement windows. Thick bars covered the arched glass at street level. She descended the concrete steps to the basement entrance, her shoes echoing grittily.

Jonathan followed behind without a word.

She dug in her handbag for the key, but before she could use it, the door cracked open. She blinked in the light, the heat from inside the building puffing against her face.

"Melissa. We've been waiting." Beatrice Britten smiled at her, reaching for her hand to draw her inside. She glanced over Melissa's shoulder and froze, eyes wide.

"I'm sorry. He made me bring him." Guilt swamped Melissa, along with anger at Jonathan for putting her in this position. "This is Jonathan Kennebrae, my. . ." She swallowed hard. "My fiancé."

Beatrice narrowed her eyes, looking Jonathan over from shiny boots to brushed hair. "What do you want here? This isn't any place for the likes of you." She put her hand to her hip, bunching her apron over her plain wool dress.

"I'll be the judge of that." Jonathan didn't back down from her scrutiny or her unwelcoming glare.

"The rest of them aren't going to like it. I don't know that we should let him in. You know what will happen—"

"Please," Melissa interrupted, "I'll vouch for him."

Beatrice gave them both one more doubt-loaded glance before stepping back. Melissa hurried inside. Jonathan entered, removing his hat.

A narrow hallway with doors on one side, lit at long intervals with electric bulbs on cords from the ceiling, led off to the right. A rumble of voices came from the far end.

"Go ahead." Beatrice waved them down the hall. "I'm still waiting for folks."

Melissa eased off her gloves as she hurried toward the far end. Jonathan kept pace easily.

At the last door she turned to plead with him one more time, but the determined look in his eyes told her it was no use. She opened the door.

∞

Jonathan steeled himself, but nothing prepared him for the scene that met his eyes.

All noise ceased. At least two dozen pairs of eyes stared at him. Women crammed every corner of the room.

Piles of fabric lay on tables in the center of the room, yellow, white, and purple. Around one small table near the door, six young women huddled with books and paper. A blackboard covered most of one wall, while pegs holding more fabric dominated another. What was this place?

"At least you now know I'm not meeting men here." Melissa crossed her arms and gave him a petulant glare. Her mouth scrunched up prettily, her thick lashes filtering her look.

For the first time he took in her dress. Plain in every respect. Dull-brown tweed coat, ordinary black skirts showing below, and a simple straw boater with a black ribbon. She dressed like the other women in the room.

"What is this place? And what is the fabric for?"

"We're organizing a rally, and the fabric is for sashes and banners."

He didn't know whether to laugh or shout. "A rally? What's so secret about a rally? What cause could necessitate all this cloak-and-dagger nonsense?"

Every eye in the room was still on him, every ear listening.

"It's all right, ladies." Melissa sought to reassure them. "This is my fiancé, Mr. Jonathan Kennebrae."

At least this time she didn't choke on the term. He chose not to analyze how content he was to have her recognize him as her intended.

She grabbed his elbow and tugged him over to the blackboard. "It's a rally for women's suffrage. Now do you understand?"

He looked about the room again.

Though the women had gone back to their work, no one was talking. They cast suspicious glances at him, particularly the group with the books in the corner.

"I'm afraid I must be obtuse. I fail to see the need to hide in a basement. The issue of women's suffrage is not a new one. Rallies for the enfranchisement of women have been held in many cities in this country."

Melissa closed her eyes and shook her head slowly, as if amazed at his denseness. "Not in this city and not with these women. Come here—maybe then you will understand." She led him to the corner table.

Wide eyes, pale hair, narrow bodies. The six women could be sisters.

"The women in this room are for the most part wives and daughters of dockworkers. They're immigrants, mostly from Scandinavia but Germany and the Slavic countries, too. We meet here at night because it is the only time many of these women are free of their other responsibilities. They sacrifice sleep to come here. And it isn't just for these women we're working. It's for women in every corner of this state. If certain people knew we were planning this rally, they would take steps to stop it. So we've kept it quiet."

"How many women are involved in this?"

"More than one hundred at last count. Obviously we can't all come every night. We take turns. And until now, no one has breathed a word of it outside the circle." Again the accusing look.

"All right." Jonathan crossed his arms, relieved her night ramblings were so benign. "But what about the books and the blackboard?"

"Some of these women barely speak English. We, the other educated ladies and myself, take turns teaching them to read and write. They want to speak and read English. They want to take part in the government of their new country, to be able to understand what their children are learning in school, to read the newspaper. They aren't stupid, like so many people think. They are intelligent, strong women who deserve a chance to speak for themselves in this country." Each word came more forcefully, her hands fisted, eyes flashing.

He rubbed his hand over the lower half of his face. The eyes of these women—worried, harried, tired—pierced him. How could he, who loved reading so much, who owed so much to his own schooling, deny them the chance to learn to read, to better themselves? As for women's suffrage, well, he had to admit, he'd not given it much thought.

"What are you going to do, Jonathan? I'm telling you right now, this movement will go on. It's too important. If you let the secret out, the meetings will just move to another place. It might slow us down, but we won't stop." Her cheeks were flushed, her eyes glowing with the passion of her cause. He had no idea she had such fire inside.

He cleared his throat, stepping back.

"Well, what are you going to do, Jonathan?" She challenged him again, hands on hips.

"I don't know. I'm going to think about it." And he'd have to do some hard thinking about how his attraction to her was growing.

She turned, tossing a glance at him over her shoulder. "Well, if you're staying, grab a needle and thread or a primer. We have work to do."

Chapter 9

S top your gloating." Jonathan pushed Grandfather's chair down the hallway toward Lawrence Brooke's office.

"Now, now, don't be cranky. You'd think you didn't sleep at all last night. Are you nervous?" Grandfather clasped his portfolio in his weathered hands. "It's a mere formality."

"I'm not signing anything today. I told you that. And if I could think of a way to delay this meeting, I would." Especially until he got his feelings for Melissa under control.

He hardly understood himself these days. Even after returning from seeing her home last night, he lay awake, hands behind his head, staring at the ceiling but seeing her face, hearing her voice as she patiently corrected pronunciation, smelling her rose perfume each time she came near.

"You're only putting off the inevitable. You'll see. It will be for the best."

A clerk stood at the end of the hall, holding the oak and glass door open. Jonathan nodded his thanks and directed the chair through the doorway.

Geoffrey met them first, his most impartial lawyer's expression firmly in place.

Lawrence Brooke sat behind a massive carved desk. An inkwell in the shape of a sinister black panther crouched on the glass top, looking ready to pounce on the unwary. Lawrence stood, grave faced. "Let's go into the conference room, shall we?"

Jonathan wheeled Grandfather through to an adjoining room. A long oval table dominated the space, surrounded by high-backed chairs. He nodded to Wasserman, not surprised to see his grandfather's favorite lawyer in attendance. At least Jonathan had Geoffrey there for moral support.

Two other occupants captured Jonathan's attention. Almina Brooke sat at the head of the table as if to conduct the meeting herself. On her right, Melissa stared at her lap. He hadn't expected her to be here.

Melissa looked up, eyes pleading with him.

His heart jumped. She had pale-gray smudges under each eye. A glare from her mother had her dropping her hand from her mouth to her lap. Jonathan was amazed at how familiar the gesture had become to him in such a short time. She always bit her nails when she was worried. A wave of protectiveness washed over him.

Jonathan strode the length of the table and took a seat beside her, ignoring the questioning look from Geoffrey and the triumphant gleam in Grandfather's eyes. No one seemed to appreciate how difficult this was, especially for Melissa. The two of them were being bartered like company assets.

He acknowledged Mrs. Brooke and listened while introductions were made. Lawrence Brooke's lawyers flanked him, while his secretary, a pale wraith of a man, sat along the wall taking notes. Wasserman sat beside Grandfather to guard his interests. Geoff sat between Jonathan and Grandfather.

Melissa put her hand on Jonathan's arm.

He bent low to hear her whisper, "Are you going to tell?"

For hours he had wrestled with this very question. If he spilled her secret, he was free. No engagement, no marriage, no merger. All he had to do was raise a fuss about her nightly jaunts, the suffrage politics, declare her unsuitable as his bride.

Lawrence Brooke had been outspoken on more than one occasion against giving women the franchise. Women—in his opinion, being the weaker sex— were unable to bear the responsibility of voting in political elections.

Grandfather would sputter and fume, but Jonathan would be free and still have Kennebrae Shipping, too. There was no way Grandfather would force him to marry a woman who was a political radical.

Jonathan shot a glance at Almina. By no stretch of the imagination could she be considered weak, but she would be mortified, humiliated if her daughter's character were called into question.

And what of Melissa herself? Could he ruin her reputation, bring down scandal and scorn on her just to extricate himself from the engagement? The thought of her wounded expression, the hurt he would cause her made him wince.

Not to mention the women associated with her in the cause. Those hardworking, immigrant women struggling to learn to read, to better themselves and fight for women's rights in a new country. Dreaming their new lives in America would be better than the oppression and poverty of their homelands. What right did he have to dash those dreams? Though he had never given much thought to women's suffrage, after seeing those women, seeing the passion Melissa had for them, he found he was inclined to support the idea.

He looked into Melissa's eyes, his heart hammering against his waistcoat. "No, your secret's safe with me." In that moment he knew he'd do whatever he could to keep her secret, to protect her in any way he could.

Relief flooded her face. For a moment he thought she might throw her arms around him and hug him. He tamped down his disappointment when she didn't. She returned her eyes to the mangled handkerchief in her lap.

He shifted in his chair. "I'm surprised to see you here."

"Mother insisted she had one item to discuss with me present. Then we would leave the rest to the men."

Jonathan nodded and sat back to endure the proceedings.

Attaché cases were opened, papers spread, and lawyers huddled, offering and counteroffering.

Jonathan listened with only half an ear, distracted by what Melissa's secret could mean for both of them and half-curious as to what Almina Brooke felt was so important she needed to oversee that part of the contract herself. He wasn't left long to wonder.

"I have to insist"—Almira interrupted his thoughts—"that a certain amount of funds be settled on Melissa at her marriage by you, Lawrence, which shall be hers alone, to be used at her discretion."

Melissa looked up. Her hands tightened into fists.

Jonathan sat up, his attention totally caught. Every man at the table did likewise.

Lawrence cleared his throat and lowered his brows at his wife. "Almina? Are you suggesting Jonathan will not give our daughter a suitable allowance?"

All eyes swiveled to Jonathan to gauge his reaction. His chest prickled. "Mr. Brooke, I fully intend—" What did he intend? Certainly he wasn't entertaining the thought of actually going through with this marriage, was he?

Almina tapped her fingers on the table. "Lawrence, this isn't about Jonathan or allowances. I feel strongly that Melissa should have a nest egg of her own. You know, for those little things a woman needs. Or even to provide a special gift for her children's birthdays or her husband's. This money should come from us, from you, on her wedding day."

An uneasy feeling climbed Jonathan's rib cage. Almina was plotting his children? He darted a look at Melissa, whose cheeks glowed. He should say something, but what?

Lawrence mulled over his wife's words, tugging at his mustache.

The lawyers sat still, pens hovering.

"Very well. How much?"

"I should think two million would be suitable." Almina didn't bother to hide the challenge in her eyes.

Jonathan wasn't sure if he gasped, but he knew Geoffrey sucked in a breath. Two million for an opening salvo. The woman had courage.

She went on. "Given the sums involved, I should think two million dollars, to be used by Melissa as she sees fit, providing she marries Mr. Kennebrae, is not too much to ask. You're talking about a merger worth ten times that much. What you do with the rest of the marriage contract is up to you, but I insist that you do right by your daughter."

No one moved.

Grandfather's eyes shone like hot coals.

Almina stared at Lawrence.

He studied her for a long moment, her challenge to his generosity hanging over the table like a sword. He pursed his lips. At last Lawrence reached forward and dipped his pen in an inkwell. "Make it three million, my wedding gift to Melissa."

Melissa stiffened and started to speak, but Almina's claw came down on her arm, squeezing it.

Jonathan frowned and took Melissa's other hand from her lap, closing his around it, surprised at her cold flesh.

Almina's triumphant look made him wonder if three million wasn't her aim all along. "Very good. That settled, Melissa and I will depart. Good day, gentlemen."

Jonathan released Melissa's hand.

When the ladies rose, every man did, too, save Grandfather.

Melissa gave Jonathan one last stunned look before following her dragon of a mother from the room.

◆

"That went well." Geoffrey tapped some files against his leg as they walked into the Kennebrae Shipping offices. "I had no idea Brooke was worth so much. A twenty-million-dollar wedding settlement, with an expected fifty-million-dollar inheritance. Not including a three-million-dollar nest egg for the bride apart from it all. It boggles the mind."

Jonathan grunted. "I didn't know Grandfather had branched out in so many areas." Admittedly Jonathan had focused his attention only on Kennebrae Shipping. To find that his family had interests in so many cities and in so many ventures astounded him.

A foundry in Cleveland. Rental properties in New York City, Boston, and Charleston. Shares in railroads, mines, and manufacturing. How many times during the meeting had Grandfather stared at Jonathan when Brooke mentioned grain contracts and new ships?

Jonathan opened his office door and stopped. Geoffrey bumped into his back.

"Thought you'd never get here. Where've you been, and where's Grandfather?" Noah lounged in Jonathan's chair, his boots propped up on the blotter. He twirled a peaked cap on one finger.

"Noah! You weren't expected for two more days. When did you get in?" Jonathan's gaze flew to the windows. Sure enough, the *Bethany* sat at the Number One Dock.

"Midmorning. The repairs weren't as extensive as first thought. They patched the leak temporarily, and we limped on home. I figured it would be better to have the majority of the work done here where our own shipbuilders can oversee the repairs. And I want the entire boiler gone over. That will take two or three weeks. Then I figure I can squeeze in one more trip through the Soo before we're iced in for winter." He swept his boots off the desk and stood.

Jonathan grabbed him in a hug. The smell of open water, windy skies, and coal smoke lingered in Noah's thick wool tunic. "When did you get so strong?"

Noah laughed. "A life on the water builds muscles. More than shuffling papers behind a desk." He rubbed his chin. "What do you think of the beard?"

Jonathan studied the bushy brown whiskers covering his brother's face. "Is that what you're calling that weed patch?"

Noah laughed and cuffed Jonathan on the shoulder. "All captains wear beards. It's a mark of authority." He turned to Geoffrey. "Hello, Geoff. Still minding Kennebrae's interests?"

Geoff grinned and shook Noah's hand. "Today more than usual, Noah. Welcome home."

Noah settled into a chair before the fireplace. "Is that where you were? Some stuffy meeting?"

Jonathan squared up the piles of paper on his desk. "Yes. And, Noah, we need to talk. Grandfather has been up to his old tricks, only this time it's worse."

"You know, sometimes I'm afraid to pull into the harbor. What's he done now?"

"Geoff, have a seat. You can clarify any points I miss." Jonathan leaned his elbows on the desk and steepled his fingers. When his lawyer was seated, Jonathan began a recounting of recent events.

"And so," he finished up, "I have to get married or forfeit Kennebrae Shipping altogether."

Noah sat, slack jawed as a sturgeon. "Are you serious?"

"Dead serious. We were just at a meeting with Brooke's lawyers to draw up the contract."

"You're not going through with it? Isn't there some way to stop it?"

Jonathan shook his head. "Not that I'm prepared to take at this time. Geoff, show him the paperwork."

Geoff dug in his file and produced a thick document.

Noah perused only the first page. "Did you sign this?" He looked at Jonathan with grave eyes.

"No, I told them I wouldn't sign anything today, and I didn't expect them to either. Each side needs a few days at least to go over the transaction. Hopefully that will give me time to find a way out without losing Kennebrae Shipping." *And without sullying Melissa's reputation.*

"But you said the engagement had already been announced. If you back out now, folks might think there's something wrong with the girl. Is there something wrong with her?"

"Not a thing." Heat crept up Jonathan's cheeks at the vehemence of his reply.

Noah sat back and studied Jonathan. A slow grin spread over Noah's face. "You like her. That's why you haven't told Grandfather what he can do with Kennebrae Shipping. You don't want to get out of this engagement."

"Don't be ridiculous. I barely know her."

"Well, what's she like?" Noah tossed the papers back to Geoff. "No, on second thought, you can't be unbiased. I'd rather hear it from Geoffrey. You've met her, haven't you, Geoff?"

Jonathan thrust his chair back and strode to the windows. Noah could be such a tease. He'd forgotten how his younger brothers could grate on him at times.

"She's beautiful." Geoffrey jumped in. "Lovely blue eyes, brown hair. I hear she plays the piano and speaks French fluently. Jonathan took me along to the luncheon where the engagement was announced." Jonathan could hear the grin in Geoff's voice and tightened his jaw.

"Grandfather's working fast. Go on, Geoff."

Jonathan groaned and hung his head. Noah was bound to hear it sometime, but Jonathan had hoped he'd be far away when his brother got the story. But perhaps it was better to get it over with now. He turned and sent a glare Geoffrey's way, knowing it wouldn't stop his lawyer from telling the tale with relish.

"Lawrence Brooke announced the engagement, and the bride-to-be jumped up, squawked a little at Jonathan, then fainted dead away." Geoff glanced guiltily in Jonathan's direction but not before Jonathan saw the amusement there, too.

Noah began to laugh. "So you're saying the thought of marrying big brother knocked her out cold?"

"He swept her off her feet."

Both men doubled over, howling.

Jonathan fisted his hands and envisioned popping both of them on their noses.

When Noah composed himself, he sat up, eyes full of mischief. "I've got to meet this girl. You'll give me an introduction, right? And I know just what to get you for an engagement present."

"What?"

"Smelling salts!"

Little brothers could be such pains. Time for some revenge.

"Noah, there's more."

"What, did she have a fit of hysteria when a wedding date was set?" He couldn't stop chuckling.

"I'm not the only one Grandfather is hustling down the aisle."

Noah quit laughing. He regarded Jonathan with a wary eye.

"He's got brides all picked out for you and Eli, too."

Noah sagged into his chair, the wind taken out of his sails.

Satisfaction settled in Jonathan's chest. Perhaps now Noah would be serious and find a way out of this mess for all of them.

"Okay, this is beyond funny now." Noah swallowed hard.

Chapter 10

Melissa stood on the low table, arms out to her sides at shoulder height, trying not to move. Pinpricks threatened with each breath. Mother and the seamstress she'd imported from New York huddled a few feet away, tossing looks over their shoulders and murmuring.

"It's so beautiful. I wish I was getting married." Her friend Zylphia wound some lace trim around her hand. "You look like a princess."

I feel like a dress-up doll. Mother's doll to dress up and show off when it suits her. Melissa forced a smile and kept her thoughts to herself. It did her little good to voice them.

"The train should be at least ten feet long. And trim it with the seed pearls." Mother lifted a handful of the opalescent beads, letting them dribble through her fingers back into the bowl.

The seamstress, a petite, dark Frenchwoman, took notes and nodded, keeping her lips pinched tight. Perhaps the habit of holding pins in her mouth had left it permanently scrunched.

"And use these crystals, too. In the floral pattern we discussed. Recreate the pattern in this lace." Mother plucked the lace from Zylphia's hand and unrolled it.

The skein landed with a thump on the rug. Zylphia rolled her eyes and shrugged, and Melissa stifled a giggle. Not more than two minutes ago Mother had insisted Zylphia roll up the excess lace to prevent its getting damaged.

Madame Lisette began removing the pins from the cotton mock-up pieces draped all over Melissa's frame.

With relief Melissa lowered her arms and stepped out of the skirt. Sarah held her dressing gown, and Melissa slipped her arms into the comforting garment. Her chemise and petticoats were no protection against the chill in the attic sewing room.

"Get dressed, Melissa, and you and Zylphia can take tea." Mother looked up from leafing through sketches. "I'll be here quite some time yet. I still can't decide if this new charmeuse fabric is the best choice or not."

Melissa hurried to her room and slipped into a yellow dress. Her hair looked a mess from pulling garments over her head. Unpinned it fell to her waist in heavy brown curls. She plaited it, her fingers quick from long practice, and left the braid hanging down her back.

The usual sense of calm Melissa experienced when entering the blue parlor failed to come over her. As always, her mother's forceful personality drove the wedding plans, drowning the household in a storm surge of details about fabric, music, flowers, attendants. And she consulted Melissa not at all. A piece of driftwood had about as much say in its destination.

Zylphia was seated on one of the velvet chairs, leafing through a photo album.

Melissa forswore being ladylike and flopped down on the ivory damask couch, plopping her feet up on a cushion.

"Well?" Zylphia pounced on her, grabbing her shoulders and giving her a little shake. "Are you going to tell me? You promised."

"Let's get through tea, and I'll tell all."

Anne, the parlor maid, entered with the tea tray, her black skirts swishing. She set the tray down on the marble-topped table. "Can I get you anything else?"

Melissa shook her head. "Thank you, Anne. That will be all. Why don't you go put your feet up for a few minutes?"

"Thank you, miss." She bobbed her head and left the parlor, her heels clicking on the parquet.

"Tell me. I can't stand it anymore." Zylphia poured her tea and stirred in a spoonful of sugar. "What's so urgent?"

Melissa regretted her rash promise to tell Zylphia her secret, but she desperately needed someone to confide in. And Zylphia could be a help if she would. The more women they had, the better. "You have to promise not to tell anyone. Not your mother, not your maid, no one."

"I promise. Now tell me."

Melissa sat up and checked that the door was closed. Then she leaned close to Zylphia. "I'm involved in underground meetings to organize a women's suffrage rally here in Duluth."

Zylphia sat back, disbelief spread over her pretty face. "Women's suffrage? Is that all? I thought it was something romantic or dangerous."

"It is, dangerous at least. Why else would I sneak out in the middle of the night and walk downtown for the meetings? And could you imagine what my father would say if he found out?"

"You sneak out at night?" Zylphia's eyes lit up. She leaned forward. "Tell me more."

Melissa described her nighttime activities, mentioning how Peter and Wilson picked her up in their family delivery wagon and watched over her to see that she came to no harm. About the women who wanted to learn to read and write, and who most of all wanted to vote, to have a say in the government that ruled them. "And there's more. Jonathan knows."

"He does? And he doesn't mind?" Zylphia's mouth opened in surprise.

"I don't think he's very happy about it, but so far he hasn't told anyone. He followed me down there. The first time he didn't make it to the building. Peter and Wilson got a little overeager and knocked him on the head. That's why he had the bruise on his temple at the sailing luncheon."

Zylphia squeezed her hands together. "What happened?"

"He was angry. I had to tell him about the meetings, or he was going straight to Father. That would've been disastrous. Father doesn't know anything about it, and I'd like to keep it that way. I took Jonathan to one of the meetings, hoping that once he saw the women and how much they were being helped and how serious we are about this, he might relent and keep quiet. I think it might have worked." Melissa picked up the teapot. "Anyway he stayed for the whole three hours and even listened to some of the ladies who were learning to read."

"He listened to lessons?"

Warmth tickled Melissa's heart. He'd sat at the table with those Norwegian ladies listening to their halting English, his long legs cramped under the rickety chair, his hair falling on his forehead. He hadn't laughed at them or belittled their lack of education, nor had he sneered at the banners and sashes, the pamphlets and placards piled about the room. "I don't know what his next move will be. I haven't even seen him since the lawyer's meeting on Monday."

"Did your father really give you three million dollars?"

Melissa twisted her mouth in a grimace. "Not exactly. None of the papers has been signed yet. If and when I marry Jonathan Kennebrae, I will receive three million dollars of my own money."

"And Jonathan agreed? No woman has money that isn't her husband's to control."

"I will, thanks to Mother's insistence."

"What are you going to do with it?"

"I don't know. I have a few ideas."

A knock sounded at the door. The housekeeper marched in, her keys jangling on the chatelaine at her waist. "A note arrived for you, Miss Brooke."

Mrs. Trolley's sallow face pinched in displeasure. She held out an envelope, wrinkled and smudged. "The man who delivered it looked rather. . .untidy."

Melissa's lips twitched at this, the most dire description one could earn from Mrs. Trolley. "Thank you."

Mrs. Trolley looked down her hooked nose, swept the tea tray with a glance, and departed.

"Who's it from?"

Melissa slit the envelope with a butter knife. She scanned the single s of paper. Her mind raced. "What are we going to do?"

"What?" Zylphia's voice rose in alarm. "What is it?"

Melissa bit her thumbnail, trying and tossing out ideas. No, that wouldn't work. No, no, no. Why now? She folded the paper and slipped it into her pocket. "I need some help. I've got to see Jonathan."

∽

Jonathan slung the papers down on his desk and rubbed his palm across the back of his neck. Why couldn't he concentrate?

Melissa. Plain and simple, she wouldn't leave his head. Even Noah had noticed his lack of concentration, his gazing into nothing, his preoccupation. Thoughts of her invaded every waking moment and even his dreams. He imagined he could smell her rose perfume, hear her laughter, see her determined little face as she stood up to him for what she believed in.

Her note crackled in his pocket, and he withdrew it. What kind of sap was he that even the sight of her handwriting stirred him? She needed to see him, as soon as possible.

He'd fired off a reply inviting her and her parents to dinner so quickly he'd smeared the ink. It pleased him that she needed him. The protective feelings he'd begun to harbor toward her swelled.

Jonathan paced his sitting room, his feet quiet on the Persian rug. He muttered to himself, sifting through his feelings, analyzing, evaluating, testing each one.

"Why are you so distracted by her? Sure, she's pretty, but there has to be more."

He stopped before the windows, pulling the drapes aside to look down on the pewter surface of the lake.

"Is it the money?" He had to face the question squarely.

An honest search of his heart told him the truth. No, his feelings had nothing to do with money.

"I'd feel this way if she had no more money in this world than those immigrant women she tutors." A rush of relief followed the statement. He paused, gripping the heavy brocade fabric.

"But what is it I feel?"

Protective. He could acknowledge that. Friendly? No, it was more than that. He had plenty of friends, and he'd never felt this way about any of them.

"Are you really as dense as that?"

[...] voice caused Jonathan to spin toward the door.

[...]ainst his door frame, ankles and arms crossed.

[...]e you been there?" Jonathan scowled, shoving his hands

[...]o know what you're too dumb to see."

[...]t that be?" Jonathan pursed his lips.

Noah rolled his eyes. "You're in love with the girl you're supposed to marry."

Jonathan tensed. "Don't be ridiculous."

"You're the one who's being ridiculous. It's as plain as a lighthouse beacon on a clear night that you love her. You've been all but walking into walls this week. You swing from wanting to talk about her all the time to not wanting to talk about her at all. You've lost your perspective and your sense of humor. If you don't love her, then you're giving a mighty good imitation."

Did he love her? How could he tell? All he knew was that he felt better when he was with her than he'd ever felt before, and when they weren't together, she was all he could think about. Maybe he did love her.

Noah crossed the room and put his hand on Jonathan's shoulder. "It's not a crime to be happy, Jonathan. If you love her, then try to win her heart. It will be worth it in the end."

Jonathan nodded slowly, his mind whirling. In love with Melissa Brooke? Wouldn't that beat all?

Chapter 11

The carriage rocked along the street in and out of pools of light cast by the street lamps. Melissa smoothed her skirts and tugged at her gloves. Sarah had done a wonderful job getting Melissa ready on such short notice.

The tone of the horses' hooves changed as they pulled off the road and onto a gravel drive. The carriage lurched to a stop. She didn't know if she'd feel better or worse if her parents had been able to accompany her. But they'd had a previous engagement. It had taken all of Melissa's persuasive powers to get her mother to allow her to accept Jonathan's invitation to dinner at Kennebrae House without her parents.

The driver helped her alight. Lamps burned on either side of the massive front doors, casting shadows under the domed roof of the porte cochere. Before she could ring the bell, the door swung open.

A silver-haired man in a black suit stepped back for her to enter. "Good evening, Miss Brooke." He inclined his head.

She hoped her smile wasn't as nervous as her quivering middle. What was the matter with her?

"May I take your cloak, miss?" His gloved hands gleamed white in the light of the chandelier.

She loosened the velvet ties at her throat, trying to swallow. The reception hall stretched at least fifty feet to the right and left. Broad steps to the second floor dominated the wall across from her, everything paneled in darkly stained oak. Oaken carved pillars stood sentinel at intervals, vines and leaves and flowers with the occasional cupid face peeking out. She'd heard about the fantastic parties held in this room in years past, but nothing had prepared her for the sheer size of the building. It was less a home than a castle. Every inch declared it the abode of men. No flowers or bright colors, nothing soft or gentle.

The butler took her wrap and draped it over his arm. "This way, if you please." He led her to the left, nearly to the end of the long hall, before stopping at a door. "The gentlemen are in the parlor." He opened the door. "Miss Brooke, sir."

When he stepped aside, Melissa entered the room. A fire blazed in the marble fireplace. Another chandelier gleamed overhead, throwing prisms of light on the painted ceiling.

"Melissa." Jonathan came forward to greet her.

She put out her hand. "Thank you for the dinner invitation. I need to speak with you."

"And I with you, but later." Jonathan tucked her hand into his elbow and led her to the fireplace. "Grandfather, Melissa's here."

"Hello, my dear. You're looking splendid. Come, sit down. Dinner will be ready in a few minutes. Warm yourself." He patted the chair beside him. "I'm delighted you could join us. It's too bad your parents couldn't come, but we'll have them over soon."

Melissa eased into the chair, trying to calm her nerves.

Abraham Kennebrae was as charming as ever, chattering away.

Jonathan stood by the mantel, looking down on her. His intent gaze heated her through more than the fire. Though she'd thought of him constantly for days, being in the same room with him made her heart skip and her breath come fast.

The door opened once more. A bearded man of Jonathan's height sauntered in, hands in his pockets. He stopped when he saw Melissa. "Well, this is a pleasant surprise. It's been years since this parlor was graced with so beautiful a woman. I'm Noah Kennebrae."

He took Melissa's offered hand and bent over it gallantly, squeezing her fingers and kissing the air above her knuckles. "You must be the girl who stole Jonathan's heart. He's been walking around like a lovesick duck for the last week." Noah grinned wickedly at his brother. "But even his description of you doesn't do you justice."

Jonathan had been talking about her? Did he think she was pretty? Melissa tried to squelch that vain thought, but it wouldn't lie down. She'd been on his mind. Was his brother's teasing true? Had she stolen his heart? Ridiculous, not when he wanted out of this engagement as badly as she did. And she did want out, didn't she?

Jonathan's brows shot down, and he glared at his brother.

Noah chuckled, his teeth white against his dark beard.

Jonathan took two steps and removed Melissa's hand from Noah's grasp. "Knock it off, Noah." His tone brooked no argument.

Melissa clasped her hands in her lap, glancing from one man to the other.

Noah didn't seem upset by Jonathan's glower. On the contrary, his grin widened, and he shoved his hands back into his pockets under his coat and rocked on his heels.

Abraham's eyes danced, a smile quivering about his lips. "Ah, this is just what I envisioned when this engagement was first spoken of. The banter of family, the softness of a woman's presence in our masculine household. If only Eli could be here to share it with us."

Melissa turned her attention away from Jonathan to his grandfather. "Eli?"

"Eli is the youngest of the Kennebrae brothers, though only by a few minutes. He and Noah are twins, similar but not identical. He's in Virginia studying shipbuilding. He'll be home in a few months."

Jonathan took a seat on the settee, stretching his long legs toward the fire. Noah leaned against the wall beside the fireplace. "And some news he'll come home to. If I were him, I'd stay away for a long time."

Abraham's hands fisted. "We've been through this." His voice, so sharp in contrast to just minutes ago, startled Melissa. "He will accede to my wishes, or he'll suffer the consequences, as will you all. I'm still the head of this family." Pink suffused his pale cheeks.

Melissa looked to Jonathan, wondering how he would take this ultimatum.

He sat up, placed his elbows on his knees, and stared into the flames. Tired lines creased his face, the barest hint of bruise still coloring his temple. "Yes, Grandfather, we know. You've made it abundantly clear on more than one occasion."

"Don't get smart with me, young man. And don't patronize me." Abraham's breath rasped, his narrow chest rising and falling quickly. "And don't think I don't know what you're up to with delaying signing the marriage contract. Mark my words, this marriage will proceed."

"Take it easy. You know the doctor says you shouldn't get worked up," Noah said, standing up straight. "And you're forgetting our guest. Melissa, don't mind them."

Apprehension fluttered across her skin. Was she to be a bone of contention between them always?

Abraham's head swiveled Melissa's way, the heat dying out of his face. "I beg your pardon, my dear. You see, this is what comes of an all-male household. We quite forget our manners."

The butler stood in the doorway. "Dinner is served."

Jonathan wiped his hand down his face and rose as if burdened with a great weight, his jaw firm, the skin drawn tight over his cheekbones. He offered Melissa his arm.

She tucked her hand into his elbow while Noah took the handle of Abraham's chair and wheeled him ahead. Melissa's heart went out to Jonathan, battling his stubborn grandfather. She knew what it was to fight her own parents for a bit of freedom, a bit of individuality.

When she squeezed his arm, he looked down at her in surprise, causing heat to rush up her cheeks. She averted her gaze, swallowing hard. They walked in silence down the long, carpeted reception hall to the dining room at the other end of the house.

Silver candelabras graced the table, throwing light toward the gleaming gilded panels of the coffered ceiling. Rich, tooled leather covered the upper walls, a luxurious forest green.

Noah wheeled Abraham to the far end of the table under the portraits.

Jonathan led Melissa down the row of chairs and pulled out the one on Abraham's left. Jonathan took the chair opposite Melissa, with Noah on his right.

Abraham held out his hand to Melissa. Confused, she placed her hand in his. The men all clasped hands and bowed their heads.

"Jonathan, will you offer the grace, please?" Abraham's voice cracked, and he cleared his throat.

Jonathan's voice comforted Melissa. He prayed, not by rote but as if he talked to a friend of long-standing, asking God's blessing on the food and those who partook of it and for a special blessing on Eli, so far from home. When he said, "Amen," Melissa looked up, catching his eye. Some of her butterflies concerning the reason for her coming tonight subsided. If he could talk to God like that, surely he would listen to her needs. But when could they be alone?

Two maids carried in the first course. Did they dine like this every night, or was this a special occasion because she was here?

Melissa and her mother often ate together in the evening. Lawrence Brooke spent long hours at his office or closeted away in his den working. He usually had a tray sent in about nine every night. Only when guests were expected did he break with his routine and dress for a formal dinner.

"The *Bethany* should be ready to pull out just after Thanksgiving. We can make one last dash to Chicago with ore and hustle back with a load of coal before the season ends." Noah picked up his fork.

Melissa studied Jonathan's younger brother. He had lines at the corners of his eyes, as if he spent a great deal of time looking out at the sun on the water. His hands were rough, calloused, and large, dwarfing his crystal water goblet. Sky blue eyes—so different from Jonathan's dark brown—didn't miss a trick. His mouth had the look of one with a sense of humor.

"That's leaving a bit late, don't you think? The weather's a bit tricky that time of year. You might be iced in by mid-November." Jonathan pursed his lips.

"Life's no fun if you don't take some risks. Anyway, I thought you wanted me to take another look at the docks in Chicago. Wasn't Jacobson headed down there to negotiate the sale?"

"What's this?" Abraham scowled. "I haven't heard about any docks in Chicago. When did this happen?"

"At the last board meeting. You weren't there, remember? You were holed up with your cronies, mapping out the future to suit yourself." Jonathan dropped his fork to his plate. "Like you have been for the last five board meetings. You said to take care of things myself, and that's just what I've done."

Abraham thumped the table with his fist. "I'm tired of this conversation. I've been over my reasons. Enough."

Melissa's skin prickled. How often this evening would she be reminded that she was a bartered bride? The food stuck in her throat, tasting of damp newspaper.

Jonathan flexed his jaw, clamping it shut on whatever he had been about to say.

Noah, his eyes filled with pity enough to make her squirm, changed the subject. "Melissa, I noticed you looking at the portraits." He waved toward the paintings in their heavy, gilded frames. "Those are our parents, Isaiah and Isabelle Kennebrae."

Melissa studied them, noting the dark hair Isaiah had passed on to his sons. Isabelle was more pleasant of feature than outright beautiful, but there was something in her expression, a liveliness, a fire, that drew Melissa's attention. She had yet to meet Eli, but both Jonathan and Noah had inherited that same passion—Jonathan for business and Noah for sailing. She made the appropriate comments and fell silent.

Dinner finished, as uncomfortable and strained as it had begun, Jonathan brooding and quiet, Abraham fuming, and Noah trying to carry the conversation. Melissa regretted coming tonight. If she married Jonathan, was this the evening entertainment she could look forward to for the rest of her life? If Noah hadn't been there, the meal would've been conducted in complete silence. Her dinner sat in her middle like an anchor.

Chapter 12

"Why don't we go to the music room? Melissa can play for us." Abraham tossed his napkin on the table, breaking his silence. "We've got a Steinway. Hasn't been played since my wife died."

Melissa shot Jonathan a pleading look.

Jonathan held her chair for her as she rose.

"I must speak with you." She kept her voice low, tucking her hand into his offered elbow.

He nodded. "Later."

She stopped, tugging on his arm. "Not later. Now."

Noah halted pushing Abraham's chair for only a second, and she realized she'd spoken louder than she'd intended.

"We'll join you in a few moments." Jonathan slid her chair under the table and waited.

"We're not competing in a race," Abraham scolded. "Slow down." Noah's reply was muffled by the doors closing.

Jonathan and Melissa stood alone in the dining room. She stepped back a pace and crossed her arms at her waist, pressing against her middle to still her nerves.

His brooding expression softened. "I'm sorry about tonight. I haven't been a very good host. Sometimes an afternoon of butting heads with Grandfather leaves me in a black mood. You had something you wanted to say?"

The enormity of what she was asking hit her. What if he wouldn't help her? Where could she turn next? Could she trust him with this? *Lord, give me courage.*

"I. . .I need your help. And I haven't much time. I got a note from the night watchman at the Cassell Building. He's leaving for St. Paul tomorrow and won't be back for several months. Tonight is his last night."

He frowned in confusion. "I fail to see how this concerns me. Surely they can find another night watchman."

"Of course they can." Was Jonathan being deliberately obtuse? "But the new watchman will hardly be likely to allow several immigrant ladies and dockworkers' wives into the building in the middle of the night. He'd drive them off or, worse, try to have them arrested for trespassing. The girls must clear the room out tonight."

Jonathan gripped the back of the carved mahogany chair, studying her. "What is it you are asking of me?"

She swallowed and wet her lips. His eyes fixed on her mouth, and a curious swirl started in her stomach. "We need another place to meet, and we need it tonight. Someplace safe."

He took a step toward her, towering over her, his gaze intent. "And did you have a place in mind?"

She nodded. He smelled of soap and spice. Her breath caught in her throat. What was he doing?

"Are you going to tell me?" His voice deepened, brushing across her like a caress.

She blinked in response and tried to remember what they were talking about. "Um. . .yes. The shipping office."

He raised an eyebrow. "You want to meet at Kennebrae Shipping? My office?" He went very still, and for a moment she thought he was going to refuse. Then he smiled, a slow, easy smile. "A good idea." He was so close she could feel his warmth through his dinner jacket. He raised his hands to caress her upper arms.

She shivered. "You are not yourself this evening, Jonathan. I expected. . ." She licked her lips again. "I thought you would be resistant to the idea."

His lips twitched. "You're right. I'm not myself. I'm tired. I'm tired to death of arguing with Grandfather." He bent a little closer. "I'm tired of wrestling with contracts, board members, and accountants' columns."

A few inches nearer, until he was only a breath away. "But most of all, I'm tired of fighting the urge to do this." He bent his head and kissed her, soft and incredibly gentle.

Her eyes fluttered closed, her heart beating so hard she thought he might feel it against his chest.

His hand came up to touch her throat, his thumb grazing her jaw. He stepped back, his eyes dark with feeling.

Her hand flew to her tingling lips. She swallowed hard and blinked, catching her breath.

"You're welcome to use the Kennebrae offices. In fact, use the private conference room connected to my office. You can haul your banners and books there, and I'll see no one disturbs them. The furnishings are much more comfortable than that basement storeroom you've been using. In fact, I'll send McKay to unlock the building and help the ladies move. He'll keep your secret safe. He's been harboring Kennebrae secrets for twenty years." Jonathan dug in his pocket and withdrew a key. "Here, take this. Then you can come and go as you please."

She didn't know which overwhelmed her more, his generosity or his kiss.

She smiled inwardly. Definitely his kiss.

Gather your wits, girl. Don't let him see how it affected you.

"What's changed your mind? I expected you to be thrilled at our predicament. I'd have to stop going out at night if we had no place to meet."

"You seem to have caught me when my resistance was low. . .in several areas." He pressed the key into her hand. "Perhaps I take solace in knowing you will be safely tucked away in my offices, in comfort, instead of in that drafty, dank basement. Or perhaps I believe in your cause and want to help you all I can."

She narrowed her eyes, appraising his sincerity. "I'd like to believe that."

"Then do. Let's join Grandfather in the music room. I have a sudden desire to hear a nocturne." He led her down the hall, and she wasn't sure her feet even touched the pale-blue carpeting.

The Steinway was beautiful with hand-carved legs like seated griffins in cherry, inlay marquetry in tendrils and leaves along the case, gleaming ivory keys, and a scrollwork music stand. But most beautiful of all, on the fallboard above the keys where the maker's name and city were usually displayed, this piano had a painting. A schooner in full sail, the rising sun picking out the details of masts and lines and rails, rode the waves of an aquamarine sea. Clouds in golds, pinks, and purples graced the sky. It was the most beautiful instrument she'd ever seen. She squelched the guilt she felt at not helping the ladies move tonight, salving her conscience that McKay would go in her stead.

She chose Beethoven's Moonlight Sonata. The music wrapped around her, carrying her away like the schooner on the melody and Jonathan's kiss.

Chapter 13

"You look different." Zylphia sipped her cup of chocolate, her eyes scanning the other diners. "Things must've gone well last night."

Melissa smiled and lowered her lashes. Last night. Her first kiss. She pressed her hand to her chest, feeling the key on a chain under her dress. The key to Kennebrae Shipping. The key to his heart?

"Things went wonderfully last night. At first it was a little rocky. Jonathan and his grandfather had been arguing, and dinner was a bit sticky, but the evening got much better after that."

"So tell me." Zylphia leaned toward her, squeezing her arm.

"They have a beautiful piano. I played Beethoven."

Her friend sagged back in her chair and rolled her eyes. "Oh phooey. I despair of you. I thought maybe something romantic had happened."

Melissa couldn't quell her smile.

Zylphia pounced. "I knew it. You are all lit up inside. Something must've happened."

"Jonathan agreed to let us—the cause, I mean—move into his office at night. Without any fuss at all. He sent a man to move the books and materials from the basement room across the street to his own conference room. We can work in comfort and safety, and he said we could use it as long as we like."

Zylphia blinked. "That's wonderful, but is that all?"

"It's all you're going to get from me." Melissa gave her a saucy grin. "Finish your chocolate. We've got shopping to do. I'm buying my trousseau, you know."

"Whatever happened, it must've been pretty nice. Yesterday you couldn't be bothered to even look at the drawings for your wedding gown, and today we're buying linens and picking out silver."

"Speaking of picking out silver, we have an appointment in ten minutes at the jeweler's. Mother selected three patterns she thought might be suitable. I'm to choose the one I like best."

"At least she gave you that much leeway. You'd think it was her getting married, not you. She's planned everything from the music to the menu to the flowers."

Melissa shook her head. "At least she has good taste. And I don't care, as long as I'm marrying Jonathan."

Zylphia's cup rattled in the saucer. "That's it! That's what's different about you."

"What?"

"You're in love. You're in love with Jonathan Kennebrae."

Melissa laughed, joy bubbling up at hearing someone say the words her heart had been singing since that kiss last night. "You make it sound horrible. What's so wrong with being in love with the man I'm going to marry?"

"But you were totally against it yesterday. You said you were embarrassed to be a bartered bride, married only for your money and your name."

"Well, I was wrong. Jonathan is rich. He doesn't need my money. If you had seen the inside of Kennebrae House, you'd know how ridiculous the idea was. All that place needs is a woman's touch. And he cares about me. I know it. He trusts me. He even gave me the key to his building."

"How romantic." Zylphia's voice dripped with sarcasm. "Almost as good as sending flowers or writing poetry. You get free run of his office."

A little gloss went off the moment for Melissa, but she lifted her chin. "Well, he didn't have to be so generous. And he does care about me. He's been nothing but nice to me."

Zylphia shrugged. "Maybe you're right. I hope you are. Let's go spend some of your father's money."

Hours later they entered Castlebrooke's foyer, arm in arm, chilled from the raw November breeze coming in off Lake Superior. The footmen carried in their parcels, and Sarah helped them with their coats and hats.

"Sarah, will you have Mrs. Trolley send tea to the parlor? I'm frozen through." Melissa checked her reflection in the hall mirror and motioned to Zylphia. "Come. We've worked hard and deserve to put our feet up. If I never see another china or flatware pattern again, it will be too soon."

Before Zylphia could answer, Mother bustled into the foyer, a hectic look in her eyes. "Melissa, where have you been?"

Melissa stopped short in surprise. "I've been downtown, the jeweler's, the stationer's, the florist's."

"Well, there's no time for that. Jonathan's here, and he's been waiting almost an hour." Mother tugged on Melissa's hand. "Hurry up. Don't dawdle. I've been trying to make small talk, but he just keeps pacing the rug."

Happiness welled up inside Melissa, and she hurried to the parlor doors without a backward glance. Jonathan was here? Was he as eager to see her as she was to see him?

She opened the door, and he stopped in midstride. "Jonathan, I'm so sorry you had to wait."

He crossed the room and took her hands in his. Heat seared her cold fingers. "I needed to see you right away."

"Is something wrong?" Her thoughts raced. Would they not be able to use the conference room for their meetings? Had something gone awry with the transferring of the supplies? She knew she should've overseen it herself, but no, she let herself be talked into staying late and playing the Kennebrae piano.

"Yes." His brown eyes were grave, his face solemn. "I'm afraid I've committed a serious error."

She blinked and stepped back, withdrawing her hands. An error?

He put a hand into his pocket. "Yes, a serious social error."

Her mouth went dry. What could it be? Did he regret kissing her?

"I've blundered badly, but I intend to make it up to you now. It seems we've been planning a wedding, but you've been cheated out of a proper proposal." He dropped to one knee and reclaimed her hand. "Melissa Brooke, will you marry me?"

Time stopped for a moment when she stared into his eyes. Then happy tears pricked her eyelids, and she put her free hand up to cover her lips. No words would come. She could only nod.

He grinned, so handsome and confident, and opened his palm. On it lay a sapphire and diamond ring. He slid it on her finger and stood, opening his arms to her.

She went into his embrace, wrapping her arms around his neck and lifting her lips to his kiss. It was everything she remembered and better. She wanted it to go on forever.

A small cough brought her to her senses. They parted reluctantly to see Mother and Zylphia standing in the doorway. Mother wore a satisfied expression, and Zylphia had her hands clasped under her chin. She let out a sigh. "That was perfect."

∽

Melissa sat beside Jonathan on the settee, listening to Mother prattle on about the wedding plans. Melissa didn't care about the music, the flowers, the choral pieces. All she cared about was that Jonathan loved her and wanted to marry her. How silly that they'd both resisted so strongly at first.

God, You are good. You work out Your plans—the ones You know are best for us—even though we might resist at first. You do know the plans You have for us. Plans of hope and a future. Thank You for Jonathan. Thank You for bringing me someone who cares for me, who is interested in my causes. I'm sorry for doubting You and Your goodness.

She adjusted the ring on her finger, its clasp unfamiliar and heavy.

Zylphia could not contain her sighs, looking all dewy and romantic every time Melissa caught her eye.

Well, it was romantic. Melissa smiled and checked her finger again to make sure she wasn't dreaming. Zylphia was right. It was perfect.

"I couldn't be happier with how things are working out." Mother offered a plate of tea sandwiches to Zylphia but kept her eyes on Jonathan. "And did you bring the papers with you?"

A prickle of irritation skipped up Melissa's spine. Why did Mother have to bring up that stupid contract? Wasn't it enough that they cared for each other? They were blessed to be marrying for love not money, no matter how much of it each family had. With his kiss still a vivid memory, she no longer felt like a bartered bride.

"They're on the table, all signed and notarized."

"Good." Mother had that cat-who-ate-the-cream look of utter satisfaction with herself and her plans. "Things are moving along nicely."

Chapter 14

"Things are proceeding nicely." Grandfather tossed his glasses onto the stack of papers on the desk.

"You needn't look so smug." Jonathan walked to the windows and looked down on the storm-thrashed waves of Lake Superior. An early November squall lashed the windows with sleet, pinging off the glass and coating everything with ice.

"I can't tell you how happy I am you've signed those papers. I'm surprised you actually proposed to the girl, as unnecessary as that was, and bought her a ring. I suppose women like that sort of thing." He shrugged his thin shoulders. "The important thing is that the wedding will take place soon, before Christmas."

Jonathan clasped his hands behind his back under his suit coat and turned from the window. "I'm glad I could please you." The manipulating old goat. It galled Jonathan that he now actually wanted to do what Grandfather had been cramming down his throat for weeks. He'd have to put up with the gloating.

"I tell you, I was worried the whole thing would fall apart. I thought maybe you didn't want Kennebrae Shipping bad enough to go through with it. You've enough of me in you to have told me to keep it all and gone off to do your own thing. Don't think I haven't heard about the offers from other shipping companies to steal you away from me."

Jonathan walked over to the desk and leaned on his palms in front of Grandfather. "I know you think I'm merely obeying your orders, but understand this: I'm marrying Melissa Brooke because I happen to have fallen in love with her, not because it means I stay with Kennebrae Shipping. Melissa is intelligent, courageous, caring, and sweet. She's unspoiled, unselfish, and everything I want in a wife. Kennebrae Shipping has nothing to do with my marriage."

Grandfather leaned forward and thumped the desk. "Your marriage has everything to do with Kennebrae Shipping, and it's high time you knew it. Why do you think I chose Lawrence Brooke's daughter for you? He's settling a huge sum on you and his daughter at her wedding, and by sugar, we need it." He sat back, his breath rasping in his throat, his eyes gleaming.

A sick feeling of dread crowded into Jonathan's chest. "What do you mean, we need it?"

"I mean we're overextended. I've kept it from you boys, hoping I could turn things around, but it hasn't worked. I took an awful beating in the Depression of '93. I sank most of my capital into silver mining in Colorado. Then the market crashed. I carried on as best I could but gave myself apoplexy in the process."

He tugged at the blanket on his legs and refused to meet Jonathan's eyes. "Kennebraes are tough, though. I weathered the storm. Things turned around, and as a gift to your grandmother, I built her Kennebrae House. She never knew how much I borrowed to build this place nor how much I borrowed to stay afloat during the recession. The only investment that has paid is Kennebrae Shipping."

Grandfather rubbed his hand along his jaw. "I can't draw any more capital from the shipping company. The shipping line needs capital to run, too. New boats, wages, fuel. We need Melissa's dowry to keep the fleet on the Great Lakes. We could lose it all without that money."

Jonathan straightened, numb, his mind frozen. "Why not just sell the other investments at a loss and get out? Keep Kennebrae Shipping viable. It's making money. I know it is. We're busier than we've ever been. You ordered four new ships."

Grandfather shook his head, his hands trembling. "Those four ships have yet to be paid for. And Kennebrae Shipping is security on the other investments. If those go down, so does the shipping line."

Jonathan swayed, reeling from this knowledge. Anger, shock, and disbelief crashed over him like the waves of the storm outside. Cold crept in from his limbs clear to his core. He turned back to the windows, unable to marshal his thoughts.

Kennebrae Shipping hung by a thread, the linchpin keeping all other aspects of the Kennebrae Empire from sinking without a trace. How had he not known? Was this partly his fault? He hadn't inquired into any of Grandfather's other dealings, concentrating only on the one business that fascinated him: shipping. And he'd concentrated on the day-to-day operations—contracts, scheduling, personnel. Grandfather had handled the financials, he and Wasserman. Jonathan had assumed it was in capable hands.

He swallowed hard, dread sinking like an anchor in his stomach. "You've duped us all. Me, Melissa, Lawrence Brooke, Almina. Even Noah and Eli. None of this has been for us—or even for Kennebrae Shipping. It's all been for you. So you don't have to look the fool for extending yourself too far. So you can keep up all this." He waved a hand at the opulent office. "This facade of wealth and power you've created. You haven't built an empire. You've built a house of cards."

Jonathan's anger grew with each word, building and cresting like a wave. "I'm ashamed. For the first time in my life, I'm ashamed to be a Kennebrae. What were you thinking, to use us all this way? It was bad enough when I thought you were just trying to manipulate me into marriage so you could get a new shipping contract. But to learn you've wagered all our futures on this stunt, I can't stand to even look at you. If I had known all this when you first raised the subject of marriage, I'd have told you to go jump in the lake. I'd have walked away from Kennebrae Shipping without a backward glance."

Grandfather challenged him with a glare. "You had that chance, and you didn't take it. You'd do anything for Kennebrae Shipping. Because you were born to it. Because you know if you don't, you'll regret it. And all those workers, your captains, your crews you've spent so much time assembling, the dockworkers, all of them out of work with the stroke of a pen if you break the marriage contract. And don't forget the pensioners you've been carrying, those who've retired from Kennebrae. They'll be destitute if we go under. Be grateful you actually like the girl, get married, and solve all our problems."

"Are you really so arrogant, so full of yourself, sitting up here in your office dictating the lives of people like you're playing some game? The livelihoods of Kennebrae employees rest more on you than on me. I didn't sign away their security trying to build an empire. You did." He shook with anger, every muscle tense. "How could you be so foolish? I've a mind to walk out and let you pump your own bilges. Noah and Eli deserve to know about this. Did you plan their marriages to shore up some other falling bit of your sand castle? Have you thought for one minute what Grandmother would think of what you've done?"

This direst of questions hit the mark. Grandfather seemed to shrink before his eyes, becoming more frail and brittle. For long moments the only sounds in the room were his rasping breath and the crackle of the fire. "What are you going to do?" His voice came out weak, more subdued than Jonathan had ever heard it.

"I don't know, but I'll tell you this. Melissa must never find out. She'd be as humiliated as I. At least I can protect her from that. I wish I'd never signed your contract. You've effectively sold me and bought her. I hope you're happy." Jonathan stalked from the room, slamming the door behind him.

∽

Melissa sat at the piano, the rhythm of the Strauss piece flowing through her. Her fingers danced over the keys, bringing the music to life, her engagement ring winking back at her as she played. She loved waltzes. Her mind floated on the melody, her foot keeping the three-four time.

Her lips lifted in a smile. Soon she would waltz with Jonathan. The Shipbuilders' Ball on Thanksgiving night, the highpoint of the social calendar and only a week away. What would it be like to be held in his arms, skimming across the floor to the strains of a violin?

And Zylphia said there was a quadrille planned, too. Melissa hadn't been issued an invitation to dance the quadrille, for this one was only for those men and women who were single. Her engagement disqualified her from that particular event of the evening. No matter. She'd be attending the dance with

Jonathan and could dance as often with him as she wanted. No frowning dowagers on the sidelines counting dances and gossiping.

The music trailed away as her fingers stilled. Mother and the modiste had designed a gown just for the occasion. Though Melissa had wanted to wear the gown she'd worn for the piano performance the night she met Jonathan, Mother's scandalized expression stilled her protests. No lady of high society appeared in the same dress twice. A social faux pas Melissa intended to commit as often as she pleased after her marriage. The expense and vanity of a new gown every night was ridiculous. If she liked something, she would wear it when it suited her.

The door opened, jarring Melissa from her reverie. "More flowers?" She turned on the piano stool. Sunlight streamed in the windows, washing the music room in a yellow glow, so much more cheerful than the steely gray skies and rain of the past few days.

"Yes, miss. Just arrived." Sarah's voice drifted through the mass of roses. She set the vase on the sideboard and brought Melissa the card. "Three bouquets this week. And perhaps another evening out?"

Melissa grinned at her maid and slit the envelope.

Dearest Melissa,
 Please accept my invitation to dine at the country club this evening, and don't forget, it's opening night at the Lyceum.

           Affectionately,
           Jonathan

Since his proposal two weeks ago, Jonathan had courted her, sending flowers, invitations, small gifts. Each came with a card in his own hand. She'd saved them all in her jewelry case. Every time they were together, she fell deeper in love. He was interesting, intelligent, serious about business and spiritual matters but able to laugh at himself. She twisted her engagement ring, shaking her head. How silly that she'd ever been opposed to this wedding. Now she counted down the days like a child before Christmas.

She walked over to the vase and leaned to bury her nose in the deep-pink blossoms. The heady and familiar scent enveloped her. Every time it was roses. Another wonderful thing about Jonathan. He listened. Once, in passing, she'd mentioned that roses were her favorite flower, and he'd remembered. Hothouse roses this time of year would be so costly, and yet he sent them often.

She checked the invitation again. Opening night at the Lyceum. She smiled and stood the card at the base of the flower arrangement, where her mother would be sure to see it. Mother would never guess the real meaning behind the words.

"Sarah, come help me do my hair. I'm going out tonight."

Chapter 15

J onathan smiled when she came into the Castlebrooke parlor. She wore his roses in her hair. They matched her pink gown perfectly. He quelled the stab of apprehension at not being forthright with her. It was for her own good that he didn't explain the Kennebrae finances.

Lawrence Brooke tucked his fingers into his vest pocket and looked her over, pride and satisfaction showing in every inch of his expression. "Ah, here you are. Very pretty."

Almina smiled indulgently. "Have a good evening. Your father and I will be out very late. We're dining at the Terrys'."

Lawrence frowned. "I don't know why you accepted their invitation, Almina. You know I don't like Roberta Terry. She's forever shoving women's suffrage down my throat. One of these times I'm going to forget myself and tell that woman just what she can do with her cause."

Jonathan's stomach muscles tightened. No wonder Melissa worried and sneaked out at night.

"Now, Lawrence, there's no harm in engaging in a discussion of the issue, and you enjoy Leonard's company. You'll have a good time."

He grumbled, checking his pocket watch. "Leonard would be wise to curb his wife's political passions. You won't see my wife touting such nonsense as women voting."

Jonathan winced at this all-too-prevalent viewpoint. He glanced at Melissa in the doorway. Her hands fisted at her sides, her chin lifted. Time to intervene.

He raised her hand, uncurling her tight fingers and placing a kiss on her fingertips. "You look stunning. I'll be the envy of every man tonight." He helped her with her cloak. "It's very cold. Will you be warm enough?"

Her jaw loosened. "I'll survive. And thank you for the flowers. I think we should be going, don't you?"

They took their leave of her parents, and Jonathan ushered her to his waiting carriage.

The maître d' showed them to an intimate table in a corner of the club dining room. Photographs and paintings of lake ships hung between high windows draped in gold fabric. Above Melissa's head, an oil of the *Bethany* hung in a gilded frame.

Jonathan lowered his gaze, not wanting to think about Kennebrae Shipping or the marriage contract in any way tonight.

Someone clapped him on the shoulder. "Well, how are you, Jonathan? It's been a long time."

Jonathan turned. "Mr. Fox." He mustered a smile, though he hated the intrusion, particularly by this small, barrel-chested man. Fox, an apt name for such a sly, cunning predator. "You're looking well." He rose and offered his hand, surprised anew at the power the older man's grip possessed. "Melissa, this is Gervase Fox of Keystone Steel. And may I introduce you to my fiancée, Miss Melissa Brooke."

"Ah yes, read about that in the paper. Delighted to meet you, my dear. It's about time someone caught this fellow and married him." Gervase beamed at Melissa then turned to Jonathan, his brow wrinkled. "Awful storms this past week. Did you suffer any damage?" He looked eager, rubbing his hands together, rocking on his toes. He licked his lips as if anticipating a juicy tidbit. Fox was the perfect name for Gervase. Even his whiskers grew up his cheeks like a fox's mask. And he didn't miss a trick.

Jonathan took delight in squashing his hopes. "No, sir, nothing important. As it happens, several of our ships were in port, here and in Two Harbors and Detroit. Only three were on the lake when the storms hit, and they were able to ride out the worst of it. A few minor repairs but nothing serious."

Gervase's mustache flattened in disappointment. "Good, good to hear it. Some weren't so lucky. Wouldn't be surprised if the season ended early. I can feel it in the air, you know? And how's your brother, Noah? I've heard great things about him, hope to meet him while I'm in Duluth. Born to be a lake captain, that fellow."

"Noah's fine. Eager to get back out on the Lakes. The *Bethany*'s laid up for repairs at the moment. He's hoping for one last run of the season just after Thanksgiving." Manners forced Jonathan to ask, though he prayed the answer was no. "Would you care to join us for dinner?"

"Ah, you're kind to ask, son, but I'm dining with colleagues across the room. Just wanted to stop by and give you my best wishes. Congratulations on your engagement, young man. Looks like you've done well for yourself." He waved and departed, a small ship creating a big wake.

Jonathan relaxed his chest and arms, surprised at how tense he was. The state of the Kennebrae family fortune sat like a ton of iron ore in his chest.

"You look tired. Are you sure you want to go tonight?" Melissa reached across the table to grasp his hand where it lay on the white linen. "I can always go alone."

He squeezed her fingers. "I wouldn't dream of it. I am a little weary. Business is. . .tricky these days. But it will right itself soon."

She released his hand when the waiter brought their meals. The food was good, but Melissa only picked at hers.

"Something wrong?"

She shook her head. "It's just my father. You heard him tonight. If he knew what I was up to, his boiler would explode. He'd lock me in my room and put a guard at the door."

"I didn't realize he was so opposed to the idea of women voting."

"A lot of men are. I'm surprised you aren't, to tell the truth."

"Before I got a bang on the head"—he touched his temple lightly, smiling ruefully—"I hadn't given the idea much thought. Now that I've had time to consider it, I don't see the harm in it. In fact, I can see that it would be the right thing to do. Women have to pay taxes, have their sons and husbands conscripted into military service from time to time, have to obey the same laws and ordinances as men. I don't see why they shouldn't have a voice in the government that rules them."

"You've been reading our literature." She gave him a saucy grin, a pleased light in her eyes that quickened his heartbeat. "We'll make a suffrager out of you before you know what's what."

"If it means spending more time with you, I'm game." He sounded like a besotted fool, but he didn't care.

After dinner he helped her into his carriage, his breath hanging in a cloud of frost. He settled in beside her, contentment wrapping around him, only a tiny, niggling sense of unease marring the night. He searched for her hand, closing his around it.

She sighed. A comfortable silence enveloped them.

They headed west on Superior Street. The clopping of the horses' hooves on the pavement and the clatter of the carriage wheels drowned out the sound of the waves on the shore two blocks to the east.

Between the buildings he caught sight of the lighthouse guarding the piers that signaled the entrance to Duluth Harbor. The stark, skeletal frame of the new gondola bridge rose high above the water.

Ahead on the right, the Lyceum towered over the street, yellow light streaming from doors and windows. Carriages stood in a queue in front, disgorging passengers in furs and feathers for the opening night of the opera season.

"Are you sorry not to be going in?" He caught her profile in the lights as the carriage rolled by.

"No." He could hear the smile in her voice. "I don't really care for opera. Now if it were the symphony. . ."

The horses turned left onto Lake Avenue, toward the bridge and away from the Lyceum.

Kennebrae Shipping stood dark and imposing. He could make out the barest cracks of light around the third-floor corner windows. "Looks like someone's here already. They've got the blinds drawn." He swung the carriage door open and jumped down.

Their shoes crunched on the damp stairs.

The door opened a crack. A pale face studied them up and down then pulled the door wider. "Evening, sir. Didn't realize you'd be coming in tonight."

"Good evening, Dawkins. Any trouble?"

"No, sir. Them ladies is upstairs. No one else's been nosing around. I'm about to do another walk around the building now."

"Good. We'll go up ourselves. Carry on." Jonathan took Melissa's arm and headed toward the stairs, bypassing Grandfather's elevator. Their steps echoed on the marble treads.

"It's kind of spooky in the moonlight, but I bet it's beautiful in the day." Melissa craned her neck, looking up the staircase at the chandelier.

"It is. Grandfather never does anything by halves. The same architectural firm who designed Kennebrae House designed the offices, too. You'll have to stop by when the sun's shining. I'll give you a tour."

They stopped before an oak door with a frosted-glass panel. The dim light from within silhouetted his name on the glass. He turned the ornate brass knob and held the door for her.

A single gaslight burned low on the far wall. Shadows draped the corners and furnishings. Their footsteps were muffled by a heavy, wool carpet. The familiar smells of paper, books, and ink wrapped around him. He breathed deeply. How he loved this place.

He led Melissa to the door beside the light. When he opened it, several ladies looked up from their work. He blinked in the sudden brightness but smiled at them. "Good evening, ladies."

"Oh, Mr. Kennebrae, thank you so much for letting us use your office. It's almost too nice to work in." One of the ladies, her hair straggling from a bun at her nape, bustled forward and all but bobbed a curtsy. She wrung his hand. "Come see what we've done."

He cast a glance over his shoulder at Melissa, who smiled at him, an imp of laughter in her eye. She loosened her cloak, revealing the pink evening gown. "Go ahead. I'll be fine."

"Mr. Kennebrae, you remember me? I'm Mrs. Britten. Beatrice Britten. We're so grateful for you helping us this way. Things are coming along so nicely for the rally. The sashes are done, see?" She pointed to the coatrack that had stood in the corner of his office only yesterday. Every peg bore dozens of purple, gold, and white sashes emblazoned with VOTES FOR WOMEN.

He admired their handiwork, glancing frequently at Melissa, who seated herself at a corner table with the English students. Fancy gown notwithstanding, he marveled at how she fit in with these ladies, most of whom wouldn't be received or even acknowledged by Almina Brooke and women of her social standing.

"And these are the banners." Mrs. Britten urged him to the conference table, awash with fabric, sewing baskets, and trim. She held up a white length of cloth. Someone had painstakingly stitched fabric letters in purple to spell out NO TAXATION WITHOUT REPRESENTATION. Gold-fringe trim swayed and caught the light.

He read snippets of other slogans among the piles. END OPPRESSION OF WOMEN, WOMEN IN BONDAGE, FREE YOUR WIVES AND MOTHERS.

"We'll be finished with these in the next week or so. Then we'll go to making the badges and ribbons. The banners won't go on the poles until we get to the rally. It's so much easier to store them folded up."

Jonathan smiled ruefully. One of the many bookcases lining the walls of his conference room had been cleared, the books piled on their sides in columns on the floor. In their place, neatly folded, lay stacks of banners, looking like the Kennebrae House linen closet. When he'd said they could make themselves at home, they'd taken him at his word.

The ladies around the table followed his progress, expressions reserved though friendly. Their scrutiny made his collar tighten, though he couldn't blame them for having reservations. In their estimation he was a member of the enemy forces.

"I've heard nothing of the rally about town. Where is it to be held? In one of the parks? Are you marching down Superior Street?"

Mrs. Britten frowned. "We're not marching in Duluth until spring. These will be used first for the march on the state capitol in January. We'll be holding the rally in St. Paul on the opening day of the new session of Congress."

His gaze flew to Melissa. St. Paul? In January? "Melissa, could I see you for a moment?"

"I'll be right back, Synove." She nodded to her pupil. "You're doing well." Her skirt rustled as she rounded the long oval table. She bit her thumbnail.

Mrs. Britten turned to the table and busied herself moving fabric that didn't need to be moved.

Jonathan could almost see Mrs. Britten's ears twitching. "Were you planning on attending this rally in St. Paul?" He kept his voice low.

"Of course. I'm on the committee. I have to be there."

"And when were you going to tell me about it?"

"I hadn't given it any thought. I wasn't keeping it from you on purpose. I didn't think you'd be interested."

"We'll be married by then. Don't you think I would've noticed if you'd left town for a few days? How were you planning to get there, and who is going with you? You can't go alone. I don't know if I'll have time to accompany you."

She stiffened. "We're going by train. There are about fifty ladies going, and even if there weren't, I would be fine going by myself. I'm not a child, you know."

"Fifty women?"

She smiled. "Yes. The number was much lower a couple weeks ago, but thanks to Mother and the marriage contract, I now have the funds to charter two railcars to take us to St. Paul. She did insist I have my own money to use however I like once we're married."

Mrs. Britten turned around and frowned, shaking her head. "Don't say something like that, lass. He'll get the idea you're marrying him for money."

A cold sweat of guilt pricked Jonathan's upper chest and back. Marrying for money. He dropped his questions. The further he steered from that rocky shoal, the better.

Chapter 16

The distinctive clang of a hammer on metal reverberated through the boiler room of the *Bethany*. Jonathan ducked to enter the cramped space on the heels of Noah. Coal dust, oil, rust, and machinery smells assaulted him. He hunched his shoulders inside his wool coat. In dock as she was, the boilers were silent and cold.

"I wanted to inspect the progress myself!" Noah shouted above the noise. "I think we're a little ahead of schedule. Might be able to pull out on time after all. Day after Thanksgiving with a full load of ore."

Jonathan nodded. "That's only two days away. At least you'll be here for the Shipbuilders' Ball." His boots crunched on the iron grating of the gangway. The massive ribs of the ship curved along the walls, necessitating a careful watch lest he bang his head.

"They're double-checking the plating on the port side. We scraped the side of the lock up at the Soo on the last trip through." Noah shook his head, pursing his lips. "Should've taken the wheel myself. Let my first mate take us out."

"You treat this ship like your baby. If you could bring her home at night and tuck her into bed, you'd be happy."

"The only girl I'll ever love." Noah rubbed his gloved hand along the bulkhead, a grin splitting his bearded face.

"Captain?" A head appeared at the top of the steep stairs. "Someone on the dock asking permission to come aboard to see you."

Noah frowned. "Did he say who he was?"

"Said his name was Gervase Fox."

Noah raised an eyebrow at Jonathan. "I've heard of him. What's he want?"

"Don't ask me." Jonathan shrugged. "I knew he was in town, saw him at dinner one night."

Noah turned to the deckhand. "Send him to the wheelhouse. We'll meet him there."

They climbed the ladderlike steps from the belly of the ship to the spar deck then another flight to the cabin deck. The aft-most hatch lay open, giving them a long view down to the bottom of the hold. Noah tromped up another flight of stairs to the pilothouse, Jonathan on his heels. Everything about the day was raw, and being surrounded by so much frozen metal only drove the

86

cold deeper into his bones. Jonathan didn't envy Noah a late November cross-ing. They had only a few minutes of stomping their feet and blowing on their hands in the tiny chart room behind the wheelhouse before the door opened.

Their visitor, rosy-cheeked and puffing, had to step rather high over the doorsill due to his small stature. "Colder than a spurned woman's heart out there." Gervase Fox stuck out his hand. "Good to see you again, Jonathan. I tried to call your office, but the operator said you aren't on the telephone line yet. When I stopped by your offices, they said you were down here. Why you'd be crawling about a hunk of steel in the harbor instead of inside by a warm fire, I'll never understand." The force of the little man's personality filled every inch of the chart room.

Jonathan shook his hand, not wincing as Gervase tried to crush his hand. "Always best to see for yourself where your money's going, don't you think? I'm sorry you had such a difficult time tracking me down. Grandfather's resist-ing installing a telephone, but he'll come around. Gervase, this is my brother Noah, captain of this vessel. Noah, this is Gervase Fox of Keystone Steel and Shipping."

Gervase's mustache bristled. "Captain. Pleased to meet you. I've heard good things about you. A hard-water captain who knows his ship and fears nothing."

Noah let the man pump his hand vigorously, while sending an inquiring look to Jonathan.

Jonathan shrugged. "I hadn't realized you'd still be in Duluth, Gervase."

Gervase's eyes never stopped their piercing journey around the room. Just like a thief sizing up his next job. He'd have some reason for coming to Duluth, for hunting them down at the wharf, but Jonathan didn't expect him to reveal it too soon. "Ah, there's always business to conduct. And as you said, best to view where your money's going yourself. I'm looking into a few ven-tures. What do you know about Three Rivers Mining?"

Jonathan crossed his arms and leaned against the chart table. "Nothing to speak of. They have a mine near Biwabik. We might have carried some of their ore through a broker before. Couldn't say for certain though. You thinking of branching out into the ore mines?"

"Oh, it's worth a look while I'm in the area. I'll be up on the Mesabi Range at the end of the week, just nosing around, you know? I have a little capital to invest. How's your grandfather? I haven't seen him since he had the apoplexy."

Jonathan shifted his cold feet. "Grandfather's fine." He had better things to do than parry thrusts from this snake oil salesman. Why didn't he get to the point?

Gervase clasped his hands behind his back and bounced on the balls of his feet. "I heard tell he was trying to sell a brickworks in Erie. That so?"

Jonathan shrugged, trying to appear casual. "Possibly. He buys and sells all the time."

"Doing more selling than buying these days, I heard." Gervase shot him an intent look.

"Nothing wrong with consolidating, is there?"

Noah's brows came down at Jonathan's offhand tone.

Gervase put on a bland expression. "No, not at all, laddie." Then he grinned. "What say we shed this boardroom politicking and be straight with each other?"

"All right." Jonathan nodded but didn't let his guard down for a minute.

"I've heard rumors that Kennebrae is in trouble. A couple of his business partners have gone under, leaving him holding the bag on some sizable loans. But he's sitting on one golden egg of an asset." He swept his arm toward the bow. "Kennebrae Shipping. The largest fleet on the Lakes, four new boats set to slide off the shipyard ways this spring, and now a contract through marriage to transport most all the grain grown in the upper Midwest."

Jonathan swallowed and took a deep breath. "Not that I'm substantiating those rumors, but I have to wonder what concern it is of yours." *And how many other vultures are circling?*

Gervase looked him straight in the eye, all blandness wiped from his face, his eyes hard and glittering like Grandfather's when he struck a particularly lucrative and satisfying deal. "I might be in the market to buy Kennebrae Shipping. A sale now, when the share prices are so high, would net more than a tidy profit for Abraham and bail him out of some rather unpleasant troubles back East. His bankers are getting antsy."

The sheer boldness, the audacity of the man to come aboard this ship and make his bald offer took Jonathan's breath away.

"Now"—Gervase put up his hands—"I can see I've startled you, but there's no point in beating about the bush. Don't think I intend to turn you out of a job. I would want you—and your brothers—to stay on with the company. You've done well growing your business and your reputation over the past eight years. I've been watching. Kennebrae ships would be added to the Keystone Steel fleet, and you would head up the offices and operations here in Duluth. Nothing would change there."

Noah bombarded Jonathan with silent questions over Gervase's head.

Jonathan pushed them aside with a "later" gesture of his hand. "That's very kind of you, Gervase, but we're not looking to sell. Whatever rumors you've heard are false."

Gervase pursed his lips then clapped Jonathan on the shoulder. "Well, if you ever change your mind, let me know. I've got a job for you, either here or in

Erie, if you ever want it. And I'll pay top dollar for Kennebrae Shipping when you're ready to sell." He wrung Jonathan's hand once more, waved a salute to Noah, and charged out the doorway. His footsteps on the metal ladder clattered through the framework of the pilothouse.

Noah crossed his arms and braced his feet apart. "What was that all about? Is Kennebrae Shipping in trouble?"

Jonathan's gut twisted. "Noah, we need to talk, but not here. Let's go to the office and warm up."

✑

Back in the familiar comfort of his office, a roaring blaze in the fireplace, a mug of hot coffee cupped in his palms, Jonathan stretched his long legs and met Noah's intent, questioning stare.

Noah blew across his own cup. "Spill it. It's eating you alive, whatever it is."

Jonathan lay his head back against the burgundy wingback. "I'm sick about it. Grandfather's been wheeling and dealing, robbing one business to cover the losses of another. He told me about it two weeks ago, though he failed to mention the part about business partners doing a bunk and leaving him in the lurch. Apparently the whole empire—mines, mills, railroads—everything is hanging by a thread. The only thing holding it together is Kennebrae Shipping. The loans are due the first of the year, his credit's extended as far as it can go, and Kennebrae Shipping is the security for the loan."

Noah bolted to his feet, arms rigid, face frozen.

Jonathan knew just how he felt. Two weeks ago, he'd felt the same way. Two weeks of constant worry had worn off the edge.

"Why didn't you tell me?" Noah's hurt showed in his eyes. He paced before the fireplace.

Jonathan put down his cup and leaned forward, resting his forehead in his palms, elbows on knees. "I've done nothing but wrestle with the numbers and try to get a handle on just how far things have slid. I hoped he was exaggerating. I hoped it was just another of his Machiavellian maneuvers to ensure I'd marry Melissa. I'm sorry I didn't tell you as soon as I found out. I should have."

"How much money are we talking about?"

The sum drained the color from Noah's cheeks above his beard. He stopped pacing and gripped the back of his chair. He stared at Jonathan, his eyes burning hot bright blue like the center of a gaslight flame.

Jonathan understood. The *Bethany*, the *Jericho*, the *Nazareth*, two dozen other ships, Kennebrae House, all gone to satisfy the debt, and even then it might not be enough.

Realization spread over Noah's face. He took a steadying breath. "So we're going under?"

"No, we're not. Not if I have anything to do about it."

"All I can say, big brother, it sure is a good thing you're marrying money. Without Melissa's dowry, we'd be sunk."

Jonathan winced and picked up his cup. "Don't even breathe those words. If Melissa found out—"

He broke off as a gasp came through his office door. He sat bolt upright, spilling his coffee.

Melissa stood in the doorway, white as a Lake Superior fog, her hand gripping the doorknob. With a small cry, she whirled and ran down the hall.

Chapter 17

Melissa burst through the bronze and glass doors of Kennebrae Shipping and out onto the frosty street. The wind whipped her hair and clothes, slapping her cheeks with cold. The tears overflowed, tracking icy rivulets from lashes to chin.

Her coachman, Weatherby, stood at the heads of the team, his breath hanging in crystals. "Miss? Wasn't he there?"

She tried to speak, but no sound came out. She couldn't seem to draw a breath. Her heart hammered against her ribs.

"Miss?" Weatherby hurried to her side and grasped her elbow.

"I—I—can't breathe—can't breathe—" Her hand fluttered, and she gulped hard, trying to force air into her lungs.

"Easy, there." His gray eyebrows came down in a worried frown. He put an arm about her waist, edging her toward the carriage. "Just one slow breath." He sucked in a deep lungful, as if that would help her.

A short pant, and the air stuck in her throat again.

"No, nice and slow." His chest rose and fell once more.

This time more air got in.

"That's it. Are you all right? What happened?"

Before she could answer, the door banged open.

She whirled.

Jonathan Kennebrae, guilt written on every inch of his frame, stood in the doorway. "Melissa, wait."

She clung to Weatherby's hand. "Get me home, please. I don't want to talk to him."

The old man's eyes clouded with questions, but he obeyed, hustling her to the carriage and handing her inside.

Jonathan hurried down the steps toward her. His hand reached for the carriage door.

"Now, sir, you must be leaving the lady alone. She doesn't want to see you right now." Weatherby interposed his frame between Jonathan and the open door. "I'll have to be asking you to step back."

"Don't be ridiculous. Melissa," he shouted over the coachman's shoulder, "if you'll just listen—" He broke off when Weatherby put his hand against Jonathan's chest and pushed him back.

Noah clattered down the stairs, blurry in Melissa's teary vision. "Jonathan, perhaps now isn't the best time." He grabbed Jonathan's elbow. "Or the place." With a nod he indicated the crowd of onlookers on the sidewalk.

Weatherby glared at both of them as he shut and fastened the carriage door. The carriage lurched and swayed. They were away.

Melissa dug in her bag for her handkerchief, pressing it to her mouth to stifle the sobs bursting from her throat.

She could only nod her thanks to Weatherby when he helped her out on the driveway at Castlebrooke. If only she could get inside without running into Mother.

The butler opened the door. "Good afternoon, miss. And how was your—" His voice broke off, eyes widening at her disheveled appearance.

She shook her head, tight-lipped, and hurried past, not bothering to take off her coat or hat. The route to her bedroom had never seemed so long before. She grabbed her skirts and ran up the stairs and down the hall to her sanctuary like a wounded animal heading to its den to nurse its wounds.

She slipped inside and leaned against the closed door. On wooden limbs she crossed the room and sank into her chair. Her hat tumbled to the floor, rocking gently on its crown. She shivered. The grate in the fireplace was cold since she'd expected to be out all afternoon.

In jerky movements she took off her gloves and unbuttoned her coat, feeling bludgeoned. Automatic motions took over as her mind whirled, refusing to settle on the one thing she must.

He lied.

It stabbed afresh, laying open her heart and dreams. Sobs clogged her throat. She rose and flung herself onto the bed, crying uncontrollably, shoulders shaking, stomach clenching.

Everything. All of it. A lie.

Eventually the crying eased to a series of hiccups and sniffs. She flopped onto her back. A heavy band of tension settled around her forehead. She rubbed her gritty eyes. Every muscle ached, and every heartbeat throbbed with pain.

How could he do this to her? And how gullible was she to believe every word he'd said? What a brilliant plan, to pretend at first to be opposed to the marriage, affronted at the idea of being bartered away by their elders. Then, when she'd come to admire him, pretending he'd fallen in love with her. The flowers, the invitations, allowing the use of his office, the ring. . .

The ring.

She scowled down at the icy blue and white gems. With a sharp tug she yanked it from her finger, scratching her skin in the process. What should she do with it? She'd like to fling it back in his face. Her lips tightened.

The cad.

The satin duvet whispered when she rolled to the edge of the bed and sat up. She weighed the ring in her palm for a moment then whipped the token of his love and affection toward the fireplace. It clacked off the mantel and clattered to the hearth.

Lord, how could You do this to me? You promised me hope and a future. Plans that were for my good. He lied to me. All Your plans are dashed. It's over. Did You lie to me, too?

A tap at the door.

"Go away."

"Miss, there's someone to see you. Mr. Jonathan Kennebrae has called." Sarah.

"I don't want to see him. Tell him to go away."

"Miss, he's most insistent."

I'll just bet he is. The charlatan.

"I'm not coming down. He can wait until he's an old man for all I care." Melissa thumped the pillows with her fists and buried her face against them. Tears burned her throat.

Footsteps dwindled down the hall. She lay perfectly still, listening, until at last the front door closed.

∽

Jonathan walked as though he dragged the *Bethany*'s anchor chain with every step. How did a man cope when his worst fears were realized?

Lord, how can this be Your plan? If You can direct rivers in their courses, why can't You give me a way out of this mess? Is this where I'm supposed to say, "The Lord gives, and the Lord takes away. Blessed be the name of the Lord"? I'm not feeling that way.

He shoved his hands into his pockets, the cold biting through his suit jacket and shirt. Why hadn't he put on a coat? A gust of frigid, damp air swirled around him, nipping and numbing his cheeks.

He'd been in too much of a hurry, that's why. Chasing Melissa, trying to get her to listen to him, grabbing the first cab he could find.

And that supercilious snob they called a butler. Glowering as if he'd like to toss Jonathan out into the street like some mendicant ruffian. And the glare from the maid on the stairs hadn't helped either.

Could this day get any worse?

A streak plummeted past his nose, quickly followed by another. In dismay he glanced up toward Skyline Drive to see clouds boiling. The heavens opened like a washerwoman throwing out the rinse water. Jonathan was soaked to the skin before he reached Kennebrae House.

∽

Melissa straightened from bathing her face with cool water and looked in the mirror at her blotchy cheeks and puffy eyes. She dabbed with a folded towel then returned to her adjoining boudoir.

The remains of tea lay scattered across the tray on the low table before the fire. A fire roared in the grate, chasing the chill from the room. Lamps blazed, the bed was turned down invitingly, and Sarah straightened the tray to return it to the kitchen.

"You didn't eat anything." Her brown eyes looked mournfully into Melissa's, her mouth drawn into a disapproving pout. "You didn't have lunch either. Aren't you hungry?"

Melissa picked up her hairbrush and dragged it through her rumpled brown tresses. She shook her head. "I don't want anything to eat. Is Mother home yet?"

As if in answer, the door was flung open. Mother glided into the room, her skirts swaying, her expression fierce.

"What's this nonsense I hear about you quarrelling with Jonathan?"

Melissa braced herself, set the brush on the dressing table, and lifted her chin. "The marriage is off."

"Fiddlesticks. What utter foolishness. I don't know what sort of slight you imagine he's done you, but I assure you, the wedding will take place as planned."

"Never." *I'll run away first.*

"Stop acting like a child, and wipe all notions of running away from your silly head."

Melissa gasped.

"Oh yes, I know what you're thinking. Your expression says it all. But I want you to listen to me and listen well. You will attend the Shipbuilders' Ball the day after tomorrow as Jonathan's fiancée, and you will do so with grace and dignity."

"But, Mother, have you any idea—"

"I don't care to know the particulars. It doesn't matter."

"It doesn't matter to you that he's marrying me for money? That he doesn't care a whit about me?"

Mother rolled her eyes heavenward, as if pleading for assistance from above. "Of course he is. What did you think, that he was marrying you for— love? Don't be ridiculous. Love is a fleeting, traitorous emotion that is beneath you. Now, pull yourself together. You have a duty to this family and to Jonathan to behave with some decorum. The wedding contract has been signed, and there's nothing you can do about it."

Melissa narrowed her eyes and bit her thumbnail.

We'll see about that.

Chapter 18

S he sent them back, sir. The envelope is unopened." McKay set the vase of roses on the table by the office door. "And the chocolates came back, too." He handed the package to Jonathan.

The confections hadn't fared as well as the envelope. The box looked decidedly as if someone had stomped on it. He pitched it into the trash can and ran his fingers through his hair. How was he supposed to make things right when she wouldn't even see him? His lone hope lay in the Shipbuilders' Ball and Almina's promise that Melissa would be there. "Thank you, McKay. That will be all."

"Dinner is served, sir."

Thanksgiving dinner at Kennebrae House was a bust. Anticipating spending it with Melissa, Jonathan had waited in vain for an invitation. Noah was dining with friends across the harbor in Superior and would be coming to the ball from there. That left Jonathan and Grandfather, who never ate much anymore, to stare at each other over the roasted bird and trimmings. Grandfather's scowl and baleful glares did nothing to improve Jonathan's digestion.

Jonathan quit the meal long before the dessert course, stalking up to his room to stare into the fire. "Lord, I don't know where this is headed. I don't know how You can pull this from despair to hope. I don't know which way to turn now. You say the king's heart is in Your hand, and You can turn it however You wish. I've been praying pretty much nonstop that You would change Melissa's heart and cause her to hear me out, but You haven't been able to manage it. I feel like I've lost my anchor here and I'm drifting in a storm."

The clock on the mantel chimed six. Time to dress. More weary than he could remember, Jonathan pushed himself up from the chair. At least it wasn't a masquerade ball this time. Last year he'd borne with stoicism maidens in costume and men in turbans and pointy shoes, Russian hussars, and three different Napoleon Bonapartes. His own costume, ordered and insisted on by Grandfather, at least had a bit of dignity to it. He'd gone as Admiral Lord Nelson.

Would she come? Would she give him a chance to explain? And if she did, what could he say? Why should she believe him? He fumbled with his tie, fingers clumsy as his mind raced. And if he couldn't make her understand, if she broke the marriage contract, what would happen to Kennebrae Shipping?

He yanked the ends of his crooked bow tie and snatched up his hat. "McKay! Where are you? Come help me with this thing!"

Finally put together with the butler's help, he trotted downstairs.

Grandfather, resplendent in evening dress with a cunningly cut jacket made especially not to bunch or wrinkle in his wheelchair, waited by the door. A black satin lap robe covered his legs. Shiny black shoes rested on the foot tread.

Jonathan stopped short. "I didn't know you were coming."

"I'm going along to see you don't foul things up more than you already have." Grandfather pulled on his gloves and accepted his cloak and hat from McKay.

A direct hit. Grandfather had the ability to pierce Jonathan's reserve like no other. Except Melissa. In fact, his desire to shout at both of them bubbled and hissed like lava under pressure. He was a man nearing explosion. He rode in stony silence to the club.

The country club lights shone like diamonds, casting winking beams on the lake. Carriages and automobiles packed the long, curved drive, passengers arriving in a steady stream at the wide front doors. The night air held the tang of snow, and the breeze off the lake hit his skin like ice water.

Jonathan clenched and unclenched his hands on his thighs as they awaited their turn to go inside. He mentally rehearsed and discarded several opening lines.

The coachman opened the door and pulled out the custom-made ramp to accommodate Grandfather's chair.

A blast of warmth hit them in the foyer. Attendants led ladies upstairs to lay aside capes and coats and freshen their appearances, while the gentlemen swirled off cloaks and stuffed gloves into top hats, and placed them in capable hands in the coatroom. Music drifted down the hallway from the ballroom.

Jonathan wheeled Grandfather toward the sound. A waltz in progress greeted their eyes beyond the gilded doors. Pinwheels of color in the ladies' dresses, stark black stiffness in the men's attire, and overall the golden glow of six crystal chandeliers bolstered by countless wall sconces.

He saw many familiar faces, business colleagues, shipping rivals, church friends, but not the one he so desperately sought. The knot in his stomach tightened. Where was she?

"Stop looking like a condemned man and get me some punch." Grandfather poked him in the leg. "She'll be here."

∽

Melissa winced as the cold beads touched her throat.

Sarah fastened the five-string choker of perfectly matched pearls. From the center a sapphire and diamond pendant hung, reflecting the dressing table lights. "It's perfect, miss."

"Almost." Mother tapped an ivory folded fan against her palm. "Where's the ring?"

Melissa glanced down at her bare hand. "I'm not wearing it."

"Yes, you are. All of Duluth society will be there tonight, they've heard about the ring, and they'll want to see it. Where is it?" She stalked to the dresser and opened the jewel case.

"I don't know. I threw it away."

Mother whirled, mouth agape. "You what? You little fool!" She advanced on Melissa, cheeks red, eyes blazing. "You're ruining everything. Do you want me to be the laughingstock of all Duluth society?"

"Why won't you listen to me? Jonathan is only marrying me so he can get his hands on Father's money. If nothing else, this marriage isn't a sound investment for Father."

"You know nothing about such things. Let the men handle the business end. You'll do your part like a dutiful daughter and keep your nose out of business affairs. Your liberal notions are making you overstep your bounds. You won't mention a word of this to your father, and if you've lost that ring. . ."

Sarah stepped forward. "Ma'am, the ring's not lost." Her voice cracked. "It was on the hearth when I swept up this morning." She hurried to Melissa's jewel case on the dresser and withdrew the ring.

Mother snatched it from her hand and pushed her aside. "Put it on."

Melissa bowed her head, shoulders slack. She held out her hand for the ring. Would she ever have a say in her own future? Pawns and bartered chattel had no say at all.

"We'll be leaving in five minutes. Do not make me come up and get you." Mother stormed from the room, her heels clacking down the hall.

"I'm sorry, miss."

"It's all right, Sarah." Melissa slipped the ring on and looked in the mirror.

Melissa came down the stairs on the dot of her mother's deadline.

Mother looked her over from coif to slippers, taking note of the engagement ring with icy satisfaction. Father frowned, preoccupied as always, then helped Melissa with her cloak.

The atmosphere in the automobile was even colder than the air outside. No one said a word.

Lord, just help me get through tonight with some dignity. I will not marry a man I cannot trust.

Her mother took her by the arm and ushered her into the ladies' changing room, standing guard with crossed arms while Melissa hung up her cloak and checked her appearance. Melissa stared into her own eyes, building her resolve. She lifted her chin. Dignity.

Thankfully one of Mother's friends drew her attention away from Melissa when they emerged into the hall, and Melissa was able to go downstairs alone.

Zylphia pounced on her at the bottom of the grand staircase, her mint-green silk swishing. "Ooo, you look beautiful. What a perfect gown. Did the modiste make it?" She squeezed Melissa's arm. "Indigo velvet. Now why didn't I think of that? It makes your eyes so blue."

Melissa tried a smile. "Your dress looks just right. You'll have men lining up for dances."

"Actually, my card's already full." She held up a wrist from which dangled a tasseled ivory booklet. "I'm having the next waltz with"—she consulted her list—"Frank Strand." A satisfied smile played on her lips. "You're lucky to be engaged. You can dance with Jonathan all you want. Where is he, by the way?" She looked over the crowd. "You can hardly find anyone in this crush."

Melissa fervently hoped Zylphia was right. Nothing would suit her more than to avoid Jonathan all evening.

God did not see fit to grant her wishes. Jonathan approached through the milling guests, tall and lean and devastatingly handsome in evening dress. She chided her traitorous heart for flipping like a landed fish in her breast.

"Good evening, ladies." He bowed from the waist. "You look lovely."

Zylphia giggled and held out her hand. "Thank you, Mr. Kennebrae."

"Please, call me Jonathan. I'm sure, as a friend of Melissa's, we shall see quite a lot of each other in the future." He smiled, but Melissa noted the strain around his eyes.

Stop it. He's feeling no pain. He knew all along it was a lie.

"Melissa"—he turned to her—"I'd like a word with you in private, if I may."

"No, you may not. Leave me alone."

Zylphia swung around to stare at Melissa. Her mouth dropped open. "Melissa?"

Jonathan set his jaw like granite.

The heat of wounded anger built in Melissa.

A voice broke into their conversation. "Ladies, Jonathan, we just got here. Wicked cold on the harbor tonight." Noah Kennebrae clapped Jonathan on the shoulder. "The music's starting, and if it isn't too brash, I'm going to steal a dance with my future sister-in-law. Come, Melissa, before he occupies all your time this evening."

Noah grabbed her hand and tugged her onto the dance floor.

Helpless to stop him without causing a scene, she went into his arms.

Chapter 19

Noah leaned to whisper in her ear. "Melissa, you have to give him a chance to explain. It isn't what you think."

She sent him a cold glance, stiff with indignation at being maneuvered into dancing with Jonathan's brother, forced to listen to him plead Jonathan's case. "It is exactly as I think. There's no mistake. Kennebrae Shipping is in trouble, and Jonathan cast about for a wealthy bride to bail him out. I don't blame him for that. It is hardly uncommon these days, though I think it is a calloused and mercenary approach to marriage."

"Then what are you blaming him for? Sending back flowers, returning gifts. Hardly the behavior of a proper fiancée." He quirked an eyebrow at her.

She swallowed hard, forcing back the ever-ready tears of late. She would not cry. "I blame him for lying to me. For pretending he felt some tenderness, that he cared for me as a person rather than a bank account. The man has a strongbox for a heart that he could perpetrate such a charade. It's cruel and unfeeling."

Noah frowned. "I think it is high time you learned a few things about my brother. Jonathan's guarded his heart and feelings for a long time, protecting them under plating thicker than the hull of my ship. But that isn't because his heart is cruel and unfeeling. It's because his heart feels too much, is too tender to trust to just anyone. I was mighty happy when I saw him falling in love with you. He was more content, more at peace than I'd ever seen him. I don't think he lied when he professed his feelings for you."

Melissa had been hurt too deeply to allow a few words to change her mind. "I know what I heard."

Noah gave her a little shake, pivoting her sharply. "You know what you think you heard. I'm the one who made the clumsy remark. Not Jonathan. I'm the one you should be angry at. Stop taking my thoughtlessness out on my poor brother. He's heartsick to think you've been hurt. If you could've heard him rounding on me after you ran away from him in the street, you'd know how badly he's taking this."

She shook her head. "But is it true? Is Kennebrae Shipping in financial trouble? Will marrying me save the company?"

Noah's lips flattened, his brows coming down. "I won't lie to you, Melissa. Grandfather's in a precarious state, moneywise. There is no denying your dowry would patch his leaky boat. But that's irrelevant to what Jonathan feels for you. I'm telling you he loves you and would marry you if you came to him with nothing more than the clothes you stood up in. Just give him a chance. Talk to him. Let him explain."

The music ended. Melissa dropped her hand from his shoulder and applauded politely for the orchestra. Could she trust Noah when he stood to gain from her believing him? Was he playing her just like Jonathan?

"Please, Melissa, give him a chance." He led her to the sidelines.

Mother waited with Abraham Kennebrae. Her icy fingers dug into Melissa's arm. "There you are, dear." The words came out falsely bright between clenched teeth. "I've been looking all over for you."

"My fault, Mrs. Brooke. I snatched her up for a dance from under Jonathan's nose." Noah bowed to Melissa. "Thank you, Melissa, and think about what I said. You won't be sorry." He winked and turned on his heel.

Abraham took Melissa's hand between his dry palms. "You look lovely, my dear girl. A credit to us all."

Melissa mustered a smile, though she longed to yank her hand from his grasp. Here sat the originator of her misery, like a king holding court, and they all danced to the tune he called. It wasn't fair, not to her and not to Jonathan either.

And Mother was no better, standing at his shoulder like a vizier, carrying out his plans with relish. And to what purpose? If Mother believed her that the Kennebrae Empire teetered on the brink of financial disaster, that it was her husband's money that would shore it up, would she be so eager to push this marriage?

A hand touched her elbow. "May I have this dance?" Jonathan's voice was velvet smooth, but there was an iron look to his eye.

"Of course you may," Mother answered for Melissa. "Go, enjoy yourself. We'll be waiting right here for you." Her tone forbade argument.

Melissa, perforce, went into Jonathan's arms, stiff as a mannequin.

"If you don't relax and stop pushing away from me, you're going to topple over backwards," Jonathan spoke to the top of her head. "You weren't this rigid when you danced with Noah just now."

"Noah is a good dancer." She refused to look up at him, refused to acknowledge the bittersweet pain of her palm in his, his hand at her waist.

"Most sailors are. But my dancing prowess, or lack of it, isn't the reason you're acting like you want to bolt from my arms. Either you listen to me here on the dance floor and stop acting like you're heading to your own execution, or I'll toss you over my shoulder and carry you out of here like the brat you're being. And believe me, I won't care a whit for the scandal it causes."

She looked up into his stormy brown eyes. He'd do it, too. She relaxed a fraction and allowed him to draw her closer to match his steps.

"That's better. Melissa, I want to apologize for Noah. He spoke without thinking. But I can assure you, I never lied to you. I didn't even know about Grandfather's problems when I proposed to you. I signed those marriage contracts as a gesture of obedience and honor to your father and my grandfather. The money means nothing." He let go of her hand to lift her chin. "Melissa Brooke, I love you. I don't care about Kennebrae Shipping. I don't care about Brooke Grain. I care about you."

She looked into his eyes, the feelings brimming there, and steeled her waffling, traitorous heart. *Don't trust him. He's lying to you again.*

They came to a stop near the edge of the dance floor. Melissa's thoughts whirled.

He led her through the crowd toward where her mother and his grandfather sat. "I'd like nothing more than to get out of here, to go someplace we could talk. I have so much to say to you, so much to ask your forgiveness for. You don't know the half of it yet."

Abraham's papery old voice reached them in a lull in the noise. "Frankly I was surprised by your letting Melissa go to those suffrage movement meetings. And in the middle of the night, too. But you don't need to worry. Jonathan will put a stop to it as soon as they're wed."

Melissa's heart felt like the bottom had opened and the contents drained out. She glanced at her mother.

Almina's eyes flashed fire, her face blazing. Her mouth opened and closed like a screened door in the wind.

Jonathan's grip tightened on Melissa's arm.

She wrenched it away. A liar and a snitch. "You told your grandfather?"

Jonathan spread his hands in an appealing gesture. "Melissa, I promise you I didn't—"

She tugged at the ring on her finger. Jagged ice coated her insides. She pressed the ring into his hand. "Good-bye, Jonathan."

Chapter 20

"Are you sure you want to do this?" Noah hoisted his duffel and stepped onto the gangplank. "I don't like it."

Jonathan nudged his brother ahead. "I'm sure. There's nothing keeping me here."

"You know you're welcome aboard, but I can't help feeling this is a mistake."

"Enough. I don't want to talk about it anymore."

Steam hissed gently, and a steady *thrum* vibrated through the ship. The firemen must have been stoking the boiler.

"Put your things in my cabin, and take my duffel, too." Noah handed Jonathan his bag. "I'll be aft checking with the engineer. We'll be underway in about half an hour."

Jonathan wove his way forward through deckhands grappling ropes, carrying provisions to the galley, and swarming over the pilothouse. Piles of slushy snow lay on the hatch covers, and ice rimed the rails. A week's snow squalls had kept a fleet of vessels in port, but the day, though cold, looked fair. Relief at their departure curled around the guilty despair in Jonathan's middle. If they could just get away.

He shouldered his way through the narrow door to Noah's cabin. Twice the size of the other accommodations aboard ship, it was still smaller than the china closet at Kennebrae House.

His brother's bag fit in the locker beside the door, but there was no room for Jonathan's possessions. He slung his valise under the desk. That would do for now. Three steps took him the length of the room. Frost prevented his looking out the portal. But the air in the cabin was warming up, steam whispering through pipes overhead heating the space.

Jonathan lay down on the bunk and clasped his hands behind his head. Footsteps on rungs, clanking pots from the galley down the hall, the ring of metal on metal, and under it all, the growl of the boilers.

Sick at heart. He'd heard the term before, but not until now did he realize the truth of it. He tried to relax, to allow the slap of water against the hull to ease his tension, but failed miserably.

He shifted, bringing his arms down and lacing his fingers over his middle. The crackle of paper made him frown. He dug in his coat pocket and withdrew several sheets of folded documents. His marriage contract. Lawrence Brooke had returned it to him three days ago, the morning after the Shipbuilders' Ball.

They'd stood in the foyer at Castlebrooke. Melissa refused to see him. Almina glowered at him, her look accusing him of ruining Melissa's reputation by revealing her suffrage activities and abetting her in conducting them under cover of darkness. He could shrug off Almina's accusations. But he couldn't shrug off Lawrence's words.

"I'm sorry, Jonathan. This isn't going to work. I've tried, Almina's tried, even Pastor Gardner tried. She's adamant. When we first put this thing together—your grandfather and I—I thought you two could come to an understanding, that Melissa would acquiesce to my wishes and you'd make a sound match. I had no idea she was entangled in this nonsense about women voting, and I wouldn't ask any man to marry her until she shed such foolishness. The fact that she remains so resistant to meeting with you shows me that the damage is irreparable. I can see now that your marriage would be a mistake. And as things stand between the families now, it would be better if we discontinued any business dealings as well." He'd thrust the papers into Jonathan's hands and walked away. "My lawyers will see to the dissolution of the contracts."

Jonathan's anger had kept him warm on the ride back to Kennebrae House. Without bothering to take off his coat, he took the stairs two at a time up to Grandfather's office.

The argument they had, the harsh words they'd hurled at one another now echoed in his head, swirling, clashing, aching.

The door swung open. Noah came in, unfolding a cot. "I know there's not much room, but I figured you'd rather bunk in here with me than with the men. We've a full crew and no racks to spare. It's either this or a hammock strung in the crew mess." He wrestled with the canvas and wood, knocking it against the wall, the bunk, and the locker until he finally crashed it down into the corner. "There, and you can have my extra pillow."

"Thanks, Noah." Jonathan swung his feet over the side of the bed and sat up. He put his head in his hands. "We should be pulling out soon, right?"

Noah closed the door and pulled the desk chair out with his foot. "There's quite a wait, I'm afraid. And we just got word the *Capernum*'s laid up. We're going to tow her consort, the *Galilee*, along with us. It's loaded and ready to go. We'll pick her up from the Number Three Dock." He sank onto the chair and clomped his boots up onto the cot. "We have time for a little chat."

"Noah, we've been through this. I don't want to talk about it." Jonathan lifted his head long enough to frown at his brother.

"Well, I do, and we've got nothing better to do until they signal us for our turn to pull out. Did you say good-bye to Grandfather?"

"No. I haven't spoken to him since Friday. We've said all we need to say to one another."

"I can think of a few things you haven't said that need saying."

"Like what?"

"How about, 'I'm sorry'?"

Jonathan looked up. "Are you serious? After what he's done? He should be apologizing to me. Manipulating, conniving, double-dealing, then dropping the boom on everyone by blabbing about Melissa's suffrage work. Then having the nerve to tell me it was all my fault things fell apart like they did. He's blaming me!" He thumped his chest with his fist. "I told him he could keep it—Kennebrae Shipping, Kennebrae House, all of it. He made his bed; now he can just lie in it. I told him to contact Gervase Fox and unload what he could to keep his head above water. That's all I can do."

Noah stroked his beard, his eyes troubled. "And what of Melissa?"

Jonathan winced at her name. "It's over, and you know it. She gave the ring back. The contract's broken. She wouldn't see me."

"Funny, when all this started, you were dead set against the marriage, couldn't wait to find a way out of it. Then you went and fell in love with the girl. Not that I blame you. She's great. If you weren't so right for her, I'd have a go at trying to win her myself." He grinned.

"Good luck." Jonathan lay back on the bunk again. He pressed his palm to his heart, feeling the cold lump of a sapphire and diamond ring in his inner coat pocket.

Noah let his feet thud to the floor. "And you say Grandfather's stubborn. You love her, and I know she loves you, too. And here you are, set to sail out of the harbor, your tail tucked firmly between your legs, afraid to fight to get her back."

Jonathan said nothing, angry and weary of the topic altogether.

"Well? Are you going to fight for her?"

"The fight is over. I lost. Now leave me alone." He rolled to face the wall.

After long minutes the door clicked shut. Noah's footsteps echoed in the passageway.

∽

Melissa's shoulders sagged. The newspaper crackled as it fell to her lap. That article, bold as brass on the front page, blaring to the world about her broken engagement. And missing the truth by several leagues.

Sarah, her only companion of the past three days, knelt by the fireplace and swept the grate. The maid had managed to smuggle the paper up to Melissa.

Mother had tried to hide it from her, but Melissa wanted to know the worst.

Melissa sighed, her chest heavy, and raised the paper again. "'November 24. Brooke-Kennebrae Wedding Sunk—The Shipbuilders' Ball of 1905 will long be remembered for its fireworks. No, not those shot off the end of the dock at midnight but those that took place in the ballroom between the Brooke and Kennebrae families. Melissa Brooke, daughter of Lawrence and Almina Brooke of Duluth, ended her engagement to Jonathan Kennebrae of Kennebrae Shipping publicly. Scuttlebutt says a difference of opinion regarding giving women the vote is at the root of this surprising turn of events. Our sources tell us Miss Brooke has been engaged in an underground suffrage movement in the Duluth area for some months. Mr. Kennebrae, left flat-footed and stunned on the dance floor, has our sympathies.'"

Tears stung Melissa's eyes, but she blinked hard and continued reading. "'For several weeks the Brooke-Kennebrae nuptials have taken a great portion of this column's ink: wedding gifts, guest lists, flowers, music, the intimate details provided us by Mrs. Almina Brooke. It seems such a waste, and the wedding of the year, set for just three weeks from tomorrow, is now officially off. Neither Miss Brooke nor Mr. Kennebrae could be reached for comment. Mr. Kennebrae's office has informed us of his imminent departure for Erie, Pa., aboard the cargo steamer, *Bethany*, at the beginning of next week. Perhaps he made a lucky escape.'"

Sarah sat back on her heels, her mouth drawn down. "I'm sorry, miss. They have no cause to talk about you that way."

"It's all right, Sarah. They got so much wrong that it's like they're talking about someone else."

"I got your note down to Mrs. Britten. She said Peter and Wilson would deliver word to all the ladies not to come tonight. And she'd arrange with Kennebrae's to get all the things out of Mr. Kennebrae's office as soon as possible."

Melissa closed her eyes and rested her head against the back of the chair. "I'll have to get word to Mrs. Britten to cancel the chartered train. I won't have the money for it now."

Mother entered, her mouth pinched, eyes narrow. She sagged into the chair opposite Melissa.

Sarah averted her gaze and hurried from the room. Melissa wished she could do likewise.

"I've spent all day canceling wedding arrangements. The florists, the food, the orchestra. You have no idea."

"I'm sorry, Mother. I wish there was something I could do to help." Melissa said the words carefully, knowing the knife-edge her mother walked with her temper these days.

"You've helped enough. I see you've read that wretched article. I'll never be able to show my face at the club again, thanks to that awful reporter. And I might as well forget ever being invited to the bridge club or the garden society. I'm a pariah in this town."

"I know how difficult all this has been for you." Melissa couldn't keep the dryness from her tone. Mother's martyrdom had grown tiresome.

"How like you to be sarcastic. You've no care at all for the consequences of your actions. You never have. If you had thought how this would play out, you'd have bitten your tongue, kept your radical ideas to yourself, and gotten married as I wanted. Now I don't know what we'll do with you. You can't stay here. Perhaps it would be best if you were to take an extended trip out to your father's aunt Persephone in San Francisco."

"Oh no, please. Her house is like a mausoleum, and she smells of vegetable tonic."

"I daresay she does. However, you have no further say in this mess of your making. You'll do as you're told for once."

Melissa sat staring at the closed door when Mother left. The ache in her heart, the yearning emptiness, threatened to swallow her whole. Alone, she could contemplate the last lines of the article. Jonathan was leaving—leaving her to face the town's curiosity alone, to take the blame that belonged to him. His betrayal was complete.

∽

Jonathan finally levered himself off the bunk and headed to the wheelhouse. He braced himself against the roll of the ship, surprised at the strength of the waves. The clanging of the channel-marker buoys and harbor sounds slid behind them. The engine hummed, propelling them through the chop. He couldn't stay in the cabin for the entire journey. He'd go mad.

Up one flight then out onto the deck. He gripped the rail and looked over the side. The *Bethany* rode low in the water, her hold laden with iron ore, showing about twelve feet of freeboard. Waves curled back, creamy white over greenish gray along her hull.

Gulls cried and keened along the shore off the port side. He looked astern, past the consort barge, *Galilee*, to Duluth growing steadily smaller.

Kennebrae House's slate mansard roof jutted skyward, its solid frame dark against the hillside. Almost abeam of them, the gray walls of Castlebrooke rose, stately and smooth. She was in there, angry and hurt, stubborn and unwilling to listen to reason. Believing he had betrayed her and refusing to let him explain.

He turned from the rail, disgusted at himself. Up another flight to the chart room and through to the wheelhouse.

A sailor stood at the wheel, Noah behind him on a high chair.

Jonathan noted his frown. "What is it?"

Noah tapped the barometer on the wall beside him. "The bottom's dropping out of this thing. Harbor forecast said cold and fair. But I don't like the look of this. The wind's picking up. I think we're in for some rough seas."

At that moment a patter of sleety rain hit the windows. A wave slapped the bows, scattering spray upward. The ship lurched but plowed on.

Jonathan shrugged. His life had been nothing but stormy seas of late. What was one more blow?

Chapter 21

Conditions worsened rapidly. Fitful snow turned into squalls then a raging blizzard. The seas grew rougher, mounting before a gusting wind.

"Keep us pointed into those waves," Noah ordered the helmsman. "If we fall sideways into a trough, we might capsize." He ducked in front of the wheel and dialed the chadburn to ALL-AHEAD FULL. A bell rang below them, and the engine room answered back with "All-ahead full." The throb of the engine increased in pitch.

Noah spoke into a tube on the wall. "Put two more men down in the boiler room. Keep those fireboxes full. We're going to need every ounce of power to stay on course."

Jonathan anchored himself against the pitching of the ship by grabbing the door frame. A bell chimed, twice, a pause, then once.

"It's seven thirty in the second dogwatch." Noah kept his eyes forward. Snow scoured the windows. "The watch will change in half an hour."

"Captain, I see the Two Harbors light."

Jonathan peered over his brother's shoulder through the growing gloom, waiting. "I don't see it."

"Wait for it, sir."

Ahead and to port, a faint, lighter spot in the haze then darkness.

A mighty wave burst over the bow, raining ice water over the pilothouse. The engine surged as the wave rippled down the vessel and lifted the propeller clear of the water for a moment.

Jonathan noted the helmsman's white face, knuckles gripping the wheel, straining to see through the dark.

Noah didn't look much better, though his voice remained calm. "Right rudder ten degrees." He consulted the compass. "Stay clear of the shoals."

"Should we try to make Agate Bay, Captain?"

"No, I don't think we could make the harbor in these conditions. I don't fancy plowing into her seawall in the dark."

For long hours they forged ahead through the worsening storm. Jonathan went between the galley and the wheelhouse, bringing coffee and food to his brother, who refused to rest. The temperature plummeted into the teens then into single digits. Ice formed on the rails and decks, making maneuvering about the boat difficult and dangerous.

A seaman, drenched and dripping, ducked into the tiny room. "Captain, the waves are breaking over the spar deck."

"Are the hatches holding?" Noah staggered as the *Bethany* slewed. He grabbed the window ledge to steady himself. "Are we taking on water?"

"The bilge pumps are coping, sir, but just barely."

"Very well. Any word from the *Galilee*?"

"None, Captain. But it's rough out there. The line's staying taut."

"Go back and watch that line. I wish we'd doubled the hawsers in harbor." The seaman tugged his hat on tight and shouldered open the door.

"Can we make Isle Royale? Anchor in the lee of the island, sir?" The helmsman's voice rose with each question.

Jonathan's unease grew. "Noah—" A monstrous wave crashed against the ship, jerking her almost sideways. Jonathan was slung to the floor, striking his head against the captain's chair bolted to the floor. For a moment stars shot through in his vision. He righted himself, accepting his brother's hand to help him up.

Water sluiced down the windows, blinding the men with every wave. Winds buffeted the ship, pushing so hard that even with the engines at maximum capacity, she made no headway.

"Captain, we're listing to starboard. The pumps are falling behind, sir."

"That's it." Grim lines of worry etched Noah's face. "We've got to turn around and make for Duluth."

The call for all hands rang through the boat. The first mate, his face ashen, climbed into the already-crowded wheelhouse. "Captain, are you sure?"

"Yes, Meroff. We've no choice. At the rate we're burning coal, we'll run out before we get halfway across the lake. Without power we'll be at the mercy of the waves."

"But those troughs! We'll roll for sure."

"Meroff!" Noah scowled at him. "Get to your station. Stand by to come about."

The man gave an abashed look, his eyes wide. "Aye, Captain."

Jonathan wiped his hand down his face. What Noah proposed was exceedingly dangerous. In order to come about, he'd be putting the *Bethany* broadside to the waves. If he couldn't swing her bow around quickly, they'd be caught in the trough and rolled over like a piece of driftwood. But with the ship listing and running short of coal, Jonathan knew his brother had no choice.

"Jonathan, would you pray?" Noah's blue eyes pierced Jonathan.

He nodded. "God, our Father, Master of the waves and the wind, we ask Your protection on this vessel and on the lives of these men." Jonathan spoke loudly over the screaming wind and pounding waves.

Noah shot him a grateful glance.

"We're humbled before the power of Your creation. But we know You hold us in the palm of Your hand. Nothing will happen to us that isn't in Your will. Give Noah clarity of mind and certainty of purpose. We thank You for bringing us this far. Please help us now. Amen."

Every man in the pilothouse echoed that Amen.

Jonathan didn't quit praying, and he knew Noah was praying, too.

"Right full rudder," Noah gave the order. "Hang on, men."

The bow swung around, blasted by water and wind. Snow scoured the windows, blocking their vision. Every man braced himself as the *Bethany* slid sideways and down. The descent seemed to last forever. Would they ever reach bottom?

Jonathan glanced out the porthole beside him. Only raging lake water was visible. Were they already rolling over?

"More steam!" Noah shouted into the talking tube.

The stern of the boat lifted clear of the water, the prop spinning wildly, shuddering through the vessel. A wave lifted them stern first, the nose plowing down.

Somewhere below a man screamed, "Father, save us!"

Jonathan's mouth dried to dust. His hands ached from gripping the door frame.

One of the front windows cracked, letting in a gust of frigid air and a fine spray of ice water. The enormous wave picked them up and slung them forward. The roar of the storm was immense, buffeting them.

The helmsman let out a cheer, grinning wildly at the captain. "We made it! You did it, sir!"

Noah didn't answer his grin. He skidded over to the ladder and shouted to the deck below, "Check on the *Galilee*! See if she made it around."

Jonathan ducked through the doorway into the chart room, peering through the water and blackness toward the stern. He could see no more than a few feet.

The ship shuddered and groaned but forged through the seas.

He returned to the wheelhouse. "I can't see a thing out there. Noah, are we going faster now?"

"The wind and waves are pushing us along now instead of us fighting through them." Noah turned to the chadburn and sent the message to dial back the engines. "We'll save some coal. It won't take as much to maintain steerage heading in this direction."

"Was that as close as I think it was?" Jonathan hunched into his coat, stepping back to get out of the draft from the cracked window.

"Closer. God sure was with us." Noah resumed his chair. "Thank you for your prayer."

"I'm not sure I've quit praying yet."

Noah grunted, fixing his gaze ahead at the inky, rain-slashed darkness. "Don't quit. We're going to need every prayer. It's going to be a very long night."

∽

Melissa leaned her head against the window, the glass frigid against her skin. What an impossibly long night it had been. She hadn't slept a moment lying in bed listening to the storm. And all morning she'd battled her conscience, her broken heart, and her sense of betrayal.

Sarah bustled behind her, folding, sorting, stowing garments into luggage.

But Melissa could drum up no enthusiasm for packing. She could only focus on the emptiness in her heart, the pain of loss and disillusionment. Sleety snow pattered on the panes; the wind howled under the eaves. Her bedroom door opened, and she turned.

"Why aren't you packing? Your train leaves this evening." Mother lifted the lid of a steamer trunk and sifted through the contents.

Melissa returned her gaze to the windows. Another gust slammed the house, sending snow swirling against the panes. Waves crashed on the rocky shore, flinging spume high in an icy veil. She closed her eyes, and the *Bethany* swam into her vision, tossed and helpless before towering seas. Had they reached a safe harbor? Anxiety tightened her chest. "Is there any word from the harbor on how the ships are faring in the storm?"

Mother gave a vinegary sound. "I've not inquired. Anyone foolhardy enough to leave port in the teeth of a storm deserves what he gets."

"But, Mother"—Melissa turned, eyes flying open—"the ships that left port yesterday afternoon left in fine weather. They couldn't know this would blow up." She waved toward the windows.

"Well, it's no business of ours. Get your belongings packed. Your father agrees that Aunt Persephone's is the best place for you. He's terribly upset about your broken engagement. I am, too. You've behaved very badly, and we're the ones who must bear the brunt of the embarrassment."

Melissa bit back all the words she wanted to say, all the protests about how she was the one wronged, how she wasn't some parcel to be mailed away at their convenience. It wouldn't matter now anyway.

Light flashed in the gray gloom outside. Thunder boomed, rattling the panes.

She pressed a hand to her throat. A chill raced up her arms. Any northerner knew thunderclaps during a snow only came during the most intense winter storms. Was Jonathan out on that raging lake, perhaps fighting for his life? "Sarah, please ask one of the footmen to go to the harbor and find out if there is any word of the *Bethany*." Melissa ignored her mother's gasp. "Tell him to ask the harbormaster and at Kennebrae Shipping if need be."

The lid of the steamer trunk slammed shut. "Melissa Brooke, I'll not have you asking after Jonathan Kennebrae like some heartbroken waif. People will think you're regretting your rash actions. How desperate do you think you'll look?"

Melissa set her jaw and turned toward her mother. "Right now I don't care how I look. Jonathan and Noah sailed out yesterday afternoon. I need to know if there is any word of them before I leave for San Francisco."

Mother huffed and frowned then shrugged. "There's nothing I can do with you. I give up." She lifted her hands and let them drop to her sides. "Your reputation's ruined as it is. Go ahead and traipse down to the docks yourself. Snivel after the Kennebraes like some needy puppy."

Melissa rolled her eyes at her mother's dramatics.

Poor Sarah had frozen, not knowing which mistress to obey.

"Please, Sarah, send word for the automobile to be brought around. Mother is right. It would be best if I went myself."

Chapter 22

Jonathan rolled his shoulders to ease his tense muscles. Cold, cramped, and exhausted, he stood at his brother's side on the bridge.

The bilge pumps chugged, trying to stay ahead of the incoming water. The wind continued to roar, driving the waves to ever-mounting heights. The ship rolled and shuddered while the helmsman fought the wheel. The *Galilee* hung behind on the towrope, slewing and bucking but holding her own.

The *Bethany* listed about two feet down on the starboard side. Noah ordered several deckhands into the hold to shift iron ore to the port side with shovels.

Jonathan didn't envy them trying to stay upright and move the filthy reddish-gray ore in the tight confines of the cargo compartments.

The Two Harbors light gave Jonathan some hope they were nearing safety.

But rather than turn broadside to the waves again to enter Agate Bay, Noah ordered the helmsman to sail on to Duluth. "I won't risk the sharp turn into Two Harbors. Duluth Harbor gives us a straight run to shelter." Noah answered the helmsman's unspoken question.

Though a seaman had nailed an oilskin over the broken window, the pilothouse remained cold.

"It will feel good to get some solid ground under my feet." Jonathan stomped his feet and blew into his gloved hands. "And I'm glad for the daylight, weak as it is in this storm. Last night was terrible."

Noah spared him a glance and a slight smile. "Good thing you're not prone to seasickness."

"You've done a marvelous job, little brother. I don't know of any captain who could've done better. We're almost home free."

Noah shook his head, his eyes on the waves crashing over the bow. He leaned in and lowered his voice. "We're not there yet. The list hasn't improved, which means we're taking on water faster than I thought. And we've got to make the harbor entrance in the worst seas I've ever seen. That opening is narrow and protected by two cement piers. We'll be lucky to get in without some hull damage."

Jonathan took in his brother's clouded eyes, his rigid expression. Responsibility for the ship, the consort barge, and the crews of both lay heavily on Noah.

"Why don't you go below for a while? Nothing's changing up here. You need some rest."

Noah shook his head. "I'll rest later. I belong here."

The watch changed. A new helmsman took the wheel. Two more hours of struggling through the storm.

Through the gloom, the green light of the south breakwater lighthouse of Duluth Harbor cast an eerie shaft toward them. Jonathan rubbed his gritty eyes, straining through the lashing water to make sure he wasn't hallucinating.

A cheer went up from the crew. Safety lay ahead.

∽

"Miss, I'm a little busy. You'll have to wait." The harbormaster pushed past Melissa. "Joe, get that tug brought around to where it can be of some use. We've already got one ship grounded on the shore. We don't need another one."

"I just want to know if there's been any word at all." She hurried after him, the wind tugging at her skirt and coat, pulling at her hair.

"Miss, go check at the shipping office." He all but thrust her away in his haste.

Melissa fought through the crowd gathered on the pier. What were so many people doing out here in this weather? The temperature couldn't be much above zero, yet folks were milling about.

The talk was all of the *R. W. England*, a brand-new steamer, beached up the shore, its hull cracked open to the surf. At least the crew had been rescued.

She could make out the hulks of a dozen ships at anchor in the harbor basin and several more outside the safety of the breakwaters straining at their anchor chains. Fog and fitful snow tussled around her. She needed to get to the Kennebrae offices. The top of the building loomed three blocks west and only one block from the lake. She wouldn't bother going back to the automobile. Getting down to the harbor had been difficult enough.

She wrapped her coat tighter about herself and ducked her head against the cutting wind. Her lungs ached with cold, and her feet were numb. If only she'd thought to ask someone—Sarah maybe—to come with her, she might not feel so alone, so anxious.

Her throat tightened when she reached the steps of the Kennebrae Building. For a moment she stood on the marble stairs, battling her pride and heartache against her need for news of the *Bethany*. Another gust ripped between the buildings, almost pushing her over.

The heavy door yielded under her hand, and the gale blew her inside. The calm warmth of the lobby pressed in on her freezing face. She panted, trying to catch her breath.

A bespectacled man behind a desk rose and came toward her. "May I help you, miss?"

For a moment she couldn't speak. Then she bolstered her courage and lifted her chin. "I'd like to see Mr. Abraham Kennebrae. Is he in?"

"I'll check. May I tell him who is calling?"

"Tell him Melissa Brooke."

She almost laughed at the man's startled glance. He must've read the papers. "Wait here." He scurried toward the stairs, stopping at the landing and peering over the banister at her.

She caught sight of herself in the mirror on the far wall. Her hair flew about her face in medusa-like swirls, her cheeks raw and red. She hadn't bothered with a hat when she left the house, but now she wished she had. She scrabbled for a handkerchief.

"This way, Miss Brooke." He led her up two flights of stairs.

A shaft of pain sliced her heart as they passed Jonathan's closed office door, but she kept her eyes forward, her hands at her sides.

The man kept darting looks at her over his shoulder, as if expecting her to burst into hysterics. They reached the end of the hallway, where he rapped twice on a door and opened it. "Miss Brooke, sir."

Melissa entered, and the man closed the door behind her.

Mr. Kennebrae sat in his wheelchair at the corner windows looking down on the harbor.

She took off her gloves and smoothed back her hair.

"Come here, child." His voice sounded frail and raspy.

She walked toward him, tucking her gloves into her pocket. A fire burned in the fireplace, casting a glow in the storm-darkened room. When she reached him, he held out his hand to her.

His skin was papery white, wrinkled, and spotted. His breath scraped in his throat. He seemed to have shrunk since the last time she'd seen him, resplendent in evening dress at the ball. Then he had been a titan of business, the head of a proud family. Now he looked like an old man broken by sorrow. His state of decline alarmed her. Had he gotten bad news?

She forced the words past the lump in her throat. "Mr. Kennebrae, I came to ask if there was any word of the *Bethany*. I know she put out yesterday."

He looked up at her with rheumy eyes. "I'm sorry, lass. More sorry than I can say. There's been no word of her." Coughs wracked him, his thin shoulders shaking under the effort of drawing breath. "Bronchitis. It comes on with the cold weather."

"Can I get you something?"

He shook his head. "Just sit with me. I have things to tell you."

She tugged off her coat and draped it on the end of his desk. Several chairs stood at attention down the side of a conference table, so she took the end one and placed it beside him where she could see his profile.

"I feel terrible about what's happened. I opened my mouth when I shouldn't have." He never took his eyes off the waves. "You see, Jonathan told me you thought he'd spilled the secret about your suffrage activities to me. But, my dear, Jonathan never said a word. In fact, I didn't know *he* knew. When I first hit on the idea of you two marrying, I had you thoroughly checked out. Didn't want any unpleasant surprises. I knew all about the meetings, and I knew when they were moved to this building. Dawkins, night guard here for years—trust him implicitly—he told me everything."

She gasped.

He took her hand, squeezing it. "Now, now, don't be upset. I knew long ago about your work with the illiterate women of the city and about your desire to see women given the right to vote. I know about your schooling, your dislike of seafood, and even your habit of biting your nails when you're worried." He took his gaze from the windows and inclined his head at her.

She took her thumbnail out of her mouth and dropped her hand to her lap, feeling heat surge up her neck.

"My dear, Jonathan didn't betray you in any way. He is as innocent in all this as you are. He knew nothing of my financial difficulties before he asked you to marry him. I deliberately kept it from him until afterwards."

Melissa swallowed hard, guilt at her accusations pressing against her chest.

"My grandson has a fearful temper. Gets it from me. We had quite a donnybrook when he found out. Don't blame Jonathan. The fault lies with me. I'll admit your mother and I jumped the gun a little with the announcement, but Jonathan proposed to you properly because he fell in love with you."

For a frozen moment Melissa was afraid to hope. Could he be telling her the truth? She wanted to believe him, wanted to with an intensity she'd never known. Reality deflated her hopes. She'd accused Jonathan of trying to marry her for money. She'd flung awful words at him, thrown his love back in his face. He might have loved her once but no more, not after what she'd done.

Mr. Kennebrae gave a rueful laugh. "You want to know the irony of it all?" He lifted some papers from his lap. "At the end of the last century, I took some property in Montana as payment for a debt. It's been sitting there, a chunk of mountain outside a little town called Butte. I got word today that the country's richest copper strike has been found out there. This is a telegram from William Rockefeller. His company, Amalgamated Copper, is offering me a scandalous amount for that patch of land. Enough to take care of all my debts and then some."

She blinked back tears. Poor old man. Trying so hard to make things work, when if he'd just trusted God to work out His plan, everything would've been fine.

Sound familiar?

Melissa frowned. Her conscience prodded her. She hadn't trusted God. She hadn't trusted anyone. And when things didn't work out the way she planned, she assumed it was God who had erred.

Oh, Lord, I'm sorry. Please forgive me. Help me to trust You with everything in my life. And, Lord, please watch over the Bethany. *Keep them safe. I need to apologize to Jonathan. You know how much I love him. Please, Lord, give me a chance to make things right. I'll try to understand if he can't forgive me, but give me the courage. . .and the chance. . .to make things right.*

Tears crept down the old man's cheeks.

She clung to his hand, praying for him, for both of them, and for his grandsons.

After a while he stirred. "I don't suppose you'd know, but Jonathan and I had a fight before he left. I said some harsh things to him that I'm ashamed of now. He's left the family business for good. He's going to work in Erie, Pennsylvania. A fellow called Fox has hired him to oversee his shipping line." His voice cracked. "I don't blame him."

Going to work in Pennsylvania? Not coming back to Duluth? Her shoulders sagged. "We're more alike than you'd think, Mr. Kennebrae. We both broke his heart."

A knock sounded at the door. The man from the front desk stuck his head inside. "Sir, the *Bethany* has been sighted heading toward the harbor."

Melissa blinked, sending tears, this time of thankfulness, down her cheeks. "I'm going down to the harbor. I have to be there when he comes in." Melissa straightened, wiping her cheeks with the backs of her hands, unable to stop her smiling.

"I couldn't imagine a better homecoming, my dear."

"He may not want to speak to me." She shrugged into her coat and buttoned it up the front.

"Then you'll have to make him listen. Kennebraes are stubborn, but when we love, it's forever. He still loves you. He just needs to be reminded."

Chapter 23

Waves pounded the *Bethany*, each one seeming larger than the last. Snow buffeted the pilothouse, scouring the windows, fine as salt.

Jonathan rubbed his sleeve on the window, swiping away condensation. Fog and snow impeded his vision so he couldn't make out individual houses and buildings of Duluth. Only the hulking shape of land and the white spray of the surf against the rocky shore flitted through swirling flakes.

Farther south, toward the harbor, watery lights shone fitfully, hazed by precipitation. Jonathan hunched his shoulders and crossed his arms, trying to hold some warmth in.

"We cannot make it into the harbor with the *Galilee* in tow. The canal's too narrow. We'll be lucky to make it in ourselves." Noah ran his hand down his face and beard.

His first mate lurched against the wall as the *Bethany* took another brutal wave. "Can't we drop the anchors here and try to ride it out?"

"No, we're taking on too much water. The pumps are falling behind. We've got to make the harbor. The hatches amidships are leaking too much." Noah straightened his shoulders. "Signal the *Galilee* we're dropping the towlines. She'll have to set her anchors and ride out the storm as best she can. If we try to take her through the canal, she'll be battered to death on the piers."

The first mate ducked out the door, struggling to close it behind himself in the wind.

Jonathan went into the chart room to look aft. The *Galilee* bucked along at the end of the steel hawser. Men clung to the rail, working their way back toward the towline, their feet slipping on the icy deck, buffeted with every step.

Light flashes and the barest glimpse of the hulk of the consort barge. Jonathan strained to see through the storm. Signal lamps, Morse code.

The door clanged open. Icy air blasted them as the first mate ducked inside the wheelhouse. "*Galilee* says she'll drop anchor, Captain."

"Very well. Release the towline."

The *Bethany* seemed to rise in the water a bit and surge forward. The towline to their consort had been dropped.

"All ahead full." Noah dialed the chadburn. He then returned to his high captain's chair. Jonathan stood at his shoulder, hanging onto the back of the chair. A wave burst over the ship, momentarily blinding them with spray.

"Left ten degrees. Line up off the south pier light."

Jonathan watched the channel between the piers grow larger as they approached. Steerage had to be corrected every few seconds, it seemed, as the storm buffeted them. Snow wreathed the steel framework of the transporter bridge across the far end of the canal. If they could just make it under the bridge, they'd be safe in the harbor. A fleet of tugs would assist them in getting to the docks.

The *Bethany* carried fifty feet of beam. The canal was one hundred thirty feet wide. Steel and concrete piers guarded the entrance through Minnesota Point into the harbor. Almost there.

The nose of the ship entered the canal fairly straight. Jonathan exhaled and lifted his hand to clap Noah on the shoulder. Before his hand descended, the boat's stern lifted high on a rogue wave, shoving the vessel forward, throwing Noah against the front wall of the wheelhouse. The helmsman crashed into him, the wheel spinning wildly.

Jonathan's feet left the deck, and he tumbled over the bolted-down chair into the wheel. His shoulder slammed one of the handles, breaking it off.

The bow gave a sickening crunch as it hit the bottom of the canal and bobbed up again.

Arms and legs scrambled. Men yelled.

Jonathan's shoulder burned, but he pushed himself off the floor.

"The captain's hurt!" The helmsman grabbed for the spinning wheel. "Look out!"

Another monstrous wave hit them, crashing them into the north pier.

Jonathan, staggering to his feet to go to Noah, was hurled into his brother.

"What do I do?" The helmsman ducked as shards from the breaking windows exploded into the tiny space.

Jonathan threw himself over Noah's defenseless form, trying to protect him from the flying glass.

Water poured into the broken window followed by a gust of icy air.

Noah groaned.

Jonathan scrambled to his feet.

Noah propped himself up on his palms, water swilling about his hands and knees. Blood dripped from a gash on his head.

Jonathan swiped the water from his eyes and tried to locate the pier wall through the window.

The *Bethany* careened crazily, her stern yawing and dragging them outside the canal walls. The engine throbbed at full throttle, but the wheel spun helplessly in the helmsman's hands. "I've got nothing. It's like the rudder's gone."

"Noah, are you all right?" Jonathan grabbed the arm of the captain's chair to keep from being tossed down again.

They were broadside to the merciless waves and being shoved toward the shore. The keel ground on the rocks of the lake bed. With a final thudding jolt, forty-eight hundred tons came to a stop, foundered on a shoal more than one hundred yards offshore.

∽

Melissa shouldered her way through the crowd, hoping to make it to pier side in time to see the *Bethany* come in. Snow spiraled around her on a cutting wind, the air damp with the spray of the waves thrashing the rock-strewn shore perpendicular to the jutting pier. Perhaps she should've gone by automobile around the harbor to the docks and met the ship there.

"She's in trouble. Look!" A man shouted just ahead of her, pointing toward the lake. "She's going to capsize!"

Melissa snaked between the onlookers, not stopping until she reached the pier wall. She scraped her wet hair out of her eyes and leaned out to catch a glimpse of the *Bethany*.

A mighty wave picked up the back end of the ship and thrust her nose downward. The scrunch as her bow hit the bottom of the canal ricocheted off the pier walls. Another storm surge swatted at her, cracking her against the north pier. The shock to the ship made it shudder.

Melissa screamed, her voice drowned out in the shriek of the storm. She gripped rough concrete, her body buffeted by onlookers trying to see better. The crowd forced her to fall back, pushing, running toward the shoreline on her left. The only thing she could see above the crowd was the top of the steamer's smokestack.

She left the sidewalk and struggled over the icy boulders, feet slipping, numb hands spread wide for balance, grasping, climbing.

"She's hit the shoal! Launch the lifeboats! Look! She's tearing apart!" Men shouted all around Melissa.

She wiped water from her face.

The *Bethany* sat abeam of the shore, barely a hundred yards away, waves pounding her amidships, spilling over the deck. Her midsection strained, then a crack appeared, wider with each slam of water.

"She's down in the stern. Look, you can see men on the deck!"

The stern settled lower in the water. A huge hiss and billow of steam jetted into the air.

"Her boiler room's flooded. They're powerless now."

The strength drained from Melissa's limbs. The wind snarled her hair, tangling it and throwing it across her face like a wet veil. No steam. No power. No heat.

"Miss! Miss Brooke!" Hands grabbed her. She swung around to look up into the face of McKay, the Kennebrae butler. His ashen face stood out in the gloom. "This way, Miss Brooke."

"How did you get here?" She'd had too many shocks to think clearly. Numbness leeched all drive and energy from her.

"I came to fetch Mr. Kennebrae from his office. We saw the crowds from the window. He wanted me to come after you and see that you came to no harm."

"Oh, McKay, they hit the pier."

"I know, miss." His strong hands helped her back up the rocks to the street.

"She's sinking. Did you see her? She's broken in two."

"Yes, miss. This way. Come back from the shore. It's too dangerous to be out there."

"Where are we going?"

"To the office. You need to get warmed and dry. The boys will be brought there when the lifesavers get them off the ship."

She followed him like an obedient child, too stunned to do anything else.

∽

Jonathan patted Noah's face. "Hey, wake up, little brother. We need you here."

Noah groaned, eyes cloudy and unfocused. "Wha' 'appen'd?"

"We're aground outside the harbor just offshore."

"My ship." Noah put his hand to his forehead. A nasty gash over his right eye bled freely.

"She's in bad shape, Noah." Jonathan squeezed his brother's shoulder. "She's down in the stern, no steam, and she's got a bad break in the middle. We're almost completely separated from the bow."

"Casualties?"

Jonathan was relieved to see sense coming back into Noah's eyes. "Some cuts and bruises, yours by far the worst. The first mate says there are men in the bow section of the ship. We don't know their status."

"Help me up."

Jonathan stood and assisted Noah to his feet.

Cold air whistled through the pilothouse from every broken window. The ship rocked hard to port with each wave pounding over her spar deck. Crew members crowded into the wheelhouse and chart room.

Jonathan tried to look away from their shocked, scared faces. He battled down his own fear, beating it back until he could think clearly.

Noah clamped a handkerchief to his bleeding head. "We're hard against the shoal, too heavy to be pushed over it. We'll be pounded apart against it." He stopped, closing his eyes and holding his chest.

"Noah?" Jonathan touched his brother's arm. *Please, God, don't take Noah.*

"I'm all right. Just knocked my ribs a bit." Noah addressed the first mate. "Light the lamp, and signal the bow. Find out what's happening up there."

"Someone's headed this way from the bow, Captain."

The men in the pilothouse surged to the windows. Four sailors picked their way across the flooded deck, clinging to the icy wire railing. Their feet slipped, bodies blown and shoved by the wind. Those in the pilothouse could do nothing but watch their perilous journey. A roll of black water broke over the men on deck, and when it receded, there were only three.

Jonathan gripped the window frame. Just like that, the lake had swallowed a victim. Jonathan willed the remaining men to be careful, his mind racing in prayer.

They reached the crack in the ship. Jonathan held his breath as first one, then another leaped the gap. A wave crashed into the ship, sending water thrusting upward into the breach like a geyser. The third man hung back, both hands tight on the rail.

The first two motioned for him to follow, but he stood still, shaking his head. Finally he turned back the way he had come. The two who remained on the deck crept forward until they reached the pilothouse.

"Captain, the ship's yawl was ripped away in the collision. There's nine men in the bow. We lost Cummings over the rail. Nobody who's left is hurt bad, just cold and scared."

Noah nodded, grim and pale.

Jonathan's heart thudded against his chest, and he had to force himself not to give in to fear.

One crewman, who couldn't be more than seventeen, pointed through the port windows. "I see the lifesavers' boat."

The white boat looked small against the angry waves. Lake Superior slapped at it, racing toward it in huge waves that thrust the bow of the little boat skyward, catapulting its occupants out like toys. Oars and sailors tumbled in the surf.

"They'll never reach us that way." Noah turned from the windows. "Bring every lantern you can find—and kerosene."

Men hurried out the starboard door.

Noah staggered.

"Sit down." Jonathan pushed him into the captain's chair and took the blood-soaked handkerchief. "Somebody get me something to bandage this cut with."

"Captain, they're signaling from the beach. They're going to try to shoot us a line with a Lyle gun and rig a breeches buoy to get us off."

Jonathan swallowed hard. As much as he desired to get off this ship, the thought of dangling like a piece of laundry from a rope over the churning water held little appeal. He dabbed at his brother's cut with the edge of the handkerchief.

"Take two more men, and see about securing that line when it comes." Noah swatted at Jonathan's ministrations. "Stop fussing. We've got to get off this ship."

∽

Jonathan put his weight into opening the port-side door. The list of the ship and the battering had bent the metal frame and bowed the steel door. Though he waited for the report of the Lyle gun, the sound couldn't reach them over the roar of the storm. Like a striking snake, a rope shot out of the fog.

Men on the deck below grappled with the line shot from the shore, making it fast to the ship.

"Won't be long now, Noah. They've got the line." Relief loosened Jonathan's jaw.

Noah pushed himself up. "Get the crew lined up. Youngest crewmen first then the officers. Jonathan, you go with the officers."

"I'll wait and go after you."

Noah's eyes hardened. "You'll do as you're told aboard my ship. The captain goes last."

They stepped outside into the swirling snow. The wind sucked Jonathan's breath from his lungs. Rigging aft of the pilothouse clanged. With every buffet the ship groaned and creaked in agony.

The breeches buoy swung out toward them, pitched by the waves. The cook's boy stepped to the rail, his face stoic but his eyes wide with fear. How old was he? Twelve, thirteen at the most? He was in for a wild ride.

Hands, numb from the cold, fumbled with the straps, sliding them up his legs. The first mate hooked the apparatus to the line. "Hold on tight. You're going to get wet as you near the shore. The line dips, so if you get stuck, reach up and start pulling yourself along. Right?"

The boy nodded, pinched with cold.

Jonathan helped swing the boy onto the rail. He tried to smile, to encourage the child. "Ready?"

Something cracked, and the line went limp, zinging into the churning water below. The boy tottered on the rail, flailing his arms.

Jonathan grabbed at the child's legs. For a moment they hung over the rail, their balance tipping them toward the water. With a supreme effort Jonathan threw himself backward onto the deck. He lay there gasping for breath, snarled in the breeches buoy and the young sailor.

"It froze. The line's gone."

Lights flashed again from the shore. Jonathan untangled himself from the broken rope and buckles, defeat pressing his shoulders. They'd have to wait for a new line. The cook's boy sat propped against the wall, eyes closed, taking great gulps of air.

"What's your name, son?" Jonathan scooted over to him, his shoulder throbbing.

"Padraig, sir." He opened sky blue eyes. "But you can call me Paddy." His brogue was as thick as his curly mop of dark hair. "Thank you, sir. I thought I was going swimming that time."

"Me, too."

The first mate turned from the rail. "They say they can't do anything more until the storm blows out. We're trapped here."

"Let's get inside the wheelhouse. It's going to be a long, cold night." Noah stood by the open door, waiting as a captain should, to be the last one inside.

Chapter 24

Melissa sat before the fire in the Kennebrae offices, sipping the tea McKay brought her. Her damp skirts steamed in the warmth.

Mr. Kennebrae sat by the window, his eyes never leaving the ship stranded in the lake.

"Do you think God's punishing me?" His breath wheezed. "Taking my grandsons from me because I've been so negligent of Him?"

She swallowed her tea, the heat sliding down her throat, warming her from within. "I don't think God is as petty as we are, Mr. Kennebrae. He doesn't play tit-for-tat schoolyard games. Everything He does is for our good and according to the purpose He's mapped out in our lives. Even when—or especially when—it isn't something that we would've chosen for ourselves."

"How do you know? You're so young."

She set her cup down and went to stand beside him at the windows. "Because the Bible says so. There's one verse I flung at God when I thought He'd abandoned me and was doing things to deliberately hurt me. But I was wrong. I know now it is true. There is nothing that happens that is outside the will of God. He doesn't follow us with a broom and dustpan, picking up the broken pieces of His plan that we smash, trying to put them back together somehow. And He doesn't shoot down lightning bolts of retribution on His children when they fall. He lifts us up, brushes us off, and forgives us."

"What verse?"

She smiled, in spite of her worry over Jonathan. "It's from Jeremiah. Chapter twenty-nine, verse eleven. 'For I know the thoughts that I think toward you, saith the Lord, thoughts of peace, and not of evil, to give you an expected end.'"

He sat silent for a moment. "So God knows our end."

She nodded. "He not only knows it, but He's planned it out ahead of time and knows it is good and not evil."

Abraham took her hand in his. "Thank you for comforting an old man in his distress. I can see what drew Jonathan to you. You are a treasure. When he gets back here, I'll do everything I can to see that you two are reconciled."

She withdrew her hand with a sad smile. "No, Mr. Kennebrae. I'll apologize to him, but that's all. If we are reconciled, it has to come from him. No more interference from well-meaning grandfathers." She sent him a pointed look. "God has things under control, right?"

Abraham chuckled. "All right, my dear."

A knock at the door and McKay entered. "I'm afraid there's bad news, sir. The lifesavers are unable to reach the ship under current conditions. They must wait until the storm dies down."

Abraham sat up in his chair. "That could take all night. And with no steam aboard ship, how will they keep warm?"

Melissa sagged against the windowsill. All night? *Oh, Lord, help me to hang on to the truth of Your Word. I know You are in control. Please, help them to survive. Please bring Jonathan and Noah back to us.*

She stood and gathered up her coat.

"Where are you going, young lady?"

"I'm going to the shore. I can't stay here in warmth and luxury when they are suffering so. I'm going to stand vigil and pray."

"I'll go with you. McKay, get my coat."

Melissa put her hand on his shoulder. "No, Abraham." He started— whether at her tone or at her use of his first name, she didn't know. "You're staying here. The weather's too raw. And there's your bronchitis to consider."

He sagged back. "Very well, but McKay, get her some proper outerwear and light a bonfire on the beach. If she starts to flag, haul her back here. I'll be in this room watching until my grandsons are rescued."

She bent and kissed him on the cheek. "Pray, Abraham."

∽

Aboard the *Bethany*, fifteen men huddled in the wheelhouse. Only three lamps had survived the wreck intact. They hung from hooks on the ceiling, rocking and swinging with the movement of the boat.

Jonathan anchored a piece of canvas to the window frame, trying to cover the gaping hole. The ship rolled and shuddered, slammed against the shoal by another frigid blast.

"Finish nailing that oilskin, and find something to brace that starboard door." Noah's voice sounded weaker by the minute. How bad were his injuries?

Jonathan spoke through lips stiffened by the cold. "Sit down, Noah, before you fall down."

"No, nobody sits. And nobody sleeps."

The men grumbled, scowling.

"That's an order. If you sit down, you'll fall asleep. If you fall asleep in this cold, you'll freeze to death. Understand?" For a moment light gleamed in Noah's eyes, the light of challenge and authority. The crew must've recognized that look, for they all nodded assent.

"Aye, Captain, no sleeping."

Paddy kept close to Jonathan's side. With no food and no water, some of the men resorted to breaking off icicles and sucking on them. Jonathan, already so cold, couldn't bring himself to do this. At least not yet.

"Is there any word from the men in the bow?" Noah wedged himself next to Jonathan in the corner of the tiny room.

Jonathan kept his voice low. "None since dark."

Concern laced Noah's voice. "Are there any lamps lit up there?"

"No, I didn't see any."

"Where there's light, there's hope, you know?"

They both looked at the three lamps throwing yellow light on the crowded room. How long would their only heat source, these three tiny flames, last?

∽

"Miss, stand back. They're going to light it." McKay tugged on Melissa's arm.

She stepped back on the street.

A burly stevedore stuck his torch into the kerosene-soaked pile of crating and firewood. Flames shot out, licking upward, throwing light and heat toward the ring of onlookers. Dockworkers, shopkeepers, housewives, and sailors crowded the pier and the streets of Minnesota Point. Several more bonfires burst up along the expanse of shoreline.

"There must be thousands of people out here keeping vigil." McKay led her to the pier wall. "And look, there's some light coming from the wheelhouse. Why, I bet those boys are in there watching us, taking heart knowing they aren't alone and haven't been forgotten."

Melissa wiped her cheeks, grateful for the heavy gloves McKay had found for her. And in the whipping snow and wind, grateful to have her hair confined under the hood of the heavy cloak he'd procured. The man was a marvel of efficiency. She almost smiled when he handed her a cup of steaming coffee. Was there anything he couldn't do?

Ladies from the church milled through the crowd, pouring coffee and offering food.

Pastor Gardner, muffled to the eyes in a buffalo coat and muskrat hat, clutched his Bible to his chest and prayed.

Melissa kept her vigil, adding her prayers to the hundreds being said on behalf of the men stranded on the ship. She spoke only to McKay and then only when he asked her a direct question. All her thoughts centered on Jonathan. She loved him. Even if he couldn't forgive her for what she'd done to him, she wanted him to know how sorry she was and how much he meant to her. She kept her eyes on the lights in the wheelhouse.

Sometime near 3:00 a.m., someone began to sing.

"Brightly beams our Father's mercy
From His lighthouse evermore,

But to us He gives the keeping
Of the lights along the shore.

Let the lower lights be burning!
Send a gleam across the wave!
Some poor fainting, struggling seaman
You may rescue, you may save."

Melissa's eyes filled with tears. A few voices joined the lone singer. She added her own, singing the familiar hymn with new understanding of the beautiful picture.

"Eager eyes are watching, longing,
For the lights along the shore."

More in the crowd began to sing, sending their message of hope across the waves to the sailors of the *Bethany*.

"Trim your feeble lamp, my brother,
Some poor sailor tempest tossed,
Trying now to make the harbor,
In the darkness may be lost."

∽

Jonathan shook his head to clear his fuzzy brain. The unending buffeting made thinking difficult. He couldn't feel his hands or feet anymore, not even when he stomped or beat his arms across his chest. The sleeves of his coat crackled with ice.

The elation he'd felt at seeing the bonfires springing up along the shore had worn off. What he wouldn't give to be standing next to one of them now. He let his mind drift to the one topic he'd been avoiding for hours.

Melissa.

Lord, I've been a knot-headed fool about her from the moment I first heard her name. Why is it that love makes a man act so stupidly? I've ignored Your Spirit's promptings, and I've tried to handle everything my own way. I've lost my temper, and I've lost my head.

"What are you mumbling about?" Noah stifled a yawn and recrossed his arms, tucking his fingers under his armpits.

"I'm telling God what a fool I've been over Melissa."

Noah grunted. "Is He agreeing with you?"

Jonathan ignored that dig. "Truth is, I prayed for weeks this Bible verse, but I think I was praying it all wrong."

"What verse?"

"Proverbs 21:1. 'The king's heart is in the hand of the Lord, as the rivers of water: he turneth it whithersoever he will.' I prayed that over Grandfather a hundred times, wanting God to change his heart about this marriage. And I prayed it over Melissa, wanting God to change her heart toward me these last few days. The only one I didn't pray it over was me."

"And God took your heart and changed it a bunch, didn't He?" Noah's words came out clipped, his jaw clamped.

"He sure did. He let me fall in love with Melissa. He opened my eyes to the plight of the immigrants we hire, particularly their wives. And the plight of women in this country who don't get a voice in its leadership." Jonathan broke off, shifting his weight, rubbing his hands on his upper arms.

"But most of all, He changed how I felt about myself and my possessions. I was and still am willing to give up Kennebrae Shipping if it means I could have Melissa forgive me. Kennebrae Shipping isn't my life. Serving God is my life. And my life would be so much better with Melissa at my side." Jonathan's teeth chattered, and he bit down hard to still them.

"That's a heap of change."

"Facing death by shipwreck will cause you to evaluate a few things."

"So God shipwrecked us so He could drill some sense into that anvil-hard head of yours? You're like Jonah." Noah's mouth barely moved. "Remind me when we get off of here to slug you a good one."

"The first thing I'm going to do when I get onshore is go to Castlebrooke and make Melissa listen to me, even if I have to break down her door."

What was that? He cocked an ear. The wind, gusting for hours, seemed to die down a bit. Was that singing?

"I must be more tired than I thought." Jonathan put his arm around little Paddy, rocking with tiredness, and briskly rubbed the lad's arms to warm him. "I could've sworn I heard Grandmother's favorite hymn. Remember how she used to sing 'Let the Lower Lights Be Burning' every night it stormed on Lake Superior?"

Chapter 25

Dawn broke, if so gray and overcast an event could be called dawn. The storm relented at last, snarling and spitting in retreat up the north shore. The waves lost their fury, subsiding slowly but steadily.

Melissa's pulse beat in her throat as the lifesavers put their boat into the water once more. With coordinated strokes, they bent the oars, taking the waves and rising over them, heading out to the *Bethany*. Melissa couldn't tell if the lights still burned in the wheelhouse.

A cheer went up when the door on the port side of the pilothouse opened and a dark-clad figure stepped out. Someone was alive!

"Please, God, let it be Jonathan." Contrition struck her. She wasn't the only woman on the beach who had a loved one on that ship. Other prayers for husbands and sons must be winging heavenward at that moment.

She tugged at her glove to bare her fingers so she could chew her thumbnail. Bad habits be hanged. She leaned against the concrete pier, straining to see.

"I have faith, my dear, that you'll see him soon."

She looked down to see Abraham Kennebrae at her elbow. Dawkins, the security guard from the Kennebrae Building, and McKay stood behind.

The butler winked at her then blew on his hands, shifting his weight. He'd not left her side all night, fetching her hot drinks, bringing a lap robe from the Kennebrae carriage to drape around her shoulders.

Abraham reached up and took her hand. "I made Dawkins bring me down. I couldn't stay up there anymore."

The white boat reached the *Bethany*, and several of the lifesavers clambered aboard. It wouldn't be long now.

She bit her nail harder. Would he be alive? Would he forgive her?

༺༻

"I'm going forward with the lifesavers. Come if you want to, but as captain it's my duty." Noah shrugged off Jonathan's hand and stepped out onto the rocking deck.

Jonathan blew out a sigh at the stubbornness of the Kennebraes and followed his brother toward the bow. His boots slipped and slid on the icy deck, but at least the waves weren't crashing over him, threatening to sweep him over the rail.

The crack in the hull was narrowest on the starboard side and a matter of a quick jump to cross. Iron ore eddied red swirls just under the surface, where the hold lay open to the lake.

The scene in the bow was grim indeed. Nine sailors had roped themselves together, lashing themselves to the deck so as not to be swept overboard. All nine lay frozen to the ship, dead.

Noah seemed to crumple from within. He staggered, his face going pale. Jonathan grabbed him to keep him from sliding to the deck.

"That's it. We're going now. No arguing." They maneuvered back to the stern of the ship and into the lifesavers' boat.

∞

Melissa insisted McKay stay with Abraham. If it was bad news, she wanted to hear it first and perhaps be able to tell Abraham gently. She picked her way down through the boulders to the shore.

Bits of flotsam and wreckage bumped against the rocks in the icy breeze. The lifesavers' boat scraped on the beach, loaded down with men. Bodies crowded around, blocking her view.

She pushed and wedged herself between the curious until she reached the front.

Strong hands lifted the survivors over the gunwale. They were so bound in blankets and coats and mufflers that she couldn't recognize any of them.

A bearded face emerged from the boat. Noah! Alive!

Her heart thudded in her ears. She elbowed a man in the side and darted forward when he moved in surprise.

Dried blood decorated Noah's pale face. What had happened to him?

Then she looked past Noah's shoulder and into Jonathan's eyes. Her heart quit beating altogether, her breath gone. He was alive! Her mouth dropped open to speak, but no sound came out. She tried again.

He leaped from the boat, staggering as his boots hit the icy water. In two strides he wrapped her in his arms, covering her face with kisses, tunneling his fingers into her hair, dislodging her hood.

She kissed him back, cupping his cold cheeks in her hands, relishing being in his embrace. All misunderstanding, all the hurt and foolishness drained away.

He pulled back to look at her face, searching for something there. "I'm reading a lot into your being here, you know?"

"I know. Jonathan, there's something I need to say to you."

"Unless it's 'I love you,' it can wait."

"Jonathan, I love you."

"Melissa, I love you, too." He crushed her to him again, kissing her, filling up her cup of happiness until it overflowed into tears of joy.

When he released her, it was only to dig in his breast pocket. He withdrew her engagement ring and slipped it on her finger. "Right where it belongs, my love."

She wiped an icy tear from his cheek and nodded, too overcome for words.

Epilogue

Y ou look lovely, my dear." Father leaned in and kissed Melissa's cheek. "Absolutely radiant."

Mother mopped her eyes. She'd cried all through the ceremony, though with happiness over Melissa's wedding to Jonathan or mourning over the fact that it wasn't the opulent festivities she'd originally planned, Melissa didn't know.

Jonathan lifted her hand, the one with the sapphire and diamond engagement ring and now the gold circlet he'd placed there only an hour before, and tucked it into his elbow. "Well, Mrs. Kennebrae."

She thrilled at both her new name and the depth of his voice brushing over her.

"Happy?"

"Deliriously." She squeezed his upper arm, leaning against him.

The reception at Castlebrooke was in full sail, guests laughing, music wafting from the piano.

"Mother's not sure how to react, but I'm glad we invited the suffragists and their families. And the Brittens. Peter and Wilson look like they're having a wonderful time. Thank you for thinking of it."

"It was the least I could do. Though Peter and Wilson won't need to act as your bodyguards any longer. No more late-night rambles to the harbor. From now on you hold your meetings in the parlor at Kennebrae House in a civilized manner. How about another dance?"

He looked at her so intently that a shiver raced up her spine. She smiled up at him and went into his arms like coming home.

He nuzzled her neck and whispered into her ear. "You look beautiful in that dress. Almost as beautiful as you looked standing on the shore in the wind and snow after a night's vigil in a storm."

She trembled, thinking of how close they'd come to losing each other forever. His grip tightened, and she knew he was thinking the same thing. "You're stuck with me now though. I heard you promise before God and all your friends."

"My bartered bride, you'll hear no complaints from me."

THE MARRIAGE
MASQUERADE

Dedication

For my wonderful church family at Cornerstone.
Thank you for all your encouragement.

Chapter 1

N oah Kennebrae tilted his head and didn't meet his brother's eyes in the mirror. "I'm through talking about this."

The razor scraped against his cheek, removing thick, brown beard in relentless swatches. The tangy smell of shaving soap mixed with bitterness. His pride lay like the whiskers in the basin, chopped off and scattered. How he'd enjoyed wearing this full beard, the mark of his captaincy. Kennebrae captains always wore a full beard.

"At least tell me where you're going. I need to be able to contact you." Jonathan put his hand on Noah's shoulder.

Noah shrugged off the gesture and rinsed the razor. He cut another patch of whiskers, careful to square off the sideburn. "I can't think why you'd need to contact me. You have everything well in hand."

Habit led him to look out the window toward Lake Superior. The hulk of his first and only command crouched on the shoal where he had grounded it last November. Ice-encased for months, it now rocked with the pounding of the recently freed surf. Jonathan would be out there later today, directing operations. Salvagers would swarm, unloading tons of iron ore, patching the hull as best they could before towing the crippled steamer into the safety of the harbor.

Though Noah mourned the loss of the *Bethany*, he mourned the loss of his crew more. Ten men dead as a direct result of Noah's arrogant foolishness. Only God's mercy had kept the entire complement of sailors from perishing during the storm, including his own brother.

"You should stay here and oversee the salvaging yourself. You're running away, and there's no need." Jonathan rammed his fingers through his hair. "What's happened to you? You've changed so much. This is nonsense."

"Is it? Is it nonsense when no one will look me in the eye? When the widows of my crew members are grieving because I couldn't bring my ship into the harbor? I need a clean break, away from Duluth." Noah's hand trembled, and he lowered the razor. Shame made it difficult to meet his own eyes in the mirror. He set his jaw, gripping the edge of the basin and forcing himself to stare into his reflection, to take the pain he so justly deserved.

Coward. Murderer.

"I know things look dark now, but you wait. Sentiment will change once the salvaging is finished. And I'm sure, once the engineers go over the *Bethany*, you'll be exonerated of any wrongdoing."

Noah snatched up a towel and wiped the excess lather from his face. The sharp smells of soap and cotton pricked his nose, and he fought to relax his gritted teeth.

Again his gaze shot to the window. At least the constant reminder of his failure would be removed from display soon. Not that he would be here to see it. He couldn't take one more day in Duluth—the stares, the whispers, the looks of pity. He had to get away before the guilt ground his soul to powder.

"Is that all you're running from?" Jonathan's stare pierced like a harpoon. "What about the wedding?"

Noah shouldered into his suspenders. "You know my views on that. Just because you fell in love with your arranged bride doesn't mean my marriage would wind up the same. Grandfather will have to break things off since it was his idea in the first place. I don't even know who he had lined up, but it won't matter now. No man is going to want to marry his daughter off to a disgraced ex-captain. I suppose I'm lucky Grandfather let me get out of the hospital and back on my feet before he started nagging about a wedding again. Broken ribs and pneumonia—a blessing in disguise. He'll have to turn his matchmaking schemes on Eli instead. It should be easy. Eli can marry whoever Grandfather chose for me."

Noah headed into his bedroom, rolling down his sleeves and buttoning the cuffs. He swept keys, watch, and coins off the dresser and into his pants pocket.

Jonathan put himself between Noah and the hall door. "Noah, I can't let you go like this. At least tell me where you're headed and when you plan to come back."

Noah noted the square jaw, the glint in his older brother's brown eyes. So much like their grandfather, Abraham Kennebrae. Bossy, dictatorial, sure of himself and his decisions. Noah envied Jonathan his confidence. He hadn't realized what a valuable commodity confidence could be until catastrophe stripped it away, leaving a husk, a shell that threatened to crumble at the first strong wind. "You have to promise you won't tell Grandfather where I am. He'll only want to drag me back and force me into marriage."

"I won't tell him where you've gone, but I will tell him you are all right. You owe him at least that much, to not have to worry after your safety." Jonathan crossed his arms.

Noah lifted his jacket from the bed and shrugged into it. He withdrew a telegram from the breast pocket and handed it to his brother.

Jonathan read the sheet aloud:

APRIL 15, 1906.
NICK KENNEDY

ARRIVE SUTTON ISLAND LIGHT VIA FERRY *JENNY KLAMATH*
APRIL 20 TO ASSUME ASSISTANT KEEPER POSITION *STOP*
STANDARD WAGES UNIFORMS AT YOUR EXPENSE *STOP*
JASPER DILLON – INSPECTOR, US LIGHTHOUSE BOARD

His eyebrows pinched over his nose. "Nick Kennedy?"

Noah stared at the door behind his brother. "You don't think they'd have given me the job if I had applied as Noah Kennebrae, do you? Nick Kennedy is close enough."

"Lying to your employers isn't the best way to start out a new job." Jonathan folded the paper into precise creases and handed it back.

Noah squashed the tickle of guilt Jonathan's accusation sent swirling through his chest. "It isn't a lie. From the moment I walk out that door, I'm Nick Kennedy, assistant keeper of the Sutton Island Light. No past, no manipulating grandfather, and no marriage to a stranger."

"You won't even meet her? At least tell her in person why you won't marry her? It's not like you to cut and run when things get tough."

The barb hit like a shot from a Lyle gun.

"Running is never the answer." Jonathan stepped aside, lines of sorrow etching his face.

Noah swallowed hard and picked up his seabag. "All I know is I can't stay here. I have to get out."

"When will you come back?"

"I don't know." Maybe never. When he could look his crew members in the eyes and not feel he'd let them down. When he could sleep through the night without nightmares of being frozen to death in his own pilothouse. When he found some way of getting through a day without wishing he had perished in the storm folks were now calling the *Bethany Blow*.

༄

Anastasia Michaels pounded up the curved staircase in an unladylike manner. She rushed down the hall to her bedroom and skidded inside. The door slammed with a *thud*, and she sagged against it, her hand still clutching the knob.

Hazel looked up from the rocker beside the fireplace. Her needle hovered over yards of white nightgown material.

"What is it this time, child?" Hazel had a dried-apple face, her eyes gleaming like two pips amid the wrinkles. She regarded Anastasia with a calm, unruffled expression. Nothing Anastasia did seemed to rile the woman who had looked after her for all of her nineteen years.

Anastasia panted, one hand on her chest, breathless more from her news than from running through the halls of Michaelton House. "Father's home from Hibbing. He went right into the study with an old man in a wheelchair. He didn't even greet me after being away for months. And do you know what they were talking about?"

Hazel eyed her shrewdly. "And how is it you overheard them if they went into the study?"

Anastasia's ears tingled with heat, and she twisted her hands at her waist. "Well, I walked by the door, and my shoe was unfastened. I had to bend over, and it just happened to bring my ear down to the keyhole. . . ."

Hazel's eyebrows lifted.

"Oh Hazel, now isn't the time to chide me for eavesdropping. It's the only way to find out anything around here. Father and that man are hatching the most awful plan." She flung her arms wide.

Hazel ran her gnarled hand across the fabric in her lap and resumed her mending. "It can't be as bad as all that. I've told you eavesdropping only gives you part of the story. Your father is an upstanding businessman. He wouldn't be doing anything underhanded."

"But he is!" Anastasia plopped onto the footstool beside the rocker and anchored her elbows onto her knees, her hands providing a perch for her chin. "They're downstairs right now arranging my marriage. To a stranger—the grandson of the man in the wheelchair. They're discussing me as if I were a company asset. Father is talking about mergers and gross tonnage and quarterly profits. And the other man is just as bad. He's gloating over railcars, loading docks, and net worth. It's disgusting."

The lines around Hazel's lips deepened, her eyes dimming. "So the time has come."

Anastasia sat up and gripped the edges of the footstool. "You don't seem surprised." Her heart fluttered like a captured bird. "Please tell me you didn't know about this." She frowned at Hazel.

Hazel poked the needle in and out furiously.

"Why didn't you tell me?"

"Your father forbade me to tell you, Annie." No one but Hazel ever called her Annie. "He told me months ago so I could look for another place if I chose. Once you're married there will be no need for me. Your husband will no doubt have his own staff. If I don't want to find a new position, your father will retire me to a cottage he owns in Hibbing to live out my days."

"How is it he wanted you to be prepared and spared no thought to warning me?" Anastasia bounded up to pace the rug. "Who has he chosen? How could he know what kind of man would be a good match for me? He's so wrapped up in his business he barely knows what I look like. He spends all his time at his mines, and then the first time he's home in months, he's making plans to rid himself of me."

Hazel set aside the mending and rose, her shoulders stooped with age but her step light. "I don't see what you can do about it, child. Your father has worked out the legal details. They'll be setting a wedding date now, I imagine. That was the last thing to do once your father got back to Duluth."

"I'll just show you what I can do about it. I'll march right down there and tell both those old schemers what they can do with their old wedding plans." She headed to the door, hands fisted at her sides.

Hazel grabbed Anastasia's elbow. "Annie, you'll just embarrass yourself and anger your father. Their plans won't be set aside by your tantrums."

"But what else can I do?" Hot tears pricked her eyes. How could he do this to her? Why wouldn't he even consult her before signing her away like one of his business contracts? He never would have treated her brother, Neville, like this. Not his son and heir. "Hazel, won't you help me?" She gripped her hands together, trying to calm her jangling nerves and think.

Hazel's eyes swept Anastasia, her wrinkled face softening into gentle lines. "Don't you even want to meet the young man? He might be nice, you know."

Anastasia waved her hands, pushing the idea away. "No, I don't want to meet him. What kind of man lets someone else decide his future? Not the kind I want to marry, that's for sure. I spent my entire childhood trying to earn Father's respect and love, and he ignored me. If I let him choose my husband, he'll pick someone just as cold and unfeeling. I can't live like that. I can't live without love."

"How do you plan to get out of this then?"

"I'll get a job. Maybe as a seamstress or a governess or something." She threaded her fingers through the heavy, blond curls lying on her shoulder. She knew precious little about sewing or caring for children, but she'd rather do that than be shackled to a stranger for the rest of her life. And Anastasia could count on Hazel for help, as she always had. She just had to wait for it.

Hazel tapped her pursed lips, eyeing Anastasia. "You're so much like your mother. Twenty-five years ago I stood in her bedroom having very nearly this same conversation. She was forced into marriage with Phillip Michaels, a perfect stranger. I couldn't do anything to help her. But I will try to help you now."

Chapter 2

Damp, chilly air swirled around Anastasia off Lake Superior. A faint red pinstripe of dawn marked the horizon. She took one last look around her opulent bedroom, hiked her skirts, and lifted her leg over the sill of her third-story window.

Her boot toe poked the air. She eased farther out the window, her fingers already aching from their death grip on the frame. Hazel's brilliant plan, hatched a week ago, didn't seem so brilliant now. But if Anastasia could just get out of the house without any of the servants seeing her, she would have crossed the most precarious of many bridges.

Stop wool-gathering and get going, girl. Time's running out.

Unable to reach the ledge, she bit her lip and eased both legs outside, rolling over until her stomach pressed against the sill. If people passed on the street below, they'd be treated to a scandalous view of her backside hanging from the window.

Scrape.

One toe ticked the rock ledge. Anastasia squirmed backward a few precious inches. Ah, at last. She slid her torso down, smacking her hat against the sash, shoving the bonnet over her eyes.

"Botheration." Curls bounced off her forehead and cheek. She pushed the hair out of the way, trying to tuck it behind her ear and right her hat at the same time, all while clinging one-handed to the outside of Michaelton House. Madam DeVries of the Duluth Ladies' Academy would have a fainting spell if she could see Anastasia now.

She steadied her breathing. First hurdle almost complete. Every muscle tense, she inched around until she faced away from the window. Strings of yellow light hung like vapors to the east.

The romance of the moment wasn't lost on her. She could be a heroine from one of those dime novels the maids liked to giggle over. Brave, intrepid, willing to risk everything for love. . .or in her case, freedom. She closed her eyes and breathed deeply.

Hooves clopping on the street jarred her back to reality. She froze until the wagon passed, grateful the driver didn't look up.

Hurry, girl.

Step, *scrape*, step, *scrape*. Her derrière scratched against the rough stone blocks of her home. If she could cross to the conservatory roof, she could ease down the gentle copper slope to the ground.

Anastasia almost laughed when she drew near the greenish metal, relief making her giddy. She took stock, squinting in the poor light to make out the best place to put her feet. Hazel's sturdy boots weighed at her feet and ankles, so unlike the dainty footgear she normally wore.

"Oh Lord, help me." She probed with a toe until she found a purchase on the slippery rooftop. So far so good. She reached for the ridgepole to steady herself, wrapping her chilly fingers on the folded metal seam.

Whump!

Her feet slid out from beneath her, and she landed on her hip, sliding, scrabbling, rushing toward the rain gutter.

A scream crowded into her throat, but she clamped her lips closed. Her eyes slammed shut as her body launched over the edge of the roof into the air. She hit the ground hard, the impact shoving the breath from her lungs and rattling her teeth. She forced her eyes open. Her backside throbbed and her wrist stung, but everything else seemed intact. Had anyone heard her?

Lamplight shone from the basement windows. The staff was up and stirring, lighting fires, preparing breakfast, but no cries of alarm or inquiry and no movement in the yard.

Dampness seeped through her heavy wool coat from the slush lying under the eaves. Her hands tingled with cold. She choked back a groan as she pushed herself up from the crocus and daffodil spears. At least she hadn't landed amongst the lilacs. Those would have been much less forgiving. A few swipes at her skirt and another adjustment to her hair and hat fortified her dignity and bolstered her courage.

Hazel's battered carpetbag lay behind the forsythia bushes along the foundation, just where Hazel had stashed it the night before. Anastasia grunted at the weight, bumping the bag against her legs and staggering across the grass toward the driveway. Hazel had sent Anastasia's trunk ahead to the docks the night before, but the valise bulged with all the things Anastasia didn't think she could do without. Next time she would pack lighter.

A chuckle escaped her lips. What next time? If this scheme failed, she'd be locked up tighter than the crown jewels until her wedding.

Her wedding. Ha! Her sentencing, more like. Father hadn't broached the subject with her, not in the entire week he'd been home. In fact, he'd barely spoken to her, closing himself up in his study when he was home and spending most evenings at his club. But whoever her intended might be, if her father approved of him, he must be deadly dull and proper. Probably not an ounce of adventure or imagination in him.

She crept along the lilacs bordering the curved drive, keeping as close to the branches as possible. She would miss the flowering of the hedge this spring.

A bit of tension eased when she reached the road. Moist pavement gritted under her boots. Duluth and Lake Superior spread out before her. Michaelton House stood atop Skyline Parkway, looking down into the lake basin—not as fashionable a location as the mansions right on the lake, but her father preferred the hilltop view.

Built just six years before, Michaelton House dominated the block with its turrets and garrets, dormers and slate roof. It looked the castle of Anastasia's dreams. Her throat squeezed at the thought of leaving Hazel and all that was familiar. The urge to go back clambered up her ribcage.

Firming up her resolve, she hurried down the block to catch the first streetcar of the morning. A grocer's cart rumbled by, making the morning deliveries, followed by the milkman's blue and white truck. Bottles clinked and rattled. The driver tipped his cap to her. She nodded, ducked her chin, and hurried on.

Anastasia had never been out this early before. Several people waited on the corner. Men in rough coats, smelling of cigar smoke and sausage. Women in plain dresses, noses pink in the chilly air, waiting for the tram to take them to their cleaning or manufacturing jobs.

Anastasia tucked herself into the back of the group so she didn't have to make eye contact with anyone. She clutched the valise handle with both hands, staring at the sidewalk. Her pulse throbbed in her throat. Concentrating on just the next step, the next obstacle, she pushed away the thought of the biggest challenge yet ahead. For now, just boarding the streetcar, making three switches, and getting to the harbor seemed enough. She half-expected someone from home to grab her and haul her back at any second.

After an age of waiting, the tram pulled up to the corner. She barely glanced at the driver or the horses. Keeping her head down, she swung herself aboard. Public transportation, another first today. Dockworkers and domestic help crowded the plain wooden seats, the smell of damp wool and sack lunches clinging to them. Anastasia had an overwhelming sense of standing out like a beacon.

She dug into her pocket for her coin, alarm shooting through her when she didn't find it right away. At last her fingers closed around it in the corner of her pocket. She dropped it into the box and edged down the center aisle, thankful for Hazel's coaching.

The bell clanged, startling her as she thumped down onto a seat. She settled her valise in her lap and placed her feet close together, tucking them as far back under the seat as she could.

A burly man with a mustache that made him look like he'd been eating a bristle broom lurched into the seat across from her. He smelled of sausage and syrup.

The tram started down the steep slope to the lake, stopping every couple of blocks to disgorge and take on more passengers. After three stops, she dared look out the window. The sun painted the business district in soft pinks and golds, burning away the low-lying fog. Businessmen in dark topcoats entered stone buildings through brass and glass doors, the commerce of Duluth waking to life.

Anastasia transferred to a cross-town streetcar, praying she had done the right thing. She should've written down Hazel's directions instead of trying to commit them to memory.

By the time she transferred to the harbor tram, she felt like a seasoned public transportation traveler. She got off at the ferry dock. A fresh breeze whipped her cheeks and tugged at her hair. Water slapped against the pilings, restless, as if seeking a way to climb the dock. She looked over the side of the quay at the chopping waves, her head swirling and her stomach churning.

Her heart thudded at what she was about to do. Could she force herself to get on a boat? Fear tightened her throat until she thought she would suffocate. Finally, air rushed into her lungs. She gasped, placing her hand on her chest, trying to quell the panic. Her arms prickled with heat, while her hands went cold. Instantly, she was a shivering six-year-old, dripping, gasping, clinging to the upturned bottom of a rocking rowboat.

∽

"Nick, pass me the wrench, will you?" A gnarled hand jutted from beneath the diesel engine.

Nick looked up from the bucket of gasoline. Greasy parts sloshed in the pungent liquid. He dug in the tool chest, implements clanking. "Think we'll get her put back together before dark? I don't fancy pumping those foghorns up by hand all night if a bank rolls in." He slapped the handle of the wrench into the grimy palm.

Fingers closed around the crescent wrench and disappeared under the engine once more. Between grunts and metallic bangs, the voice of his boss, Ezra Batson, drifted out. "We'll get her put right. Just needed a new seal. You finished washing the grease off those parts?"

"Almost." Nick gave them a final swish then tossed them onto a flannel rag. The gasoline evaporated quickly in the sunshine slicing through the door. He pulled another cloth from his back pocket and wiped his hands. "How often does the fog-engine break down? I've been here a week and this is the third time we've worked on her." He didn't really mind. The release his spirit felt at leaving Duluth made him take small annoyances like broken machinery in stride. The more he got used to being Nick Kennedy, the less he felt the drag of Noah Kennebrae's recent problems. He found himself smiling more, even able to tease a bit. How odd to feel like a new man and yet feel like his old self all at the same time.

Ezra scooted across the concrete floor on his back, emerging into the light. Grease smeared his cheek, and dirt flecked his gray hair. "It's just working out the kinks, since the equipment sits idle all winter." He rubbed his nose with the back of his hand. "Takes a lot of maintenance to stay on top of things. I can't tell you how glad I am the Lighthouse Board sent you and the boy along this year. Last year I had to make do with one helper who quit after a month. Said it was too remote out here. He was lonely for the lights of Duluth."

Nick sorted through the parts, fitting some together, lining up nuts and bolts for reassembling the engine cover. "I guess what some see as a burden, others see as a blessing."

Ezra tossed the wrench into the toolbox and rolled to his knees to stand. "You don't seem to mind it, that's sure. I'd think a handsome young feller like you would have a lady at home missing him."

Only some well-heeled heiress Grandfather wants to shove at me. He shrugged, shaking his head. "No lady at home. I think I'm destined to be a bachelor forever. I like peace and quiet."

His boss chuckled. "That's what they all say until the right girl comes along and knocks all their previous notions into the lake. Mark my words, son, if you meet the right girl, you'll never be the same."

Nick inserted a bolt and spun a nut on the shaft. "Maybe you got the last, best girl." He smothered a grin, anticipating Ezra's answer.

"I got the best one, that's a fact." The old man's face softened, his eyes going warm as they did whenever he talked about his wife. "Imogen's a treasure. Like the Good Book says, 'Her price is far above rubies,' and I wouldn't trade her, not even for an ore boat of gems." He walked to the door and stared out at the lake, his eyes squinting in the bright light glinting off the restless waves. "This year will be easier on my Imogen. The Board is sending a woman out to help with the housekeeping and cooking. Should arrive on the *Jenny Klamath* this afternoon." He palmed his pocket watch. "In an hour or so, if they're running on time. I want you and Clyde to meet the ferry. You can pick up the mail and tote this woman's baggage up to the house."

A woman? *Hmm.* That would be good for Mrs. Batson. Though neither Ezra nor his wife ever spoke of it in Nick's hearing, he had a feeling Mrs. Batson was ailing somehow. Her skin had a transparent, papery look to it, and Ezra had mentioned her trouble with headaches. Nick wondered at his boss for bringing her to such an inaccessible spot. She looked like she needed to be under a physician's care, not marooned on a rock in the middle of Lake

Superior, miles from shore and leagues from a hospital.

"Hope this lady's better than the last one they tried." Ezra handed Nick another bolt from the cloth on the floor. "Don't know where she hid the liquor, but she managed to get some here to the island. That gal was drunk as a skunk from noon till dark every day. And she sang when she was drunk, songs no woman should know. And when her liquor ran out, she got mean. Imogen tried to help her, but she wasn't having any. We put up with her for two weeks, till the *Jenny Klamath* made her return trip down-lake; then I packed her up and sent her back to Duluth. I can't abide a drunk, and a drunk woman's even worse."

Nick tried to imagine the upright and steadfast Ezra faced with a rollicking drunk in his kitchen. A smile tugged at his lips. "Sounds like you were better off without her. Surely the Lighthouse Board will have found someone more suitable this time."

Ezra grunted. "I think they jump at anyone willing to come here. Sometimes I don't think they even interview these ladies. I've heard stories that would curl your hair. Women running from the law, women with compromised morals looking to find a lonely lighthouse keeper to latch onto. If we didn't need the help, I never would've applied for a housekeeper in the first place. But there's no way Imogen could keep things up to the mark. Not with inspections being like they are."

"The inspector's pretty thorough?" Nick tightened the last bolt and began cleaning up the tools.

"Hear my words: Jasper Dillon is the most thorough, most disagreeable inspector the Lighthouse Board has ever employed. Most folks just talk about a white-gloved inspection. Dillon actually does them. Everything on this rock is owned by the Board, but Dillon acts like it belongs to him personally. Every windowsill, every pane of glass, every blade of grass on Sutton Island will be inspected for cleanliness and adherence to the code set forth by the Board. Sometimes I think Dillon must sleep with that book under his pillow. He's got every line memorized, and he enforces every rule to the maximum."

Nick's eyebrows rose. "That bad, huh? How often does he come to inspect?"

"That's the trouble. There's no schedule. He just pops up like a summer squall, blows in, wreaks havoc and threatens to fire us all, then blows out. It might be a month from now or it might be this afternoon. But he'll come. And if he finds anything out of order, he'll be back with a vengeance the next time."

"He sounds charming. I can't wait to meet him." Nick grinned.

"Don't take him lightly." Ezra's frown brought Nick up short. "When you see him coming, you'd best scramble into your uniform coat and look smart. He's not a man to trifle with."

Nick pursed his lips, bringing his hand up to stroke his beard. He stopped when his fingers touched his bare cheek, a wry smile twisting his lips. When was he going to stop doing that? "We'd best test this engine out. I can only imagine what would happen if Inspector Dillon showed up and it wasn't working."

The engine turned over and rumbled to life, the sound filling the small fog-house, making conversation impossible. Nick watched the needle on the pressure gauge rise, pressure building in the cylinder. When it reached the right level, the twin foghorns on the roof bellowed out a long *beeee-yooooo-ouuuu*. Nick grinned at Ezra, who killed the engine.

In the silence, a steam-whistle blast piped across the water, a cheerful and impertinent echo of the mighty foghorn. Ezra stuck his head out the doorway, shading his eyes to see down-lake. "It's the ferry. You best go meet her. I'll finish up here and see you at the house."

Nick rolled down his sleeves and plucked his hat from a peg on the wall. He'd best look presentable to meet this new housekeeper. He checked his appearance, whisking some dirt from his pant leg. At least his boots gleamed. He'd spent most of last night rubbing them with mink oil to waterproof them, then applying polish and elbow grease to buff them to a glossy shine. An inspector would find nothing to quibble about there.

Chapter 3

Annie clutched her valise to her quivering stomach and wished for the thousandth time she had never set foot on the *Jenny Klamath*. Why did this have to be the first job to present itself? Why hadn't something come along where she could keep her feet on dry land?

Mist coated her clothing and hair. She closed her eyes, willing herself not to be sick. The gentle-rise and fall of the ferry played havoc with her senses, sending waves of pea-green clamminess sloshing through her. She tried to make herself one with the bench.

The ship's whistle pierced the air, laughing at her frailty. She jerked, her eyes popping open. Cold sweat bathed her skin, her neck and back aching with tension. If only this nightmare would end. She dared a look out of the corner of her eye, not moving her head. Purplish-grey cliffs rose ahead of the ferry, white surf pounding their jagged, rock-strewn edges. Dark trees poked the sky high overhead, and looming above that, sunlight shattering off its prisms, the red and white tower of the Sutton Island Light.

Annie swallowed hard, forcing down her rising gorge. *Almost there. Almost there. Almost there.* The chant, growing faster to match her heart rate, swirled in her ears.

Around her, crew members prepared to pull into the dock, shouting to one another, swarming over the lashed-down cargo as if they hadn't a care in the world. Lines whizzed through the air, and at last, the ferry bumped softly into the dock.

Thank You, Lord. Thank You, Lord.

"Miss Fairfax?" A crewmember stopped in front of her. "Sutton Island, miss."

She nodded, trying to smile, though her cheeks refused to budge. Her breath caught against the lump in her throat. Time to go. She inched forward on the hard bench. Weakness spiraled down her legs.

With a death grip on the rail, she baby-stepped along the deck. Her head swam with nausea. She reached the gap in the rail where the gangway was supposed to be. Open space down to restless blue-green water yawned before her. No gangway? How was she supposed to reach the dock?

"Toss your bag down, ma'am." The deckhand stood at her elbow. When she didn't move, he took the valise from her grasp and heaved it across the

149

chasm. It landed on the dock safe and sound.

A tall young man stood beside her bag, looking up at her. "Afternoon, Jenkins. This the new housekeeper for the light?" He scrutinized her, the breeze ruffling his dark hair. She couldn't read his expression, but his close observation did nothing to quell her fears or her queasy stomach.

"This is her. Give her a hand down, will you? I need to make sure the boys offload all the mail. Last time they forgot two packages."

"Sure." The man held up his hand to Annie. "C'mon, miss. I'll help you."

They expected her to leap across open water? Were they mad? She'd fall in and be sucked under the dock. "I can't." She shook her head, her hands icy. Tremors of weakness flowed down the backs of her legs.

He rolled his eyes. "I don't have all day. I have work to do."

She squeezed the rail harder, tears of fear and frustration pricking her eyes. "I can't. It's too far." Her voice rasped in her dry mouth.

The man blew out a long breath and swung aboard the ferry. She both marveled at and resented his casual grace all in the same instant. Without warning, he scooped her up into his arms.

She squealed, grasping him about the neck. "Sir, what are you—"

Ignoring her, he leaped. His boots thumped on the boards, and wondrously, the pitching and rocking stopped. Annie looked over his shoulder at the ferry then into his eyes—blue, the same color as the sky. He set her down and backed up a pace, looking over her head up the dock.

Relief at being off the boat surged through her, relaxing her icy control. "Thank you, sir. I'm so—" To her complete and utter mortification, she lost the fight with her nausea and retched on the man's immaculate black boots.

His jaw slacked, his eyes going wide. He looked at his boots then at her.

She clapped her hand over her mouth. "I—I–I'm so sorry."

He didn't move, blinking in shock.

She backed away. Embarrassment flooded her cheeks with heat. Humiliated, she whirled and ran up the dock.

Someone's laughter chased at her, mocking.

Halfway to shore, something rocketed into her side, flinging her through the air. She screamed, arms flailing, grasping for something, anything to hold on to, but finding nothing. Her backside smacked the water, and the icy lake closed over her head.

∽

A scream ripped through the air.

Nick looked up from his ruined boots to see the lady responsible sailing over the side of the dock. Clyde Moore let the mailbag drop to the ground. It took Nick a moment to realize Clyde must've sideswiped the new housekeeper with the bag and pitched her into the water.

Nick ran, dodging ferrymen. When he reached the spot where she'd gone in, he peered into the water. Nothing. He flung off his hat then heaved off his boots. "Get a rope ready, you fools! Clyde, launch the boat!"

Nick leaped feet first into the frigid waves, tucking his knees up when he hit the water, trying to jump shallow so as not to hit any submerged rocks. The icy water sucked his breath away, instantly numbing his fingers and toes. He took a deep breath then went under, hands wide and grasping. He scraped his knuckles on a boulder. The surf slammed him into the base of the cliff.

For eternal seconds he peered through the murky green water, arms sweeping, legs forcing him to go deeper along the cliff. Waves pummeled him. His lungs screamed for air, even while his feet went numb. He could feel his strength being sapped by the cold.

At the moment when he knew he must surface, something soft tangled around his fingers. He grabbed a fistful of cloth. He turned toward the surface, pushing off a rock to gain momentum, dragging her after him. She gave him no help, limp as a rug. It was probably too late. Of all the stupid accidents, falling off a dock.

His head broke the surface, and he sucked in a great lungful of air. The girl's face lolled out of the water on his shoulder, her mouth open, eyes closed. He wrapped his arms around her middle and squeezed. Water gushed from her mouth, her eyes popped open, and she moaned. Relief surged through him at her coughing and wheezing. She wasn't dead, at least not yet.

He spun in the water to locate the dock. The current had taken them more than twenty yards away and they were getting farther all the time. Nick swiped at her long, clinging hair that tangled across his face, obscuring his vision.

Men swarmed the dock, scrambling to get the lighthouse rowboat launched.

The girl seemed to suddenly become aware of her circumstances. She stiffened, screamed loud enough to drown a foghorn, and tried to climb on top of him. His head went under, water filling his nose and eyes and ears. She clawed at him, flailing and swinging. Her elbow connected with his cheekbone, sending stars exploding through his vision. Stupid girl would drown them both.

When he resurfaced he clamped his arms around her, pinning her flailing limbs to her sides. "Stop it, you little fool!"

She seemed not to hear him, screaming and going under, writhing as he tried to kick hard enough to keep them above the waves. His shoulder hit a submerged rock, and his grip on her loosened. He reached out for the rock with one hand, the other grasping her wrist, tugging her toward him. White ringed her eyes, her hair straggling over her face and shoulders. He could barely feel her wrist in his grasp. The rock allowed him a moment's breather, even as a wave splashed over them.

When she screamed again, he did something he had never contemplated before. He let go of the rock for an instant and slapped her with his open hand across her cheek.

Stunned, her scream died. He used the moment to pull her toward him again, clinging to the rock. She subsided. Had he knocked her senseless?

Oars smacked the water, and before she could regroup for another bout at drowning him, Clyde's face appeared over the edge of the rowboat.

"Take her." Nick knew his lips must be blue, they were so stiff. Strong arms lifted the woman over the side of the boat. They reached back down for him, and to his shame, he was too cold to assist himself. They lifted him like a child and settled him in the rocking craft. The wind on his wet skin and clothes bit colder than the lake. His teeth chattered, his muscles cramping.

"Hang on, Nick."

He huddled on the bottom of the boat, shivers wracking him. The woman lay only inches from him, eyes closed, skin white as new snow. Hanks of gold hair clung to her pale features, and her long lashes, gathered in points by the water, lay against her cheeks. Her chest rose and fell in short gasps. At least she was still alive. Which was more than he could say for the way he felt.

"Almost there, Nick." Clyde swung the oars to turn the boat alongside the pilings.

Strength trickled back, sending pins and needles into his hands and feet. Nick stumbled onto the dock. Someone threw a jacket around his shoulders. He brushed him aside, teeth chattering. "Take care of the girl."

Clyde lifted her, still limp, onto the boards. Jenkins appeared with a blanket to cover her.

"Got to get her. . .up the hill." Nick shoved his dripping hair out of his eyes, his hand trembling. Shivers wracked him until he thought he'd never get his boots back on. His soiled boots seemed a small matter now. He struggled into them, the leather sticking to his wet socks and legs.

The *Jenny Klamath* gave a toot of the whistle. The captain eased her away from the dock, evidently intent on keeping his schedule, a near drowning or not. Jenkins swung aboard at the last moment, waving back at Nick with an apologetic smile.

Clyde and Nick loaded the woman onto the handcart used to haul supplies up the track to the lighthouse at the top of the cliff. Nick sneezed and coughed, his lungs protesting their dunking. Silt stung his eyes, blurring his vision. Frigid water dripped from his clothes. They lifted the cart handle and began the trek through the trees, the iron tracks of the cart path glinting where the sunlight dappled through the pines.

Chapter 4

Annie pressed her hand against her chest, coughing. Her hair hung in dripping rats' tails. Every movement brought an unpleasant gush of water from her clothing and shoes. But nothing could compare to the guilt and embarrassment sloshing through her. As if it weren't bad enough to throw up on someone, she had to nearly drown him.

The cart rumbled and bumped over the ground, winding up a steep grade through trees and into the open. The wind rippled over her, chill fingers stroking her skin. She lay shivering, her body wracking with cold.

The two men stopped the cart before a two-story brick house. The younger one, red hair blazing, grinned at her. The older one, her rescuer, reached into the cart and scooped her up like a child. What little breath she had fled. She should say something, protest that she could make her own way up the steps, but her teeth chattered so hard she couldn't form the words. His arms held her secure, and she found her eyes closing, her head tipping to lie against his shoulder.

His boots clomped on the steps. Then a screen door squeaked and banged shut. She really should pay attention, but all she could concentrate on was the cold.

"Oh, dear, what happened?"

Annie's eyes flew open. A tiny, white-haired woman with dark eyes stood beside the stove.

"This is the new housekeeper. She fell in the lake."

Indignation rose in Annie's chest. She had *not* fallen in. She was pushed.

Before she could say anything, her rescuer continued. "I'll leave her to your care, Imogen. And you might want to give her something for a bilious stomach. She doesn't seem to have taken too well to boat travel." Without another word, he dumped—well, eased—her into a straight-backed kitchen chair and strode out the door, like a man glad to be done with an unpleasant task.

The screen door squeaked again, and the redheaded fellow tossed Annie's valise in where it landed with a *thump*. "There's a trunk at the dock with your name on it. I'll fetch it up as quick as I can." A flash of white teeth and a multitude of freckles and he was gone.

The elderly woman tut-tutted, stoking the fire and pulling the teakettle forward. "Oh, you poor thing. You must get into dry things immediately. Let's get you up to your room. I'm Imogen Batson. What a poor welcome you've had."

Annie followed her employer up the stairs. Imogen took each step slowly. Annie couldn't help but wonder what such a delicate and fragile woman was doing at a lighthouse station.

"Now, you get into dry clothes and come down for a hot cup of tea." Imogen showed her into the bedroom. "I'm sorry. I don't know your name."

"Ana—Annie. Annie Fairfax, Mrs. Batson."

"Pleased to meet you, Annie. Call me Imogen. We don't stand on much ceremony around here." Imogen closed the door behind her.

Water dripped in a circle from Annie's skirts. Weariness rolled over her, making her fingers clumsy. She peeled the drenched clothes off and let them fall in a sodden heap. Two coarse towels hung on the back of the washstand. She plucked them off, rubbing her skin hard to restore circulation. Then she rummaged through her valise. When she couldn't find what she sought, she dumped the contents onto the bed in a jumble.

Dressed again, though sans her soggy shoes, she draped a towel over her shoulders to keep her wet hair off her blouse and ventured downstairs.

Imogen waited in the parlor. "You sit here by the fire, and I'll get you some hot tea."

As she warmed by the fire with the cup of tea Imogen prepared for her, shame spread over Annie. The man who saved her life—that poor man she'd almost killed—had dumped her on Imogen like a puppy that had been naughty on the rug.

"How are you feeling, dear? Such a dreadful thing to happen, falling in the lake like that. It's a wonder you survived. God was surely looking out for you, having Nick close by. A blessing, it was." Imogen tucked a hot water bottle into the chair beside Annie and pulled an afghan up around her shoulders. "The water's terribly deep there at the base of the cliff. And it's not long since ice-out."

Annie breathed in the aroma rising from her teacup. So his name was Nick. It suited him. "I'm not sure he would share your opinion." Her teeth only rattled a little against the porcelain. After all the trauma of the day, Annie had no more energy than a dust rag. Her escape from Michaelton House early that morning seemed to have happened in another lifetime.

"I have a feeling we're going to do well together, you and I." Imogen patted Annie's shoulder. "Are you warming?"

"Yes, thank you." Annie smiled. Imogen reminded her a bit of Hazel: kind, uncomplicated, easy to be around, by turns starchy and sweet. Perhaps this job wouldn't be so hard after all. Her fears of getting a mean taskmistress of an employer seemed unfounded.

Imogen took the chair across from Annie and picked up her tatting. The shuttle poked in and out of the white lace slowly in the older woman's hands.

How many times had Hazel tried to teach Annie to tat? Annie had no patience for handwork—snarling thread and pricking her finger more than she stitched. She'd rather read a book, taken away to exotic, exciting places in her imagination, than, in the words of the old nursery rhyme, "sit on a cushion and sew a fine seam." Hazel had relented and done the sewing for Annie, allowing Annie to read aloud while Hazel worked.

Homesickness weighed her shoulders. When would she see Hazel again? When would she sit beside a fire and read aloud to someone eager to hear the adventure of a good book? She shook her head to clear her thoughts. "Do you think Nick will be all right?"

Imogen nodded. "He's a tough one, that Nick Kennedy. And private. Keeps to himself most of the time. But a good worker. My Ezra says he's never seen a man so careful to follow all the rules. Never shirks a duty. I doubt a dunking will set him back."

Annie breathed a prayer of relief. Though the accident wasn't her fault—after all, she'd been knocked into the water by a flying mailbag—she would hate to think she'd caused her rescuer any permanent damage. She couldn't bear something like that to happen to her again. Echoes of the panic she'd felt when she hit the water fluttered through her. All her worst fears and memories collided, and she had to force herself to breathe slowly. She set her cup aside, afraid she might drop it.

"Imogen, please tell me about my duties here." Her gaze traveled over the simple parlor, noting the rag rugs, the white lace curtains, the brown sofa and chairs, everything clean and shining. So normal and ordinary, it calmed Annie once more.

"Oh, you don't want to hear about that now. Time enough in the morning to start work."

"No, really, I'd rather know now. Otherwise, I won't sleep well wondering." Annie didn't want to admit she had no idea what tasks a housekeeper might do in a place like this. The housekeeper at home walked around like a prison warden, keys jangling from the chatelaine on her belt, a permanent persimmon pucker on her lips as if disapproving of even the air she breathed. The maids scurried at the sight of her, and only the butler remained undaunted by her ramrod posture and formidable face. Annie avoided her as much as possible. Hazel and the housekeeper were at permanent daggers drawn where Annie's room and possessions were concerned.

"There's the cooking, the cleaning, and the laundry—those are the main things. Then we do a bit of gardening, and if need be, we help with the light. The light comes first here, always. From dusk to dawn the beacon must shine."

A gentle smile creased her face. "You'll come to love Old Sutton. I've lived around lighthouses so long I find it difficult to rest comfortably unless I fall asleep to the steady flash of a beacon."

Annie didn't care about the light at that moment. Her thoughts centered on one thing—cooking. There was no cook here? Cleaning she could probably do—dusting, even mopping—but cooking? Annie had never so much as boiled water for tea before. How was she supposed to cook meals?

Don't panic, girl. You can do this.

Perhaps she could find a book of recipes at the general store. Her confidence climbed back up a notch. A cookbook would solve all her problems. "How many people live on Sutton Island, and how far is it to town?"

Imogen glanced up. Her delicate eyebrows came together. "There is no town on Sutton Island."

Annie sat up, the blankets dropping away from her shoulders. "No town?" Her heart bumped an erratic beat.

"Annie, Sutton Island is uninhabited except for the people needed to man the light. My husband is the head keeper, Nick is first assistant, and Clyde Moore is the second assistant. Then there's you and I. That's all."

Her mind froze. Five people. No stores, no church, no neighborhoods. No roads, no sidewalks, no milk delivery to the door. What had she gotten herself into?

"Didn't the inspector tell you when you applied for the job? We're eight miles off shore. Halfway between Two Harbors and Split Rock where they're slated to build a lighthouse. The closest town of any size is Duluth." Imogen picked up her tatting again, but an arrow of concern remained between her brows. "You'll get used to it. Supplies are delivered by one of the lighthouse tenders, on either the *Marigold* or the *Amaranth*, though if there is a passenger to be dropped off at the island the *Jenny Klamath* will stop. If we need the ferry to pull in for some reason, we run a flag up at the end of the dock to let her know. And there's always plenty to do here. I never seem to get it all done."

Annie threaded her fingers through her hair to aid the drying. Five people, miles from any town. She, who had never lived outside Duluth, now perched on a rocky island in the middle of Lake Superior. Still, it might not be so bad. Her father would never think to look for her here, and the chances of running into someone who would recognize her were on the slim side.

"I think you should spend the rest of the afternoon in bed. We don't want you coming down with a cold. I thought I heard Clyde taking your trunk upstairs." Imogen tucked her handwork into a basket beside her chair. "I'll feed the men tonight and bring you up a supper tray. You can start your duties by cooking breakfast in the morning. The men like to eat at seven."

Breakfast for five people by seven tomorrow morning. Annie gathered her blankets and trekked up the narrow stairway. She'd have to come up with a plan, for to admit she couldn't cook would invite Imogen to send her packing back to Duluth and her father. Surely breakfast couldn't be that hard. . . .

∽

Nick tucked his hands behind his head and stared at the ceiling. A shaft of light raced across the room. He'd grown used to it by now, but the first few days had driven him nearly mad. The thin curtains did little to filter the powerful beam. He'd best close the blind if he wanted to get any sleep before his shift started at two. The green shade rattled down, blocking most of the light. At regular intervals, a white frame showed around the fabric then vanished.

His body ached, both from his lifesaving gambit this afternoon and from returning to the dock to help Clyde stow the boat. The girl invaded his thoughts. He scowled in the darkness then winced as his eye stung. She'd nailed him with her elbow. Good thing she hadn't knocked him out with the blow or they'd both have gone down to feed the fishes.

What was a girl like that doing on Sutton Island? Seasick and unable to swim, and from the look of her, barely old enough to be on her own. What were her parents thinking to let her take such a remote job?

His split knuckle throbbed. Scrubbing his boots hadn't done his hand any favors. He still couldn't believe she'd been sick on him.

She wouldn't last, not here. He gave her two weeks, just until the ferry returned and they flagged it down to pick her up. She'd be waiting on the dock with her bags packed, if he was any judge.

That water sure had been cold. Cold like he hadn't felt since. . .

Sleep crept over him.

Wind shrieked through the broken window, carrying swirling snow and icy pellets of spray. The captain huddled shoulder to shoulder with his men in the cramped pilothouse. The storm surge slammed the side of the ship, rolling her, pounding her against the shoal.

He lurched, his ribs throbbing, inhaling daggers with each breath. He'd lost feeling in his feet long ago, and now the cold crept up his legs. He shivered, ice hanging on his eyebrows and lashes, his breath a frosty plume that rimed his collar. Would the storm never end?

Then the deck heaved beneath his feet as he picked his way over ice-encrusted hatches and lines to the stern, clinging to the rail while surf surged over the ship. Low clouds scudded across the sky, the wind blowing them back out on the lake after the receding storm. He had to get to his crew in the stern. They would be all right if he could just get to them in time.

The men clung together, tied to the deck to keep from being swept overboard. The man nearest him had his face covered with his coat. The captain's hand trembled, but he forced himself to look.

He recoiled in horror. It wasn't a crewman. His brother's face, encased in a blue-white pallor, stared blankly up at him, frozen to death. His gaze darted from one face to the next. Jonathan. . .every face was Jonathan's. Dead, frozen, killed by his own brother's careless stupidity.

"Murderer!"

"Killer!"

"Coward!"

The accusations came from everywhere, hurled at him on the wind like shards of glass, slicing, ripping, shredding his soul. A mighty wave swept over the broken vessel, dousing him in frigid water, sweeping the bodies toward the rail.

"No, Jonathan, I'm so sorry. Please forgive me! Jonathan!" He tried to hang on to the body nearest him, but the lake pulled and sucked, tearing in a relentless battle until he lost his tenuous grip on Jonathan's sleeve.

"Jonathan!" He clawed and kicked, trying to swim in the icy waves, trying to grab Jonathan before he was towed under by the lake.

A giant seagull flapped over him, cawing and beating its wings. A blast of light hit his face, blinding him.

Nick woke, gasping, bathed in sweat. His heart bucked and surged. The window shade had snapped up, the cord and ring still swaying against the window. Another shaft of light coated the room and was gone.

The nightmare. Always the same, always horrible, always leaving him wrung out and exhausted.

He sat up and rubbed his hand down his face. Several deep breaths later, he assured himself that the dream wasn't real, that he hadn't killed his own brother. Jonathan was very much alive, probably at Kennebrae House sleeping beside his bride, Melissa, at this moment.

Nick swung his feet out of bed. He might as well relieve Ezra at the light. When the nightmare hit, there was no going back to sleep. As long as he was at the lighthouse, he was Nick, not Noah. If he worked hard enough, maybe he could forget.

Chapter 5

Annie squinted at the kitchen clock and placed her hands at the small of her back, arching to stretch out the stiffness of a night in a strange bed. A yawn forced its way out, nearly cracking her jaw. Her eyelids sagged as if they had anchors attached to them. On a few occasions—first nights, galas, soirees, and such—she'd come home at this hour, but never had she risen from her bed so early.

The bacon sputtered and popped in the skillet. Annie poked the ragged strips with a fork. She had no idea how long to cook it. Just getting the stove lit had seemed a monumental task, the pungent odor of smoke still lingering in the air as a testament to the wisdom of opening the damper first thing.

"Good morning."

Annie whirled at the sound.

Mr. Batson, white shirtfront gleaming in the early morning light, stood in the doorway.

"Good morning. . .sir," she remembered to add.

"Imogen won't be down for breakfast, I'm afraid. She's feeling a bit under the weather. All the excitement yesterday, no doubt." He fingered his tie, as if checking that all was in order. "Clyde should be here soon, and Nick. Nick had the early morning watch."

She nodded, her middle flopping as if seagulls were fighting over a piece of bread inside her stomach. "Should I take a tray up to her?"

Mr. Batson nodded, and a rush of satisfaction bubbled through Annie. She'd said the right thing.

"Perhaps midmorning. And keep her in bed as long as you can. She's worn herself out trying to get things shipshape before Inspector Dillon shows up."

Inspector? The very thought made anxiety wriggle up her spine. *Please, Lord, let me figure out what I'm doing before You bring down inspectors.*

Steam spurted from the oatmeal pot, rattling the lid. A mist of sweat coated Annie's forehead when she checked the contents. The cereal popped and bubbled like the tar the workmen had used to patch a neighbor's roof last spring in Duluth. Was it supposed to be this thick? Her shoulder complained when she tried to stir the sticky mass.

The kitchen door opened and banged shut.

She dropped the lid from nervous fingers, and it bounced off the corner

159

of the stove and clattered to the floor. Nick. She prayed he wouldn't bring up her seasickness or her sudden departure from the dock. If he did, she might just melt right through the floor. She would thank him eventually, but she wanted to do it without onlookers.

Nick didn't even glance her way. Instead, he removed his cap and hung it on a peg by the door. He scanned the kitchen, breathed deeply, and frowned, looking at the ceiling.

Annie followed his gaze. She chewed her lip in consternation. Scarves of smoke lingered near the crown molding, evidence of her fight with the stove and the first batch of bacon she'd burned. She lowered her eyes and went back to fretting about breakfast.

But Nick drew her attention without even trying, making her pulse speed up. His shoulders seemed so broad he must've had to turn to get in the door. While he exchanged good mornings with Mr. Batson, Annie studied him. Dark brows shaded deep-blue eyes, eyes that seemed to hold a wealth of sorrow. His somber expression didn't keep him from being handsome though. If anything, it gave him an air of vulnerability that made Annie want to offer him solace. Had he suffered a heartbreak? Had he lost someone dear to him? She suddenly wanted to know all about this man who had saved her life.

His glance right into her eyes yanked her back from spinning fanciful yarns. She grasped for some cool aplomb but failed. Nothing witty came to mind to say, so she lifted a hand in a slight wave.

He tilted his head to the side and looked at the stove behind her, eyebrows raised.

Annie sucked in a deep breath then coughed as air caught in her throat.

His left eye bore the faint shadow of a bruise. With a rush, Annie remembered flailing at him in the water. She must've given him that shiner during the rescue. Embarrassment trickled from her crown to her heels.

A scorching odor wafted around her. The bacon! Annie pivoted back to the stove, greeted by spitting, snarling, smoking grease. The strips of meat lay stiff in the hot fat, coated with charred blackness. She'd ruined another batch. But there was no time to cook more.

Chairs scraped behind her. She caught sight of Clyde sliding into his seat at the table, his hair sleep-tousled.

She plunked the meat onto a platter, wincing as hot bacon grease hit the top of her thumb. Good thing she'd set the table when she'd first come down. If they were going to be this prompt for breakfast, she might have to get up even earlier. The oatmeal defied her attempts to get it out of the pot, sticking like concrete to the metal. She finally tossed a trivet on the tablecloth, grabbed two cloths, and horsed the heavy pot to the table. They could serve themselves.

When everyone was seated, Mr. Batson bowed his head. "Almighty God, we thank You for Your bounty. Make us worthy. Amen."

Annie clenched her fists in her lap. *And please don't let anyone die from my cooking*.

Mr. Batson cleared his throat, and Annie looked up. He lifted a strip of bacon onto his plate, frowning.

Clyde reached for the spoon sticking out of the oatmeal. He tugged, but when the spoon wouldn't budge, he let go, his eyes wide. He shot a look at Nick, who shrugged. "This cereal's sure"—Clyde scratched the hair over his right ear—"hearty." He smiled, as if relieved to have come up with a good word.

Nick grabbed the serving spoon and wrenched out a hunk of doughy oatmeal. The gray material defied gravity, clinging to the spoon, refusing to drop into his bowl—not even when he held it upside down and whacked the heel of his hand against the table to jar the oatmeal loose.

Annie closed her eyes. Humiliation coursed up her neck, through her cheeks, and into her ears. It prickled across her chest. She opened her eyes in time to see Clyde cover his mouth with his hand and shoot Nick a sympathetic look. Her chin went up. Who did they think they were, laughing at her?

"What did you say this was again?" Nick picked up his fork and scraped the cereal off the serving spoon and into his bowl. It landed without changing shape.

She shifted in her chair, wringing the life out of her napkin. "It's oat—meal." She enunciated each syllable.

"Hmm." He poked the mass with his fork. "I'll have to take your word for it."

Clyde snickered then wrestled his own spoonful of oatmeal. "Sure wish we had some fresh milk to thin this out a bit."

Annie sat helpless. So far, no one had braved to taste the food.

Mr. Batson touched his fork to a slice of bacon and it cracked into black bits.

She supposed she would have to be the first to eat a bite. When she lifted her bowl, Nick obliged her by dumping a spoonful of cereal in. Her arm wobbled at the unexpected weight.

She took her fork, licked her dry lips, and pried off a hunk of cereal. She put it in her mouth and was immediately reminded of damp newspaper and glue.

She chewed, keeping a pleasant expression on her face. Her hand gripped her water glass, and she took several big swallows to get the horrid stuff down. "Mmm. Just like home." She stared Nick in the eye, daring him to contradict her.

Clyde sniffed his before he put it in his mouth. He, too, must've needed water to coax it down his throat. "Ma'am, if this is what you ate at home, I have to say, I'm impressed."

As if on cue, all three men pushed back their plates. Annie tried not to look at their stares at one another.

"I guess we're not all that hungry this morning." Mr. Batson smoothed his already smooth shirt. "Don't forget to check on Imogen." His eyes twinkled. "And I don't believe she's hungry this morning either. Just tea should do her until she can come downstairs." He went into his office and shut the door.

Nick headed toward the porch, pushing Clyde before him. Annie couldn't help but notice both men take an apple from the bowl on the table by the door.

She hung her head. She'd be lucky if they didn't put her off the island at the first opportunity. Then what would she do?

"Lord, why aren't You helping me? Are You even listening? I can't do this by myself."

She clacked knives and forks together, scraping everything into the heavy pot of oatmeal to dump into the lake later. Plates clattered into the washtub. With a guilty start she remembered Imogen trying to rest upstairs. Poor lady. At least she'd missed having to eat breakfast.

A smile tugged at Annie's lips. Maybe God had answered one of her prayers. No one had actually died from eating her cooking. At least not yet.

∽

Nick wrinkled his nose at the pungent smell of vinegar. He dampened the cloth and rubbed a spot on the window.

Waves crashed against the rocks over one hundred feet below, an incessant accompaniment, especially loud when, as now, the wind from the north pounded the waves into the caves just at the waterline. The Sutton Island Light perched on the edge of the cliff, embedded in the rock, as solid as the cliff itself.

Nick gripped the black rail of the catwalk with one hand and bent to the bucket at his feet. He enjoyed his task of washing the windows every day, inside and out, as well as wiping down the prisms of the clamshell Fresnel lens; but he would be glad when warmer weather came along. His hands, chapped by the vinegar and the wind, stung in the cold.

The glass gleamed, throwing back the sunlight. Rainbows ran along the curved prisms surrounding the kerosene lantern inside.

A sense of satisfaction settled over Nick. How quickly he'd dropped into his new routine. Familiar with the discipline of being a captain, the many regulations and duties of keeping a lighthouse didn't chafe him as they did Clyde. Nick's shoulder ached pleasantly from the scrubbing, and he dropped the rag in the bucket with a *plop*. Never again would he underestimate the efforts of his ship's crew when they swabbed the deck.

Nick brought himself up short. That all belonged to his past life. He narrowed his eyes and forced the thoughts aside. His life was here now, where he couldn't hurt anyone.

Several gulls shot up from the cliff face, squabbling and circling, pulling his attention away from the past. Noisy, messy birds, but as familiar to him as the waves lapping the shore.

A flash of gold caught his eye. Sunlight glinted off hair the color of ripe wheat. Miss Annie Fairfax. She lugged a bucket toward the edge of the cliff, the birds swooping and darting overhead. What was she doing? The rocky edge was stable, but the winds could be tricky. She should be more careful.

He ducked through the open window into the lantern deck, set the vinegar solution on the floor, and all but sprinted down the spiral staircase, through the watch room, and out into the sunshine. "Miss Fairfax," he called to her above the sound of the gulls diving on the contents of the bucket as he crossed the open space.

She gave a guilty start, lowering the pail.

The birds pecked at the gray lumps on the ground, flapping and hopping. They stole bits from each other, dropped them, and attacked the oatmeal again. Poor birds were in for a bit of indigestion.

"You shouldn't be so close to the edge." Nick took her elbow and guided her back a few steps. "We don't want you taking another tumble into the lake. I might not be able to fish you out from up here."

Her cheeks reddened, and her eyelashes fell to cover her surprisingly dark eyes. What an odd combination with hair so fair. It caught the light and threw it back, so shiny and bright. He'd never seen hair that color before. She wore it piled up, like one of those Gibson girl pictures. A few wisps touched her temples and cheeks, the breeze playing with the strands.

He realized he was staring and cleared his throat. "What are you doing up here?"

The tip of her tongue darted out to touch the corner of her mouth. "I was getting rid of the leftovers." She waved a hand toward the bucket.

"Ah, disposing of the evidence?" He cocked his head to one side. "I doubt the birds will thank you."

She dipped her chin, and he immediately regretted teasing her. Every cook could have a bad day, and the first attempt in a strange kitchen should be allowed some leeway. No doubt lunch would be better.

Before he could apologize, she looked up. "I'll try not to kill the local fauna." She skewered him with a stare.

Hmm, not the delicate flower he first thought. She had some fight in her. And she looked so pretty all riled up he couldn't resist pushing her a bit further. "See that you don't kill the local human population either. And stay away from the cliff. I don't have time to keep an eye on you every minute of the day."

Her mouth dropped open.

A tingle of warmth raced through him at her hot glare.

"No one is asking you to." She bunched her skirts in one hand and stooped to pick up the bucket.

The gulls keened, swooping closer.

She turned away from the cliff and brushed past him.

Without thought, his hand jumped out and caught her arm. "Wait. Has anyone given you a tour of the buildings?"

"No, there's been no time." She tugged her elbow, trying to get away from him.

He tightened his grip. Why was he reluctant to part with her? "There's time now. You'll need to know what is safe and what isn't. Come, let me show you around." That was it. He was concerned for her safety.

Annie studied him out of the corner of her eye, her mouth pursed, her chin high. She looked like she would refuse him but finally said, "Very well."

An unreasonable happiness surged through him. What was the matter with him? He released her arm and took the bucket from her. "Let's start with the lighthouse."

She walked beside him to the red brick tower, looking up and blocking the sunlight with her hand.

"This lighthouse was built in 1899, so it's just seven years old. This little ell off the side of the tower is the watch room." He set the bucket down, held the door for her, and showed her through the sparse, tile-walled office that consisted of a plain desk, a wall lamp, and a small stove. They entered the tower, and he motioned for her to precede him up the shiny, black staircase. Their footsteps rang on the metal. The higher they climbed, the tighter the spiral, and the tighter her grip grew on the handrail.

They stepped into the lantern deck. Light shattered into a thousand rainbows through the prisms of the lens, dancing in the air, on her cheeks, in her eyes. Her hair glowed even brighter.

She sucked in a breath and laced her fingers together, tucking them under her chin. "It's so beautiful. Look how far you can see."

He followed her gaze across the cobalt water to the thin, white line of the horizon. Puffball clouds graced the pale sky. Foamy wave tips appeared and disappeared on the ever-moving lake. Far to the north, he could just make out the dark blot of a ship approaching. He turned to study Annie once more.

With her lips parted, eyes wide in wonder, she enchanted him. No one had ever affected him this way, making his heart thump faster, his palms sweat. Her lips, rosy pink, smiled at the vista before her.

Reality nudged him. *Kill those thoughts, buddy. There's no way she'd ever fall for you. If she knew the real you, she'd despise you.*

He turned his back to her. "This is a third-order Fresnel lens made in Paris with an incandescent oil-vapor lamp. Its official range is twenty-two miles. It gives a half-second flash every ten seconds." Much better. Keep the conversation on facts. He clasped his hands behind his back, staring at the top of the light above his head.

"It's quite impressive."

"I clean the windows every morning, wipe down the prisms, and trim the wicks, ready for lighting at dusk. According to the manual, the light must be completely ready for service by 10:00 a.m."

"Do you always follow the manual?" She held his gaze. "I can see the need for it, but don't you tire of the rigidity? The monotony?"

"No. I used to think life was no fun if you didn't take some risks, but I've learned better. The rules are there for a reason. They make the choices for you so you don't make mistakes that can be costly. There's safety in following routine. Without rules, you have disorder, chaos, and unnecessary risk." He crossed his arms and leaned against the window.

She shrugged, curling a tendril of hair around her slender finger. "I suppose, but if you only live inside the rules, there's no spontaneity. And you miss an awful lot of adventure."

"Adventure isn't all it's cracked up to be. Even if you do everything right it can still end badly, but doing things spontaneously always leads to disaster."

She regarded him skeptically and with what he thought might be a tinge of pity. He put it down to her age and inexperience. She'd soon learn how hard life could be.

"Let me go down the stairs first. That way, if you stumble, I'll be able to stop you from going all the way to the bottom." He started down the steps before her, listening to the *clang* of her shoes on each tread. They emerged into the sunshine once more.

"In addition to the lighthouse tower, there are four buildings on the island." He motioned to the two-story dwelling sitting at the foot of the light-house, the same red brick construction. "The main house, as you know, is for the head keeper and his family. Then there's the fog-house. A gasoline engine drives the air compressor that sounds the horn. We have to use it pretty often. The fogs can be bad on the lake."

They walked across the open space on a gravel path as he pointed out the various buildings and what role each played in the daily operations. He surprised himself at how much he was talking. He hadn't said so much to anyone since he'd been here, mostly preferring to work alone and retire to his room to read rather than socialize. But with Annie, he found himself more at ease than he'd been since arriving on the island.

They turned at the sound of a screen door slapping shut. Clyde jumped off the porch of the little house, a ladder over his shoulder, a paint can dangling from one hand. He lifted his chin in greeting, sauntering to a square wooden building set apart from the brick structures. He leaned the ladder against the eave and bent to open the paint. With broad strokes, he began painting another coat of white to the already-gleaming siding.

"What's that building then?" Annie waved toward Clyde.

"That's the fuel store. It's full of kerosene for the lighthouse and gasoline for the engines in the fog-house. You won't need to go in there. Just tell me or Clyde if you need kerosene for the house lamps, and we'll get it for you."

She crossed her arms at her waist, the ties of her apron fluttering behind her. "I had no idea Sutton Island would be so isolated. Odd to think there's not another person for miles. It's disconcerting."

Nick rubbed his chin. The isolation didn't bother him. In fact, it suited him just fine, but it was a good reminder as to why he should steer clear of any entanglements with Annie Fairfax. No man with a past like his had any business getting mixed up with a girl like her.

She studied the horseshoe-shaped clearing then turned to look him in the eye. "I haven't had a chance to thank you properly for saving my life. And I'm sorry for being sick on the dock." Her delicate ears reddened, and her gaze dropped.

Uncomfortable, both with being thanked for something he'd done instinctively and with the protective feelings expanding in his chest, he shrugged and half-turned away from her. "Don't mention it." He waved away her thanks. "You've seen the most dangerous places on the island. Stay away from the cliff, the fuel stores, and the tower. And it's against the rules for you to enter the lighthouse without one of the keepers. That should keep you safe. And considering the state of this morning's breakfast, I'll stay away from the kitchen. That should keep *me* safe." He grinned, waiting to hear her laugh.

She gasped, dropped her arms to her sides, and stalked off toward the house.

So much for his attempt at humor.

Chapter 6

Pique carried Annie through heating water and preparing a tray for Imogen. High-and-mighty Nick Kennedy. See if she ever thanked him again. She threw teaspoons onto the tray more forcefully than she'd intended.

Still, it had been a little funny. Annie shook her head, smiling. The oatmeal had been truly awful. And the bacon...well, the bacon was best forgotten.

She carried the tray up the stairs, glancing out the window on the landing. Nick stood at the base of Clyde's ladder, speaking up to him. Interest and indignation battled within her.

"Come in," Imogen answered Annie's knock.

Annie backed into the room, trying to keep the tray steady. "Good morning. Mr. Batson thought you might like a cup of tea."

The room lay in dusk, light forcing its way around the edges of the dark shade. Imogen struggled up onto her elbows, her white hair lying over her shoulder in a narrow braid. "Aren't you a dear?" She patted her nightcap and tweaked the covers. Imogen's voice trembled a bit, sounding exhausted, though she'd lain in bed most of the morning.

"Here, let me help you." Annie propped pillows behind Imogen's head and shoulders. Annie set the tray before Imogen then turned to open the blinds on the east-facing windows.

Morning sun illuminated the room. Bold colors galloped across the bed in cheerful blocks of quilt fabric. An overstuffed chair draped with a crocheted afghan in bright granny squares sat on a braided rag rug beside a square oak dresser.

Imogen poured her tea then held the cup to her nose, breathing in the wisps of steam rising from the fragrant liquid. She blinked in the bright light, her forehead screwed up. "I'm sorry I couldn't be downstairs to help with your first meal here. My head, you see. Sometimes the pain just wears me down."

"Oh, does it still hurt? Should I close the blinds?" Annie twisted her hands in her apron.

"That's all right, dear. Ezra brought me a headache powder early this morning. That usually pushes the pain down enough to be bearable."

Annie stood still for a moment then remembered her place in the household. She gave a quick nod to the mistress and started for the door.

Imogen's voice halted her. "I know you're busy, but please, sit down and visit with me a moment. There are a few things we need to talk about."

Apprehension quickened Annie's breathing. Had Imogen learned of the breakfast debacle? The guilt of her subterfuge—she balked at calling it outright lying—weighed in her chest like a lump of her own oatmeal. When she tried to perch on the edge of the upholstered chair, the squishy cushion gave way until she feared she might be swallowed.

Imogen set her teacup on the tray and regarded Annie with sober, dark eyes. She had such a look of patient strength, of serenity hard won through adversity, of total honesty, Annie wanted to squirm. "Tell me about yourself. I'm curious how you came to be in the Lighthouse Board's employ."

Surprised at not being chastised, Annie smiled. Then she realized what a giant pit yawned in front of her. Time to choose her words carefully. She didn't want to mislead this kind woman any more than she already had, especially when she was obviously suffering, but Annie also couldn't afford for the truth to come out. The Lighthouse Board would fire her and promptly pack her back to her father.

She cleared her throat, her mind racing. "My father works the mines up on the Mesabi mostly, though sometimes on the Vermillion." Well, that was true enough. He did own three mines, two on the Mesabi Iron Range and a smaller one on the Vermillion Range. "My mother passed away when I was young."

"So you grew up in a mining camp?" Imogen smoothed the edge of the blanket. "You've got very refined manners for being brought up by a miner. Or did your father remarry?" The question hung in the air between them.

Annie frowned. She'd never even seen one of the mining camps. Her father refused to take her up onto the range. She'd only be in his way. And the range was no place for a proper young lady. "My father never remarried. He left me in the care of a kind woman in Duluth. Now that I'm grown up, I need to be making my own way in the world. I saw an advertisement in the Duluth papers for a housekeeper and companion and applied." She kept her head down, her eyes on her hands in her lap. "The Lighthouse Board notified me by telegram that I had obtained the position, and here I am." She shrugged.

"Was there no young man set on winning your affection? Surely a girl as pretty as you would have her pick of suitors in Duluth?"

Annie heard again the muffled voices of her father and that old man in the wheelchair, plotting, arguing, and ultimately putting a price on her future, building a matrimonial cage around her bar by bar. An uprush of honesty propelled the words from her throat. "My father had someone in mind, but I'm not ready to get married, especially to my father's idea of a good husband. I want to be free to choose my own way. If I get married, it will be to someone who has nothing in common with my father. I want someone who will love me enough to stay with me, not to be racing off to his job, putting money ahead of his family. I want someone who will understand that people make mistakes, that they deserve forgiveness and second chances. I want someone who will love me first, last, and always. I won't be someone's second best."

She stopped, shocked at how much had poured out. She took a ragged breath and tried to smile to lessen the force of her words. "I'm sorry. I got a little carried away."

Imogen nodded, her lips twitching. "Ezra wasn't my father's pick for me either. Papa had me paired up with a stuffy banker back in Detroit. But I knew my future lay with Ezra from the moment I first saw him."

Annie tried to picture a young Ezra and Imogen falling in love. One look at Imogen's face made the picture easy to see. Love shone in every wrinkle, line, and tremble of the older woman's face. Her eyes, so dark in her pale face, glowed. Even with the headache dragging at her, she looked the part of a bride in love. Annie wondered if she would ever look that way when she spoke of a man.

"I have to ask how breakfast went. I thought I caught the scent of scorched bacon drifting up the stairs this morning. Was the stove giving you trouble? It can be such a beast sometimes."

Annie closed her eyes and lifted her chin. There was no way she could hide her lack of experience from this kind woman. "The stove was the least of my worries. Breakfast was a disaster. I burned two batches of bacon, and something happened to the oatmeal to make it suitable for chinking a log cabin. The truth is I haven't a clue how to cook. I can just about boil water for tea, but that's it." Her shoulders drooped, and a lump formed in her throat, cutting off her words. She was about to be fired, and she hadn't even held this job for twenty-four hours.

Imogen's soft laughter made Annie look up, blinking the moisture from her eyes. "Oh, Annie, I think you and I are going to get along just fine. When Ezra and I took our first lighthouse appointment, I couldn't cook either." The tray shook. "I burned a batch of biscuits so bad they turned to ash when I touched them. Took me a week to get the smoke smell out of the kitchen."

Tensed muscles relaxed, and Annie sagged against the back of the chair. She joined in the laughter weakly, strength drained from her for the moment. She never knew how exhausting relief could be.

Imogen put her hands on the sides of the tray to lift it away, but Annie struggled up from the chair. "Let me."

Imogen smiled up at her. "Don't you worry. I'll help. We'll have you as proficient as a sea cook in no time."

Before Annie could thank Imogen, a strange sound, like the buzzing of a hornet, filled the room.

"Oh no." Imogen halted halfway out of bed. "That's the *Marigold*'s ship horn. The inspector is on his way."

Chapter 7

Nick raised his head from the logbook and looked out one of the watch room's diamond-paned windows. Was that a ship's horn? He grabbed the field glasses from the window ledge and headed outside. A plume of smoke rose from a small ship to the north.

Ezra barreled around the corner.

Nick sidestepped at the last instant to avoid a collision.

"Follow me." Ezra hurried down the path toward the house.

"There's no fog." Nick easily kept up with the older man. "Is there a ship in trouble?"

"No, but we are. The captain of the *Marigold* and I have a little deal worked out. If the inspector is aboard the tender, the captain gives me a double blast of the ship's horn. We'll have about twenty minutes before Dillon sets out on the launch. I have to meet him at the dock."

Nick's heart rate increased. "What do you want me to do?" He tightened his grip on the field glasses.

"Go get into your uniform and make sure it's done up as per regulations. Then check that everything is ready in the tower. If you get time, stick your head in the fog-house for a quick look-see. I'll head for the dock to meet Dillon. And find Clyde. He was supposed to finish painting the fuel house. If he isn't there, he's probably down at the dock. I told him to haul the rowboat out and start painting it. He'll be needed to unload supplies." The last words floated over Ezra's shoulder as he disappeared into the house.

Nick jogged to his quarters, grimacing. Enough had been said about inspections to make him dread this one. He leaped onto the porch and hurried into the assistant keepers' house. Though it was dark, he wasted no time on raising the blinds. Two crates sat in the small front room. With the tender's arrival, more supplies would crowd the space by nightfall.

His own quarters, square, stark, and cleaner than a silver spoon at Kennebrae House, pleased him. He shucked out of his shirt and opened the locker at the foot of his bed. His uniform, purchased at his own expense, lay still wrapped in the brown paper the shopkeeper had tied it up in. When he'd asked Ezra upon arriving, his boss had said ordinary work clothes would suffice and to save the uniform for the inspector. Nick ripped off the paper and lifted the navy jacket out. A pang shot through his heart. The coat resembled his captain's uniform with bright brass buttons and a bit of gold braid on the lapels.

A snowy-white shirt with new celluloid collar lay in the top drawer of the bureau. He donned it, tucking it in, grimacing at the tightness around his neck. He knotted the black tie at his throat then shrugged into the jacket.

The clock on the bedside table ticked away the seconds. Nick ran through his list of morning chores. He could think of nothing he'd failed to do.

He took his hat from the locker and placed it on his head, glancing in the mirror to make sure it sat at the proper angle. The collar pinched, and he dug his finger under it, tugging. His heart thumped.

Nick shook his head. It annoyed him that the arrival of one man could throw the entire complement of keepers into such a fuss. He understood about maintaining standards and ensuring the working order and operation of government property, but from the level of anxiety produced, it was as if President Teddy Roosevelt himself were arriving at the dock.

He stepped out of the house into the sunshine, shooting his cuffs and picking a stray string from his jacket front.

"*Wooeee*, if you don't clean up nice." Clyde leaned the ladder against the porch rail and propped his elbow on one rung. "Did you hear that ship's horn?"

"Get that ladder out of sight and change your clothes. Then head to the dock to help unload supplies." Nick snapped out orders as to a crewman. "Inspector Dillon is arriving in a few minutes."

Clyde's eyes went wide, his pepper-pot freckles standing out in his pale face. He scooped up the ladder and paint can and disappeared.

Nick checked the watch room and the tower and took a quick glance into the fog-house as instructed. Everything looked shipshape. He took a deep breath then headed to the dock to support Ezra.

The *Marigold* rounded the north end of the island. Nick stepped onto the dock. Waves surged along the base of the cliff in restless, ceaseless movement. Within moments of dropping anchor, the steam-powered launch putted toward shore.

Clyde leaned against the cart, arms crossed, red hair blowing in the breeze.

Ezra paced the end of the dock, hands clasped behind him, head down. He snapped to attention when the boat bumped the pilings.

Nick caught the rope the deckhand tossed to him and made the launch fast.

Whatever Nick had expected Dillon to look like flew out of his head upon sight of the inspector. Jasper Dillon stepped over the gunwale and imposed his presence upon Sutton Island.

Nick topped him by at least ten inches. Even in his hat, Eleventh District

Lighthouse Superintendent Jasper Dillon stood no more than five feet, two inches. Everything about the man was tiny, from his hands to his feet to his coal-black eyes. If not for the hostile, defensive expression in those eyes, Nick might have been looking at a child.

Dillon made a sucking noise through his teeth, nodded to Nick and Clyde, and turned to Ezra. "Ah, Batson, I hope everything is in order?" He dug with slender fingers into his breast pocket and pulled out a toothpick. The wind fluttered the pages on the clipboard under his arm.

"Good to see you again, Inspector. I'm sure you'll find everything to standard."

Nick noted that neither man shook hands. With Dillon's ramrod posture and militant glare, perhaps a salute would have been in order.

Dillon whipped his head around to glare at Nick, almost as if he'd read Nick's mind. "You must be Kennedy." Dillon thrust his chin out, daring Nick to deny it.

"That's right." Something in him refused to cower or back down from this little bantam rooster. "I've heard a lot about you, sir." He deliberately let his tone indicate that not all he'd heard had been good. Nick was not accustomed to being talked down to, especially by a man who needed to look up to do it.

The inspector sucked hard through his teeth again, and the toothpick took a mauling. For a long moment he skewered Nick with his eyes. A smug smile tugged at his thin lips. "Mr. Kennedy, I should like you to accompany me on my inspection. Mr. Batson can oversee the unloading of the supplies." He lowered his clipboard and tapped his narrow thigh.

Ezra gave Nick a wide-eyed glance full of despair over Dillon's head. Nick nodded, as if Dillon's idea was the best he'd heard in a long time. "Right this way." He indicated the steep path up through the trees.

Dillon proved to be as demanding as Nick had been told. From the foundations to the roof vent, no surface in the tower went without scrutiny. The inspector ran his white glove over every sill, molding, and piece of furniture. Dillon got so close to the lens, his breath fogged the prisms.

Nick resisted the urge to sigh. He'd be the one to have to polish them again.

The fuel house received the same treatment, each barrel and container of fuel accounted for. This didn't take long, as the bulk of their summer supplies was even now being unloaded on the dock. The only fuel in the place was that dropped off by the *Jenny Klamath* when Nick and the Batsons had arrived to open the light for the season two weeks ago.

Clyde arrived with the first load of kerosene drums from the shore just as Dillon started toward the fog-house. Clyde gave Nick an impudent grin behind the inspector's back.

Nick averted his face to keep from laughing aloud.

In the fog-house, Dillon went over every inch of the gasoline engines, making marks on his clipboard, sucking on his teeth. Through it all, Nick stood silent by the door. Dillon would find nothing amiss. Everything, from the shingles to the doorsill, was exactly as prescribed in the manual.

Thank You, Lord, for Ezra Batson and his insistence on everything being by the book.

Dillon's mouth twisted in a persimmon pucker. "I should like to inventory the tools now." He sucked in a giant breath that moved his shirtfront only a little. A solid gust of wind would sweep the man right over the cliff face.

"Tools are kept in the assistants' quarters. Right this way."

"Fine. I'll come back for the house inspection."

They crossed the clearing, Nick careful to keep pace with the inspector. He refused to walk behind the pompous little man.

They passed the front porch of Ezra's house. From within, a pot clanged against metal, and a mutter followed. He shrugged away his unease. Surely Annie would have everything under control there.

⟡

Annie scrunched her eyes up tight and sucked on her throbbing finger. In her haste to get the dirty dishes out of sight, she'd pinched her finger in a door. Hot tears smarted at the corners of her eyes, but she blinked them away. There was no time to cry.

She wrestled with the window over the sink, trying to get it open to rid the kitchen of the stale smoky smell. Slow footsteps overhead indicated Imogen moving about, no doubt dressing and putting up her hair.

Her hair! Annie's hands flew to her straggling bun. Being outside in the wind had tousled it, and tearing about the house hadn't improved the job. At least this was one task she was comfortable with. Though Hazel had usually done Annie's hair for going out, Annie had enjoyed styling her own hair most days.

She sped up the stairs to her bedroom and grabbed her hairbrush from the dresser. The pins snarled in her hair, her fingers clumsy in haste. She brushed it then began the process of winding it up into a perfectly relaxed knot. She winced when a hairpin jabbed her scalp, but in moments every lock was in place.

Looking behind her in the mirror, she screwed up her face at the mess. Never having had to care for her own belongings, she had scattered possessions hither and yon last night and this morning in her search for a suitable outfit. Good thing the inspector wasn't likely to come up here. The very idea of a strange man invading a girl's sleeping quarters!

Imogen met her in the hall, her face pale, her fingers chilly when she grabbed Annie's hands. "Did you get the kitchen squared away?"

"There wasn't much time. I did the best I could." Annie helped Imogen down the stairs. "You should've stayed in bed."

"I'll be fine. I'll sit in the parlor. You'll have to be in the kitchen, but don't say much. Dillon doesn't like back talk, and he won't overlook anything."

"I'll hold my tongue." Even as she said it, Annie wondered if she could. She wasn't accustomed to stifling her words.

Annie got Imogen settled on the sofa and went into the kitchen. She arrived none too soon.

Nick held the door open to allow a small man to precede him inside. "This is Inspector Dillon. Inspector, Miss Fairfax." Nick stepped inside and leaned against the wall beside the door. He crossed his arms, his face impassive.

A shiver raced across Annie's shoulders at the intense way Nick's eyes bored into hers. She licked her lips, and when he gave her a quick wink, she giggled.

"Madam? You find something amusing?" The inspector crossed his wrists behind his back and rocked heel to toe, pausing on his forward movement momentarily, as if trying to make himself taller. He gave an obnoxious suck on his teeth, the air whistling in moistly. The clipboard stuck out from one hand.

"Ah, no, I'm sorry. Pleased to meet you, sir. Won't you make yourself comfortable? Would you like a cup of tea?" Annie winced at her rapid-fire words.

"No, thank you. This is not a social visit. Just keep out of my way."

Annie backed up until she ran into a counter. Her hands suddenly seemed to be too large and in the way. She put them behind her and gripped the rolled edge of the enamel sink.

"I'll start with the pantry. I'd like to see the inventory of goods." The inspector held out his hand, tapping his foot on the bare kitchen floor.

Annie shot a look at Nick, who shrugged. She had no idea what the inspector wanted.

"Well? Where is it?"

"I. . .I. . ." She shook her head.

"Hmm." The clipboard came up, and he dug a pencil from his pocket. "No inventory sheets."

Annie closed her eyes. Surely Imogen had them somewhere. Her eyes shot open when the pantry door squeaked.

Dillon disappeared, and soon, the sounds of tins clanking, stone crocks scraping the floor, and glass tinkling filtered out.

Nick moved to her side. "Inventory sheets?"

Her heart accelerated at his closeness. He smelled of soap and lake breeze. "I haven't seen any. Do you suppose it's important?" Her voice rasped low. "How did the rest of the inspection go?"

"No idea. He doesn't say much, just barks his questions and orders and struts on." His voice held a laugh, and when she looked up into his eyes, he grinned at her.

Was it hot in here?

"I have a bad feeling about this. I've only been here one day. Surely he can't expect me to know where everything is. That's unreasonable."

"The inspector seems to deal in unreasonable." Nick straightened up.

Dillon emerged from the pantry, his mouth in a hard line. "Someone"—he glared at Annie—"spilled oatmeal on the floor. And there are several pots missing, as well as the washtub."

Annie gulped. Before she could speak, Dillon began yanking open cupboards and drawers. Cutlery clattered, wood scraped, and Annie's nerves stretched.

Please, please, please, God, if You're listening, don't let him—

Too late. The inspector opened the oven door. Annie grimaced. The dishpan, stacked high with dirty pots and dishes, cowered in the oven where she'd shoved it out of sight only a few minutes before.

"What is this?" Dillon puffed up with outrage. His small white forefinger pointed first to the dishes then to Annie. His chin lifted until he was staring down either side of his narrow nose.

Hot embarrassment shot through her. She looked at the floor, not wanting to see Nick's reaction.

"Get these out of here." Dillon tapped his foot.

Annie stepped forward, but Nick put his hand on her arm. In two strides he crossed the kitchen and slid the washtub from the oven. Annie answered his inquiring look by nodding toward the counter beside her.

Dillon gave them each a sharp glare then pivoted on one heel and entered the parlor.

"Thank you." Annie choked on the whisper.

"You'd better follow him. I'll be out on the porch." His kind smile shot warmth through her that had nothing to do with embarrassment.

She found Dillon and Imogen in the front room. Imogen, though pale, held herself regally, the match of any inspector.

Dillon seemed to realize this, for he treated her with a deference that had been decidedly lacking in his behavior toward Annie. But his eyes never stopped moving, calculating, assessing. "I'll just check a few more things, Mrs. Batson, and then the men will convene to the fog-house to discuss issues at this station." He bowed quickly then ducked out of the room.

"How did it go in the kitchen, dear?" Imogen laid her head back against the chair and sighed.

"He found where I'd stashed the dirty dishes." Annie spread her hands wide.

A soft chuckle escaped Imogen's lips. "You didn't put the dishes in the oven, did you? That's the first place they look."

Annie laughed ruefully in return. "I wish you'd have told me that sooner. I'd have hidden them in my room."

"They wouldn't be safe there either. He's checking the bedrooms right—"

"Miss Fairfax!" For such a little man, he had a loud voice.

Dread and hot anger gushed through Annie. She grabbed her skirts and hustled up the stairs. How dare he!

He stood in the doorway to her room, his face red, eyes blazing hot enough to start a fire. "What is the meaning of this?" He held up one of her petticoats.

The sight of Dillon holding her undergarment knocked all sense of caution out of Annie. She snatched the item from his hand. "Sir, this station may belong to the Lighthouse Board, but the Board does not lay claim to my personal items. I will thank you to stop pawing through my possessions. It is unseemly." Annie stood to her full height, topping the inspector by several inches. She refused to cower, and she refused to allow him to push her around any longer, the picky prig.

His mouth gaped and his eyes glassed over until he resembled a fish fresh from the lake. His nostrils flared, a dull redness suffusing his cheeks.

Annie tightened her lips. She'd gone too far. Imogen had only asked that Annie hold her tongue, and what had Annie done? Lashed out like a cornered badger at the first opportunity. She waited for the hammer to fall, for Dillon to order her to gather her strewn belongings and get off his island.

They stood toe-to-toe for a moment longer. Then, to her surprise, Dillon whirled and stomped down the stairs without a word.

Annie walked on unsteady legs to the bed and sank down, causing the springs to squeak. Her heart thundered against her ribs, and her breath came in quick pants. She'd faced him down, but now what? Would he write her up in some wretched report? She'd be lucky if he didn't send her packing on the next ferry south.

She looked about her room. Her traveling costume from the day before huddled in a damp and sorry heap where she'd stepped out of it. Petticoats and stockings snarled together in a pile beside her valise, which lay on its side open and spilling out her spare chemises and drawers. Her trunk stood open, a heap of clothing piled in the tray.

Heat scorched her face at the thought of any man, much less the insufferable inspector, seeing her possessions in such disarray. She rose and, for the first time in her life, began folding and putting away her own clothing.

Chapter 8

Dillon made his departure midafternoon. Though everyone but Imogen assembled on the dock to see him off, he spoke only to Mr. Batson.

Nick stood off to the side, watching, impatient for the inspector to be gone. The routine of Nick's day had been thrown awry, and he was anxious to get it back on track. And his stomach growled. He'd had nothing to eat since yesterday evening but an apple. Dillon had kept them talking in the fog-house through the lunch hour.

He wondered how things in the house had gone after he left. Annie stood at the foot of the dock, not venturing out over the water, her hands clenched at her waist, the wind blowing her skirt and hair. She didn't look at Dillon, or anyone else for that matter. A thrust of pity for her jabbed him. She was too young, too green for this job. What had driven her to take this position, so obviously wrong for her?

Dillon's nasal voice punched into his thoughts. "The lighthouse, fog-house, and fuel stores are all in fine condition. I commend you on their orderliness and cleanliness." He rocked on his toes, mauling another toothpick in his teeth. "The buildings and grounds are in excellent condition, better than I had expected considering how early in the season it is."

Clyde shot Nick an eyebrow-wobbly look, grinning through his freckles. The kid had a reckless zest for life that made Nick smile. Oh to be that naive again, to roll through life with few cares, little baggage, and a sense of adventure.

"However," Dillon went on, "the domestic side of things is another matter altogether. The kitchen, pantry, and sleeping quarters were disastrous."

Nick glanced at Annie. She winced, seeming to shrink a little with each barb. He had a sudden urge to go to her, to put his arm around her and tell her it would be all right. Where had that come from? She was nothing to him. Why then did he have the desire to shove his fist through Dillon's face for upsetting her?

"Because housekeepers are so difficult to obtain for remote stations such as Sutton Island, I am not going to fire Miss Fairfax at this time, no matter how much she may deserve it. Mrs. Batson tells me she is satisfied with Miss Fairfax's work, though I don't know how she could be. No, I'm not going to fire Miss Fairfax, but I am putting her on notice. I will return to inspect the station again, and if I find anything out of place, her employment will be terminated. From this moment on, Miss Fairfax is on probation. And while she is on probation, I will be looking for another candidate to fill her position. Should a suitable housekeeper apply, I will replace Miss Fairfax. Is that understood?" He tossed his toothpick onto the dock and dug in his pocket for another. The breeze flapped the papers on his ever-present clipboard, and Nick imagined himself ripping the clipboard from Dillon's hands and tossing it into the lake.

Ezra nodded, eyes sober, glancing between Dillon and Annie. "I understand. Thank you, Inspector. Are you sure you won't stay for some lunch?"

Nick looked heavenward. That was tempting things. If Annie cooked him a lunch anything like her breakfast, Dillon might set her adrift in a rowboat to find her own way back to Duluth.

"No, no, not this time. I can still inspect Two Harbors if I leave now. Good day, Batson, and don't forget what I said about a new housekeeper." Dillon clambered aboard the launch, sat stiffly upright in the bow, and pointed his face toward the *Marigold* lying at anchor a few hundred yards offshore. The launch puttered away, plowing through the waves, taking the inspector to wreak havoc elsewhere.

Nick laughed when he realized everyone on the dock had let out a big sigh of relief.

Ezra's mouth twisted in a wry smile. "I always look forward to that man's departure."

"What a way to live." Clyde hopped up onto a barrel of kerosene and gently drummed his heels against the metal side. "Folks never glad to see you come, always happy to see the back of you. What makes him so disagreeable?"

Nick unbuttoned his heavy wool tunic and slid out of the sleeves. Ezra did the same, and removed his hat as well.

"I try to be a little more understanding of him than most, I suppose." Ezra threaded his fingers through his flattened hair. "I met him once in Duluth, with his wife. She must be twice his size and has the disposition of a mule with a toothache. That man is oppressed, henpecked, and altogether dominated at home. I suppose he had to exert his will somewhere, and he takes it out on the folks in his employ."

Nick tried to imagine Dillon's domestic situation. It boggled the mind.

"I'd be nicer to people then, if it was me." Clyde hunched his shoulders. "'Cause I would know how it felt to be bossed and pushed around."

"I think I would, too, though I can't see either of us as henpecked husbands." Ezra smiled. "Imogen isn't the bossy type, and I imagine you'd have more sense than to marry someone like Mrs. Dillon in the first place. How about we get these supplies up the hill and stowed away...according to regulations." The corners of his eyes crinkled in humor.

Nick tossed his coat over a crate and picked the box up to move it to the cart for transport up the hill. A tiny part of him felt sorry for the inspector, and a larger part felt grateful to have escaped the same fate himself. Who knew what kind of woman his grandfather had picked out for him? Just because she was the daughter of Grandfather's crony didn't mean she wasn't a shrew.

Annie still stood at the foot of the dock, staring out over the water toward the *Marigold*. A sort of forlorn resignation rested on her pretty features, drawing down the corners of her eyes and mouth.

"Don't take it to heart, Annie. A few dishes in the oven aren't the end of the world."

She nodded, blinking her brown eyes hard a few times. A deep sigh escaped her lips as the lighthouse tender weighed anchor, gave a blast of the horn, and headed southwest to Two Harbors. "If that's all it was, I wouldn't be too worried. I lost my temper with him and made him look foolish." Her mouth quirked up. "Inquisitive, nosy, bothersome man. I wish he had stayed to lunch. I'd have fed him some of my oatmeal."

Nick laughed, surprised at her ability to joke about something that had angered her only a short while ago. Were all women this mercurial in temperament?

When he turned around from placing the crate on the cart, Annie was making her way up the footpath, occasionally glancing back over her shoulder toward the lake. Probably making sure the nasty little inspector wasn't returning.

"Clyde, head up the hill and light a bonfire. Throw some green leaves on it to make it smoke good." Ezra set two five-gallon containers of gasoline into the cart. "You can just see a good smoke column from here at Two Harbors. We'll try to warn them he's coming their way."

Clyde grinned. "Smoke signals. Great idea."

"Only fair. A little warning makes all the difference."

Nick slung the mailbag into the cart. A little warning. If he'd had a little warning about the storm last fall, he'd never have left the harbor. He wouldn't have been caught in the storm, and he wouldn't have found himself in the Lighthouse Board's employ, subservient to a tyrannical inspector.

Another glance up the hill. Sunlight gleamed off her golden hair. And he'd never have met a feisty girl named Annie Fairfax.

✺

Sunday dawned clear and bright. Imogen, feeling better this morning, gave Annie a cooking lesson. Pride glowed around Annie's heart when the men sat down to an edible meal for the first time since her foray into the culinary arts. Black frills decorated the edges of the fried ham, and the eggs were past hard, but the biscuits more than made up for any shortcomings. They were light, hot, and fluffy, just begging for honey.

179

When the dishes were cleared away—washed this time, not stuck in the oven—everyone gathered in the parlor for Sunday services. Annie entered the room last, her Bible clutched in her hand, to find the only available seat was on the davenport between Clyde and Nick. She sat between them, trying to make herself small so as not to touch either of them. Her shoulder brushed Nick's. She glanced up to see him staring down at her, intense and focused. Her mouth went dry, and she dropped her gaze to her Bible in her lap.

Ezra prayed. He spoke formally but as if he prayed often.

Annie wondered what it would've been like to grow up with a man like Ezra as her father.

"Our text for today is found in Proverbs 18:10. Nick, would you read that for us?"

Nick opened his Bible, the onion papers rustling like poplar leaves in a breeze. " 'The name of the Lord is a strong tower: the righteous runneth into it, and is safe.' "

"What does that mean to you?" Ezra looked at Clyde.

"We have a safe place to run when things get tough."

Annie froze, hoping Ezra wouldn't call on her for her opinion. She hadn't even opened her Bible. What did the verse say again? Her hands went cold.

"Annie?"

She shook her head, mind racing.

"That's all right. Nick?"

"We serve such a powerful God that even His name holds safety for us. He has promised never to leave us, and we know that if we are in trouble, He is waiting to help us. He won't abandon us."

Abandonment. Annie knew a thing or two about that. Maybe God didn't abandon good men like Nick or Clyde, or good people like the Batsons, but why hadn't He saved Neville? Why hadn't He stopped Mother from losing her reason or Father from shunning Annie after Neville died? Annie's thoughts whirled like a mini-tornado, memories and old hurts clashing with the words of the verse. *A strong tower. A strong tower.*

Ezra spoke again. "This promise is supported again and again in the Old Testament. I can believe this promise now because God kept His promises to the Israelites way back. Every time they called on Him, He heard them. He was a strong tower for them in their times of trouble. He never once left them, and He won't leave us either. All we have to do is run to Him. I take great comfort in that."

Imogen nodded, her face peaceful and loving, eyes intent on her husband.

Sure, she can agree with him. Ezra adores her. They've been together a long time. He's never abandoned her. Annie feared she would never know that closeness with anyone. Certainly not with someone her father chose for her out of greediness for money and power.

At Ezra's bidding, Clyde stood and picked up his guitar. With a nod to Imogen, he put his foot on the low table and settled the instrument on his knee. He strummed the strings, sending music vibrating through the room. In a clear tenor, he sang a few words of a familiar hymn.

Everyone joined in, Annie doing so automatically, though her thoughts remained on the Bible verse and her reaction to it.

∽

Clyde opened the mailbag for everyone, a treat put off in the busyness of yesterday to be savored in the quiet of a Sunday afternoon.

Annie knew there would be nothing for her since she'd only just arrived at the island, though she couldn't help but catch some of the excitement from the others.

Clyde received a package and letter from his mother in Superior. "Socks. She knows me well." Clyde held up a handful of gray wool. "And Pa's got a new job at Kennebrae Shipping. He's working on the *Bethany*. Guess they were able to salvage her."

Nick had a letter he tucked into his pocket without reading. He must want privacy. Annie could appreciate that. Was it from a sweetheart at home? She couldn't tell. He didn't look particularly eager to read the letter, nor excited about the sender. Surely if it was from a girl, he'd be less grim.

She chided herself for being so inquisitive and turned her attention to Imogen. Imogen received two letters and Ezra one.

Then there were the papers. Everyone took a Duluth newspaper, regardless of the date, and began reading. Annie found herself looking at yesterday's paper. She smoothed the crisp pages in her lap then held them up to hide her smile. At home, Father never would've approved of Annie reading the newspaper. Such behavior was unbecoming to a lady. She wondered at how much her life had changed in just a single week. Washing dishes, folding clothes, sweeping floors, and now reading newspapers.

Annie's eyes finally focused on the article under the masthead:

LOCAL HEIRESS DISAPPEARS

Anastasia Fairfax Michaels, only daughter and heir to Phillip Michaels, was reported missing early Friday morning. Phillip Michaels, owner of Michaels Mining and Manufacturing, reportedly worth more than one hundred million dollars, told police early yesterday morning that his daughter had disappeared from their Skyline Parkway mansion. Anastasia (19), a recent graduate of the Duluth Ladies' Academy, stands to inherit the Michaels fortune someday. The family is distraught. Michaels told this reporter his daughter was betrothed to a prominent Duluth businessman, though the formal announcement had yet to be made. Michaels refused to give us the name of the groom-to-be at this time.

Authorities are baffled by the case. So far, no ransom demand has been made and no plausible theories as to how a kidnap could have occurred have been put forth. Is this a kidnapping? Or did the young lady elope?

When the possibility of his daughter's running away was broached, Michaels became violently angry, shouting at reporters and police alike. "She wouldn't do anything so foolish. All her things are here, even her jewelry. If she ran away, why didn't she take them with her? I demand you find her and bring her back. I'll pay five thousand dollars' reward to anyone who will help get my daughter back." He then ordered his footmen to escort all news personnel off his property.

Annie glanced up.

No one looked at her. All were engrossed in their reading.

She stood. "I believe I'll take this upstairs to finish reading." Her pulse throbbed in her throat. The paper shook in her hands.

She reached her bedroom and leaned against the closed door. She quickly scanned the article again. Annie hadn't thought about the press or the police when she'd fled, only escaping her father's marriage plans for her. Leaving everything behind and being outfitted by Hazel in ordinary clothes, not even writing a note to anyone, had all been necessary to her escape. Just getting away wouldn't have been enough. She had to get away without anyone knowing her whereabouts. Well, no one but Hazel, and she'd never tell.

That must be why Hazel hadn't told the police it wasn't a kidnapping. She could hardly say she knew Annie had fled without saying she also knew where Annie had gone. Anyway, Hazel was probably on her way to Hibbing to that retirement cottage promised to her by Father.

Father. Annie rolled her eyes. Just like him to demand people help him then throw them out. And she couldn't believe he'd mentioned the betrothal. How could he still be planning the wedding when she wasn't even there? "I bet if I showed up in Duluth today, he'd have me married by tomorrow."

Guilt gnawed at her for causing such a fuss. Surely all the uproar would die down in a week or so, wouldn't it? She folded the paper, wondering where to hide it. Another headline below the fold caught her eye. SALVAGE CONTINUES ON *KENNEBRAE BETHANY*." Evidently the *Bethany*'s captain had left Duluth. Poor fellow, she didn't blame him. Folks would be talking about the wreck of the *Bethany* for years to come. Annie finished the article and stuffed the paper into a drawer. She'd take it down to the kitchen before breakfast tomorrow and burn it. It just wouldn't do for anyone here to see it. They'd make the connection between Anastasia Fairfax Michaels and Annie Fairfax in two blasts of a foghorn.

Chapter 9

Nick pumped air into the fuel tanks to pressurize them to the proper level. He tested them, a fine mist of kerosene spraying out of the nozzle. Perfect. He shielded his eyes and lit the oil-vapor lamps inside the lens. The lantern deck burst into white hot light.

One last squinting glance around the edge of his hand to confirm all was well and Nick clanged down the spiral staircase to the bottom of the tower. He checked the chains in the column then wound them slowly and evenly, cranking at a steady pace to ensure they didn't tangle. He checked his watch then engaged the gears. The light above began to revolve. He watched for four complete revolutions, timing them with his pocket watch. Perfect, one flash every ten seconds.

The chair creaked familiarly beneath him. He scooted it up to the desk and reached for his pen to update the log.

> *Tanks pumped and lantern lit at 7:34. Chains wound and light timed. Weather clear, slight breeze from the northeast. Three ships sighted before dusk, one ore carrier and one lumber boat with hooker in tow.*
> *N. Kennebr—*

He stopped in frustration. He'd almost signed his real name. He dipped his pen into the ink and deliberately let a blob fall on his signature. Good thing he'd noticed his slip. Ezra might ask some awkward questions.

Rules dictated every action taken concerning the light be logged while on watch. Past logs entries made for some interesting reading. The first keeper here, a man named Orrin Olden, was particularly wordy. His entries spoke of bad weather, a ship just off the coast whose boiler exploded, causing the ship to go down so quickly the keeper didn't even have time to launch a rowboat to save anyone aboard. One entry told of a lightning storm over the island. Not even the lightning rods on the tower kept bolts from striking the buildings. Nick flipped back to that entry.

> *Terrible lightning storm last night. Windows broke in the tower, but the lens, thank the Lord, is still intact. Lightning shot out of the faucets and raced in fist-sized balls across the floor and into the parlor.*

By far the strangest oddity of the storm was the lard bucket I'd set beside the downspout on the corner of the house. When I looked at it this morning, it had hundreds of tiny holes pierced through it. Guess I won't be using that as my bait bucket anymore. –Orrin Olden.

Nick flipped back to the current page and signed "Nick Kennedy" next to the ink blotch. He checked the wall clock, then his watch, then stepped outside.

Clyde sat on the back porch of the Batsons' house, strumming his guitar and singing. In the twilight, Nick picked out Annie's form leaning against a porch post, her hair pale in the growing dusk. Every ten seconds the soft edge-glow of the lighthouse's beam circled overhead, briefly illuminating the Batsons sitting on the porch swing.

An owl hooted in the trees behind the house, preparing for his night hunt. From below the cliff, a fish jumped, flopping into the water with a *smack*. Must have been a big one. Perhaps Nick could find a little time tomorrow to fish off the dock, though he wondered what Annie would do if he presented her with a half-dozen fish to cook.

Had that last rotation of the light been slow? Nick counted, waiting for the next flash to hit the chimney of the house. Eleven. He'd better check. He was probably counting too fast.

He stepped into the tower and held his watch to the wall sconce. Eleven, almost twelve. A quick check told him the weights weren't fouled in the shaft, nor were the cables tangled. The rotations continued, but each was just a few seconds slow.

Ezra arrived before Nick got halfway up the stairs. "Is the light slow?"

"Yes, I'm just headed up to check on the mechanism from up there." Nick shielded his eyes when he reached the lantern deck and ducked down to observe the clockworks at the base of the light. The hot smell of burning kerosene filled his nose. The heat generated by the lantern was intense, though much of it drifted up through the vent ball in the roof. He saw nothing wrong. The light hurt his eyes even though he tried not to look at it.

He rejoined Ezra in the watch room. "I can't tell. Everything seems to be running well. We won't be able to tear it apart and look at it until tomorrow." Nick blinked, still seeing spots.

Ezra stroked his chin. "We'll have to turn it by hand then. I'll get Clyde."

Nick rolled up his sleeves, turning back the cuffs in precise folds. It was going to be a long night. He looked up when Ezra returned with Clyde. Nick jumped to his feet when Annie entered the watch room.

Ezra crossed his arms. "I've decided we'll work in shifts. Nick, you'll take the first watch. Annie has volunteered to keep the time for you. We'll alternate two-hour watches until daylight. Annie"—he turned to her, handing her a marine stopwatch—"ten seconds exactly for each flash of the light, twenty for the clamshell to turn once around completely, right?"

She nodded, her dark eyes appearing black in the light from the wall sconce.

Ezra and Clyde left to try to get some sleep before their watch, leaving Nick and Annie alone in the watch room.

Nick studied her then picked up the chair from the desk and took it into the tower. He set it along the wall under a lamp for her.

She wrapped her shawl tighter around her shoulders and sat down. "How do you want me to do this?" Two narrow vertical lines appeared between her eyebrows. Her bottom lip disappeared behind her upper teeth.

"Count out the seconds. You'll have to do it loud enough that I can hear. I'll be turning this crank." He motioned to the lever. "It's attached to the gears that turn the light."

"Why is it so important that the light flash at ten second intervals? What's wrong with eleven or twelve? Isn't the fact that the light is shining at all enough?"

Nick began the process of disengaging the chains and weights from the gears. "Every light on the lake has its own signal, its own timing, and its own color. Some of the lanterns are green, some are white, some are red. The precise timing of the light lets mariners know which light they are near. There's a whale of difference between, say, the lighthouse at Two Harbors and the lighthouse at Devil's Island. If the captain doesn't know or can't tell the difference, just having the light won't be enough to keep him from running aground if he thinks he is somewhere he's not. Even then, you can't always avert disaster. A lighthouse shouldn't give a captain a feeling of safety. It should increase his awareness of danger."

"It makes me think of all the ships that were lost last fall. Remember the *Bethany*? Her captain was within sight of the Duluth Harbor Light when he ran aground. All winter that ship sat there in the ice. I wonder what happened to that captain."

Nick bent to the lever without answering her. Guilt, shame, anger, everything he'd been trying to escape by coming to Sutton Island was trapped within his chest. "Start counting."

∽

"Four, five, six, seven, eight, nine, ten. One, two, three. . ." Annie continued to count aloud. Her tongue stuck to the roof of her mouth, and she longed for a cup of hot tea.

Nick bent over the crank, turning, turning, turning, never stopping. Sweat dripped from his forehead, and patches soaked the back of his white shirt, sticking it to muscles that moved and rippled with each turn.

Annie tugged her shawl tighter around her shoulders and wiggled her toes in her boots. The temperature had dropped as the hours passed. Soon she would be able to see her breath. Sitting in a stone-and-iron tower during a Lake Superior April night was enough to bring on pneumonia.

"Six, seven, eight, nine, ten. One, two, three, four. . ." *This is how people go insane. Whoever says lighthouse keepers' jobs are easy is a fool.* They were on watch every hour of every day. What made them choose this work? They had to be men of extraordinary commitment. Men who wouldn't run away when things got tough. Not like her father—

She shut that line of thought down and concentrated on counting. And she watched Nick.

Nick would be a good husband. He was kind, honorable, and hardworking. He loved God and never shirked a duty. Imogen sang his praises, and Ezra and Clyde got along with him so well. And a girl would have to be blind not to see how handsome he was. His behavior toward Annie had been perfect. Well, except for a little teasing about her cooking, but only the once. Yes, he would be a good husband.

"Nine, ten. One, two. . ." Not like the worm her father had chosen for her. Annie envisioned a miserly, middle-aged grump with bad breath and thinning hair. He probably smoked foul-smelling cigars and maybe even wore a monocle. He'd drone on endlessly about capital ventures and voting shares when he bothered to speak to her at all. She would be expected to run his house smoothly, see to all his comforts, and, above all, produce an heir and preferably a spare within the first five years of marriage. As a proper wife, she would be required to attend such functions as he permitted and to overlook all his faults, particularly those involving breaking the seventh commandment. And he would magnanimously overlook her past sins so he could get his grubby mitts on her inheritance. Annie's fingers gripped the stopwatch so hard, her hand shook.

"Five, six, seven. . ." If her father had chosen a man like Nick instead of some spineless grub with dollar signs in his eyes, she never would've fled Michaelton House. But no man of Nick's fine character would want to be mixed up with someone like her, money or no money.

"We'll take over now." Annie looked up to see Clyde taking over the crank and Ezra reaching for the watch.

Annie handed it over and attempted to rise. Her muscles had stiffened in the cold and inactivity. Pain pressed into her lower back like pushpins. Her feet were blocks of ice.

Nick held out his hand to help her rise. "You look worn out. We'd best go get some sleep before we have to come back in a couple hours and do it all over again." He brushed a lock of hair off her cheek, the contact of his fingers on her skin sending spiraling jitters through her middle.

Her breath caught in her throat, and she told herself not to be silly, he was just being kind. She had let her imagination get away from her a bit, that was all. Her mouth trembled into a smile. "Good idea. I'll set my alarm clock."

They had gone only a few steps toward the door when a *crash* and shattering of glass sounded over their heads.

"What in the world?" Ezra stopped counting. "The lens!" He shot up from the chair and hurried up the stairs.

Nick was only a few steps behind him.

Annie and Clyde stared at each other. A second *thud*, then a third ricocheted down the spiral steps. Annie could stand it no longer. She grabbed up her long skirts and ran to the stairs.

She reached the lantern deck. The beacon blazed, momentarily blinding her. She cried out and threw up her hands. At her feet on the top step a bundle of feathers flopped weakly. Glass shards peppered the floor. Another *thud* and another pelted the glass. "What is it?" She had to shout to be heard above the sound of a hundred wings.

"A bird barrage." Ezra held the door to the catwalk for Nick to squeeze through. "Get below."

"Let me help. What can I do?" A Canada goose flew through the open window and crashed into the center prism of the light. Glass rattled, but nothing broke.

"Get below and help Clyde time the light. We'll worry about the birds."

Annie turned and hurried down the steps, wincing at each impact of a feathered body with glass or metal or brick. Why would geese do this?

Clyde continued to turn, trying to crank with one hand while holding the stopwatch in the other.

She took the watch and held it for him so he could see while he turned. "It's geese. They're flying into the light. One broke a windowpane. Nick went out onto the catwalk. I think he had a broom with him. What would make birds fly into the tower?"

Clyde kept his eyes on the watch. "I've heard of it before. Something goes sideways with them. They act like moths around a candle." Concentration lined his youthful face, his red hair darkening and sticking to his forehead with sweat. "Count for me."

Nick's and Ezra's muffled voices came from overhead. The thudding went on.

Annie took up counting again, huddled on her chair, wondering if the next bird through the window would disable the light completely.

After what seemed like hours—though Annie's watch indicated twenty minutes—the bombardment ceased. Clyde continued to turn the gears, and

Annie kept on counting, but she strained to hear what was happening upstairs.

At last, feet sounded on the stairs. Ezra came first, his face ashen. Nick followed, shoulders slumped, a smear of blood standing out boldly on his white shirt.

Annie thrust the watch into Ezra's hands and hurried to Nick. "Are you hurt? What happened up there? Is it over?" She touched the red patch, worry over his safety making her hands jerk with small, fluttery movements.

He looked down at her, puzzlement quirking his eyebrows. "I'm fine. The blood isn't mine." His hand covered hers and he brought it down to his side. He didn't let go. Instead he twined their fingers together. With his other hand, he brushed the hair back from her forehead.

A shaken-up feeling jangled through her, like a quarter in a tin can. His handclasp tightened, his palm pressed warmly to hers. She stared into his eyes, wondering what he was thinking, wondering if he knew what affect his presence, his kindness, had on her.

Ezra cleared his throat. "I think you and I, Nick, should stay on watch. Bird barrages are strange things, and quite often they happen in bunches. It wouldn't surprise me if we got another one tonight. Annie, can you handle the timing duties with Clyde?" He held up the silver stopwatch.

Annie nodded. With reluctance, she released Nick's hand. Her shawl had fallen off one shoulder. She groped for it, numbness stealing over her. *Please, God, don't let it happen again. I couldn't stand it. Watch over Nick and Ezra. The catwalk is so small. Don't let them fall.*

"One, two, three. . ."

Chapter 10

Nick rubbed his hand across his forehead. Lack of sleep burned his eyes. Only once had he spent a more miserable night, that aboard the freezing, grounded *Bethany* in the teeth of a November gale. This night of battling birds bent on self-destruction, though bad enough, paled in comparison to those nightmare hours.

Stiffness clung stubbornly to his back and shoulders. He rolled his neck. Sleep would be a long way off. They still had to find out why the light was running slow, and they had to clean up the mess. His shoulder ached from the kick of the shotgun. Ezra had brought them each a shotgun from the house when the second attack came. Nick fired so many shells, the barrel of his gun bent from the heat.

Three times the birds came. Several windows in the lantern room were cracked and broken, but the prisms of the lens remained intact. The precious curved glass bore the marks of battle, blood-smeared and smudged, but none had broken. Several dead birds lay on the catwalk and lantern deck. Below, they counted sixteen feathered corpses. Many others had dropped into the lake far below.

Nick doused the beacon and followed Ezra down the stairs into the base of the tower.

Annie sat on the straight-backed chair, her bright hair slipping from its knot. She leaned back, resting her head against the slick, enameled tile on the wall, her face pale, lashes dark against her cheeks. The stopwatch lay in her lap, her fingers curled around it.

Clyde sat along the wall opposite her, arms propped on his upraised knees, wrists limp, hands hanging. He, too, rested his head against the wall, eyes shut. The poor lad had cranked the light for more than five hours straight. He'd probably sleep the clock around.

Ezra went through into the watch room, his shoulders bent. His hair seemed to have whitened overnight, the lines deepening on his face, his eyes growing more sober and haggard as the night wore on.

Soft sunlight crept through the small windows, marching in a spiral around the tower and following the curve of the stairs.

Nick lifted the stopwatch from Annie's relaxed fingers and slipped it into his pocket. He put her arms around his neck and slipped one hand under her knees, the other behind her back. She weighed next to nothing. Her eyelashes fluttered for a moment before falling again, and her head rested against his shoulder. He breathed in the scent of lilacs from her hair.

His heart bumped crazily against his ribs. She felt right in his arms. He recalled how she'd rushed to him, checking to make sure he was all right after his first battle with the birds and how he'd enjoyed her concern, her attention.

That thought brought him up short. What was he thinking? He had no right to court her, to stake a claim. Not only was he unworthy of her after the fiasco with the *Bethany*, but he was also sort of engaged thanks to his grandfather's machination. Unless or until he was released from that engagement, he had no business entertaining thoughts of another woman. Though none of these thoughts kept him from enjoying the feel of her in his arms as he carried her across the grass toward the house.

Imogen met him at the porch door, her face pallid. Her hand shielded the sunlight from her face. She must be in the grips of another headache. "Bring her through here," Imogen whispered and motioned for him to follow her into the parlor.

Nick entered the parlor and knelt to lay Annie on the sofa. Imogen held a bright crocheted blanket to cover her. He found himself strangely reluctant to let Annie go. He finally withdrew his arms, gently easing her head onto the pillow.

She opened her eyes for a brief instant, her brown gaze looking right into his soul. He blinked, and her eyes closed. A small sigh escaped her. She snuggled into the pillow and slept.

Imogen tucked the blanket around her, edging Nick back. He went into the kitchen, trying to sort out his jumbled feelings.

Imogen met him there. "Poor lass. What a dreadful night for you all. I've got coffee on."

He took a steaming mug from her, blowing across the top to cool the fragrant liquid. "You look done in yourself. Maybe you should lie down for a while, too." The gentle way she eased herself down into a chair, as if her head might come off if she jarred it, caused him concern.

"It's nothing. Just one of my headaches. I took some powders." She rested her cheek on her hand. "Anyway, I got more sleep than anyone on the island last night. The least I can do is keep the coffee hot and get you some breakfast when you're ready."

Nick took a long swallow of coffee, feeling it wash his middle, warming him from the inside out. Though she tried to hide it, he knew her headaches were more than "nothing."

"We won't need breakfast anytime soon, I shouldn't think. Clyde's sleeping like the dead in the tower. Ezra and I have to figure out what's wrong with the light, and we have to reglaze a few windows. We can rustle up some grub when the time comes."

She looked at him shrewdly. "I doubt you've ever cooked for yourself in your life. You have no more notion what goes on in a kitchen than Annie does."

He raised his eyebrows. "What would make you say that?"

"I've been watching you, Nick. You have the best manners and the most cultivated speech of any assistant lightkeeper I've ever come across. I have a notion you were brought up privileged. You know everything there is to know about the lake and the ships on it, but you're no ordinary deckhand. You have the air of a naval officer about you. You're not hiding something from us that we need to know, are you?"

Nick tried not to squirm under her scrutiny, nor show just how close her evaluation had come to unmasking him. "No, ma'am. I'm not hiding anything from you that you need to know."

Even through the pain in her eyes he could see her brain working. "And I notice how you look at our Annie. You're not planning on breaking her heart, are you? She's a sweet, naive thing, head in the clouds half the time. I won't have you misleading her." Imogen pointed her finger at his chest. "You're a handsome man, Nick Kennedy. Annie's been watching you, too. It wouldn't take much of an effort from you to make her fall in love. Unless your intentions are honorable, I don't think you should trifle with her affections."

Heat curled through Nick's ears and raced up his neck. Not since his grandmother had passed away had he been lectured in such a manner. Imogen reminded him of his grandmother: tiny, energetic, frustrated when her health kept her from living life at a gallop, caring and concerned for those in her charge. "Ma'am, I assure you, I have no intention of dallying with Miss Fairfax. I have other commitments back in Duluth that make a romantic liaison impossible. My fiancée would frown upon such doings." There, that should set Imogen's mind at rest.

Lines formed between her brows. "You're betrothed? I had no idea."

"It's not been publicly announced yet." He was getting in deeper and deeper. "And I'd just as soon keep it quiet around here, too, if you don't mind."

Imogen nodded, though her face bore skepticism.

Nick finished his coffee and headed back to the lighthouse.

~

"We've been over every inch of the mechanism. I can't find anything wrong. The gears mesh perfectly, the springs are tight, no screws are loose." Nick wiped his hands on a rag and stuffed it into his pocket. "That just leaves one thing."

Ezra and Clyde groaned in unison. "The float."

The lens mechanism "floated" on two hundred fifty ounces of mercury. At a pound per fluid ounce, that meant two hundred fifty pounds of liquid metal to drain and purify.

"Do we have any extra?" Nick eased his tired muscles down until he sat on the floor. He stared out at the lake, listening to the sound of waves gently slapping the rocks at the cliff base that drifted up through the broken windows. Window repair was next on the list of things to do after fixing the light.

"We have one eight-ounce bottle for emergencies." Ezra smoothed his mustache. Earlier he'd put forth the idea that the mercury under the lens had somehow gotten contaminated. It had happened to him once before. Rust flakes had fouled the mercury so the lens wouldn't turn smoothly. They'd kicked around the idea for a while but decided to leave it as a last resort.

Nick turned to Clyde, whose bloodshot eyes bespoke his lack of sleep. "Get two clean buckets and bring a fuel can of kerosene."

"I'll go get the extra mercury should we need it." Ezra started down the stairs after Clyde.

Ezra's hypothesis proved correct. They washed the mercury with kerosene, letting the heavy metal fall through several inches of the oily fuel in the bottom of a bucket. Impurities and rust flakes floated atop the kerosene, easily picked out with a newspaper. The entire operation took about two hours to complete.

When they finished refilling the tank under the lens, Clyde swirled the few drops of mercury left in the bottom of the bucket. "Stuff's amazing." Bright quicksilver beads raced and collided, merged and separated in the bucket.

Nick smiled at how young Clyde looked. The boy had done well. Responsible, polite, conscientious. A good candidate for a ship's officer, given some seasoning.

Nick pulled himself up. How easy it was to slip back into that old frame of mind.

They tested the lamp. With the mercury purified, the beacon rotated with precision.

Nick sighed with relief and clapped Ezra on the back. "Why don't you and Clyde get some shut-eye? The window repair is a one-man job. I can take care of it. Then I'll come in for some food and a nap." He swallowed a yawn. A nap sounded like heaven at the moment.

Glass, glazing points, putty. How thankful Nick was for the supplies. That, at least, he owed to Jasper Dillon. The man kept his lighthouses stocked and ready. Carrying the tools up the stairs, Nick grimaced at how he'd let the little man get under his skin. Henpecked at home. The idea made Nick grin. That explained a lot. Guess he could give the inspector a little leeway.

As he worked, Nick marveled again at the beauty of God's creation. The vista before him couldn't be more spectacular. Aquamarine water, white-tipped waves creaming over, brilliant white-blue sky, snowy clouds, and the north shoreline a faint, dark ribbon in the west. Gulls keened and hovered on the breeze, squawking and bickering.

An ore boat chugged into view. Nick swept up the glasses and held them to his eyes, toying with the focus until the image became clear. The *Kennebrae Cana*, with the *Galilee* in tow.

A lump lodged in his throat. The *Bethany* had been towing the *Galilee* the night the storm hit. Like a fool, he'd cut the *Galilee* loose just outside the harbor to ride out the storm at anchor in the basin. Why hadn't he done the same? Why had he tried to enter the harbor? The listing and water intake on the *Bethany* hadn't been that bad, had it? The crew might have been able to shift the load and pump out the water if only he'd just dropped anchor like the *Galilee* had. He'd acted in haste, and the cost had been high.

His hands ached, and he realized he was gripping the binoculars hard enough to break them. He set the glasses down on the ledge and picked up the putty knife. The glazer's points pricked his fingers, but he welcomed the distraction. Anything to take his mind off his past.

Regular maintenance on the light took him the rest of the morning. He washed every pane and prism. He scrubbed the lantern deck, sweeping up feathers and debris from the repair efforts. Then he trimmed the lamp, setting everything ready for sundown.

He pushed aside thoughts of his old life, of his family, of how things used to be. And he tried without success to ignore the fact that his heart wasn't in the lighthouse. His heart rode the waves racing to catch up with the Kennebrae ships just disappearing over the horizon.

Chapter 11

L ife fell into an easy pattern over the next few weeks.

Annie, under Imogen's tutelage, discovered an aptitude for baking, hitherto unknown. She continued to burn, over-season, and otherwise ruin all attempts at stovetop cooking, but she was a marvel with the oven. Her desserts and breads were such a success, the men forgave much in the way of culinary disasters.

Annie managed to secret the Duluth paper out of her bedroom and into the firebox, breathing a sigh of relief as the pages curled and blackened, obliterating news of her escape. She pushed thoughts of her life in Duluth into the back of her mind and concentrated on the here and now, enjoying a freedom she'd never known, blossoming, gaining confidence, deepening her relationships, and finding new facets of her character to explore and strengthen.

Imogen spoke often of spiritual things, teaching Annie through her gentle ways of a deeper, more satisfying relationship with God, one where God wasn't a vengeful or indifferent parent but a loving Father who cared for His children. Annie's faith grew, day by day.

Evenings were her favorite times, especially those evenings when Nick didn't have the early watch. Everyone gathered in the parlor. Imogen would crochet or tat, her rocker creaking softly. Nick would play checkers with Clyde or Ezra. And Annie would read. Though she detested Jasper Dillon, she fell gratefully upon the wooden cupboard of books he'd left, part of the lighthouse library. Each lighthouse on his route received one of the crates of books, to be exchanged at the next inspection.

One night she picked up *King Solomon's Mines*—a choice that would've sent her father into a tirade—and settled herself into a corner of the davenport. Allan Quatermain was such an interesting hero. So stalwart and fearless, and so sad and introspective at times. Annie caressed the cloth cover of the book, her fingers tracing the indentations of vines and leaves, of gold lettering on the spine.

"Since you're starting that book over again, why don't you read it aloud, dear?" Imogen's hook flew in her fingers, poking in and out of the yarn. The ball of wool at her feet tumbled in the basket when she pulled some slack.

Annie cast a glance in the direction of the checkers players. Clyde's bright eyes and grin encouraged her. Nick's darker blue eyes set her breath crowding into the top of her lungs. No matter how she tried to dissuade her heart, she couldn't make herself see sense. He was everything she wanted in a man. It took much discipline on her part to avoid letting her growing feelings for him show.

She opened the book to the dedication and cleared her throat. She had read aloud to Hazel nearly every night while Hazel rocked and knitted or mended. Tears pricked Annie's eyes as she wondered where Hazel was now and if she missed Annie at all. A wave of homesickness rushed over her, receded, then returned to lap about her heart like combers on the beach.

Clyde shifted in his chair, his boots scraping the floor.

The sound brought Annie back, and she began to read.

∞

Nick lost all interest in checkers the moment Annie spoke. Did she know how her voice took on the various characters, each one sounding different?

Clyde, too, ignored the game, wrapped up in the story. Imogen's crochet hook moved slower and slower until it stilled in her hands.

Lamplight raced along Annie's bright curls, and her cheeks flushed slightly. Slender hands held the book, tilting it toward the table lamp next to her.

Nick couldn't help but notice the delicate curve of her neck and the gentle slope of her shoulders. Her shoes stood side by side in front of the sofa, her feet tucked up. He remembered the feel of her in his arms when he carried her in to place her on that very sofa. She had never mentioned it. Neither had he, but he cherished the memory. Even now he imagined he could smell the faint scent of lilacs on her hair.

Nick forced himself to concentrate on the story. He'd look a fool if someone asked him about the plot right now. Annie had a gift, a real gift, for bringing a story to life. In spite of the distractions, he found himself drawn into the tale.

Ezra stomped into the room, breaking the mood.

Nick rose at the expression on Ezra's face.

"There's a ferry off the east side of the island. I could just make it out with the glasses. They're signaling distress. I think they've struck the submerged rocks out there near the bell buoy. We'll have to launch the boat and help them."

Nick nodded. "I'll take Clyde and go. Ezra, you and Annie get down to the dock with blankets. Imogen, get a fire going. There may be injuries." He barely noticed that he'd taken charge of the situation, usurping the authority that rightfully belonged to Ezra. Getting to a wounded vessel quickly meant saving lives.

Clyde sprinted down the dark path through the trees to the dock. Nick followed quickly, picking his way in the lantern light. By the time he reached the dock, Clyde had the canvas tarp off the boat and was loading in the oars.

Nick joined him in the rocking craft. He fastened the lantern to the pole in the stern and sat at the tiller. "Row hard, boy. I'll relieve you when you tire."

Clyde fixed the oars in the oarlocks and bent his back to the task.

Nick leaned on the tiller, curving the boat around the north end of the island. Once free of the shielding cliff, the bleat of the ship's horn reached them. Above that, faintly, the clang of the bell buoy kept time with the waves.

How had a ferry ended up on the east side of the island? Every lake captain knew of the dangers of the razor-sharp shoals there. All traffic larger than a canoe passed to the west side of Sutton Island.

Fine mist sprayed Nick each time the bow dipped into a trough.

Clyde grunted with effort, but his stroke remained smooth.

"Where'd you learn to row like this?" Nick raised his voice to be heard.

"Father was a lifesaver off the coast of Cape Cod before we moved west." Clyde's teeth gleamed white in the moonlight. "Been rowing since I was a little gupper."

Nick marveled at how God worked, bringing the right people to the right place at the right time. *Please, Lord, let us get to the boat in time.*

From a hundred yards away the ferry's lights flickered on the water. People crowded the deck, shouting. The ship listed hard to port.

Nick caught the tang of smoke in the air from the twin stacks far overhead. He leaned harder on the tiller, and the boat swung around and bumped into the starboard side of the ferry. He read the name *Olivia Star* on the side wheel of the boat.

People rushed forward.

"Hold there!" Nick shouted. "Women and children first. We'll take as many as we can each trip."

Heedless of his words, a wall of humanity surged toward the small craft. One man missed his footing and shot out into the air, landing in the water with a yelp.

When he surfaced, Nick leaned out of the boat and grabbed him by the collar. He dragged the man around the rowboat toward the ferry. "Get up there and wait your turn."

Clyde lifted a child of about six or seven into the boat then reached up for another. "Here you go, lassie. A ride in my nice boat. You sit still, and we'll have you to land in a jiffy." His matter-of-fact voice seemed to calm the children. They huddled together on the seat, eyes wide, but not crying.

"Where's the captain?" Nick scanned the crowd for anyone in authority. "How many passengers are aboard?"

A deckhand in a dirty uniform leaned over the rail. "There's sixteen passengers and eight crew, counting the captain."

"Any injuries?"

"Beyond a few cuts and bruises, I don't think so."

Clyde continued to load passengers until the gunwales dipped toward the water. "This is all we can take this load. We'll be back."

On the return trip, Nick gave the tiller over to a white-faced woman and grasped a pair of oars. Rowing in such a crowd proved difficult, but it hastened their speed.

The water grew choppy when they rounded the west side of the island. "Bail!" Nick's jaw tightened. Waves lapped over the sides of the overloaded boat. "Bail!"

Passengers cupped their hands, throwing the water overboard. One woman removed her hat and used it as a bucket, shoving, pushing, tossing water out.

Relief swamped Nick as the dock came into sight. Annie and Ezra held lanterns high, Ezra out on the end of the dock, Annie on the shore. Nick and Clyde handed passengers up as quickly as they could and started back around the island for another load.

The second return trip was faster, as the passengers were mostly male. The boat could hold fewer of them, but they helped row and bail. On the final trip out to the damaged steamer, nearing exhaustion, Nick and Clyde picked up the last remaining crew members, the first officer, and the captain.

The *Olivia Star* listed farther in the water, her lowest deck now awash. She seemed to have run aground on a single sharp point of rock, tottering and balancing, sliding ever lower as she took on water.

A crew member dumped the captain, a limp tangle of arms and legs in a dark suit, into the bottom of the rowboat. The captain lolled beneath the seats, a livid bruise darkening half his face, a trickle of blood oozing from the corner of his mouth. He mumbled but didn't open his eyes.

"Was he injured in the wreck?" Clyde eased the man's arms aside so he could brace himself at the oars.

The first officer grunted and rolled his eyes. He held his ribs with one arm across his middle, his face ashen. None of the other crewmen said a word.

"You hurt?" Nick steadied the man, placing his hand on the officer's shoulder.

"Ribs."

"Well, rest easy now. We'll have you on shore in no time. Somebody hold this tiller."

Though his arms resembled lake kelp, Nick took up the oars again. Several spots on his fingers and palms burned. He'd have blisters by morning, no doubt.

The rising wind worked against them, blowing against their backs, bucking the small craft.

At last they reached the dock again. Ezra leaned down to pull them up from the boat.

Nick grasped his hand gratefully. "That's all of them. The ship's listing bad, but it's perched on a submerged rock. If it doesn't take on too much water and slide off whatever it's grounded on, it might be salvageable." *Like the* Bethany. Nick leaned against the dock piling, wrapping the bowline of the rowboat securely. The thought jabbed him like a poke in the eye.

Annie stood at the far end of the dock. Why didn't she come out?

He beckoned to her, but she shook her head, her face ghostly in the light of the lantern she held up to guide the refugees toward the path. He staggered toward her, body screaming from the rescue efforts.

When he got close, she bit her lip, tears wetting her cheeks. "You're all right? You got everyone?"

"We got everyone." He gave in to the urge and put his arm around her shoulders, hugging her into his side. "Nice to know someone was here worrying about us."

She stayed in his embrace a moment then seemed to collect herself.

He dropped his arm from around her and stepped back, wondering if he had offended her with his familiarity.

"I'm glad you're all right. I prayed for you as hard as I could." She brushed her skirts and ducked her head. "We'd best get up the hill and help Imogen. I don't know where we're going to put all these people."

He took the lantern and offered her his arm for the hike up the hill.

෧

The smell of damp wool and coffee hit Annie in the face when she walked into the kitchen. Woebegone looks greeted her. People huddled near the stove, and Imogen filled cups. A kettle whistled.

"I'll take that." Annie lifted the coffeepot from Imogen's hands. She bent her head to whisper in Imogen's ear, "What are we going to do? Where can we put so many people?"

"We'll manage, dear. They'll have to sleep on the floor, that's all. It's how we're going to feed them that has me praying." Imogen patted Annie's hand. "God will figure things out. He hasn't failed us yet."

Annie shook her head, smiling. God *was* going to have to figure things out, because Annie was fresh out of ideas. If she fed them any of her own cooking, they'd likely take to the lake and try to swim to shore just to escape.

Imogen tore up a bed sheet and Annie helped her wrap the ribs of the first officer. That man, clammy and gray, they put on the sofa, propped up with plenty of pillows. He thanked them over and over in a shallow, breathy voice. Imogen dosed him with tea and a bit of laudanum from the medical kit, and he drifted off to sleep moments later.

The captain proved a more difficult patient. He mumbled and thrashed, face screwed up in a thundercloud grimace. Annie tried to hold a cold compress to his bruised head, but he kept swatting her away. He reeked of a most foul odor, one Annie couldn't place. Obviously the smack on the head had disoriented the man to the point of delirium. He finally subsided in Imogen's rocker, so Annie left him there, snoring like a fog signal.

Clyde and Nick got most of the men bedded down in the assistant keepers' quarters. Three had to settle for pallets on the parlor floor in the main house. Annie gave up her room to a mother and her two small daughters and moved in with Imogen. Nick, Clyde, and Ezra would take turns sleeping on a cot in the fog-house.

By the time everyone was settled for the night, the clock struck two. Annie dragged herself up the stairs. Her hair had long since given up staying in its knot. She flipped it back over her shoulder with a tired hand. Breakfast for thirty? It didn't bear thinking about.

She shrugged into her nightgown, keeping the lamp low in deference to Imogen, who was already asleep. Annie slipped between the sheets, not bothering to braid her hair for the night. She'd battle the snarls in the morning. If she wasn't so tired, she'd take the time to examine just how relieved she was to see Nick come back safe and sound. . .that and how wonderful his embrace had been.

Chapter 12

God proved Himself trustworthy again the next morning. One of the women rescued from the ferry was the ship's cook. She took over the kitchen, fixing breakfast for thirty without displaying any of the panic Annie would've felt. Annie turned the entire operation over to the five women from the ship and concentrated on caring for Imogen, who once more found herself victim of a sick headache.

The children, the most resilient of the group, bounced outside to explore the moment they were excused from the table. Annie took one look at the overloaded dishpan and blew out a breath, fanning wisps of hair off her forehead. She needn't have worried. The women were more than willing to pitch in and help. Annie left them to it and went into the parlor to check on the two wounded men.

How Hazel would laugh to see Annie now, changing bed linens, administering medicine, acting the hostess for two dozen unexpected guests. Annie, who had never cooked, cleaned, or cared for her own clothing. Hazel would hardly know her. Annie hardly knew herself.

She opened the drapes a crack, saw that the man on the sofa was awake, and pulled them a bit wider. Sunlight streamed in, tracking across the polished maple floor, picking out motes in the air. "How are you feeling?" She pulled the blanket higher around the injured man.

He tried to speak, but only a croak came out.

Annie helped him sit a little straighter and held a glass of water to his cracked lips.

"My name is Saunders. Jared Saunders." He hugged his ribs, his lips tight. "Thank you for all you are doing. Are the passengers all right?"

Annie nodded, twisting her hands in her apron. "They're fine. Everyone's breakfasted but you two." She gestured to the captain, sagging in the rocker, face slack. "Would you like me to bring you some food?"

He shook his head, throwing a look of disgust toward the captain. "No, I couldn't eat a thing. Perhaps some coffee?"

"Coffee it is. What about the captain? Should I wake him?"

"I wouldn't advise it." Saunders's voice held a dry irony.

The captain must not be a morning person. She'd let him sleep. After the trauma last night, sleep was probably the best thing for him.

She whirled to go back to the kitchen, colliding with Nick in the doorway. His hands came up and cupped her shoulders, turning her insides to water. She hadn't seen him since last night. He'd had the early watch in the tower. Shadows clouded his blue eyes. No wonder, with the rescue and then having to stand watch.

"Nick, good morning." Did that sound as breathless as she felt?

"Good morning, Annie. How are your patients?" He backed up a step and dropped his hands to his sides. A faint bristle of whiskers covered his unshaven cheeks, and tired lines spidered out from the corners of his eyes.

"Mr. Saunders asked for a cup of coffee. I haven't checked on the captain yet. He seems to be sleeping quite soundly."

Nick bent over the captain, scrutinizing the bruise on the man's temple. He sniffed, frowned, and then poked the man in the shoulder. "Quite soundly." Nick's voice held a strange tightness.

"Come into the kitchen and I'll get you breakfast." She laughed. "Don't worry, it wasn't cooked by me. It will be quite edible, I assure you." She turned to Saunders. "I'll be right back with your coffee."

∽

Nick followed Annie into the kitchen. Women washed and wiped plates, carrying them into the pantry, bustling back out, chattering. He'd come through the front door of the house, hoping to catch Ezra alone in his office and avoid talking to anyone else until he spoke with his boss.

"There he is." One of the women, tall, with wiry red hair, rushed over to him and wrung his hand. "We want to thank you for saving us last night. I don't know what would've become of us if you hadn't come along." The women crowded around him, professing their gratitude, some wiping tears. One even kissed his cheek.

Annie caught his eye, obviously enjoying his embarrassment. She filled a coffee cup and went back into the parlor.

All the while, anger simmered in his gut. Last night had been too fraught with danger and exertion to be sure, but one look at the captain this morning had confirmed Nick's suspicions. He had to talk to Ezra.

The tall redhead pushed him down into a chair and plunked a bowl of steaming oatmeal in front of him. "Now, you eat up, Mr. Kennedy. There's plenty more where that came from."

Nick reached for a biscuit in the basket on the table, broke it open, and spread it with jam. He bit into it. It was good, but nothing like his Annie's biscuits. He stopped chewing. *His* Annie?

As if his thoughts conjured her up, she came back into the kitchen. He rose. "Have you seen Ezra?"

"Sit down, please. He and Clyde went to the east side of the island to look at the ferry awhile ago. He said they'd be back shortly."

Nick nodded. He finished the biscuit, ate a few bites of the oatmeal to be polite, and then stood. Before he could wend his way through the women, Ezra opened the back porch door and stepped in.

"The ferry survived, still perched on that rock. She's about a hundred yards east of the bell buoy. Looks like she might've run smack over it, the way it's bent. Someone will need to get out there and repair that buoy before too long."

"Can you come into the parlor?" Nick jerked his head toward the door.

Annie took up the coffeepot and headed into the parlor just ahead of them. She filled Saunder's cup again then picked up the bottle of laudanum from the end table.

Nick waited until she'd given the man a dose. "Annie, if you don't mind, I need to speak to—"

Nick's words were cut off by a growl from the captain. He stirred in his chair like a bear waking from hibernation, gripped his temples between his meaty paws, and groaned. "It hurts."

Annie darted to his side and knelt down. "Don't try to move, sir. You've had quite a knock on the head. I'll get you a headache powder right away."

Nick took hold of Annie's arm and lifted her out of the way. "Don't bring him anything." His voice was sharper than he'd intended.

Her eyes widened, and she looked down at his grip on her elbow.

His hand fell away. "I'm sorry. I need to speak to the captain before you give him any medicine."

Saunders propped himself up on his elbows. "His name is—"

"I don't care what his name is. To me, he's just another bottom feeder." Nick hauled the captain up by his lapels. He sniffed. Alcoholic fumes emanated from the man to the point Nick thought the captain might burst into flames if he got too near a candle. "You're drunk."

"Leave me alone." The captain's words slurred. His eyes looked terrible, bloodshot, with pinprick pupils.

"Were you manning the pilothouse when the ship went aground?" Nick glared at the sodden excuse for a lake captain. When the man didn't answer, Nick turned to the injured officer on the sofa.

Saunders lay back, eyes closed to mere slits. He nodded. "Captain had the wheel. Threw us all out of the pilothouse just after sundown. I went below to talk to the crew. The captain had been drinking off and on all day."

"And you let him take the wheel?"

Saunders gave a low chuckle then groaned and held his ribs, panting in shallow puffs. His face twisted in a wry grimace, half pain, half shame. "He used considerable force. He's a brute when he's drinking. I didn't get these bad ribs in the wreck. He tossed me out of the pilothouse like a piece of driftwood. I hit against the rail. Lucky I didn't go over into the water. I made it down to the engine room, barely. We were discussing a mutiny when the ferry ran aground."

The captain wavered on unsteady legs. "A mutiny? I'll have your liver, you two-faced coyote." He clutched his head again, his complexion turning gray-green. "Where's my whiskey?"

"How dare you!" Nick's jaw ached, his teeth clamped hard. He shook the man.

The captain howled. "My head."

Ezra stepped forward and placed his hand on Nick's forearm. "Maybe we should sober him up before—"

Nick shrugged Ezra off, too angry to think. "He wounded his own crew-man on purpose. He's soaked with liquor. This is dereliction of duty in all its worst forms, putting women and children at risk for no reason other than unbridled lust for liquor." A nasty taste grew in Nick's mouth. He turned back to the pathetic officer. "You were so drunk you ran over a bell buoy and grounded your ship at the foot of a lighthouse. You endangered the lives of your passengers and crew. You don't deserve to be a lake captain."

The drunkard's chin came up, a look of belligerent contempt gleaming from his bloodshot eyes. "Hah. You're one to talk. I know who you are, Kenne—"

Nick's fist shot out and caught the captain in the jaw.

The man's head snapped back, his eyes rolled, and he sagged in Nick's grasp.

Pain shot up Nick's arm, but he disregarded it.

Annie gasped.

Nick saw her out of the corner of his eye.

She put her hand over her mouth, her brown eyes wide in shock.

He gulped for air, tense as an anchor chain in a storm.

Annie blinked, staring at him as if at a stranger.

The anger drained from him. He released the man's lapels.

The captain sagged to the floor, sniffling and moaning.

Nick held up his hand to Annie, wanting to apologize, but the words lodged in his throat. He wasn't sorry for the punch. He'd gag if he tried to say he was. But he was sorry to have been such a brute in her presence. He swung away from her shocked face, shoulders quivering, fists clenched.

Ezra's troubled eyes met Nick's. "I wish you hadn't done that, son."

Before Nick could respond, the captain pushed himself to his knees. Spittle and blood flew when he opened his mouth. Though slurred, Nick understood him perfectly. "You'll be sorry for this. I'm Grover Dillon. My brother Jasper is your boss. He'll have your job for this." A thick sausage-like finger poked the air.

Annie's gasp sliced through Nick's heart. A ton weight pushed against his chest. He had to get away before he took another swing at that pathetic man. The doorframe wavered. He blinked, clearing his vision, then turned on his heel and strode out through the kitchen into the sunshine.

Emotions bounced around inside him like ball bearings dropped on a concrete floor. He turned his face to the warm rays, taking deep breaths, trying to calm himself. What had possessed him to punch that man? Violence hadn't solved anything. It only made his situation worse. Nick's hand throbbed in time with his heart.

What hurt the most was knowing that not all of his anger had been righteous. Had he punched the man for being a drunkard, or had he punched him to keep him from revealing Nick's identity? Nick knew the truth, though admitting it shamed him to the core.

He hung his head. *Lord, I'm a fool. I acted without thinking. Forgive me, please. And help me to bear it if the captain broadcasts the truth.*

The thought of the hurt in Annie's eyes should the truth come out made Nick wince. He had to avoid that at all costs. Nick flexed his hand and lifted his chin. At least his day couldn't get any worse. He nodded to two of the ferry refugees on the cobbled path.

"Say"—one of the men stopped on his way into the house and turned to study Nick's face—"you look awfully familiar. Haven't I seen you in Duluth?"

Chapter 13

When Nick volunteered to handle extra watches in the tower, Ezra couldn't hide his relief. A man of peace, Ezra no doubt wanted to keep Nick from punching anyone else.

In the two days since putting his fist into the drunk's face, Nick had remained in the tower and watch room. Clyde or Ezra brought him his meals, making him feel like a prisoner. Of Annie he'd seen nothing. His gut churned each time he thought of her. What might she say if the truth came out?

Would Dillon keep his mouth shut? Perhaps Nick should come clean with Ezra at least. For two days he waited for his secret to come home to roost, but nothing happened. His only escape from the lighthouse came when he and Clyde took one of the ferry's crew over to the grounded ship to offload some of their supplies to help feed and house the passengers.

Nick now stood on the catwalk outside the lantern deck, a fresh breeze ruffling his hair and making his pant legs flap like flags. He swept the horizon with the field glasses.

A tiny blot to the north gradually became more defined. A stack emerged, white steam trailing back. Gleaming decks and a red side wheel plowing the water. He waited. The boat came close enough for him to read the name, though he knew it by heart. *Jenny Klamath* in black and gold letters.

A gull rose above the level of the cliff and hung in the air only a dozen feet from the tower.

"We'll get these passengers loaded, especially *Captain* Grover Dillon"—contempt dripped from Nick's words—"and anyone else who might recognize me. Then things can return to normal."

The gull cocked his head, pinfeathers fluttering. He keened as if in answer then plummeted toward the water.

Several hours before, Ezra had raised the flag on the pole at the end of the dock, signaling for the ferry to stop on its way down-lake. The *Jenny Klamath* would be on the watch for it, as they always were when passing the light, and would soon slow and head toward the dock. The ferry's shallow draw allowed it to pull right up to the dock, unlike the supply ships which had to anchor well offshore and use a launch.

Would Annie be at the dock? Maybe he should go down there. No, better not to risk Dillon or one of the other passengers blowing the whistle.

A blast of the ferry's horn indicated she'd seen the flag. Nick kept the glasses on her until she disappeared behind the trees on the west side of the island.

The screen door on the house slapped repeatedly as refugees ventured out and headed across the clearing toward the gap in the trees that marked the path down to the dock.

Footsteps clanged on the metal staircase, and the heavy iron door scraped open behind Nick. He turned.

Clyde's blazing mop poked through the small opening. His blue eyes squinted in the sunshine. "Thought you'd be up here. Guess you'll be gladder than anyone to have all these people gone." His white shirt fluttered and flapped, molding to his narrow chest and wiry arms. "Captain Dillon is still growling like a bear with a bee-stung behind."

Nick lifted the glasses to his eyes once again. "Did he say anything more about me?"

"No, and that's mighty odd, because he's complained about everything else. Whenever your name comes up, he gets a weird gleam in his eye. I'd watch out if I were you. He means you no good, and that's the truth."

Clyde's open, sunny personality both refreshed and chided Nick. So many weeks of hiding his own identity, of watching every word, grated on him. The more he grew to like and admire Ezra, Imogen, and Clyde—and Annie, particularly Annie—the more distasteful his duplicity grew.

Clyde leaned his hip against the rail and crossed his arms, seemingly oblivious to the one-hundred-plus-foot drop to the water below. "Nick, have you ever courted a girl?"

The glasses came down. "What?"

Clyde's cheeks reddened until his freckles disappeared. He shrugged, whipped out his handkerchief, and rubbed a spot on one of the windowpanes. "A girl. Have you ever courted one?"

"I can't say that I have."

Clyde sighed. "Well, it's about time you did."

"Excuse me?"

"Miss Annie. I think you should court her. I was going to give it a try myself, her being so pretty and nice and all, but she'd never go for a guy like me. Anyone who's been around you both for more than ten minutes can see she's got feelings for you."

Warmth blossomed in Nick's chest. She did? In spite of himself he had to ask, "How do you know?"

"The last two days while you've been hiding in the tower"—he gave Nick a knowing look—"she's been wandering around like a lost kitten. No smiles, no laughter, and every time one of us comes back from bringing a meal to you, she asks how you are."

Nick pondered Clyde's words. Was it true? Could she have feelings for him? "If she cares so much, why didn't she come over and see me for herself?"

Clyde's boots scraped on the metal grating. "I don't know. Maybe she thought you didn't want her to. Or maybe she didn't want to look like she was setting her cap for you, especially since you haven't let her know you'd like to court her. Girls are funny that way." His lips pursed, and he nodded, all the wisdom of his twenty years gleaming in his eyes.

"And how is it you know so much about women?"

"I have nine sisters. A fellow has to learn a few things just to survive in a house like that."

Nick handed him the field glasses. "You can take the watch. I'm going to get cleaned up."

He mulled over Clyde's words. Did he want them to be true? And if so, what was he prepared to do about them?

∽

Annie took the last glass from Imogen and placed it on the pantry shelf. She squared up the bottles and tins of spices, each label facing frontward, each container even with the ones next to it. "We'll have to make note of the extra supplies we used for the guests."

"You've made marvelous progress, Annie." Imogen spread the damp tea towel on the bar on the inside of the pantry door. "Inspector Dillon won't find anything to cavil at when he returns."

Annie laughed, grimacing. "After the first disastrous inspection, I had nowhere to go but up. And I owe it all to you. You've been so patient. And the men. They've borne my ruined attempts at cooking with great fortitude. I think Nick wondered if he might starve to death when he caught sight of my first attempt at cooking oatmeal."

Imogen preceded Annie into the kitchen and poured them each a cup of coffee. "It's a good thing you've become such a marvelous baker. Cookies and pies and apple dumplings cover a multitude of sins." She smiled, her dark eyes glowing with friendship.

Annie took the cup Imogen offered and sat at the table. The silence wrapped around her like supple silk. No more crowds, no more people asking her for things, no more surly captain holding his head and swearing at her. Now things could return to the tranquil pattern of before. And Nick could come down from the tower once more.

Nick. She could admit to herself how much she'd missed him over the past few days, missed his easy banter with Clyde, missed reading aloud with him in the room, missed their discussions of novels and politics and nature when the reading was done. And most of all she had missed him during yesterday morning's worship service. Though the parlor had been crowded with people, for Annie it had seemed empty without Nick to lead them in prayer, to discuss the passage read.

Imogen sat down opposite Annie, a worried frown on her brow. "Annie, I know it isn't any of my business, but I've noticed how you watch Nick and how your face lights up when he comes into the house."

Annie focused her gaze on Imogen, heat easing into her neck and up her cheeks.

Imogen moved her cup in small circles, staring into it. "Nick is a fine man, to be sure, but you need to be careful. Living here in such close quarters, sometimes you can feel things for someone, or think someone feels things for you, when it's really just a matter of proximity." She looked up, dark eyes entreating Annie to understand. "I just ask you to take care. You're young, and Nick's very handsome. But we all have lives away from here: other things, family, commitments, and such. Just go slow, all right?"

Annie dropped her gaze to her lap and twined her fingers together. Was it just proximity? Would she feel the same about Nick if she'd met him on a busy street in Duluth? "I appreciate the warning, Imogen. I really do. You don't have to worry. I won't rush into anything. I'd best get back to work, and you should rest. You've worked too hard the past few days. I'll straighten up the parlor myself."

She was still folding blankets and moving chairs when Nick came into the house. She knew his footsteps instantly, and her heart thumped more quickly in response. In spite of her words to Imogen about not rushing, she couldn't help her response to him.

"Annie." He stood in the doorway, his hair windblown. Caution clouded his eyes, a wariness she hadn't seen in him before.

"Nick." She dropped the afghan onto the back of the rocker, so happy to see him after his self-imposed isolation. "There's fresh coffee." She joined him in the kitchen, lifting down an enamel mug.

"Annie, I want to apologize for my behavior." He sounded as if he had a ball of yarn in his throat.

She handed him the coffee, puzzled.

"I shouldn't have been such a brute in your presence." His blue eyes studied her, making her skin tingle. "That captain deserved a thrashing, but I should've taken things outside. I'm sorry. No lady should have to watch such undignified behavior."

"Please don't apologize. The captain got nowhere near what he deserved. I'm only sorry it drove you out of the house for a few days."

He took her hand, sending ribbons of heat swirling through her. "You're most generous. I'd like to make it up to you somehow. I'll tell you what. I have to fix the bell buoy on the east side of the island and check on the ship.

Salvagers showed up this morning to start patching her and getting her off the rocks. Why don't you come with me on the lake? It's a warm day. We might even do a little fishing."

Annie's mouth went dry. Go out on the lake in that tiny boat? Cold sweat prickled her skin like hundreds of ants. With everything in her heart she wanted to go with him, to spend time alone with him. But fear cloaked her. Memories mocked her.

"Annie?" He stepped closer, his clasp on her hand tightening.

"I'd like to, Nick, but—"

"I know you don't like the water much." He stood close. "I've seen how you won't venture out on the dock. Falling into the lake your first day here must've been terribly frightening. But that's in the past, and you're fine now. I wouldn't let anything happen to you. I'd really like you to come."

No. I can't. Never. I'd die of fright.

"Yes, Nick. I'd love to go."

Chapter 14

Walking down the trail through the trees to the dock, Annie wondered for the thousandth time in the past hour what had possessed her to agree to this. Her other hand rested in the crook of Nick's elbow, the muscles playing beneath his shirtsleeve doing nothing to calm her jumping heart.

Lord, what was I thinking? I can't do this. I can't. How can I cry off without looking a fool? Help me. Help me get through this. I can't do this.

Her mind kept up a constant prayer. She cast a glance back up the slope through the trees to the tower. The beginning of the Proverb Ezra had read at services her first Sunday on the island played through her head.

"The name of the Lord is a strong tower: the righteous runneth into it, and is safe."

A strong tower. God is a strong tower. A refuge.

A trickle of calm flowed into the maelstrom inside her. They reached the foot of the dock. She could do this. With God's help, she could do this.

"I can't do this." She stopped the instant her feet scraped on the damp wood. Her hand slipped out of Nick's arm, and she scooted back to the safety of dry land. "I can't."

He turned quizzical eyes upon her. "The dock's sturdy. Look." He jumped and landed on the boards with a *thud*. "Solid as the cliff she's fastened to." He smiled, his teeth white against his tanned skin. "Well, maybe not that solid, but no woman as small as you is going to unsettle it." He held out his hand, beckoning her to follow. "I'll keep you from falling in again."

A strong tower. A strong tower. A strong tower.

Against everything within her, her hand reached out for his. Here in the lea of the island, the breeze sighed, and the waves swished and gurgled almost playfully. She looked down but quickly raised her eyes. She didn't want to see the water moving between the boards under the dock. It might sound playful, but she knew the dangers lurking there.

She suddenly recalled his last words. "I didn't fall off. I was pushed." Her chin came up. The very idea that she'd fall off the dock like some ninnyhammer.

He shook his head. "Naw, I think you weren't looking where you were going and tumbled in."

"I did not. Clyde hit me with a mailbag. You were there. You saw the

210

whole—" She stopped when he laughed.

"Look, you made it all the way to the boat." Nick nodded toward the small craft bobbing on the waves. He wore a smug expression.

"You teased me on purpose." The knot in her stomach loosened a coil.

"Worked, didn't it?" He stepped into the boat and braced his feet against the rocking motion. "I'll help you in. And this time, no throwing up on my boots. It's calm as a baby's naptime out there today. You shouldn't get seasick." His eyes twinkled. He beckoned for her to come closer to the edge.

What on earth was she doing getting into a rowboat? Her feelings for Nick had addled her brains.

He put his hands on her waist. Her fingers shook as she settled them on his broad shoulders. As if she weighed nothing, he lifted her, swinging her into the boat. She sagged onto a seat, her heart knocking wildly as the boat wobbled.

Tools lay in the bottom of the rowboat, clanking gently. Nick slipped the rope from its mooring and used an oar to shove away from the dock.

Annie put her hand on her chest, trying to assist her breathing. How was it all the wide outdoors didn't have enough air to fill her lungs? Her knuckles turned white and ached from her one-handed grip on the gunwale.

Nick fitted the oars into the oarlocks and pulled. The boat shot away from the dock.

A strong tower, a strong tower, astrongtowerastrongtower. "A strong tower."

"What's that?"

She opened her eyes, barely realizing she'd closed them.

Nick eyed her questioningly.

"I was quoting that Bible verse we read the first Sunday I was here. Proverbs 18:10. 'The name of the Lord is a strong tower: the righteous runneth into it, and is safe.' I've read that verse over and over, and I learn something new each day about how God is a strong tower."

Water rushed against the hull, slapping, chuckling, taunting her. She stared at Nick's face, trying to draw strength from him, trying not to let the memories clawing inside her head overtake her.

Nick looked over his shoulder and up the cliff face to where the lighthouse emerged as they rounded the north end of the island. "That's a good verse for here."

A shout reached them from overhead. Clyde leaned over the rail, waving down to them.

"He's a nice boy." Annie pried her hand from the edge of the seat and dared a quick wave up to him.

Nick laughed. "He's older than you are."

"Is he? He seems so young."

"Tell me about yourself, Annie. I know nothing about you except you love to read and you make a terrific apple pie. Oh, and to steer clear of your oatmeal." He eyed her with a grin, waiting for her response.

She made a face at his teasing. What could she say? *My name is really Anastasia, and I've run away from home? I'm the daughter of a mining tycoon who wants me to marry a complete stranger in order to bolster his fortune?*

She settled for the story she'd told Imogen. It was true, if not complete. "I grew up in Duluth. My father works in mining, in Hibbing mostly. My mother passed away when I was young."

"Any brothers or sisters?"

A hard lump formed in Annie's throat. "One brother, but he died when I was small. What about you? Any siblings?"

"Two brothers." He shrugged. "One older and one a few minutes younger. I'm a twin."

"Really? Does he look like you?" She shook her head at the thought. There couldn't be another man as handsome as Nick Kennedy.

"Similar, but not identical. He's back East right now learning a trade."

"What about your parents?" She relished this chance to get to know him better.

"My mother died in childbirth. My father followed not long after in a carriage crash. My brothers and I were raised by my grandparents."

"Have you always been in the lighthouse service?"

He shook his head, looking past her shoulder. "No, but I've always worked around or on the lake." The chop increased, the breeze tugging at his hair. He pulled on the oars, eyes staring far away, watching the water, the cliffs, the sky. He had no fear, completely at ease. "A great day for making good time on the lake. The *Jenny Klamath* should be almost to Duluth by now."

She nodded, not taking her eyes from his face. If only this boat weren't so wide, she could grip both sides. Her muscles ached with tension.

Gulls squabbled overhead, diving and hovering, white-gray flashes in the afternoon sunshine. A loon bobbed on the waves near the cliff base. It dived, disappearing from view only to pop up a dozen yards away, lightning fast.

"There are some mighty big fish that live amongst these rocks. Sturgeon the size of lifeboats."

She questioned him with a glance. "Lifeboats?" She didn't want to think about lifeboats, nor the need for them.

"Well, maybe not that big. But there are some monsters down there just waiting to be caught."

Monsters. "Do you think Captain Dillon will cause trouble? I've never seen a man so angry."

Nick shrugged. "He might, but it would be risky for him. The passengers and crew can testify that he was stone drunk the night of the wreck. He'll lose his job if nothing else, and he might even face criminal charges. Getting revenge on me might be the least of his worries."

"Was he telling the truth about being the inspector's brother?"

Nick grinned. "Who would claim to be Jasper Dillon's brother if he really wasn't?"

Annie surprised herself by laughing. "True. Though I didn't see any family resemblance, unless you count overall crankiness."

They swung around the north side of the island and headed east. The chop increased, small creaming froth appearing on the tops of some of the waves.

"You all right? No seasickness?" He pulled his feet away from her. "My boots aren't in danger, are they?"

Annie shook her head, smiling in spite of the fear. This wasn't so bad. *A strong tower. A strong tower.*

Nick steered them away from the island, covering an expanse of open water.

Annie caught her first glimpse of the stranded ferry. Several boats dotted the surface around the ship, men striding the decks, throwing ropes to one another, hammering and pounding.

"They've started the repairs. I don't think it will take them long. She isn't really wounded as much as just stuck. If they can get her off the rocks without inflicting too much damage, they can tow her in. I see they've brought bilge pumps. Maybe they can pump fast enough to compensate for the water she might take on between here and Two Harbors. If she isn't too badly crippled, they might even tow her to Duluth, where they can more easily make the repairs." Nick swung their boat around to get a better look at the lakeward side of the ferry. "Good thing she's shallow drafted. An oar boat would've ripped wide open on these rocks." His voice sounded far away and sad, as if recalling events that brought him pain. He shook his head and pulled on the oars again.

From a distance a faint clanking reached Annie's ears. The bell buoy. She prayed it wouldn't take Nick long to make the repairs, though she had to admit, being out here in a boat wasn't as bad as she'd feared.

They approached the buoy. Nick whistled. "He hit her square. All she needs is a little hammering to straighten her out. That and a new coat of paint, but we'll have to wait on that until we get some on the next tender." Nick shipped his oars, allowing the boat to glide alongside the red and white frame of the buoy. He reached out and grabbed the buoy, halting their forward progress. "Hand me that line, would you, please?"

Annie glanced down to the pile of rope at her feet. She groped for the end with one hand, frustration clenching her stomach when she couldn't unwind it properly. She'd have to let go and use both hands. Finger by finger she peeled away from the gunwale. Her heart thudded in her ears. She almost laughed when she realized she was pushing down with her legs, trying to anchor herself more firmly in the boat. The line untwisted, and she handed it to Nick. A rickety breath rushed into her lungs. This wasn't so bad, was it?

Then Nick stood up. The boat bucked side to side, a little water slipping in over the edge.

Annie pitched toward the lake, a shriek erupting from her throat. At the last instant her hands locked onto the seat.

Nick looked at her over his shoulder, tying the boat to the buoy. "What?" He scanned the water around them. He studied her as he bent to pick up a hammer, sending the boat rocking again.

"Don't! Please!" To her shame, sobs bolted out of her throat. She sank to the floor of the boat, still gripping the seat, eyes clamped shut. The sound of water roared in her ears. She imagined it closing over her head, shutting out the world of light and air, imprisoning her within its frigid clasp.

"What's all this?" Nick's warm hands closed over her shoulders.

She clutched at him, eyes popping open, lungs gulping air in great gasps.

He knelt in the bottom of the boat, enfolded her in his arms, and stroked her hair. "Annie? What happened? You were doing so well."

She gripped his shirtfront. "Don't stand up. Don't. You'll tip us over. Please, don't stand up."

"I won't." He held her tight against his chest, letting her cry. "Shh, it's all right. You're safe, Annie. I won't tip the boat over. I promise."

The bell clanked over and over with the rocking of the boat.

She sniffed and hiccupped.

He gallantly pushed a handkerchief into her icy hands.

She gripped it in her fist as she clung to his shirtfront. "I'm sorry. I thought I could do this. I'm so sorry. Please, take me back."

"I'm the one who should apologize. I pushed you too hard. We'll go back now." He settled her on the seat and picked up his oars. With mighty pulls they surged over the surface of the water.

Annie couldn't bear to look at Nick. She had failed. He must think she was an idiot. She *was* an idiot. One little lurch of the boat and she turned into a quivering mass of hysteria. She bent her head and kept her eyes on her shoe tips until the boat bumped into the dock.

Nick began to tie the craft off.

Annie didn't wait for him to help her. She scrambled onto the planks and all but ran to dry land.

Hard thuds followed her, and Nick's hand gripped her elbow. "Annie, wait."

214

Tears of humiliation and guilt ran down her cheeks. "Let me go, please, Nick."

"I can't let you go like this. Tell me what happened out there."

"No, I can't." She struggled in his grasp, but his grip tightened.

He gave her a little shake. "Annie, tell me."

The truth burst out, though it cost her mightily to voice the words. "My brother died on that lake. And I killed him."

His hands fell away from her, and she made her escape, sobs nearly strangling her as she struggled up the steep slope, away from his look of shocked horror.

∽

Nick stood still for one moment then headed after her. He castigated himself for being so prideful, thinking if he just got her out in a boat she'd be fine, that *he* could cure her of her fear. When was he going to learn not to be so arrogant?

He heard her before he saw her. Her dry, rasping sobs pierced his heart. She reached the clearing, panting, shoulders shaking.

"Annie, stop."

She halted, arms stiff at her sides, one hand clutching his handkerchief. Her chin nearly touched her chest. A tear dropped to the ground.

He couldn't help it. She looked so forlorn and helpless. He put his arms around her, tucking her head under his chin. She smelled of flowers and sunshine, and he didn't care that someone might see them. He only wanted to take away her hurt or share it somehow.

"I'm sorry, Annie. I had no idea." He brushed a kiss across her hair. "Please tell me what happened. I don't believe for one minute you killed your brother."

Contentment settled into his chest when she put her arms around his waist. They stood like that for a long moment, too short a time in his mind, before she pulled back, wiping her eyes with his handkerchief.

He led her to a fallen log on the edge of the clearing, crouching on one knee before her and keeping hold of her hands. "Tell me, please."

"It happened a long time ago, when I was six. Neville was eight. We were visiting friends of my parents who had a house on the lake. There were no other children to play with and nothing to do, so Neville and I ventured down to the shore to throw rocks into the water." She twisted her fingers together in his grasp, not looking at him.

"Go on."

Her delicate throat worked as she swallowed and continued. "Father told us to stay off the dock, but we were bored. Neville bet me I couldn't run to the end of the dock, touch the boat shed, and run back faster than he could." A wisp of a smile tugged the corner of her mouth. "He was always betting me one thing or another, and I was always trying to prove I was as good as he was. Father never had much time for me, but he doted on Neville. Took him everywhere, treated him like a pet. I guess I always wanted to be as good as Neville so my father would love me, too." She hiccuped.

"We raced a couple times. Each time Neville won. I couldn't bear his taunting, so I challenged him to get into the rowboat tied to the dock. Neither of us could swim, and this was the height of daring, especially considering how furious Father would be if he caught us." Her voice caught for a moment. Nick released one of her hands to brush several strands of hair off her cheek and tuck them behind her ear. He cupped her cheek and stared into her troubled brown eyes, trying to give her strength.

"Neville said just getting into the boat would be too easy. He bet me I'd never have the nerve to get in the boat with him and row out a ways. He told me no girl would ever be that brave."

She hung her head, but he put his finger under her chin and raised her face to the light. When he opened his mouth to tell her she didn't have to go on, she shook her head and rushed on as if now that she'd begun she had to finish the story. "We got in the boat, and Neville untied it. He pushed us away from the dock. I couldn't believe he'd actually done it. The oars were so big, Neville couldn't manage them both. He ended up pulling on only one, and we twisted and turned circles, all the while drifting farther and farther away from the dock. I got more and more scared, and I started to cry. I begged Neville to get us to shore. He shouted at me to quit crying and grab the other oar. I tried to, but I knocked it into the water and it floated too far away for me to reach."

Her tears flowed freely. Sorrowful memories filled her eyes. She didn't see Nick at all, it seemed, so focused on the past, only long-ago images filled her mind. "Neville yelled at me, calling me stupid. I suppose if we'd both kept our heads, someone would've rescued us, but we panicked. Neville stood up in the boat to try to reach out with his paddle to get back the oar I'd dropped. The boat rocked and flipped over, pitching us both into the lake."

She closed her eyes, her hands gripping his in her lap. For long moments she sat perfectly still. His heart ached for her. She roused and looked into his eyes. "I managed to climb onto the upturned boat and cling to it until help came. I called and called for Neville, but he had disappeared. They found him the next day, but they wouldn't let me see him. I wasn't even allowed to go to the funeral. My mother went into a decline and passed away not long after. My father has barely spoken to me since. He blames me for Neville's death, but no more than I blame myself."

She disengaged her hands. "So now you know my worst secret, Nick Kennedy. I killed my brother. If I hadn't been trying to best him, he'd still be alive today." An empty look came into her eyes, utter defeat.

He smoothed his palms down her upper arms and gripped her elbows. "Annie Fairfax, what utter nonsense. You were a child. Your brother's death was an accident. You were no more culpable in his death than I."

She shrugged his hands away. "If it wasn't my fault, then why does my father think it is? Why won't he talk to me? Why won't he love me?"

She rose and tried to brush past him, but he blocked her way. "Grief makes people do strange things. Maybe your father didn't know how to handle his sorrow. Maybe he didn't know how to treat a little girl who was also grieving. But Neville's death wasn't your fault. It was an accidental drowning. You have to stop blaming yourself."

"How?" The cry burst from her throat as if under pressure. "How can I not blame myself? Everyone who has ever loved me has blamed me for his death. My mother, my father, I think even Haze—" Her voice broke on a sob.

Nick brought her into his arms again. "Annie, those people are wrong. And you're wrong. Stop punishing yourself. If you don't, this will eat you alive." Guilt stabbed him.

What a hypocrite I am. I'm preaching what I don't practice. But this is different. I was a grown man, not a little girl trying to outdo her brother. I should've known better than to try that harbor run. I should've done something different. If I had, my crew would still be alive.

Annie relaxed in his arms, spent with emotion.

Nick cradled her against his chest for a moment, then stepped back a half pace. He took her face in his hands, using his thumbs to swipe away the last of her tears. He was all kinds of a fool, but he couldn't stop himself.

∽

The instant Nick's lips settled on hers, Annie knew she'd been waiting for this moment for a long time. Clasped in his arms, sheltered, secure, she gave herself over to the wonder of his kiss. The salty taste of her tears mingled with the sweetness of knowing herself cherished by the man she'd come to care for so deeply. In that instant, she dreamed a thousand dreams, made a thousand plans, let her heart soar.

With the abruptness of being thrown in the lake, Nick broke the kiss and pushed her from him.

Annie blinked, stunned. Had she done something wrong?

His hands fisted at his sides, and his breath came in gasps. Those lips that had so recently caressed hers formed a hard line. He swallowed hard. "My apologies. I had no right to do that. It won't happen again, I assure you."

"Nick?" Her hand went out to him. "You don't need to apologize."

He shook his head, staring past her shoulder toward the lighthouse. "You have no idea, Annie. There are things that prevent me from—" He broke off and turned away from her. "I'm sorry." He strode across the clearing and disappeared into the watch room.

Annie sank to the fallen log and buried her face in her hands. Great sobs wracked her shoulders, sticking in her throat. She wiped her eyes once more with his handkerchief, noting the bold NNK embroidered in navy blue on the white linen. How could he be so kind and gallant on the one hand, and so cold and distant on the other?

She had bared her soul, her deepest shameful secret to him, had dared to dream he might be able to look past that and love her anyway; but in the end, she was as alone and unlovable as ever. And she had no one to blame but herself.

Chapter 15

I t's your turn, Annie." Clyde twirled his mallet like a baton.

Annie nodded and bent over her ball. How incongruous, to be playing croquet when the entire world had crashed to bits around her. Imogen and Ezra seemed oblivious, seated on the porch swing, rocking gently, shaded from the Sunday afternoon sun. Against her will, her eyes strayed to Nick. He stood beside the porch, arms crossed, staring past the lighthouse to the waves beyond. In the two days since he'd kissed her and walked away, he hadn't said a word to her.

His kiss. As she had done a thousand times, she allowed her mind to race back, to remember every second in his arms, the feel of his lips on hers. Then, like a bucket of lake water in the face, the cold shock of his dismissal struck her. She blamed herself. Her actions had been too emotional, too forward. She should've kept control, held her tongue and buried the truth about her brother's death. By baring her soul, she'd opened herself up for rejection.

For an hour after he left her in the clearing, Annie had cried out to God, opening places in her heart that she'd tried to keep hidden from Him. Broken, she laid it bare before Him. All her guilt, her feelings of abandonment, of loneliness, she brought out for Him to touch, to heal. She asked for and received forgiveness and peace.

With His forgiveness came the knowledge that she had to confess her identity to her employers. A great weight lifted from her when she determined to do the right thing. Though her heart ached for Nick, she felt cleansed and renewed. "Thank You, Father, for loving me in spite of who I am. Please give me the strength to do what You want me to do." Now she just needed to find a way to tell Imogen and Ezra the truth about who she really was. And Nick. She'd have to confess to Nick one more of her secrets.

She whacked the ball, sending it well past the wicket. It rolled across the grass and came to rest under a hawthorn bush. If only she knew how to broach the subject with Nick, to apologize and somehow get their relationship on an even keel again.

Clyde rubbed his ear and sauntered over to her. "You all right, Miss Annie?"

She tried to smile but had a feeling she didn't pull it off too well. "I guess I'm just not in the mood to play today. I can't seem to concentrate."

219

He nodded then inclined his head toward Nick. "Like someone else. Guess he's got a lot on his mind these days waiting to see if the boom is going to be lowered for him poking Grover Dillon in the nose. Rotten luck him turning out to be the inspector's brother." Clyde took the mallet from her hand. "Nick's been touchier than a nest of wasps for a couple days now. Though I shouldn't complain. He's taken extra watches in the tower the past two nights."

So that's where Nick had been. Annie had missed him at mealtimes and especially in the evenings in the parlor. She hadn't been able to make herself ask after him. It mortified her that he would avoid her this way.

"I'll put the game away, Miss Annie. It's almost time for the sing-along."

"Thank you, Clyde. Maybe we can try again next Sunday." *If I'm still here next Sunday*. She mounted the steps to the porch and sank into a chair.

Imogen lay with her head back against the swing. Her mouth tensed in a line, patient forbearance stamped on her expression.

"Headache again?" Annie leaned forward and took Imogen's hand where it lay limp on the arm of the swing.

Imogen nodded, not opening her eyes. "Just a touch."

"Can I get you anything? Tea? A cold cloth?"

"Thank you, child. I'll just rest here. The fresh air helps."

Ezra looked up from his newspaper and frowned. "Perhaps we should cancel the sing-along today."

"Oh no, Ezra. I love the music." Imogen shifted and opened her dark eyes, entreating him. "And Clyde plays so well. Please?"

Ezra nodded, smiling, but eyes still clouded with worry.

Annie envied them their closeness, the assurance and security of their love for one another. Imogen, willing to brave being ill in this isolated spot so she could be with her husband. Ezra, doing all he could to make his wife happy, to ease her suffering as much as possible, allowing her to be here with him because that's what she wanted most. Just yesterday he'd come into the house with a bouquet of spring wildflowers, eager as a young suitor. And hadn't Imogen blushed like a bride at his attention?

Annie's gaze went to Nick again. He stood with his back to the porch, studying the west horizon. His white shirt stretched taut across his shoulders. She could see his face in three-quarter profile—the strong jaw, the dark brows, watchful eyes scanning the water. A fitful breeze gusted, blowing his hair and fluttering his sleeves. Though he stood no more than twenty feet away, the gulf between them yawned. She longed to go to him, to recapture the closeness of the past. But she couldn't risk his rejection again.

"Looks like some weather building in the northwest." Nick didn't turn around when he spoke.

Annie followed his gaze. A low smudge of gray hung in the sky, ominous, but far off. Another gust of air scurried past, whipping up puffs of dust from the path and bringing the smell of rain.

Ezra nodded. "It's been a quiet spring so far. We're due for a storm or two. Is the dingy in the boat shed?"

"All secure." Nick crossed his arms. "It will be a good night to be inside, I think."

Clyde came up the walk from his quarters, guitar in his hand. He settled himself on the steps and strummed the strings. "Any requests?"

"'It Is Well with My Soul.'" Imogen lay back again, her voice barely above a whisper.

Clyde's clear tenor drifted out. Annie lay back, allowing the music to soothe her rumpled spirits. As he sang of the great forgiveness that was hers through Christ, she relaxed, her heart unclenching. God's forgiveness was unconditional. He already knew her deepest secrets, and He loved her anyway. That would have to be enough.

She watched Nick through half-closed eyes. Though his actions had hurt her, she didn't blame him, not exactly. There could be no hope of a future together unless she told him who she really was. Would it make a difference? Would the fact that she was a wealthy heiress matter to him? The entire charade had become so burdensome, a barricade between her and the people she had come to care about. All at once the situation was intolerable. Annie sat up, resolved to come clean. She braced herself to rise. Nick deserved to know first, in private. She would apologize for her emotional display of two days ago and tell him the truth about running away from home. Then she would tell Imogen and Ezra. She owed them that much for their kindness to her.

A whistle blasted the air, freezing Annie in a half-standing position.

"That sounded like the *Marigold*." Ezra bolted up, his paper falling to the porch floor in a rustling fan.

Imogen sat up, holding her hand to her head, squinting against the pain. "The *Marigold*? Isn't that just like Dillon, calling on a Sunday with a surprise inspection?"

Annie's heart turned to ice. The lighthouse tender. Inspector Dillon. She did a mental gallop through the house. The kitchen was spotless. Fresh cinnamon rolls sat on the counter under a cloth. Would he consider them a bribe? The kitchen inventory lists hung on a clipboard by the pantry door, as up to the minute as she could make them. And her room. He wouldn't recognize the place. Neat as a sheet. Bed made, belongings in the drawers, not a hint of dust, not even under the iron bedstead. She'd even washed the windows yesterday.

The group burst into activity. Nick and Clyde sprinted across the grass to their quarters to don their uniforms. Ezra scooped up the newspapers and thrust them into Annie's arms. He checked his buttons and cuffs while Imogen straightened the cushions and folded the afghan she'd used as a shawl.

Annie hurried inside to put the paper on the shelf in the parlor and to check her appearance in the mirror in the tiny hall. She repinned a few locks the breeze had displaced and made sure her blouse was neatly tucked into her skirt. She made a face at her reflection. If only the inspector had held off another half hour she might have been able to get Nick alone. At least she would have been able to confess her identity and get out from under this load of guilt.

At the door, she hesitated. Should she don her apron over her dress? No, not on a Sunday afternoon. Inspector Dillon would have to take her as she was.

When Annie stepped back onto the porch, Imogen took her hand. "The men have gone down to the dock. We'll wait here for them."

Annie's hands trembled. She took a deep, shuddering breath. *"The name of the Lord is a strong tower." Lord, we're running to You. Keep us safe.*

∽

Nick braced his legs apart and clasped his hands behind his back, never taking his eyes off the launch that bobbed toward the dock. The west wind shoved the waves before it into the shore, whitecaps crashing on the rocks, sucking and slurping under the dock beneath his feet. Storm clouds continued to build to the northwest, black and surly.

Ezra stood beside him. "You know I'll speak on your behalf to the inspector."

Nick shook his head. "Don't jeopardize your career for me. Sutton Island needs you. The Lighthouse Board needs you. Don't throw away a thirty-year career fighting with Jasper Dillon. I can take whatever he dishes out."

"That may be true, but I don't want to see you hung out to dry because of a personal matter. If Grover Dillon wasn't his brother, he would've read the report and put it out of his mind instead of showing up here to condemn you for it."

"Maybe he dislikes his brother and is here to give me a medal." Nick's lips twitched, and he cast Ezra a sidelong glance.

"This is no joking matter." Ezra frowned. "If he fires you, where will you go? Do you have funds to live on until you find another job? You know I'll give you a reference."

Guilt raced across the back of Nick's neck. He had more funds than Ezra Batson had seen in his lifetime. He had a name, power, finances, a share in the largest shipping company on the lake, not to mention a mansion and a family—all of which he'd turned his back on and hidden as if he were ashamed of them. But he wasn't ashamed of his family, only of himself.

"I'll be fine if he cuts me loose." But would he really? Being fired meant leaving the island, leaving Annie. The past two days had been horrible, wanting to go to her and tell all but knowing he had no right to. Knowing she would reject him if she knew who he was and what he had done. And how could he ask for her hand when, in truth, he was betrothed to another? The pain of knowing he'd hurt her, that she didn't understand why he had walked away, ground upon his soul. He longed to be free of the entanglements of his past so he could pursue and win her.

The launch neared the dock, and Clyde hurried out to grab the lines and make her fast.

Inspector Dillon climbed out of the boat, belligerent expression in place, reminding Nick of a pugnacious rooster.

Nick forced himself to relax, to unclench his fists and loosen his jaw.

Dillon turned back to the boat and assisted a woman onto the dock. She stood no more than five feet tall, her face wrinkled, eyes bright. A bonnet covered most of her hair, but what Nick could see was pure white. He glanced at Ezra, who shrugged and shook his head.

Leaving the woman to trail behind, Dillon strutted up the dock. Clyde lifted bags, presumably the woman's, and followed. The inspector stopped before them, scowling at Nick. His nose wrinkled as if he had encountered a foul smell.

"Inspector." Nick stepped forward.

Dillon looked him over from head to toe. "If you thought I wouldn't hear about your behavior, you are sadly mistaken. However, I have no intention of conducting business here on the dock with weather coming in. We'll discuss your situation in the house like civilized individuals." The words burst from him, as if he expected Nick to wrestle him to the ground and demand to know his punishment that moment. Dillon looked over their shoulders to where the path disappeared through the trees. "I see Miss Fairfax didn't come down to the dock. Well, I'll deal with her in good time as well." He motioned to the old woman. "This is Miss Thorpe. She'll be taking over Miss Fairfax's duties beginning today."

Nick's heart lurched. Annie was leaving the station?

Dillon smirked. Pompous little fool, swelled up with his own power. He needed a proper lesson—like a dunking in the lake.

Lord, help me keep my temper. And help Annie. She's going to be devastated.

"Is that really necessary?" Ezra smoothed his hands over his brass buttons. "We have no complaints with Miss Fairfax. She's settled in quite well."

"You may have no complaints, Mr. Batson, but the Lighthouse Board feels differently."

"The Lighthouse Board or just you?" Nick's eyes narrowed.

Dillon's lips curled in scorn. "You are in no position to chide me, sir. I would suggest you concern yourself with your own situation. I'll concern myself with

Miss Fairfax." He turned his back and started up through the trees.

Clyde shouldered past with the bags, eyes downcast, freckles standing out across his pale face. Nick stood aside to let him pass.

Ezra's brows came together, but he offered Miss Thorpe his arm to assist her up the steep path. "Welcome to Sutton Island, Miss Thorpe."

"Please, call me Hazel."

Chapter 16

Annie recognized the stooped figure instantly. Emotions clashed in her chest—homesickness so sharp she wanted to cry, regret that she hadn't been able to confess to Nick before he found out on his own who she was, resignation at her father sending Hazel to fetch her home, a tinge of anxiety at the welcome she would receive when she faced him.

She searched Nick's face for the disappointment she knew would be there. But he bore only a look of concern, his brows down, his eyes troubled.

Dillon sneered and puffed out his chest, small in stature, small in mind. Seeing him again left a stale taste in her mouth, and she found her lips tightening. He'd no doubt relish her unmasking. She braced herself for his unsavory comments.

"Miss Fairfax, this is your replacement, Miss Thorpe. I'm officially relieving you of your duties, effective immediately. Miss Thorpe is more than capable of running the household and assisting Mrs. Batson. You may pack your things. The ferry will pick you up tomorrow morning and return you to Duluth. You are no longer needed here."

Annie blinked.

Hazel stared hard at her, her eyes willing Annie to keep silent. Her former governess stepped forward, holding out her wrinkled hand. "Pleased to meet you, Miss Fairfax. I'm sure you'll be able to show me over the house and my duties before the morrow." Hazel gripped Annie's hand so hard Annie's knuckles popped.

She cleared her throat. "Miss Thorpe." The words came out strained. Annie now knew how the birds felt when they flew into the tower windows. Blinded, stunned, reeling.

Dillon mounted the stairs and swept the group with an imperious glare. "If the gentlemen will assemble in the parlor. You women won't be needed for our discussions."

"I'd like the ladies to be present." Nick's face was casual, but his voice held a challenging edge.

Dillon pursed his lips, his weedy mustache poking out. "Very well, but I warn you, this is not a social gathering." He swept into the house, his shoes squeaking on the polished floor.

Annie didn't know what to think.

Hazel pulled her down to whisper in her ear. "Not a word until we can talk."

Annie nodded, sure she couldn't speak even if she knew what to say. Her legs resembled wooden planks as she shuffled, stiff-kneed, into the house. Hazel was here, Annie had been fired, and now Nick's livelihood was on the chopping block. This day couldn't possibly get any worse.

∽

They filed into the parlor like a jury into a courtroom. Nick elected to stand by the fireplace, not wanting Inspector Dillon to look down at him. He'd take whatever the inspector had to say standing up.

Something about Annie's demeanor disturbed him. She kept darting glances at the new housekeeper as if she expected that lady to do something unpredictable. And Miss Thorpe missed nothing, her black eyes moving from face to face, studying, evaluating. He doubted anyone could fool Miss Thorpe for long.

Dillon sat in the wingback chair and placed his feet primly side by side, withdrawing a sheaf of papers from an inner pocket. He perched a pair of glasses on his narrow nose and studied the pages, though Nick was sure the inspector knew the contents by heart.

The silence stretched.

Clyde coughed and dug for his handkerchief, snorting loudly. "Sorry," he muttered, stuffing the red cloth back into his hip pocket.

"Mr. Batson, I am here to inform you that I shall be making further changes to your staff effective immediately. This man"—he gestured toward Nick—"has been deemed unsuitable as an employee of the Lighthouse Board."

Ezra straightened. "Mr. Dillon, Nick is an exemplary worker, and his character is of the highest quality. I agree that in this one instance he might've chosen a better way to express his opinion, but he had considerable provocation. Your brother was quite drunk and belligerent."

Nick winced. *Don't do it, Ezra. Think of your career.*

Dillon scowled. "Mr. Batson, I have reviewed the incident fully. While my brother's actions were regrettable, this man had no right to assault him. That sort of behavior is unworthy of an employee of the Lighthouse Board. But that is not why he is being released. You say his character is above reproach? I beg to differ."

Nick's gut clenched. A terrible sense of foreboding swept through him, leaving him weak and unsettled.

A sneer spread across the inspector's face. "This man has been lying to you from the day you met him. He obtained this position under false pretenses. The man you know as Nick Kennedy is, in truth, Noah Kennebrae, disgraced captain of the ship *Bethany*. If I had known his identity when he applied for employment, I never would've hired him. He knew this and lied to gain this position."

Shame thrust up in Nick's chest. He looked from one face to another.

Ezra and Imogen regarded him with shock. Clyde with stunned awe. Dillon bared his teeth in a feral smile of triumph. But Annie, the one he cared the most about, sat like a stone, face pale, eyes wide.

"Annie, I—" He what? How could he explain to her?

Dillon tapped the papers on his knee then put the last nail in Nick's coffin. "Mr. Kennebrae, now would be a good time for you to return to Duluth. I spoke with your grandfather just yesterday. He informs me that your betrothal is on the verge of being announced in the papers. No doubt your bride will wish you to attend your own engagement party. She must be most anxious for your return."

Grandfather! Nick grimaced. He should've known the old man wouldn't take his defection lying down. But to announce the engagement in the papers? Without even knowing where Nick was? No, Abraham Kennebrae wouldn't do that. Jonathan must've told Grandfather where Nick had gone. His fists tightened. He'd have a word or two for his older brother when they met again.

A sob caught his ear. Annie rose, her eyes wide and accusing. "Engaged?" She blinked, sending a tear cascading down her cheek. "You're engaged to be married?" Without waiting for an answer, she fled, shoulders shaking, head bent.

Dillon rose, snickering. "Well, it seems your betrothal comes as a shock to the young lady. Just what sort of relationship do you have with the girl? Perhaps it is best both of you are leaving the island. The Lighthouse Board will not tolerate loose morals amongst its workforce."

Nick's hands shot out and grabbed Dillon by the lapels. He hauled the shorter man up until he stood on tiptoe.

Blood drained from Dillon's face, his eyes stretching open until white showed all the way around his irises.

Nick towered over him, panting. "How dare you besmirch that girl's character! She's as innocent and pure as spring rain. Don't judge everyone by your low standards, you guttersnipe." He shook the inspector. "You've waltzed in here, eager to hurt and ruin and destroy. Well, you've accomplished your mission. But know this, if you ever cross my path again, if you ever utter one word against Annie Fairfax, I'll see you pay for it. I'll throw every bit of influence the Kennebrae name has behind seeing you ruined and thrown out of the Lighthouse Service." Nick released his grasp, and Dillon fell back in the chair in a heap. Nick's hand shook with the urge to haul the petty little man upright again and punch him as he had the drunken captain.

Ezra stepped between them, putting his hands on Nick's upper arms. "No more, son. You've defended her honor. Anything more would be wrong."

For a long moment, Nick stood still, muscles tense, pulse throbbing. Then his head dropped, his shoulders sagging. He had to go after Annie, to try to explain. If only he'd come clean two days ago instead of walking away from her.

Lord, I know I shouldn't ask You for help getting out of my own tangled lies, but if You could please help me find a way out of this, a way of telling Annie the truth, I'd be grateful.

He headed into the kitchen. A gust of wind caught the screen door, yanking it open then whipping it shut with a *crack*. With quick steps he crossed the floor to stick his head outside. A gust pushed against his face, chill and moist, a precursor to rain. Black clouds tumbled overhead, darkening the sky. Annie would have to wait. He started toward the tower. With inclement weather rolling in, he must get the lamps lit.

His footsteps clanged on the metal stairs. He jogged upward, eager to do his duty and then find Annie. Though his hands raced, pumping the fuel tanks, checking the gauges, lighting the kerosene wicks, his mind raced faster. What could he say to her? How could he make her understand about his grandfather and his family and the loss of his ship that prompted his escape in the first place? Would she listen to him? Would she understand?

The lamps flared to life, momentarily blinding him as he shut the panel and ducked out from under the lens. He hustled down the stairs to release the pin holding the chained weights. The lantern began to revolve. Nick blinked, grasping his watch to check the timing. Perfect. Ironic, that. Everything in his life had exploded into chaos, but the light mechanisms rolled on.

He stepped outside the watch room and from habit scanned the lake. The dark hulk of a freighter plowed through the rising waves. Nick grabbed a pair of field glasses from the hook inside the door and held them to his eyes. No name showed on the bows. Every inch of the ship gleamed with new paint. She bucked, her nose slewing a bit. Why didn't her captain straighten her out to face the waves instead of taking them quarterways? If the storm broke in a fury, the boat could swamp, or worse, roll completely over.

Nick jerked the glasses down. He didn't have time for this. He had to find Annie. Before he could return the binoculars to their hook, a distress whistle pierced the stormy air.

Chapter 17

Morse flashes began from the pilothouse. Nick grabbed a pencil and paper from the watch room desk and began transcribing the signals.

CAPTAIN INJURED. MUST REACH DULUTH QUICKLY. NEED YOUR HELP, NOAH. WILL SEND LAUNCH. ELI. CAPTAIN INJURED. MUST REACH DULUTH QUICKLY. NEED YOUR HELP, NOAH. WILL SEND LAUNCH. ELI. CAPTAIN—

Nick quit transcribing, the pencil falling to the grass. Eli was on that ship? And he knew Nick was on Sutton Island? The distress whistle pierced the air again.

Clyde and Ezra hurried around the corner of the watch room. "What is it?" Nick held out the paper to Ezra. "It's my brother. They need help."

Ezra scanned the page. "Clyde, you're on the watch. Make the proper journal notation. Nick, er, Noah? I hardly know what to call you. Captain Kennebrae?" He stared intently at Nick's face.

Familiar guilt pierced Nick's chest at the mention of his former title. All the doubt, the pain, the shame he'd been running from for months crowded back, rooting him to the spot.

Captain.

He couldn't go, couldn't step onto the deck and assume command ever again. He couldn't run the risk of making another mistake, of taking the lives of innocent crewmen.

Ezra peered through the glasses. "They're putting out a launch. Water's getting wild out there."

A fat raindrop pelted Nick's cheek. The cold water startled him, shaking him to life. "What does he think I can do?"

"You can get that ship into the harbor safely."

Nick studied the ship. A brand new boat, probably only a skeleton crew aboard. With the captain out of action, there likely wasn't another crewman aboard who could take a ship into Duluth in a storm. Especially riding light and getting kicked around in a wind that would only worsen as the storm rolled over.

"You have to go, son." Ezra lowered the glasses. "You're the only one who can help them."

Still Nick stood, rain falling faster. He couldn't do it. And yet, if he didn't, wouldn't he be condemned anyway? *God, what are You trying to do to me?* "I'll go. Have Clyde pack my gear on the ferry tomorrow." He thrust out his hand. "I know I have a lot of explaining to do, and if I had time I would. For now, know that I appreciate everything you've done for me and that I regret deceiving you."

Ezra shook his hand, looking him square in the eyes. "Son, I can guess at your reasons. And I don't hold anything against you. Your brother needs your help. Get down to the dock quick now, and go with God."

"Signal the ship that I'll meet the launch." Nick tossed the words back over his shoulder as he headed for the path to the water. "And tell Annie I'm sorry."

∽

Annie stood beside the window of her bedroom, arms crossed at her waist, head leaning against the curtains. Raindrops streamed down the panes, making the trees and buildings outside watery blobs of color. Every ten seconds the beacon swept overhead, its light shaft spearing the downpour.

No wonder he walked away from me. He's got a fiancée in Duluth.

What was she like? Was she beautiful? Nick. . .no, Noah—she must think of him as Noah Kennebrae now—was returning to his family to marry someone else. Another tear slipped down her cheek.

At least she hadn't broken down and told him her own identity. He never would've believed her. Here she was running from an engagement set up by her father, straight into the arms of a man who had a woman he loved back in Duluth. Of all the idiotic things to do. Why hadn't Ni—Noah told her? She never would've dreamed such fanciful, impossible dreams about him if she'd known he was in love with someone else.

Someone tapped on the door. She didn't answer. She didn't want to talk to anyone, especially not Noah Kennebrae.

The door opened. "Annie, child." Hazel.

Annie stood still. She'd grown up enough in the past six weeks to resist the urge to throw herself into Hazel's comforting arms and let her governess soothe away some of the hurt. A hard lump formed in Annie's throat.

"Anastasia, stop pouting and listen to me. I didn't come all this way for you to ignore me." Hazel's sharp, familiar tone forced Annie to turn around, but she kept her arms crossed in a defiant gesture. "Now sit down and let me talk."

Annie walked to the end of the bed and sat, pressing her hip into the footboard.

Hazel took the chair beside the dresser and positioned it so she could sit face-to-face with Annie. She eased her small body down.

"Child, I've regretted helping you leave Michaelton House since the moment you escaped. I've wrestled with my Lord and with my conscience every day. I had no right to help you defy your father, and I'm guilty of lying to him. But no more. I know you won't like it, but I've told him exactly where you are. I contacted Jasper Dillon and arranged to take your place. Jasper doesn't know who you are, and that's just the way your father wants it. Mercy, was he angry." She rolled her eyes and shook her head. "They've had the police looking for you and everything. I could hardly stand not telling them you were all right. Your father was so worried about you. I couldn't have him fearing the worst, and I couldn't stand lying to him anymore."

Lies. Everywhere lies. Annie let her hands fall to her lap. She was so tired of the lies. "It's all right, Hazel. You know, just this afternoon I screwed up my courage to come clean, to tell everyone here who I was. I guess it doesn't matter now. The one person I really wanted to tell was hiding secrets of his own."

Hazel's dark eyes searched Annie's face. "Just what do you feel for that man, Noah Kennebrae?"

The sound of his name made prickles of shame race up her arms. "I don't feel anything for Noah Kennebrae. I thought I loved Nick Kennedy, though." Her voice came out in a whisper. "I did love him."

Hazel crossed the room and sat beside Annie. Her thin, old arms came around Annie's shoulders. "Annie, girl, I'm sorry. I wish I'd never gone along with helping you escape. I didn't think of all the trouble it would cause. Your father is sending a launch for you in the morning. He didn't want you on the ferry for fear someone might recognize you and ask awkward questions. He'll meet you in the harbor as soon as you dock. Do exactly as he says. He's going to bluster at you, but trust me, he loves you, and he was worried about you. Things will turn out for the best. Just trust me."

"Trust you? Trust isn't coming easy these days. I can't even trust myself."

"Well, if you can't trust me, then trust the Good Lord. He knows what is best for you, and He says to obey your father. Have a little faith."

Annie said no more. She had never felt so alone, so abandoned before. Even Hazel had taken her father's part. But it didn't matter anymore. She'd lost Nick forever. Without him, she might as well fall in line with whatever future her father had planned.

∽

Nick met the dingy at the dock and hopped aboard without even waiting for them to tie up. Now that he'd made the decision to go, he wanted to get there as quickly as possible. Rain lashed his face; spray kicked up before the bow of the launch, splashing into the boat. The two-man crew fought to keep the craft pointed into the waves. Nick grabbed a bucket and bailed the water sloshing around his boots.

The ship lurched on the rough seas, bobbing as the surf increased. Lightning split the sky, followed by a *boom* of thunder. Nick ducked instinctively. The clouds opened. He swiped the water from his eyes and shivered. Even in early June, the storm chilled to the bone. His mind balked at what he was about to do, but his heart had no choice. Not when his brother, his twin, needed him.

The small boat pulled alongside the freighter, the boats crashing together. A rope ladder flopped over the side. Nick grabbed the wet hemp, his boot slipping on the soaked wooden rung. A wave slapped the side of the freighter, dousing him with icy lake water. His teeth clattered together.

Hands reached down from the railing above and grabbed his shoulders and arms, heaving him onto the deck. Around him, ropes were hurled down to the men in the launch to make fast so the small craft could be winched aloft and lashed to the deck.

Nick clung to the rail, getting his sea legs, then made his way to the pilothouse. Warm light showed in fuzzy, rain-smeared halos from the windows. He couldn't help but notice that this ship was designed exactly like the *Bethany*, from the pilothouse to the deck to the smokestack. Horrible feelings of déjà vu swept over him. Familiar, terrible, walking-through-his-own-nightmare feelings.

Eli met him at the pilothouse door. His brother—younger by twenty-three minutes—grabbed him by the shoulders and pulled him into a mighty hug. Relief etched his features. "I can't tell you how glad I am to see you. We're in a mess."

And Nick was supposed to get them out of it? His stomach roiled, weakness radiating out from his middle and draining his limbs of strength. What was he doing here?

Eli pulled him into the pilothouse.

A gust of warmth hit Nick's face. Steam heat. Water dripped from his clothes onto the floor. Everything was just the same—the pilothouse, the chart room behind, the brass chadburn, all exactly like the *Bethany*.

"Get out of that wet jacket. Here, put this on." Eli swept a coat off a hook beside the door to the chart room.

Nick shucked the sodden garment and shouldered into the rough, dry wool coat Eli handed him. In the center of the pilothouse, behind and to the right of the wheel and helmsman, the captain's chair stood bolted to the floor. Nick averted his eyes. He couldn't sit there. He couldn't let these men place their lives in his hands. "Where's the captain?" Perhaps the injury wasn't too bad. Perhaps the captain would be here soon to take over.

"We put him in his cabin. He slipped going down the ladder into the engine room and hit his head. Bled like crazy and he hasn't woken up. I think he broke some ribs in the fall, too. The cook is sitting with him. He needs more doctoring than we can give him."

The helmsman gripped the wheel, brow scrunched, face pale. The ship took another broadside wave and rolled.

Nick grabbed the back of the captain's chair, bracing himself. "Helm, ten degrees right rudder." He hadn't meant to bark the order, but the words forced their way out of his throat. "All ahead two-thirds." His hand grasped the cold brass handle of the chadburn, and he dialed down to the engine room for more power. "Keep the bow pointed into the waves." The mantle of command crowded about him with uneasy familiarity.

Eli clapped him on the back. "Boy, am I glad you answered my call."

"What are you doing on the lake in a green boat with a skeleton crew? I thought you were in Virginia."

Eli braced against the pitch of the hull. "She's the *Kennebrae Siloam*, fresh off the ways of the shipyard. Grandfather cabled me to pick her up in Detroit on the way home and get back to Duluth on the double. Said I couldn't miss your engagement party. He's still sore I didn't make it back for Jonathan's wedding. The question is what are you doing on Sutton Island?"

Noah shook his head. Grandfather's scheming was another thing he'd have to deal with, but not now. "Later." He tapped the helmsman on the shoulder. "Straighten out that bow and stop looking at the compass. The pull of the iron ranges throws the compass off course. Keep your eyes peeled for the Two Harbors light. Even in these conditions, you should be able to pick it up fairly soon." Like they had that fateful night last November. He should've tried the turn into Two Harbors instead of running for Duluth. Then maybe his men wouldn't have perished.

Lord, I can't do this. Why have You brought me back here to this place? Why have You put another crew's fate in my hands?

To take his mind off his reeling thoughts, he turned to Eli. "I suppose Jonathan told you where I was?"

Eli braced his legs and held onto the rail running under the pilothouse windows. "Don't be sore at Jonathan. He was all set to come get you himself a month ago, but Grandfather told him to wait. Something about the wedding plans being on hold and Sutton Island being as good a place as any for you to wait. Jonathan's letter wasn't all that clear."

"I'll bet." Noah rubbed his face.

"Sir?" The helmsman gripped the wheel, holding it hard against the force of the wind and waves. "Will we be trying to make Two Harbors?"

At that moment another scalding shaft of lightning arced across the sky. Noah blinked against the black spots hovering in his view.

Eli spoke up, "The captain needs doctoring, but I think Duluth is his best chance. I'm not even sure if there is a doctor in Two Harbors."

Memories swamped Noah. The *Bethany* bucking and heaving in the storm. The decision not to try to make the turn into Two Harbors. Jonathan's face, so pale. Everyone relying on Noah to know what to do. He swallowed hard. "How many crew members aboard?"

"Eight, counting the cook. Two stokers—they came to get you in the launch—two deckhands, an engineer, the helmsman, the cook, and the captain. Then there's you and me." Eli ticked them off on his fingers. "Ten, all together. And, Noah, we're light on fuel. With no load and a quick run from Detroit to Duluth, they didn't top up the coal bunkers."

A hollow pit Noah had been trying to ignore swelled in his middle. Low on fuel, green boat, skeleton crew, huge storm. If the captain downstairs weren't in such dire need of medical attention, the smart thing to do would be to drop anchor and ride out the storm, maintaining just enough power to keep them headed into the waves. Noah tugged on his bottom lip, wishing he had his whiskers back to rub while he thought.

"Call everyone to the pilothouse."

Chapter 18

Men crowded the bridge. The cook elected to remain below with the captain. Every face regarded Noah solemnly. The helmsman continued at his position; the others lined the walls of the small room.

"Men, there's no sugarcoating the situation. The safest course is to drop anchor and wait out the storm. You all know the risks of attempting a harbor run in rough seas. The captain is in a bad way. I don't know if he's going to make it, but his chances are better if we can get him to a doctor."

One of the crewmen, a grizzled man with enormous white side-whiskers, shifted a plug of tobacco in his mouth. "I say we risk it. I been with the cap'n for nigh onto twelve years now, and he deserves a chance." Several voiced their agreement.

Noah nodded. "We're riding light with no load. Fuel's low, so we have to commit one way or the other soon. Either we shut down all but the bare minimum and ride things out, or we pile on the coal and get to Duluth as quickly as possible. You all know me, you know what happened the last time I captained a ship in a storm." He braced himself, but not one crewmember cast him a reviling glance. "But I'm willing to try to get us into the harbor."

Eli clasped him on the shoulder. "Noah, you're the best captain on the lake, and these men know it. We'll do everything we can to help you."

Fear churned in Noah, hot and cold by turns. Their faith humbled him. "Very well. Stokers, get down to the boilers, and get to work." He turned to the engineer. "Throw her wide open. You and you, you're the deckhands, right?" Two narrow, lean men nodded, their slickers dripping water. "One of you get downstairs and relieve the cook and tell him to make sandwiches and coffee, lots of coffee. The other will stand by to relay messages and carry the food to the crew."

"What shall I do, Noah?" Eli raised his brows.

"Stay here and watch with the glasses. Daylight's fading. The instant you spot the harbor light, give a shout. I'll be watching, too." Noah settled into the captain's chair and gripped the arms. "And all of you, pray."

The men dispersed to their stations.

In less than five minutes the ship surged ahead, the engine throbbing. Waves broke over the bow, sending water pouring over the deck. With no cargo, the ship bobbed like an empty bottle on the waves. Noah braced himself for each roll.

235

Eli clung with one hand to the window frame, the other pressing the glasses to his eyes. "Awfully hard to see anything. The sky and the water are starting to merge."

Nick nodded. "It will get worse before it gets better." Images of the *Bethany*, of the storm, the faces of his crew members, flashed in his head. He second-guessed his decision a hundred times. What if he failed? What if history repeated itself and he lost another ship?

He thrust the thoughts aside. For the sake of the man lying injured on the bunk below, the crew would risk the narrow harbor entrance. For the captain's sake and his own, Noah would return to Duluth and all he'd fled two months ago.

"What did Jonathan say about the engagement?" He didn't really want to know, but it gave him something else to think about.

Eli shrugged. "Just that it would be in the papers by the end of the week. Noah Kennebrae to wed the daughter of Phillip Michaels."

"Michaels? The iron tycoon Michaels?" Noah remembered seeing his name on a few Kennebrae manifests, but most of his ore was handled by their archrival, Gervase Fox's company, Keystone Steel. "So, Grandfather plans to get all of the Michaels shipping contracts, does he?"

"Yeah, didn't he tell you who the girl was?"

"I didn't discuss it with him. I guess I didn't want to know. Maybe I thought if I ignored it, the problem would go away." How foolish. By stepping out of the discussion, he'd done nothing but give Grandfather a free hand.

"The Michaels's business would certainly keep the fleet busy. Between the grain from Jonathan's marriage and the ore from yours, we'll need half as many ships again just to cover the contracts. Which will give me the perfect opportunity to test out my new ship design." The pilothouse lurched, rolling as a wave caught her off the port side.

"Don't get ahead of yourself there. I'm not marrying the Michaels heiress."

Eli whipped around. "That's not what Grandfather says. How're you going to get out of it?"

"I'll just tell Grandfather I'm in love with someone else, and I intend to marry her." *If she'll have me. If she can forgive me. And if I can find her again once she's left Sutton Island.* His heart thudded thickly in his throat. His beautiful Annie. He hadn't even gotten to say good-bye. As soon as he confronted his grandfather and this girl he was supposed to wed, he would begin his search.

Eli grinned. "In love with someone else? Who is she? And boy, is Grandfather going to be surprised. I can't wait to see what he says. That should be some show."

"I wouldn't be so complacent if I were you. He might just have you take my place with this Michaels girl."

Eli shook his head. "I'm married to my work. Grandfather will have to accept that. I wouldn't give up shipbuilding to marry any woman."

"Eli, you've never been in love. That's your trouble. If you had, you'd give up anything, any dream, any hope, to win the woman you love." The ache around Noah's heart intensified. He had to find Annie, to make her understand how much he loved her. And he had to get free of his grandfather's entanglements.

"Two Harbors Light, sir."

Noah's jaw tightened. He could play it safe and swing the boat into the security of Agate Bay. He could dodge the gauntlet of the Duluth ship channel. But the injured captain needed a doctor in Duluth.

The helmsman flicked a questioning glance his way.

"All ahead full, helm." The light at Two Harbors slid by on their starboard side. No turning back now.

The ship pitched and plowed through the waves for what seemed an eternity before a faint glow appeared through the gloom ahead.

"Duluth Harbor Light, sir." The helmsman peered through the window.

Noah tensed. "Left rudder five degrees. Line up on the starboard light. Bring her around." *Lord, help us. You promised to be a strong tower. We need that strength now.*

Several ships lay at anchor beyond the channel, riding out the storm before trying to enter the docks. Noah scanned the shoreline. The *Bethany* no longer lay broken on the shoal just outside the piers. He could be grateful for that at least.

Waves thrashed the piers, spewing up gray white foam, surging over the seawall higher than a man's head. The *Kennebrae Siloam* bucked and heaved, her nose plowing the water, targeting the window formed by the transport bridge.

"Reduce power." Noah's mouth went dry. He had little recollection of the *Bethany's* wreck, having been tossed to the floor and rendered unconscious when she bottomed out in the channel. But what he'd awakened to was something he had no desire to relive. "Correct your course, helm. Waves hitting three-quarter on the port bow. Steady at the wheel."

Eli moved to stand behind Noah, holding the back of the captain's chair just as Jonathan had done seven months before.

Noah's hands ached from gripping the arms of the chair.

The bridge loomed ahead. Green water heaved against the bows. Lightning streaked the sky, precursor to a clap of thunder that shuddered through the steel hull and rattled the panes of the pilothouse.

The nose of the ship entered the canal. Rain ran down the windows. The green light of the pier lighthouse bathed the ship momentarily in an eerie light.

Noah could barely breathe. "Steady, helm." A heavy wave smacked the ship mid-keel. She slewed, kicking the stern toward the pier. "Watch the cross current as soon as she noses through the channel."

The helmsman hung on as the ship bucked, spinning the wheel to edge the nose toward the starboard pier and bring the stern back in line. He wasn't quick enough, and the stern bounced off the steel and concrete pier, the impact vibrating through the ship.

For a moment, Noah closed his eyes, certain a repeat of the *Bethany* disaster was about to occur.

Eli grabbed Noah's shoulder.

Noah's eyes popped open. He dialed the chadburn, asking the engineer for more power. A rumble shot through the ship as the pistons responded to the increased steam from the boiler. The ship surged forward, scraping momentarily against the pier but righting herself and leaping under the bridge supports.

"You did it!" Eli grinned and punched Noah's arm. "I knew you could."

Noah brushed his brother's praise aside. "Signal the tugs. Take us into any empty Kennebrae dock, and signal that we require medical assistance."

"Aye, aye, Captain Kennebrae."

Captain Kennebrae. A bittersweet homecoming indeed.

∽

Two hours later, Noah shouldered through the doors of Kennebrae House into the foyer, stripping off his coat as he went. Carved oak pillars stretched to his right and left down the grand hall, and overhead crystal chandeliers winked. The imposing staircase dominated the space, curving off on either hand to the balcony above. The sound of cutlery and china clinking drifted from the dining room at the end of the house.

The butler took his coat, eyes bright with welcome. "Mr. Noah. It is good to have you home, sir." The seasoned servant concealed whatever surprise he might have felt at Noah's appearance behind a long-practiced mask of imperturbability. Some things never changed.

"McKay, is Grandfather at supper?"

Eli shoved his way in the front door. He dropped bags, coat, and an armful of chart papers in a heap on the marble mosaic of the entryway. "McKay! Now I know I'm home." Ignoring protocol, he wrapped the butler in a bear hug.

"Mr. Eli, it's been too long, sir."

"That it has. And I brought the prodigal home with me." Eli flashed a boyish grin. "Or maybe he brought me home. We had to make a harbor run in the dark in the teeth of this storm." As if to punctuate his words, lightning flashed through the stained glass windows above the landing before them, bringing to colorful life the lotus blossoms and birds held captive in the leaded design. The thick walls and slate roof of Kennebrae House muffled the thunder to a distant roar.

McKay motioned for them to follow him toward the dining room.

"Mr. Noah and Mr. Eli, sir." He announced them and withdrew.

Massive silver candelabra graced the mahogany table. In the flickering candlelight, Grandfather's dark eyes gleamed but registered no surprise.

Jonathan rose from his position at Grandfather's right hand, a smile splitting his normally sober expression. "Noah, Eli, welcome home." Jonathan advanced to shake hands with them. His eyes studied Noah's face. "I had no idea you were coming home tonight."

Melissa pushed back her chair and joined them, kissing Noah on the cheek. "Welcome home, Noah." Her face held questions and compassion in equal measure. She squeezed his arm. "I'm glad you're back. I've missed you." She turned to Eli. "And you must be Eli. It is so good to meet you at last."

Eli grinned. "Johnny, old boy, you sure came out the winner catching this gal. Melissa, Grandfather sent me a copy of your wedding photo. Your picture doesn't do you justice. You are loveliness itself." He kissed her warmly on the cheek and hugged her. "Too bad I wasn't here at the time. I'd have snatched you up before Jonathan knew what hit him."

Jonathan cocked an eyebrow at Eli, who stalked around the table to greet Grandfather.

Noah braced himself for battle and followed.

Grandfather sat straight in his chair. Gaslight from the wall sconces ran along the metal arcs on his wheelchair. His snowy hair lay like a helmet on his large head. The Kennebrae tartan blanket in his lap covered his stick-thin legs. Everything Noah loved and everything he resented about this man clashed in his breast.

"Noah, Eli, I'm pleased you've returned. Sit down, have some dinner." Grandfather motioned to the discreet screen in the corner beside the silver hutch.

A maid's white cap bobbed, and she disappeared into the kitchen.

"I was just about to tell Jonathan and Melissa about the party tomorrow night at Michaelton House."

Eli pulled out a chair beside Melissa, leaving Noah to sit beside Jonathan. "Party? What a nice homecoming." McKay set a plate before him and placed cutlery and glasses. Eli dug into the meal as if he hadn't eaten in a week.

When the butler set food before him, Noah's gut churned and tightened.

"Though it is nice that your homecoming coincided with Noah's, the party is intended to announce and celebrate Noah's engagement." Grandfather took up his glass and sipped, staring at Noah with a challenge in his eyes.

Noah stared at his plate for a moment then raised his chin. "Grandfather,

I have no intention of going through with this marriage. I won't put myself or some girl through it. Call off the party, extend my regrets, and get this notion out of your head."

Jonathan turned to Noah. "Noah, you don't have to call things off. I know you were upset when you left, but I have some news for you that might change things. We hauled the *Bethany* into dry dock, and the engineers have been going over her."

Noah braced himself to hear what he already knew.

"We've conducted interviews with the remaining crew, and we've had two independent shipbuilders go over her. The wealth of evidence states that you made the only choice you could under those circumstances." Jonathan's gaze pierced Noah.

Noah leaned forward, his hands gripping his knife and fork.

Jonathan continued. "You remember how she was listing even before she hit the canal wall? The engineers say part of her hull had buckled and was taking on water. You had no choice but to attempt the harbor run. If you had laid out at anchor, she'd have gone down in a matter of an hour or so." He grinned broadly. "Everyone agrees that you saved our lives. Though some were lost, and we grieve for them and their families, more were rescued. You can stop blaming yourself. The *Bethany* will be out of commission for a while, but she'll be back on the lake next spring, maybe even this fall. You're not a failure. You're a hero. In fact, a reporter from the Duluth paper was at the shipyard today to hear the verdict. It will be all over town by tomorrow that you deserve the highest praise."

"Here, here." Eli raised his water glass. "I knew it. And you saved our necks today. This hero gambit is getting to be quite a habit with you."

Noah sat in stunned silence, processing Jonathan's words. For so long he'd assumed he'd made the wrong choice, that he'd jeopardized his crew. Could his brother's words be true? Had he made the right decision? Relief, questions, absolution, all crowded his mind.

"I'd like to go look at her when I have a chance." He forced the words through his thick throat. After he found Annie. Everything else was second to that. Surely she'd be aboard the *Jenny Klamath* when it returned to Duluth. He'd meet her at the dock tomorrow and confess everything.

"Me, too," Eli agreed. "And I want to talk to you, Grandfather, about implementing some of my new designs. The *Bethany* refit would be just the opportunity I need to try them out."

Grandfather nodded, his fingers steepled beneath his chin. "Good idea. Go tomorrow. Just be back here in time to leave for the party."

Noah's shoulders sagged. "I told you, Grandfather, I'm not getting married, at least not to the Michaels girl."

Grandfather's fingers fisted and he banged the table. "You will. The contracts are ready. Philip Michaels has already signed. The invitations to the party went out last week."

Noah narrowed his eyes. "Last week? But you didn't even know I'd be back in town. Or did you?"

The old man's chin lifted. "I knew it. I planned it. How do you think that unctuous little inspector knew your real name? When those ferry passengers you rescued returned to town, one of them came to see me. He recognized you as the captain of the *Bethany*, but you were using a different name. That's when I contacted the Lighthouse Board and let them know they had an imposter in their ranks. I knew they'd fire you and you'd be back here within the week."

"You had me fired?" Noah pushed his chair back.

"I wanted you home." Grandfather's back straightened. "I wanted you to stop running from your responsibilities. Now you're here, and you're exonerated from any wrongdoing regarding the *Bethany*. You're free to marry."

Noah stood. "When will you stop manipulating people? I'm not a chess piece for you to shove around and use to conquer your opposition. I have no intention of marrying this Michaels girl. Cancel the party, inform her family, and leave me alone. You don't have the hold over me that you had over Jonathan, though I'm pleased at how that all turned out."

He nodded toward Melissa, who smiled softly in return.

"I've proven these past two months that I can take care of myself. I'm not afraid to walk away from all this." He waved his hand toward the ornate room. "In truth, my heart belongs to another. I have every intention of marrying her when I find her again."

Grandfather scowled and tossed his napkin down. "Don't be a fool. Think of what your marriage would mean to the company, to Eli, who is filled to bursting with new shipbuilding ideas. If you marry into the Michaels family, we'll need at least six new ships, probably ten, to carry their ore. If you won't do it for yourself, then do it for your family. And who is this girl you say you love? Is she wealthy?"

"She's as poor as a fishwife, but I don't care. I'm not marrying her for money."

Noah regarded each of them—Grandfather, imperious and demanding; Jonathan, sober, staring at his hands in his lap; Eli, eager-eyed, chewing thoughtfully. And Melissa, her blue eyes filled with compassion.

Jonathan cleared his throat. "Don't blackmail him, Grandfather. Noah should marry for love. If he loves another, he should be free to pursue her."

Grandfather wheeled his chair back, expression dark. "Well, I'm not going to do his dirty work for him if he's as ungrateful as that for all the work I've done. He owes the girl and her family an explanation. He should at least meet his fiancée before he ruins her character by refusing to marry her."

Melissa nodded. "Noah, I don't deny you should have the right to marry whomever you choose, and I wish you success in winning the girl you say you love. But having been in this situation myself"—she smiled at Jonathan—"I know I would've been devastated and ashamed if I'd heard secondhand that my fiancé had broken the engagement. Please, at least meet the girl and tell her yourself. She might be grateful, and she might even be sympathetic to your cause."

Eli swallowed his last bite. "What about the party?"

Melissa's mouth firmed up. "If the invitations to a party have already gone out, it's too late to call things off." She turned to Grandfather who still fumed, glaring at Noah. "I wish you had informed me before now. I would've offered to help with the preparations."

"Don't be daft." He cleared his throat and softened his tone. "Michaels has it under control, I'm sure. I wanted it to be a surprise. You shouldn't be working so hard, not in your condition." His voice softened. "You have to take care of yourself."

A delicate blush colored her cheeks, and her eyes went soft.

Jonathan stood and placed his hand on her shoulder. "Noah, Eli, you can be the first to congratulate us. Another Kennebrae will join us late this fall."

Eli surged to his feet and enveloped Melissa in a hug.

Noah offered his congratulations, but his mind seethed against his grandfather.

"I can't believe you would do this to your family, Noah. My reputation is on the line, millions of dollars at stake, and you're just thinking about yourself." Grandfather wheeled himself from the room.

Jonathan shook his head. "Don't worry about it, Noah. You know how he is. He'll get over it."

Noah shook his head. "I wish I could do as he wants, but I can't. I can't marry someone when I love another." He imagined Annie's face when he met her at the dock. His lips twitched. Perhaps he should wear an old pair of boots.

Chapter 19

Annie gathered her belongings around her. What would her father say? At least the trip had been smooth, all traces of the previous day's storm washed away. The *Lady Genevieve*, the private yacht of one of her father's friends—at least that's what one of the crew told her before showing her to the forward salon and shutting her inside—slid through the channel, the gulls dipping and wheeling around the steel girders of the bridge.

Had Hazel given Imogen Annie's letter explaining everything? Would Imogen, so kind and gentle, be able to forgive Annie for deceiving her? Would Hazel be able to explain all that Annie couldn't?

She leaned close to the porthole and took in the familiar skyline. A bittersweet smile twisted her lips when they passed the ferry dock. How long ago it seemed that she'd forced herself onto the ferry to begin her journey to Sutton Island.

The vessel eased into a berth. Annie stood and adjusted her hat, tugged her gloves on tighter, and picked up her valise. She could hardly believe how little she cared that she was on a boat. Evidently a broken heart was an excellent cure for an unreasonable fear. She supposed she had Noah Kennebrae to thank for helping her get over her terror of boats and water...and she had him to thank for the broken heart, too.

Stop it, Anastasia. Stop thinking about him, and concentrate on what you're going to say to your father.

Even the gangplank gave her only a moment's unease. She nodded to the crewman and headed down the incline. Her boots hit the dock, her valise bumping against her leg.

A hand grabbed her elbow. "Anastasia." Her father's voice was like a breath of icy air in the late-June afternoon. "This way."

So, he'd come to meet her. She swallowed and dared a look at his face. His expression was as cold as his voice. His grip tightened, as if he feared she would disappear if he let go.

"Hello, Father." Guilt at the trouble and worry she'd caused him sat like a sodden stone in her chest. Her apology rushed out. "I'm sorry. I never should've—"

"For goodness' sake, Anastasia, not here. Wait until we get home." He took her valise and tugged her up the dock.

She trotted along behind, trying to hold her hat on. Shame heated her cheeks. No welcome, no thankfulness for her return. Instead she got a frigid reception and a reprimand for showing emotion in public.

They stopped beside a shiny new automobile. A chauffeur in a long white duster and driving gloves stood beside the curb. He stepped up to take the bag from her father's hand.

Her father held the back door and motioned to Anastasia. "Get in."

"Is this yours?" Anastasia gawked at the gleaming black paint and the shining windows. Her father had been skeptical of the newfangled automobiles and had resisted purchasing one before now.

"Of course. It arrived just after you left." He pursed his lips. "It won't bite you. Get in."

Anastasia gathered her skirts and ducked to enter the rear seat. Plush velvet yielded to her touch. She tried to make herself smaller when her father seated himself beside her. She couldn't help noticing the brass and wood, the wool carpet, even the crystal bud vases hanging on the divider between the front and back windows on each side. Work conveyance or not, her father had spared no expense when he finally decided to purchase an auto.

The chauffeur stepped to the front of the car and bent down to crank the engine to life. They jounced over the rough streets, heading up toward Michaelton House.

Anastasia gathered her courage for another try. She licked her dry lips. "Father, I apologize for running away. It was heedless of me. I should have stayed and spoken to you about your plans for me. I'm sorry I caused you such worry."

His fists tightened on his knees. Not once did he look her direction. "You *have* caused me worry, as well as a great deal of trouble. I should've known you'd do something harebrained like this. Do you have any idea how humiliating it was for me? Do you know the jeopardy you put my business reputation in? I did not enter into your marriage contract lightly, nor do I enjoy being made to look a fool. I'm lucky Abraham didn't cancel the contracts when he heard of your childish prank. It's a good thing your groom has been away recently."

"The wedding is still going to happen?" Anastasia's insides turned to water. "But I thought—"

"You *didn't* think, that's what. Yes, the wedding will happen, and you will be under lock and key until it does. When I think of all the trouble you've caused me, all the maneuvering I've had to do, I could shake you. I couldn't keep the story out of the papers. The police treated it like a kidnapping. Once I knew where you were and when you'd be returning home, I had to pay a steep 'fee' to an insufferable newspaper editor to have an article published saying you'd gone to visit friends. I looked like an imbecile, claiming not to know the traveling plans of my own daughter. But better that than the truth leaking out. From this moment on, you will not set foot outside Michaelton House unless you are in my presence. You will keep to your room and be thankful someone is still willing to marry you. If your fiancé saw you right now, he'd no doubt call off the wedding. I'm ashamed to admit you're my daughter, clothed like a servant, doing menial work. Your engagement party is tonight, and you will dress appropriately. After all, your betrothed will be present, and I'll be announcing your engagement."

Anastasia shrank back into her corner of the seat, her courage and will draining from her like beans from a sack. Nothing had changed in all the weeks she'd been away.

A fatalistic malaise came over her, pouring through the cracks of her broken heart. What did it matter now? The man she loved was marrying another. She might as well do the same.

∞

Her room was just as she had left it. White furniture with pale-gold accents, light-blue drapery on the canopy bed, gold rugs, white marble fireplace. The only thing missing was Hazel in the rocker. The emptiness enveloped Anastasia like a cold shawl.

She unpinned her hat, tugging it off and letting her hair straggle from its knot. The clock on the mantel ticked loudly announcing the time—just after five. Anastasia looked down at her humble dress. Brown wool skirt, sensible white blouse, unadorned brown jacket. So suitable for her life on Sutton Island, and so very wrong for a formal party in Duluth society. She decided against ringing for a maid to assist her.

During her preparations she prayed, tossed about in spirit between obedience to her father and brokenhearted loss and betrayal. She strove to cling to the serenity she had found at Sutton Island Light.

"Lord, thank You for being my strong tower. Help me to obey my father. Give me the strength to hold myself together when I meet this man I'm supposed to marry. Help me be gracious to him and obedient to my father."

The aromas of lilac sachets and cedar greeted her when she pulled open the wardrobe. Lavish gowns in silks and velvets hung on padded hangers, sleeves stuffed with tissue to hold their shape. What apparel would suit an engagement party? The fabrics, cool and soft, wrapped around her work-roughened fingertips. She'd need gloves tonight. Her gaze settled on a navy-blue gown with golden stars sprinkled over the skirts and bodice. Perfect.

Two hours later, the butler knocked on her door. "Mr. Michaels requests your presence downstairs to receive your guests, miss."

Annie scanned her appearance once more, checking the heavily coiled

245

braid and ostrich feathers at the back of her head, touching the pearl choker at her throat. With a final tug to her gloves, she opened the hallway door.

Male voices rose up the curved staircase, echoing against the ceiling and bouncing off the marble entryway.

She took extra care descending, stopping at the landing to bolster her courage before turning to go down the last, wide flight to the hall below. Somewhere down there, her husband-to-be waited. With a resigned and broken heart that longed to be back on Sutton Island, she walked down the stairs.

Halfway down, the voices stopped and the five men in the hall looked up. Anastasia found herself staring into the blue eyes of Noah Kennebrae.

Chapter 20

Anastasia froze on the stairway, her hand coming to her mouth too late to stop the cry of distress. It had never entered her head that her father might have the Kennebraes on the guest list. She tried to ignore how devastatingly handsome he looked in evening dress, how dear and familiar his features were to her. Did this mean he knew her fiancé? Worse yet, could he possibly be related to him?

He too seemed dumbstruck. His mouth opened, but no sound came out. Finally, he whispered, "Annie?"

The sound of her name on his lips shot through her like sparks. In spite of herself, she couldn't help but look for the woman who must be his betrothed. But the only other woman present was on the arm of a tall fellow who bore a slight resemblance to Ni—Noah Kennebrae.

Her father stalked to the bottom of the stairs and slammed his hands onto his waist. "Go back upstairs, Anastasia." His brows lowered, giving him a thundercloud look. "These people are leaving. According to the Kennebraes, the engagement is off. Noah Kennebrae asked for permission to tell you himself, but I won't allow him to humiliate you like this." He made shooing motions for her to go back up.

Her father's voice shook with anger when he turned toward the Kennebraes. "You'll rue the day you went back on your word, Kennebrae. I'll see the entire state knows you've broken our agreement."

Noah moved to the foot of the stairs until he stood directly in front of Anastasia. Tears pricked her eyes, and heat skittered up her arms at having him so close. "*You're* Anastasia Michaels?"

She nodded, still unable to speak. She was so confused she couldn't catch and hold a single thought.

Noah turned to her father. "Sir, could you give us a few minutes alone to sort things out? Please?"

"Never. You've made yourself plain enough." Her father pounded up the steps and tugged on her arm, but she stood fast.

After a false start, she found her voice. "Nick. . .I mean, Noah. What are you doing here? What is my father talking about?" She moved down until she stood eye level with him, taking in every line of his face, searching for answers. "Tell me what's going on here."

He blinked and rubbed the palm of his hand across the nape of his neck. "If I knew, I'd tell you. It seems we've all gotten our lines crossed. Annie, I can't tell you how glad I am you're here. I was sick at heart when you weren't on the ferry this morning." He turned to Phillip Michaels. "Sir, we really need a few moments in private."

Father wasn't ready to be rational. "How dare you humiliate us this way! After all the work I went to getting Anastasia here in time for the party. I even borrowed your grandfather's yacht to go fetch her from that wretched island. Your grandfather promised the wedding would take place, no matter what, and you're in my house not five minutes before you want to call it all off? Get out of my house, the whole lot of you."

Before anyone could move, the butler opened the front door to a dozen or so party guests. Women in satin and jewels and men in evening dress, laughing, talking, and anticipating an enjoyable occasion, poured into the massive foyer.

Anastasia's father held fast to her elbow, his hand shaking. She dared a look up at him. His face set in hard lines, and his jaw muscles worked. They were trapped.

Anastasia's knees turned to pudding. She never should have come home. Once more she'd let her father down.

"Congratulations, Noah." A man with a florid complexion and the shoulders of a bear smacked Noah on the back. "'Bout time you put your neck into the matrimonial noose."

Noah took Anastasia's hand. He gave it a hard squeeze, as if to say, "*Play along and we'll sort it out later.*"

"Thank you, Titus. Allow me to introduce my bride-to-be, Anastasia Michaels. You know her father, Phillip." Noah flashed Anastasia a loaded look. "If you'll excuse us, we have a few matters to talk about privately."

"Oh no you don't, my boy. You'll have enough time to bill and coo later. Come meet some friends of mine." The man named Titus pulled Noah toward the door.

Noah glanced back over his shoulder as he was tugged away.

A beautiful brown-haired young woman introduced herself as Melissa Kennebrae, welcoming Annie to the Kennebrae family. Anastasia shook hands with Noah's brothers and briefly with Abraham Kennebrae himself. His dark eyes pierced her, taking her measure.

Father grabbed her elbow and leaned down to whisper harshly into her ear, "What is the meaning of this, Anastasia? Why did he call you Annie?" Father glowered at her, his eyes like hot coals. "Do you know each other?"

She swallowed, feeling as if she'd missed a step in the dark.

"I'm waiting for an explanation, Anastasia."

Rebellion flashed in her chest. "So am I. Why didn't you think to tell me the name of the man you were forcing me to marry? If I'd known. . ." Would it have changed anything? What game was Noah playing? Surely after all that had passed between them, he didn't think a wedding could take place? How could a marriage founded on lies and secrets and guilt ever work?

Anastasia found herself standing in a kind of receiving line, accepting congratulations and teasing remarks. Her father stood between her and Noah, his forbidding glare reminding her that a reckoning was coming. She'd never wanted to escape more. But where could she go?

"The name of the Lord is a strong tower: the righteous runneth into it, and is safe." Lord, help me. Be my strong tower in the middle of this storm.

More guests flocked in, and Anastasia got separated from her father and Noah. Everywhere she turned, another smiling face offered her best wishes.

How could this be straightened out? Duluth society filled the house, and not a soul knew of the lies, the sneaking around, the secret masquerade that stood like a wall between her and any future happiness. And Noah—when he thought this out, when he remembered how they'd deceived one another—she was sure he'd go through with calling things off.

As society matrons gathered around her, Anastasia watched Noah from the corner of her eye. He spoke to her father, whose eyes narrowed. But finally, when Father stalked down the hallway to his office, Noah followed close behind. No doubt Noah intended to explain all, after which someone would make an announcement that would end this farce.

She watched that door, ignoring everyone around her. After what seemed an age, Anastasia's father returned, looking like he'd bitten a wasp. Though she expected him to swoop down on her and hustle her upstairs with loud threats, he merely nodded to her.

Noah emerged, his face set in a determined expression. He marched straight up to Anastasia and took her hand. Ignoring comments and gasps from the onlookers, he pulled her down the hall to the room he'd just left. Anastasia had no choice but to trot in his wake.

Once inside the office, he released her hand and shut the door. He leaned against it and crossed his arms.

Anastasia didn't know what to think. So she just stood beside her father's desk and waited.

"You look beautiful. Blue suits you."

Her tongue sprang to life. "What a ridiculous thing to say at a time like this. What are we going to do? Half of Duluth seems to think we're getting married." Pain stabbed her heart.

He laughed. "Good. If I know my grandfather, by tomorrow, the other half will think so, too."

He'd obviously lost his wits. She twisted the diamond bracelet on her wrist, sliding it along her satin glove. "I've never seen my father so angry. He'll never forgive me."

"Don't worry about your father. I've had a word with him, and I think he understands. At least to the extent that he would rather have the marriage go ahead than everything to come out. He went to arrange for the toasts to be made. In fact, we only have a few minutes to get our lines uncrossed before someone breaks down this door and hauls us out to raise a glass of punch."

Tears pricked her eyes. "It's impossible. How could you even think of going forward with the engagement? You let me believe you were a fraud, that you had dallied with me then run off to marry another woman—" Her hands fisted at her sides.

When she tried to turn away from him, he pulled her into his arms. She pushed at him, struggling in his embrace, but he held on.

"Annie, stop it. Stop it!" He hugged her tight. "Let me explain."

"You can't. You can't explain anything. Do you know how much you hurt me?"

Sobs crowded her throat. As much as she wanted to loathe him, to lash out, to wound him, she couldn't.

When she stilled, he loosened his hold but didn't let her go. Instead he stroked her shoulders and hair, whispering against her temple. "I'm sorry, but hear me out." He put his finger under her chin and raised her face. "We have a lot of lines to untangle, but I want you to know I love you with all my heart, and I'd never knowingly hurt you. I had no idea who Grandfather was arranging for me to marry, and I certainly didn't think he'd go ahead with his plans after I left town."

She could barely take in his words. Too much heartbreak, too many guilty secrets stood between them. He said he loved her, but how could she be sure?

"Annie, please." He brushed a kiss across her forehead. "I don't want there to be any secrets between us ever again. I ran away from Duluth because I was ashamed. I felt so guilty over the wreck of the *Bethany*. I wanted to start a new life. But the guilt came with me. I thought I'd never be happy again. But then I met you. I've wanted to tell you the truth so many times. I wish now I had."

"You broke my heart when you left. You were engaged to someone else."

A smile tugged his lips. "Actually, when you think about it, I wasn't. I was engaged to you." He grasped her hands, his eyes pleading with her. "Annie, I promise you I was going to end the engagement my grandfather had arranged for me and find you as soon as possible. I don't want to spend another day without you. When you weren't on the ferry this morning, Eli had to nearly tie me down to keep me from setting sail for Sutton Island right then."

Hope leaped in her heart. "After everything, all the secrets, you still want to marry me? You're willing to forgive me for not telling you who I was and why I'd run away?"

"I'd be a real hypocrite if I didn't forgive you, wouldn't I? You had secrets from me. I had secrets from you. Annie, my love, I'm done with secrets. I'm done with being haunted by the past. From this moment on, I'm just Noah—Nick, if you prefer—forgiven by God and, I hope, by you. Say you forgive me for being so stupid as to walk away from you without telling you the truth. Say you love me as I love you. And please, darling Annie, say you'll marry me." He stepped back and opened his arms, waiting for her response.

All the walls of hurt and hiding crumbled from around her heart. Without hesitation, she went into his embrace. "I do forgive you, and I do love you." Her heart pounded at admitting it aloud for the first time.

His eyes glowed with warmth and love, making her heart beat faster. "There's only one more thing I need to hear from you before I kiss you like I've been wanting to all night."

"And what's that?" She stroked her fingers down his cheek, delighting in the roughness of his stubbly whiskers. A stray thought flitted through her mind, wondering why he hadn't shaved. His question blew the thought from her mind.

"Anastasia Michaels, will you marry me?"

She cupped his cheeks and stared deeply into his blue eyes. "Noah Kennebrae, I would be honored." Her arms slipped around his neck.

He lowered his head and kissed her, lightly at first but then deeper. His kiss was everything she remembered and better.

When they pulled apart, he caressed her hair. "I love you, Annie. I don't think I can call you Anastasia. Will you mind? You'll always be Annie to me."

"I love you, too. I won't mind a bit, Nick." Her heart threatened to burst with happiness.

"Your father will be breaking down this door soon." He smiled into her eyes, pulling her close for another kiss, then rested his cheek on her hair. "There's only one thing that worries me."

"What?" She nestled her head under his chin, reveling in his embrace, almost weak from relief and joy.

"Do you have any idea how my grandfather is going to gloat? He's won again."

She smiled, hearing the laughter in his voice. "You don't sound like you mind very much."

A chuckle rumbled under her ear. "I don't suppose I do at that. But when he hears the whole story of our little marriage masquerade, he's never going to let me live it down."

Annie sighed, loathe to return to the party. "Marriage masquerade. That's what it's been, hasn't it? But no more."

"No more, my love." He hugged her tight.

THE ENGINEERED
ENGAGEMENT

Dedication

For Georgiana Daniels.
Thank you.

Chapter 1

Duluth, Minnesota, 1906

Josephine Zahn. Josie." Her sister's urgent whisper pierced the quiet of the front hall. "Why aren't you dressed? We're going to be late."

Josie glanced up the stairs at Clarice leaning over the banister and made a shushing motion with her hand. She strained to hear the conversation going on in the parlor.

"Radcliffe, you don't seem to grasp the situation. Josephine is brilliant, I tell you, and she should be allowed to continue her schooling. The world needs mathematicians like your daughter." Good old Grandma Bess. Josie twisted her fingers and bit her lip.

"I've said all I'm going to say on this subject. Girls have no need of higher education. I'll thank you not to fill her head with such nonsense—no doubt gleaned from those wretched magazines you insist on bringing into this house. Josephine won't need higher education to run a household, and that's what she's destined for—to marry well and see to the needs of her house and husband. I knew I never should've let you talk me into hiring that engineer to tutor her. I'm tired of tripping over her blueprints and scratch paper, and I'm tired of hearing of trips to the harbor to study the ships. I scotched that behavior quickly. No daughter of mine is going to be hanging around the shipyards, and no daughter of mine is going to go to college."

Josie's heart dropped from her throat to her toes. If Grandma Bess couldn't change Papa's mind, it wasn't going to get changed.

"Jo—*sie*." Clarice spoke louder this time, drawing out the second syllable in admonition.

Josie glanced at the clock and turned away from the parlor doors. Grabbing up her skirts, she bolted up the stairs in a most unladylike manner. "I'll be quick."

Clarice sighed. "We'll be late again. Papa's going to be mad."

"Papa's already mad," Josie muttered. She ducked into her room. Dropping onto the padded stool in front of her dressing table, she unpinned her black hair and picked up her hairbrush. Shrieks from down the hall made her roll her eyes at her reflection. Giselle and Antoinette, ever ready to jump into sister-squabbling chaos.

"They're mine! Give them back!"

"You stole them from me!"

Scuffles and thumps from the nursery.

Josie laid the brush aside and swept her hair back over her shoulders in preparation for going into battle against the younger forces in the house. Before she could rise, little feet thudded on the runner in the hall.

Her door burst open, and Giselle flew in, Antoinette in full chase.

"Josie, help!" Giselle clutched a pair of white kid boots to her chest, her black hair floating wildly around her pale face. Her dark-blue eyes pleaded with her older sister.

Josie stood, and Giselle took refuge behind her.

Antoinette put her hands on her hips, panting, cheeks red. "Jo, she's got my shoes. Make her give them to me."

Josie glanced over her shoulder at the enamel mantel clock while she tried to disengage Giselle's grip from her skirt.

The moment Giselle appeared from behind Josie's back, Antoinette made a wild lunge for the coveted footwear. The sprightly Giselle scampered away, leaping onto the canopied bed. The curtains swayed, and the bedsprings creaked. Antoinette's momentum carried her into Josie's desk. A column of books teetered for a moment then crashed to the floor, followed by a cascade of papers. In a final *coup de grâce*, the ink bottle tipped over onto the blotter. Undaunted, Antoinette started after Giselle, who shrieked again—a particular talent of hers—and scooted farther out of reach.

Josie sprang for the ink bottle, scooping it up before the stopper could free itself entirely but garnering a healthy dose of ink on her hand in the process. She held her dripping hand away from herself over the spattered blotter and dug with her clean hand for her handkerchief.

"Girls, stop it this instant!" Mama's voice cut through the chaos like a thunderclap. Everyone froze, Josie included. Mama rarely ventured into the girls' wing of the upstairs.

Josie swallowed hard and clutched her handkerchief over her stained fingers.

Giselle dropped onto her backside on the mattress. Josie almost smiled at the horrified expressions on her younger sisters' faces. To be caught in an unladylike brawl by Mama certainly topped their "worst deeds" list.

Antoinette rushed into speech. "Mama, she took my—"

Giselle's mouth opened for another wail, but Mama's raised hand stopped her mid-inhale.

Mama turned to Josie. "I don't know why you encourage their hoyden-ish behavior. Whatever their discrepancy is, fix it and do it quietly. I knew it was a mistake to bring them along to this wedding. The social event of the summer is no place for children. But when your father insists, we obey." She looked at the rumpled bed and the glacier-tongue of papers and books on the floor. "This room is a disaster. Why must you always be surrounded by clutter? I have no intention of assigning a maid just to clean up after you. They have more than enough duties as it is. Take care of your own things."

Protest of her innocence in the matter clogged Josie's throat, but she knew it was pointless to argue. Mama saw things the way Mama wanted to see things, and that was that. Josie sent her sisters each a warning glare to keep their mouths shut.

Mama consulted the silver timepiece pinned to her lapel. "We will leave this house in exactly twenty-two minutes. Anyone not downstairs at that time can explain to her father why she made us late." She swept out of the room.

Josie's shoulders sagged, and her chin lowered to her chest. Just like Mama. If one Zahn girl was at fault, all were at fault.

Giselle's lower lip quivered, and two blobby tears tumbled down her cheeks.

Antoinette shrugged and stared at the floor. A suspicious moisture appeared at the corners of her eyes. The tongue-lashing Josie had intended to impart evaporated. Antoinette never cried.

"Antoinette, you go first and make it snappy. I'm not even dressed yet, and I don't want to have to explain to Father what made me late."

"She took my shoes. She can't find hers, so she pinched mine."

"Did not! These're mine."

Knowing if she didn't jump in now they'd be back to shouting and chasing each other again, Josie stepped between them, dabbing at the ink blotches on the edge of her hand. "Stop it, both of you. Giselle, give me those shoes."

Giselle handed over one boot then looked about the bed for the other one.

"Well, where is it?"

"I don't know. I must've dropped it." She shrugged, sending a hank of hair sliding over her shoulder and into her eyes.

"You'd lose the Canal Bridge if it was in your possession for two minutes. Give me your foot." Josie grabbed Giselle's ankle and held the boot sole against the little girl's foot. "Look at that. It's way too big. Toni was telling the truth."

"I told you so." Antoinette stuck her tongue out at Giselle and grabbed the boot. "Where's the other one?"

Giselle slid off the bed and shrugged again.

"Well, you had them both when you came in, so help me find it." Josie tossed her soiled handkerchief onto the dressing table.

They found the shoe well back under the bed, though how it had gotten there, Josie couldn't imagine. She had to lie flat on the floor and stretch out until she could grab the heel and drag it out.

257

"There, order restored, at least to Toni's footwear. Now, both of you, scoot. Giselle, find your shoes. I have to dress."

Antoinette sat on the edge of the bed to put on her boots. While she tugged at the buttons with the buttonhook, Josie opened her wardrobe and pulled out the pale-blue dress her mother had chosen. She glanced over her shoulder to her sister. The fabric matched Antoinette's. Mama insisted all her girls dress alike. Josie stuck her tongue out at the despised dress that made her one of the herd.

Antoinette straightened and stuck her foot out, rolling the ankle as much as the high boots would allow. "Stupid old boots." She watched Josie shrug into the dress. "I wish I had my own room like you. Giselle is always taking my things."

"Having your own room doesn't always keep your things safe from little sisters." Josie glanced at the mess of papers and books on the floor. At Antoinette's guilty expression, she laughed. "I know just how you feel, chicken."

She moved to the dressing table to pin up her hair. Getting her black hair into the relaxed bun dictated by current fashion never came easily to Josie. She turned her head this way and that, poking in pins until she was satisfied it looked as near the newspaper clipping of Charles Gibson's "Gibson Girl"—conveniently stuck into the corner of the mirror for reference—as she could make it. She tilted her chin up and lowered her eyelashes, comparing her reflection to the print ad. Who was she kidding? Her face was too round, her nose tilted too much at the tip, and her mouth. . .her lips would never form that perfect little bow.

She turned on the stool and saw her own features, ten years younger, looking back at her from Antoinette's face. "Maybe you can do what I do, Toni. Find little ways to break out, to be your own person." She glanced at the clock. "Let's go. It's almost time."

Josie scooped up her handbag and gloves and followed Antoinette down the stairs. Giselle bounced down the steps ahead of them, hair tied up in pale-blue bows and feet shod in her own kid boots. Clarice waited with Mama and Papa in the foyer.

"Line up." Papa's side-whiskers jutted out as he pursed his lips.

Josie prayed for patience as they went through the familiar ritual. Clarice, Josie, Antoinette, and Giselle lined up shoulder to shoulder for his inspection. Four Zahn girls, black of hair, blue of eye, pale of skin.

"Very nice." Papa walked down the line like a general inspecting his troops. "I'm expecting stellar behavior from you young ladies today. This is a momentous occasion, and I want you all there to celebrate it."

Josie shot Clarice a questioning look. Why was Papa so interested in a society wedding? Clarice shrugged and shook her head.

"Now, the carriages are here. Octavia?" He offered his arm. "Bring—" He stopped, frowning and staring at the two youngest girls for a moment.

"Antoinette and Giselle?" Mama prompted.

"Yes, yes, Antoinette and Giselle. I knew that. Though why you had to give them all those fancy French names I'll never know. As if good old-fashioned American names weren't good enough. Should've called them Ann and Jane, like I suggested." He continued this familiar rant out the door to the waiting carriages.

Josie sighed and followed Clarice out into the hot August sunshine. In this one instance she was in complete agreement with her father. Plain old American names would've served them better. But Mama had insisted on French names, and that was that

"Where's Grandma Bess?" She waited for Clarice to climb into the second carriage.

"I'm right here."

Josie smiled as Grandma descended the steps. Here was one woman no one would confuse for someone else. Grandma Bess, tall, spare, ramrod-straight, wore her customary lavender dress with black bead-and-lace trim and wide, swooping black hat with lavender ribbons trailing. Over her arm she carried an enormous black and lavender carpetbag that went everywhere with her.

Josie took her place in the corner of the carriage and looked out as they drove through the streets of Minnesota Point toward the Canal Bridge. She imagined Antoinette and Giselle in the carriage ahead would be squirming with anticipation. They loved riding the gondola across the water.

The steel structure of the bridge loomed ahead. A familiar tightening started in Josie's middle. The five-minute ride on the suspended car across the open water of the canal always made her palms sweat and her heart beat fast.

But that wasn't the only reason her pulse jumped. Every time she thought of seeing *him* again, she found it difficult to breathe. And she'd surely see him today. He was the brother of the groom, after all.

❧

Eli Kennebrae twirled his pencil like a baton, walking it up and down his fingers absently as he stared out the window past Grandfather's head.

"Look at me when I'm talking to you." Grandfather smacked the arm of his invalid chair. "You haven't heard a word I've said."

"Yes, I have. I just don't like it. I thought you'd given up on these schemes."

"When has a Kennebrae ever given up? You don't have to like the idea. You just have to do it."

"I don't think so. You don't have the same hold over me you had over Jonathan. As for Noah, well, you're just lucky he fell in love with the girl, or today's wedding wouldn't be happening either."

"No hold over you?" Abraham Kennebrae stiffened, challenge lighting his dark eyes. "I believe I do."

Eli tucked the pencil behind his ear and tapped his papers neatly into a file folder. He leaned back on the settee and propped his ankle on his knee. "And just what is it you think you have that can force me into doing your bidding?"

"I have the *Bethany*."

Eli's leg came down, and he straightened. "What about the *Bethany*? You just agreed I could have her to modify with the new loading and storage system. She's almost repaired to the point where I can start my modifications."

"That's right, I did. But I forgot to mention the conditions."

Eli's collar tightened.

"You can have the *Bethany*, and I'll foot all the bills to convert her, but you have to agree to marry Radcliffe Zahn's daughter before winter." The cane back of Grandfather's chair creaked a bit as he leaned into it and propped his elbows on the arms. He steepled his fingers under his chin and smiled complacently.

Eli met his stare, his mind racing. "And if I refuse?"

"No ship and no funding."

He squeezed his eyes shut and clamped his lips tight. How like his grandfather to connive and manipulate to get his way. Stubborn old goat.

"Why? Why can't you be happy with the way things turned out for Jonathan and Noah and leave me alone?"

"I gave Zahn my word months ago that a wedding would take place. And when a Kennebrae gives his word, he keeps it."

"But you're not keeping it. You're expecting *me* to keep it."

Again Grandfather's hand pounded the arm of his chair. "That's right, I am. Think of it as a business deal, between you and me. You get what you want; I get what I want. Zahn's shipping more than a million board feet of lumber out of Duluth every year. Kennebrae Shipping should have a slice of that pie. Zahn as good as promised that a marriage between the families would guarantee we didn't get just a slice but the whole pie, crust, filling, and meringue."

Lumber, the perfect cargo for his new ship design. If he didn't get the *Bethany* and the money from Grandfather for the modifications, he'd be forced to abandon ideas of building this summer. The year would be spent raising finance and cajoling investors, a job Eli hated. A whole year would be wasted, assuming he could find anyone to back his ideas anyway. Why couldn't he just build ships?

Jonathan ran the family shipping business with an ease Eli could never hope to duplicate. Eli's twin, Noah, captained Kennebrae vessels on the lake, making a name for himself as a hard water captain who feared nothing. And what did Eli do? What mark had he made on the company? Nothing. *Yet*.

But he could, with this new design. All he had to do was say yes to Grandfather's plans. And those plans hadn't worked out too badly for Jonathan and Noah, had they? "I'll think about it."

Grandfather's mouth curled in a satisfied smile. "I knew you'd come around."

"I haven't promised anything. I said I'd *think* about it." Eli stood and gathered his papers. "The wedding is in half an hour. Guess I'd better change."

"She'll be here, you know."

"Who?"

"The girl." Grandfather let out an exasperated breath. "The whole Zahn family is invited."

Eli frowned. This was all happening way too fast. Still, he didn't have time to discuss it further right now. As the best man, he couldn't be late for the wedding. As to meeting his future bride, well, he'd cross that bridge when he came to it. Jonathan and Noah hadn't done too badly for themselves. Perhaps he would be the same.

Chapter 2

Josie tried not to stare as she stepped down from the carriage in front of Kennebrae House. The massive mansion built of stone filled her view and seemed to blot out the sunshine. *Imposing* was the only possible word for this place. Though she'd never been inside, she'd heard of its impressive opulence.

Her own father's house, *Belle Maison*, named by her mother, was quite impressive, with three stories, a turret, and a wide, inviting porch that looked out upon Lake Superior. Though in a less fashionable part of town out on Minnesota Point, it still rivaled most of the mansions in Duluth. Except this one.

The family ascended the steps in a group, Josie and Grandma Bess bringing up the rear of the line. She wasn't sure what held her back. This day had loomed large in her mind for weeks. Now that it had arrived, she wanted only to duck back into the carriage and speed home.

Pull yourself together. Don't be a silly goose. He probably won't even speak to you.

They stepped into a foyer so grand, Josie sucked in a surprised gasp. *Foyer* was hardly the word for it. To her right and left, a wide area with carved oak paneling stretched through the middle of the house. Before her, across the carpeted expanse, an immense staircase rose to a landing that broke off to the right and left to curve upward to the next floor. On the landing, rainbows of light filtered through stained-glass windows featuring swans and lotus flowers in whites and pinks and yellows.

Garlands of greenery and flowers draped the banisters, and ribbons hung from the wall sconces. The chandeliers—she counted five—lit and further softened the austerity of the room. Women in large hats and impossibly wide-sleeved dresses and men in frock coats and starched white shirts headed to the left.

"Good afternoon, sir." A man Josie assumed was the butler noted the embossed invitation Papa held out for his inspection. "The wedding will take place in the gallery, sir. At the end of the Grand Hall."

Grand Hall. That was certainly the right name for it. Josie fell into line with her sisters and headed toward the far end. Organ music began. Josie searched every face as they entered the room, looking for him while trying not to appear so.

An elbow nudged her ribs. Antoinette pointed up. Light streamed through a gabled glass roof overhead. Oil paintings, some as large as a double quilt, hung in ornate gilded frames on both side walls.

Giselle slipped her hand into Josie's and whispered, "Look at the flowers."

White blossoms—lilies, roses, chrysanthemums, and others Josie couldn't name—nearly obscured the fireplace at the far end of the room. Even from this distance, Josie could smell their fragrance. She squeezed Giselle's hand and bent to say, "Beautiful, aren't they?"

Giselle, a garden lover from birth, nodded, not taking her eyes from the bouquets. Josie had to guide her down the center aisle to the row of white chairs Papa had chosen.

Grandma Bess went in first, followed by Clarice, then Josie, and on down the line until Giselle. Mother sat between Giselle and Papa. Just as she did in church. Just as she always did everywhere.

Antoinette kept craning her neck to look behind them at the organist and the pipes extending up more than two floors above. Clarice, to Josie's left, twisted her handkerchief and chewed her bottom lip.

"Is something wrong?" Josie kept her voice low.

Clarice looked at her lap and gave a short, quick shake of her head.

Josie shrugged. Clarice had always been an intensely private person, keeping her thoughts to herself, holding herself apart from her sisters. Where Antoinette said any and everything that came into her head, where Giselle showed every emotion on her face, Clarice remained aloof and self-contained, always a mystery. Josie went back to watching people.

He came in before she was ready. Following the groom up the far aisle, his presence sent a jolt from the top of her head to the soles of her feet. Her mouth went dry. He was even more handsome than she remembered. Older. After all, it was three—almost four—years since she'd seen him last.

Dark-brown hair, smooth and shining, blue eyes that glistened when he laughed, and white teeth that flashed often. That's how she remembered him, smiling, laughing, enjoying himself. He'd teased her a bit, a girl of just fifteen, gauche and uncertain at her first Shipbuilder's Ball. He hadn't danced with her, conferring that honor on Clarice instead, but Josie hadn't really minded. Just watching him had been enough.

Eli Kennebrae. He looked in her direction, his face sober. Her pulse quickened, and the butterflies in her stomach turned to seagulls.

The groom, Noah Kennebrae, on the other hand, smiled so wide, Josie wondered if his cheeks ached. Thick brown whiskers covered the lower half of his face. He shifted his weight from foot to foot and clasped and unclasped his hands in front of him, watching the doors at the back of the room.

Pachelbel's Canon swelled out from the organ. Josie lost sight of Eli behind the ostrich-feather-adorned hat of the woman in front of her.

Through her misty veil, the bride's smile beamed even brighter than her beautiful golden hair.

Josie didn't pay much attention to the ceremony. She kept her gaze on Eli, noting his broad shoulders, strong profile, and erect stance. Did he still smell of shaving soap? What would it be like to be a bride, walking up the aisle to exchange vows with Eli Kennebrae? She blushed for having such intimate thoughts about a man she barely knew. And yet, the fantasy lingered in her mind.

When the preacher said, "You may now kiss the bride," Noah took his new wife, Anastasia Kennebrae, into his arms and kissed her long enough and with such tenderness that every woman in the room from Grandma Bess to Giselle sighed in satisfaction. Josie caught Mama wiping a tear with her lace handkerchief.

Josie followed her family outside onto the spreading back lawn for the reception. The breeze from the lake cooled her cheeks, though the sun was fierce. Tablecloths fluttered, and more massive bouquets of flowers in urns along the walk enveloped Josie in their perfume.

Expecting to be seated at a table with her younger siblings, Papa surprised Josie by directing her and Clarice to a table of adults.

Her heart jumped into her throat and stayed there.

Eli Kennebrae rose, and his easy smile flowed over her like a warm blanket. "Mr. Zahn." He shook Papa's hand.

"My daughters—" Papa turned to them and hesitated, his brows coming together slightly. "Clarice and Josephine." He smiled broadly, as if relieved to have come up with the answer without a prompt.

Josie winced at the sound of her whole name.

Eli held their chairs for them and made introductions. "My grandfather, Abraham Kennebrae, and family friend, Geoffrey Fordham."

Josie nodded to the elder Mr. Kennebrae. His white hair reflected the sunshine, and his black eyes glittered. She had the impression, invalid chair or not, of great strength and mental sharpness. He seemed to miss nothing going on around him. The other man smiled politely at her but made no real impression. Her attention shot back to Eli across the table.

Mama and Grandma Bess took their places, balancing out the numbers. Josie turned to see where her other sisters had gotten to. Giselle and Antoinette sat at a long table near the bottom of the garden, being attended to by a white-coated waiter.

"A lovely wedding, Mr. Kennebrae." Mama smoothed her dress at the waist and tilted her head so her wide-brimmed hat would shade her face. "They're an ideal couple, aren't they? I predict they'll be very happy together."

"I agree. They had some rough sailing, but that's all behind them now."

Abraham Kennebrae turned to Grandma Bess. "You're looking well, Elizabeth. It's been some time since I saw you."

"I keep myself busy. Always a lot for a grandmother to do with a houseful of granddaughters."

He grinned. "I have a feeling they won't be underfoot too long. Girls as pretty as these will have suitors hanging about the front gate sooner than you think." He elbowed Eli, who rolled his eyes and looked out over the lake. "Yes, indeed, fine-looking girls you have there, Radcliffe. You should be proud. Shouldn't be surprised if an engagement was announced soon."

"Stop it, Grandfather. This isn't the time or the place." Eli's blue eyes flashed.

Undercurrents sucked around the table like the tide. Josie didn't know where to look or what to do with her hands. Meeting Eli again wasn't supposed to be this awkward.

✑

Eli excused himself from the table as soon as he decently could and mingled with the guests. How could he be thinking of selling his freedom, even for a chance of fulfilling his dreams? Not that he should complain too much. Radcliffe Zahn did have some fine-looking daughters. But it was the principle of the thing that galled him. He couldn't go through with it. He'd tell Grandfather tomorrow. No ship was worth tying himself to a virtual stranger for the rest of his life, no matter how pretty she was.

"Eli Kennebrae?" A short, barrel-chested man with silvery whiskers bristling outward from his cheeks stopped Eli on his way toward the punch table. "Gervase Fox. Glad to know you."

Eli shook the man's hand, surprised at the strength generated by such a small fellow. "Glad you could come."

"Now, don't run away. I've been meaning to talk to you." Fox held Eli's elbow when Eli would've moved on. "I hear you've been in Virginia learning the shipbuilding trade."

"That's right." Eli's interest was caught, as it was whenever shipbuilding came up for discussion.

"Why Virginia? Not enough shipbuilders on the lakes for you to learn from?"

Eli frowned at the challenge in Fox's question but brushed it off. "I wanted to learn the mechanics of oceangoing vessels to see which ones would best apply to lake ships. I'd already studied in the Kennebrae shipyards here."

"And did you learn anything?"

The way Fox leaned in, eyes trained on Eli's face, caused Eli to step back a pace. "A few things, here and there. What did you say you did again?"

"Didn't say. Figured you'd know. I'm Gervase Fox, Keystone Steel and

Shipping. Surely your brothers have mentioned me. We're friends, Jonathan, Noah, and I."

"Excuse me, sir." McKay touched Eli's arm, and Eli turned to the Kennebrae butler. "Mr. Kennebrae would like to see you."

"Thank you, McKay. Nice to have met you, Fox." Eli walked away from the little man with the distinct feeling that he was being watched.

Grandfather met him on the back veranda. "Where have you been? It's time for the photographs."

Eli allowed himself to be positioned here and there in the family photos, glad for his brother about the marriage but bored with the proceedings.

Jonathan wore a concerned look and watched his wife, Melissa, like she was a stick of dynamite. Just over a month away from her confinement, Melissa bore his anxiety with good humor.

"How're you holding up?" Eli sat beside her while the photographer set up shots of the bride and groom.

"Fine. It was a lovely wedding. They look so happy, don't they?"

Eli had to agree. The grin hadn't left Noah's face for a month. And his bride couldn't seem to take her eyes off him. A stirring of something—was it jealousy?—flickered in Eli's middle. If he got married, he'd want his bride to look at him like Annie looked at Noah. His resolve to tell Grandfather to call off ideas of an arranged marriage strengthened.

Laughter drew his attention. Geoffrey stood with the two oldest Zahn girls near the table with the wedding cake. Wouldn't it be nice to be Geoffrey, no one trying to force him into marriage, free to just chat with pretty girls on a nice afternoon?

Eli excused himself from Melissa and sauntered over to his friend.

"Almost done?" Geoffrey lifted his chin in the direction of the photographer.

"Yes, though I'm nearly blind with all those flashes." Eli accepted a glass of punch from a passing tray. He looked at the younger Zahn girl over the rim as he drank. Something about her face caught his attention as it had when he first saw her. He liked the way her nose tilted up a bit at the end and the way her lashes fringed her blue eyes. Why did she seem so familiar to him? Had they met somewhere before?

"I think I'll stroll down toward the water," Geoffrey spoke to no one in particular. "Would you care to join me, Miss Zahn?" Geoff held out his arm to the older Zahn girl—Clarice, wasn't it?

She nodded and accepted his offered arm, leaving Eli standing with her sister.

He set his cup on the table behind him. "Josephine, right?"

She winced. "Please, call me Josie. Josephine always makes me feel like a pet poodle on a satin pillow."

He grinned. "Josie it is, then. I hate to be so forward, but I feel as if we've met somewhere before."

The way her eyes lit up told him he'd been right. "Yes, we have, though I'm surprised you remember. It was some years ago." She flicked a glance up at him through her lashes then looked out over the lake once more. Captivating.

"Some years ago? Let's see. Was it at the yacht races? No?" He cast back in his mind. "Founder's Day Picnic?"

She shook her head and hooked her little finger through a strand of hair that had blown across her cheek. He studied the curve of her jaw and the slender column of her neck before dragging his mind back to the question at hand. "I'm sorry. You'll have to jog my memory."

"The Shipbuilder's Ball of '03."

He snapped his fingers. "That's where it was. We danced together, didn't we?"

Her expression went from happy to sad in an instant, like snuffing out a candle. "No, that was my sister. You danced with Clarice that night."

∽

Josie stood on the front lawn and watched the bridal couple drive away. Women waved handkerchiefs, and men clapped. She prayed they could go home soon. No matter how she looked at it, it always came up the same. She would always and forever be just one of the Zahn girls, interchangeable, identical in everyone's eyes. The moment Eli had confused her with her sister, it was like someone had set a cold sadiron on her heart and left it there, pushing all the life out of her. Would he, or anyone else, ever see her as an individual?

That Eli, of all people, had done it only made it hurt more. And yet, could she blame him? It had been a long time ago, and she and Clarice did look so much alike. Perhaps she should solace herself with the fact that he remembered that night at all.

Her gaze found him, leaning against the gatepost, talking to his friend, Mr. Fordham. His hands gestured as he spoke, and Mr. Fordham laughed. They must be good friends.

The tinkling of a bell caught her attention. The Kennebrae butler stood on the front steps beckoning the guests near. Beside him, Abraham Kennebrae sat stately and proud. On the far side of the invalid chair stood her father. Puzzlement knit Josie's brow as she moved to stand with the others to hear what they had to say.

Her mother edged close and clasped her arm, drawing her through the crowd to stand at the front of the semi-circle of guests. Josie found herself in her familiar spot in line between Clarice and Antoinette, a place both comforting and exasperating at the same time.

"Ladies and gentlemen." Their host cleared his throat. "We didn't want to take any of the attention away from the bridal couple, so we waited until their departure to make this announcement." He motioned to Papa, who stepped forward, smiling.

"It is with great pleasure that I announce the engagement of my daughter—" He paused and looked frantically down at the row of girls in pale blue.

Josie's breath stuck in her throat, and all thought ceased. Her heart beat against her ribs like a captured bird, and her mouth went dry. Engagement?

Her father continued, "Clarice to Eli Kennebrae."

All the air whooshed out of Josie's lungs.

Clarice gave a strangled little cry of surprise.

Papa beamed. "Come up here, Clarice, Eli." He beckoned.

Mama gave Clarice a shove to get her started.

Clarice moved as if in a dream.

Josie knew exactly how she felt. This whole day had been a nightmare.

Chapter 3

A band of steel settled around Josie's forehead and tightened a little with each new comment from her parents.

"A fall wedding, don't you think?"

"Consolidating the shipping makes sense."

"I hear charmeuse is the new thing for wedding gowns. But I think you should get married in silk."

"Abraham and I have been planning this for over a year."

"Do you think we should have the wedding at Belle Maison or at Kennebrae House? Today's wedding was so lovely, but I want my girl married at her own home."

And so it went on through their arrival home and continued all through the light supper. A supper neither Josie nor Clarice was able to choke down.

Josie looked at Clarice again. Her sister sat as if in a stupor, eyes blank with shock. Josie knew just how she felt. A lightning bolt from a clear blue sky couldn't have hit with more surprise.

Clarice was engaged. To Eli Kennebrae.

Josie looked to Grandma Bess to see how she was taking the situation. Grandma sat in her customary chair, paying no attention to the ebb and flow of conversation going on around her, totally engrossed in one of her magazines. How could she read her serial stories at a time like this?

Josie wanted to stand and scream at her parents for being so cruel. How could they just spring this on everyone? And why did it have to be Eli?

Josie's train of thought stopped when she realized everyone was looking at her. She didn't remember getting to her feet.

"You wanted to say something, Josephine?" Mama raised her eyebrows expectantly.

Heat coursed through Josie's face and neck and spun in her ears. "It's been such a big day. I think I'm developing a headache. May I be excused, please?"

"Yes, of course, and Clarice, you may go, too. We'll talk more in the morning."

Josie dragged herself up to her room. The mess of papers and books beside the desk remained. She had no energy or enthusiasm to clean it up. It would have to wait until morning. And with her tutoring cut off and no hope of college, why bother to keep the books out anyway?

She was turning back the rumpled comforter and getting ready to climb into bed when someone tapped on the door.

Clarice entered when Josie called.

Surprised, Josie slid into bed and pulled the covers up over her lap. Clarice wasn't one for midnight confidences, though Josie supposed if ever she needed someone to talk to, it would be now.

Clarice sat on the end of the bed and leaned against the footboard, pulling her knees up and tucking her toes under the hem of her dressing gown. "I can't believe any of this is happening." She grabbed the cuffs of her sleeves and put the heels of her hands up to cover her eyes.

"I know. Didn't they give you any warning at all?"

"None. I nearly fainted. How could they do this to me?" Clarice dragged her hands down her face. Her black hair hung in twin braids on her shoulders.

Josie hadn't bothered to braid her hair for the night, too mixed up in her emotions for such a mundane task. Evidently not even a cataclysmic shock could keep Clarice from her evening routine.

"What are you going to do?" The question had burned in Josie's mind for hours.

"What *can* I do?" Clarice's brow wrinkled. "I don't see that I have a choice in the matter."

Josie shrugged. It was an impossible situation. A formal engagement had been announced in front of nearly a hundred witnesses. Mama and Papa were thrilled with the match. And what Mama and Papa wanted, Mama and Papa got. Clarice was right. She had no choice.

"This is terrible." A tear slipped down Clarice's cheek.

Josie watched it glisten in the light of the bedside lamp, and her own eyes filled. She blinked hard, hating to cry even worse than Antoinette did.

Clarice's shoulders shook. "I don't love him."

"Of course you don't. You barely know him." Josie no sooner said the words than she had to chide herself. *You barely know him either, and you've been in love with him for more than three years.*

"You don't understand. I love someone else." The words seemed wrung from Clarice. She put her forehead down on her knees.

Josie blinked. The self-contained and ultra-private Clarice in love? "Who?" Josie leaned forward.

Clarice shook her head, either unable to tell or unwilling. Her muffled sobs continued.

Josie sat back against the pillows and stared at the organza curtains of the canopy bed. What a mess. Clarice engaged to the man Josie wanted. . .and in love with someone else altogether.

∽

As family dinners went, Eli had to judge theirs less than a success. His anger carried him through the first two courses, and Grandfather thrashed him verbally until he was goaded into responding in kind.

Melissa finally laid down her fork and leveled them both with a glare that reminded him of Grandmother back when Eli was a young boy. "Enough, both of you. Grandfather, I thought you'd finally learned your lesson about these engagements, but I see you need another dose of humility. Be careful the Lord doesn't teach it to you. And Eli, stop saying such terrible things you'll regret. Nothing will be settled tonight. Either finish your supper in peace, or leave the table so Jonathan and I can."

The anger simmering in Jonathan's eyes at them for upsetting Melissa in her delicate condition drove Eli from the table like a naughty child. Good thing after all that wedding food he wasn't very hungry anyway.

Eli entered his workroom and paused to let the familiarity of his sanctuary sink in. He leaned against the door and crossed his arms, his eyes taking in the familiar drafting table, bookcases, and shabby, overstuffed chair by the small fireplace. The eaves sloped down on two sides, but the wide window permitted sunlight to fall across the desk for most of the day. Though darkness had fallen hours ago, he still sought his attic workroom as a safe port in the storm.

McKay must've anticipated his need. The lamp on the mantel flickered, and a pot of coffee sat on the table beside the chair. That man had an uncanny ability to serve that amazed and humbled Eli.

Eli dropped into the chair, allowing its familiar comfort to soothe the tense muscles in his neck, and poured himself a cup. He drew the warm fragrance deep into his lungs and tried to relax. He hadn't been able to think clearly since Grandfather had dropped the cat amongst the pigeons at the reception. Always a deliberate thinker, Eli needed quiet and time to process what had transpired and what he was prepared to do about it. He should've anticipated this move from Grandfather—making the engagement public so no one could back out. The old man had pulled it on both Eli's older brothers to varying degrees.

The door creaked open, and Geoffrey's head came around the edge. "Eli?"

"Come in." Eli made to stand.

Geoff motioned him back. "McKay told me you'd be up here." He stepped into the room and looked around. "Nice bolt-hole you've got. Wish I had someplace like it."

Eli put down his coffee cup and gathered up the books and papers littering the footstool. It was the only other place to sit, since Eli always stood to work at the drafting table.

McKay tapped on the door and entered with a small tray holding another coffee cup.

Again Eli was amazed at the man's ability to do the right thing at the right time. "Thank you, McKay."

Geoff waited until the butler had closed the door before he looked at Eli. "Wanted to see how you were holding up after such a big day." He blew across his coffee cup and took a sip.

Eli shrugged. "He ambushed me."

"He ambushed all of us—again."

"Humph. I told Grandfather I'd think about it. *Think* about it. I didn't know today was the day. And I have the distinct feeling that the girl didn't know it either. She turned to a pillar of salt when they trotted out their announcement." Eli shifted in his chair, remembering her ghost-like pallor and trembling hands. "Either it was a tremendous shock to her or distinctly unflattering toward me as a prospective husband." He tried to raise a smile from Geoff, but the lawyer's expression didn't change.

"What do you think of her?"

"What's to think?" Eli spread his hands wide in a helpless gesture. "I don't know her. I've barely spoken to her. I shared more words with her younger sister today than with Clarice herself."

"Will you go through with it?" Geoff leaned forward, elbows on knees, his stare boring into Eli.

"I hardly know where I am at the moment. The engagement has been announced. Now I know just how my brothers felt when Grandfather pulled this stunt on them. And I'm just as trussed up. If I back out now, not only will the girl's reputation be called into question, but I'll lose—" He hesitated, not wanting Geoffrey to know he'd been contemplating exchanging matrimony for a chance to fulfill his dreams. What had he been thinking to let Grandfather maneuver him into this corner? One moment of weakness, and the old man had pounced.

"You'll lose what?"

"My self-respect," he substituted lamely. "When a Kennebrae gives his word, he keeps it." The irony of using Grandfather's own words stung him enough to make him laugh bitterly.

Again, Geoffrey didn't share the humor.

"Let's talk about something else."

"What? What else is there?" Geoff's coffee cup hit the table hard enough to slosh some of the liquid out over the rim.

"Let's talk about my ship." Eli shoved aside thoughts of matrimony and machinations in favor of metal and machinery, an infinitely more interesting and safer subject to consider. "I have the preliminary drawings done and the go-ahead to start the work, but I'm having trouble with some of the calculations." He rose and picked up his latest sketches. "I'm no mathematical genius. I can do the basic stuff, but I need some help with calculating the stress on these beams here and just how much I'll need to reinforce the hull here and here to compensate for the removal of this angle support and this one." He pointed to the cross-section of the hull. "And I'll need to recalculate the other measurements, now that I have an actual ship to use."

Geoffrey joined him at the table but hardly seemed to be listening. A muscle flexed in his jaw, and his hand gripped the edge of the drawing.

Eli sorted through the chart rack beside the drawing table. "I've studied her blueprints a little bit, just based on the repairs I knew were underway, but I haven't fit my ideas to her quite yet." He tugged out the drawings of the *Bethany* and unrolled them. "I'd sure like to find someone to go over the calculations for me. I need someone who can keep his mouth shut. My design is going to revolutionize lumber shipping, and I want to keep it quiet until I launch the ship." His mind skipped ahead to that glorious day when the ship would come off the ways and he would make his mark on the shipping industry. And he would become a valuable member of Kennebrae Shipping at last. "Keep your ear open for me. If you come across someone you think could help, let me know." He rolled out another schematic. "What do you think?"

"I think it's monstrous." The words shot out of Geoffrey's mouth like bullets from a gun.

"What?" Eli's head came up.

"What you Kennebraes do to people. You treat folks like pawns, pushing them here and there, making them do things they don't want to do, just to get yourself ahead. I know it's worked out for Jonathan and Noah, but what happened today—" Geoffrey broke off. "I'm sorry." His lips were so stiff, Eli could barely understand him. "I've said too much." He blew out a breath, his shoulders sagging. "I know today wasn't your doing. It was your grandfather, as it usually is. You know, when it happened to Jonathan, I thought it was funny. Even when Noah got led a merry chase by Annie, I thought it a lark. But today, I suddenly had it to the back teeth. People shouldn't be treated this way."

Eli turned around and leaned against the table, crossing his arms on his chest. "I know. I just don't know how to change things."

Geoffrey had never spoken so vehemently about anything not business related. In the boardroom or the courtroom, Geoff was a tiger, fighting on behalf of his client for all he was worth, but anywhere else, he was as easygoing a man as one could find. To see him so upset drove home what an impossible situation Eli was in.

Geoff smacked Eli on the back, an apologetic look lingering in his expression. "I'd better go before I jeopardize my job as legal counsel to the Kennebraes."

"Like that could ever happen." The idea made Eli smile. "You're the only one who gets along with all of us at the same time. Grandfather will never let you go. In fact, if you're not careful, he might find a bride for you, too."

Chapter 4

S it up straight, Josephine. You look like a wilting vine." Mama tapped her palm with her closed fan. "Proper young ladies must have impeccable posture at all times." She snapped the fan open and fluttered it below her chin. "Once more, if you please, from the beginning."

Josie sighed and straightened her spine. Listening to an instrument or singer was pleasant, but having to play as her sisters performed chafed. She liked music theory well enough but couldn't carry a tune in a valise with the clasp padlocked. Her mother had relegated her to playing the piano while her sisters sang.

She cast a longing glance through the music room window toward the lake then turned her attention back to the lesson. Antoinette's sweet soprano held a note, while Giselle's little-girl voice chimed in. Though Josie cocked her ear ever so slightly toward Clarice, she couldn't hear any of the song from that direction. Clarice hadn't said a word this morning about the engagement. Her already pale skin looked even whiter, and her eyes showed the strain of sleeplessness.

"That's fine, ladies. You may go now." Mama levered herself to her feet when the song finally ended. "Clarice and Josephine, I'd like you to stay. We have further lessons to accomplish today."

Josie tucked her lips in and stifled another sigh. These infernal daily etiquette lessons would send her mad before too long. She spun on the piano stool and put her feet side by side under her hem.

Clarice sat on the chaise, not allowing her back to touch the puffy, berib-boned pillows leaning along the wall behind her. Her hands lay in her lap, and her downcast lashes hid her expression. All she would tell Josie about the man she loved was that she had met him at the Lyceum and they had arranged to meet there several times through the opera season. No one in the Zahn household liked opera save for Clarice, but because Mama thought it a status symbol, she'd allowed Clarice to attend through the winter in the company of several girls from her class. Now Clarice's shoulders slumped in defeat.

Josie frowned. If it were her, she'd fight. She'd stand up to Mama and Papa. No way would she allow them to push her into a marriage.

"Just a few things I wanted to go over." Mama lifted a book from the table beside the door. Her movement set the bead fringe around the lampshade swinging. "Clarice, you're an engaged woman now."

Clarice flinched, and Josie tried to ignore the pain that jabbed just under her heart at Mama's words.

Mama continued. "You'll be inundated with callers and opportunities to attend social functions. We shan't give anyone reason to cavil at our social skills. That's why we're going to study each and every chapter of *Mrs. Catherine Morris's Proper Etiquette for All Occasions*." Mama tapped the book in her lap.

Josie put her elbows on her knees and propped her chin in her hands. "Why do I have to be here? I'm not engaged."

"For the tenth time, sit up straight. I despair of you, child. And keep your chin level with the floor. You will be accompanying your sister on many of her outings, especially those Eli Kennebrae cannot attend, or to ladies, only events like teas and the garden club. It wouldn't do for Clarice to attend alone, nor should she attend with only her mother as company. Besides, this will make an excellent entrance for you into societal circles we've only just begun to crack. We may well find a suitable match for you as a result."

"So I'm to be part of Clarice's entourage so you can trot me out to potential buyers?" Outrage flowed through Josie's limbs. She had no trouble straightening her back or keeping her chin level with the floor.

"Modulate your voice. You know full well Mrs. Morris insists a lady must always keep her tone civil and her words sweet."

Josie bit the inside of her cheek to keep from pointing out that Mama's own voice was less than civil or sweet at the moment.

Grandma Bess entered the room, her footsteps slow, leaning heavily on her cane. Her black bag thumped against her side. "Octavia, I hope you don't mind if I take a chair in here. I was out on the veranda, but the breeze became too strong."

Mama smiled, but tight lines formed at the corners of her mouth. "Of course I don't mind, Mother Zahn." The lines deepened when Grandma took the chair between Mama and Clarice and dug in her bag until she found her latest periodical.

"A new magazine arrived in the post today. I just have to find out what happened to the countess. She was in a dreadful bind when the story left off last month."

Josie craned her neck to see the cover picture. *Ainslee's*, *Atlantic Monthly*, *The Monthly Story Magazine*, *Saturday Evening Post*, Grandma subscribed to them all, and several more. Much to Mama's despair, Grandma insisted on speaking of the "lurid characters," as Mama called them, in the serial stories as if they were real people.

"Clarice, I've had new calling cards printed for you. They should arrive this afternoon. Also, we need to make plans for your trousseau. Evening wear and tea gowns first. Then sporting costumes, day dresses, and undergarments."

Clarice, who adored new clothes, only nodded.

Josie let her mind drift from the conversation to a particularly stubborn geometry problem she'd encountered in one of her books. Perhaps she was approaching it wrong. She often found if she backed off a problem and started from another angle, the solution would come to her. If only real life were as organized and simple as mathematics. If only she had her tutor to talk to. But he'd moved to Detroit when Papa fired him. Poor Mr. Clement.

Mother leaned over and rapped Josie on the knee with her fan. "Josephine, stop wool-gathering. If you don't learn these rules, you'll perform a frightful gaffe in front of the wrong people, and that will be the end of your hopes of a fine match. Why must you always daydream when important matters are being discussed?"

"Important to you maybe," Josie muttered under her breath.

"Josephine!" Mama reared back and glared. "That will be quite enough from you. You are excused. If you wind up an old maid because no one will marry such an uncivilized, disobedient horror, don't blame me."

Heat suffused Josie's cheeks. She knew better than to talk back to Mama, and yet she did it time and again. She caught Grandma's eye.

Grandma gave her a slow, deliberate wink then buried her nose in her magazine again.

Josie rose, nodded to Mama, and escaped to the library.

∽

Late afternoon sun fell across the book in Josie's lap. She sat curled in a wide wingback chair, her geometry book and tablet in her lap, feet tucked under her hem. The library was the one place in the house where she could almost always be alone. The little girls felt at liberty to wander—or run—in and out of her room all day for the slightest reason. But the dark, quiet, scholarly atmosphere of Papa's library held no appeal for them.

She really should formulate her apology to Mama for talking back, but it was so hard to drum up the proper humility. Mama could exasperate Josie so quickly. Sometimes Josie wondered if she had been dropped into the wrong family by mistake. She might look like her siblings, but often she felt a stranger in their midst. Only Grandma Bess really seemed to understand her or see her as an individual. But that was probably only because they were both so often in trouble with Mama.

The library door opened behind her, rubbing on the Aubusson rug Mama was so proud of. Josie froze, hoping whoever it was would go away. Nobody could see her from the door, hidden as she was by the high back of the chair, and, if she stayed quiet, they would probably leave.

"No one will see us in here. It's the one place we can be alone." Clarice.

Who would she be bringing to the library?

"Are you sure? I'd be hard-pressed to explain my presence if we're discovered."

Josie's mouth dropped open. A man's voice. Her fingers curled around the edge of her book. Curiosity feathered up her arms.

"No one but Josie ever comes in here. I don't know why Papa even put a library in the house, except it's expected for rich men to have one. I've never seen him crack a book."

Josie kept her breathing shallow. It sounded as if they'd moved to stand almost directly behind her chair. Should she interrupt?

"Enough about your papa. Clarice, it's been torturous. What are we going to do?"

"I don't know. There's nothing we can do. It's too late." The flat, fatalistic tone of Clarice's voice caused sadness to weigh down Josie's chest.

"I don't believe that. There has to be something. I'm going to speak to your father."

Where had she heard that voice before? It tantalized her, just at the edge of her memory.

"It won't do any good. Papa doesn't change his mind. And anyway, there's your job to consider. If you speak up, the Kennebraes will fire you."

He worked for the Kennebraes?

"I don't care. Clarice, I can't live without you. I love you."

The rustling of movement and steps on the carpet, and Josie could tell Clarice was being embraced. In an instant she knew she shouldn't be hearing this, that she was eavesdropping in the worst way. But how could she get out of the room without their knowing?

"Please, Geoffrey, don't. It only makes it harder."

Geoffrey, that's who it was, the man who had been with Eli at the wedding reception.

"Harder? I don't see how it can be. I'd like to shake you, Clarice. How can you even dream of going through with this? I know you love me. You must."

Josie leaned over and dropped her book flat on the hearth. It smacked, and the sound ricocheted off the glass-front bookcases surrounding the room.

Clarice squealed.

Geoffrey rounded the chair, his hands fisted.

Josie blinked and stretched like a cat waking up, then shook her head as if surprised to see a man before her. "Hello." She put her hand up to cover a fake yawn. "Do I know you?"

"Josie!" Clarice crossed her arms at her waist, her lower lip darting behind her teeth for a moment as she looked at Geoffrey then back at Josie. "Stop pretending you were asleep and didn't hear a thing. I know you better." She pointed to the book. "You never fall asleep over math."

Josie shrugged and straightened. She'd tried to give them a graceful way of saving face. It wasn't her fault if Clarice didn't take it.

Geoffrey shoved his hands into his pockets, his face like a thundercloud. "So much for a private place to talk. Getting a Zahn girl away from her sisters is impossible."

Josie put her tablet on her math book and stood. "So I gather this is the man you met at the opera?"

Clarice nodded and stepped closer to Geoffrey. "Geoffrey Fordham, this is Josie."

He nodded but didn't take his eyes off Clarice. He looked like a man dying of thirst and she was a tall glass of water. "There has to be something we can do. I went to talk to Eli about it last night, but I had to leave before I punched him in the teeth."

"Why? What did he say?" The words leaped out before Josie could stop them. It really was none of her business. In fact, she should find a way to escape, but mention of Eli kept her rooted to the rug.

"He's so busy with his shipbuilding plans, I wonder if he even knows he's engaged. All he could talk about was his ship and his math problems." Disgust laced Geoffrey's words. "He's engaged to the woman I love, and he acts like he doesn't even care."

"Math problems? What math problems?" Josie's mind leaped up to chase the idea.

"Who cares? Something about his new ship design. He had the gall to ask me to help him find a mathematician, when all I wanted to do was throttle him for treating Clarice so cavalierly." Geoffrey paced to the window and back.

Clarice stopped him from repeating his steps by placing her hand on his arm. He took it and tucked it into his elbow.

"What did you expect him to do?" Josie asked. "He barely knows her. It would've made you madder if he'd have pretended he was in love with her. If Eli didn't know the engagement would be announced, then he's as much a victim as Clarice. Perhaps he's coping the only way he knows how."

Geoffrey gave Josie a curious glance, and she realized how hotly she'd come to Eli's defense. Embarrassment heated her cheeks and climbed into her ears.

"I suppose you're right. If he knew about Clarice and me, he'd feel terrible. We've been friends a long time. He'd never steal another man's girl." He patted Clarice's hand and squeezed it close to his body with his elbow. "The question is, how can we fix this?"

Josie tapped her chin. "I doubt it will be Eli you need to pacify. It will be

Mama and Papa and old Mr. Kennebrae. They're the ones who cooked up this batch of catastrophe."

Clarice pulled her hand away from Geoffrey's grasp. "Stop it, you two. There's nothing we can do. I can't defy Mama and Papa." Her blue eyes looked agonized, but her expression was resolute. She moistened her lips and crossed her arms at her waist again. "I'm sorry, Geoffrey. You know how I feel about you, but I cannot go against my parents' wishes." She didn't cry, but her voice broke at the end. She turned and fled.

Geoffrey took a step to follow her, but Josie stopped him. "Don't. She's upset. She's like Papa. Once she makes up her mind, it's awfully hard to change it, especially right away. Let her cool down. Maybe there's a way out of this." She plopped down in the chair and put her elbows on her knees, defying Mama's nagging about posture that echoed in her head. Her chin rested in her palms, and she nodded for Geoffrey to sit in the opposite chair. "Tell me more about Eli's math situation."

He perched on the edge of the chair and looked toward the door. "I don't want to talk about math. I want to know what to do to get Clarice to change her mind and back out of this engagement."

"Maybe one is related to another." An idea, or the ghost of an idea, flitted on the edge of Josie's mind.

"How?"

"What you need now is time. Time for Clarice to get her courage up. Time to figure out what you're going to do. If you keep Eli focused on his ship, he'd have less time to spend with Clarice, and you'd have more time to map out a plan of attack. All you need is a mathematician to keep him busy."

"And where am I going to get one of those? They don't grow on all the bushes around here."

"How about me?" She spread her hands wide.

"You?" Geoffrey smiled then quelled it, looking at her in a patronizing way she was so familiar with when a man found out she liked math. "This is a little more complicated than figuring out needed yard goods for a ball gown or converting a recipe for two to feed a dinner party of twelve."

Josie took a deep breath, then bent to her tablet, flipped through a couple of pages, and turned it to face him. "This isn't exactly recipe conversions. Although I can do those, too."

He took the tablet and frowned at the rows of numbers and symbols. "What is this?"

"It's a line graph for flow dynamics. I was calculating the approximate rate of flow of water past a whaleback ship's bow versus a conventional steamer's bow."

"A line graph?"

"A handy tool for solving complex equations."

"And you can do this? Nobody's helping you?" He leafed through the pages.

She shrugged. "I've always been good at math. I guess you could say I think in numbers. You could write to my tutor, Mr. Clement, if you doubt my abilities. He taught me for over two years, though most of it was theoretical study when Papa forbade me to go to the shipyards anymore."

"You could do what Eli's looking for? He wants help calculating stress loads and hull bracing, and I don't know what all."

Her mind raced with the possibilities. Helping Eli, helping Clarice and Geoffrey, and getting to work on an actual ship—real-world problems. A hint of doubt nudged her. Real-world problems required real-world solutions. And being wrong held consequences. But she wanted to try.

"The dilemma will lie in keeping my identity a secret. You're a perfect example. No man is going to think a woman is capable of the complicated mathematics necessary for structural engineering."

"And how can we keep your identity a secret? He's bound to notice you're a girl." Geoffrey tunneled his fingers through his hair in exasperation.

"Then we'll just have to make sure he doesn't find out."

Chapter 5

Enough wooden scaffolding shrouded the *Bethany* as to resemble a log jam in spring. Eli mounted the ramp and climbed toward the deck.

Jonathan's footsteps scraped behind him. "Have you been to see her yet?"

"No. Not yet." Eli ignored both his brother's snort and the nasty nudge his conscience gave him. "I've been busy."

"Too busy to go see your fiancée?"

Eli climbed faster, as if he could outrace Jonathan's pestering. The immense cleft amidships came into view. "She sure hit that shoal hard. The surf nearly broke her in two." Eli stopped for a moment to survey the damage. "I don't know how you survived."

Jonathan paused beside him and shuddered, though the August sun beamed down and a soft breeze flowed through the shipyard, cooled by the lake. "God's mercy. A lot of good men didn't survive that storm."

"Must've been hard, being so close to land and still so far from safety."

"The longest night of my life." Jonathan turned away to watch a man scurry up a ladder near the smokestack, his shoulders bowed under an immense coil of rope.

Eli sensed his brother was done talking about it. Both Jonathan and Noah had little to say about the events of that night, and Eli supposed he didn't blame them. Things could've gone much differently during that storm.

Jonathan crossed his arms. "You didn't say when you were going to go see Clarice. Don't you think you should make some time in your busy schedule?"

"I will. Like I said, I've been busy." Eli turned his back and headed up the next ramp.

They reached the deck near the pilothouse, their footsteps echoing on the metal decking.

"She looks about down to scrap iron right now, but just you wait. You won't even know her when I'm done." Eli patted the building plans rolled up under his arm.

"You haven't said just what you're doing to change her." Jonathan stuck his head into the pilothouse, his expression sober. For a long moment he stared at the tiny space, no doubt reliving moments of the previous November when the ship had grounded just outside the safety of the harbor, a victim of the worst storm in Duluth's history.

"Come into the chartroom, and I'll give you a quick peek." Eli shouldered the door open farther and stepped inside the wheelhouse. He ducked his head to enter the small room just behind and spread his papers on the chart table.

Jonathan followed and leaned against the railing guarding the steep steps to the hold.

"Which dock job pays the most?" Eli reached for two books to weigh down the edges of the curling blueprints.

"Lumber loaders," Jonathan answered quickly. "Every stick loaded by hand. Hard work. They deserve the pay. One of the reasons we've steered clear of hauling lumber, though I suppose with your marriage that will change."

Eli grimaced and sighed. "Look here. This is a plan for a typical lumber hooker. One hundred sixty feet long, thirty feet wide. In order to make hauling lumber efficient, a shipper usually has a steamer and a tow barge, loaded to the gunwales, with lumber stacked on the deck and in the hold." He loosened the edge of the plan, and it rolled across the table to reveal the sheet underneath. "But look at this. The *Bethany* is four hundred fifty feet long. Her capacity for lumber would be huge."

Jonathan scanned the drawing, already shaking his head. "The labor to load and unload her would erase any profit for filling her with pine. No doubt she'd hold a lot, but it would all be for nothing if you couldn't turn a profit. And she'd be laid up in the harbor for days on every trip. It would take a full crew of lumber loaders several days to fill her up. Add another several days at the other end to unload her, and you've really bottomed out the number of trips she could make in a season."

Eli grinned. "Exactly. But that's if you're loading her by hand. What if I told you I had a design that would allow you to load her by crane, and in less than five hours?"

"I'd say you're barmy." Jonathan straightened away from the chart table and crossed his arms. "But I'd be willing to listen to more."

Eli grabbed a pencil from the mug in the rack on the wall and, with a few strokes, sketched out his design. "Look, if we alter the deck hatches, it would allow enough access that an entire unit of lumber could be lowered at one time. Then, I plan to add a sliding storage system to move the lumber from side to side in the ship. By orchestrating the loading process, you could balance the lumber as you loaded it, lock it into place on the sliders, and *voilà*!"

Jonathan scratched his chin, his dark eyes keen on the sketch. "And you've thought all this out? It's really possible?"

A grimace tugged Eli's mouth, and he used the end of the pencil to scratch his hairline. "In theory. The math is a little fuzzy, but I'm working on that. It just needs a few kinks ironed out. I need to hit on just the right hatch construction that will open wide but close down to be watertight. But think what it would mean, not just to Kennebrae Shipping but to the lumbermen of Minnesota and all over the Great Lakes. Fast, efficient ways to get their lumber to purchasers."

His older brother looked thoughtful. "If it worked, it would revolutionize the industry."

"That's what I aim to do. Put Kennebrae Shipping on the map as the leader in Great Lakes shipping. And this invention and this ship will lead the way."

A knock rang on the open metal door, and Gervase Fox stepped in. "Afternoon, boys." His stare darted into every crevasse of the room, and he rubbed his hands together in relish. "Hope you don't mind my coming here to see you. I was over at my own shipyard and thought I'd stop by to see how repairs were coming on the *Bethany*."

Jonathan stepped forward, all but crowding Gervase in the small space, shielding the chart table from prying eyes.

Eli quickly picked up the books and allowed the drawings to roll up with a dry rustle.

"Gervase, just the man I wanted to see." Jonathan stuck out his hand. "I've been meaning to ask you to dine with me at the club. I want to hear all the news about this new ship you're building at your yard. Word has it she'll dwarf anything else on the lake. You'll have to be careful you don't build her so big you can't get her through the Soo Lock." He herded Gervase to the door, and before he exited, he shot a warning glance over his shoulder.

Eli nodded. Their footsteps rang on the deck, and as soon as Eli could no longer hear them, he grabbed his plans and headed down the steps to the hold.

A man in filthy overalls lay on his back half in one of the boiler fireboxes, his boots braced on the floor, his torso straining. Metal clanked on metal. The smell of coal dust, oil, and iron filled the air.

"Hey!" Eli had to shout above the noise. He leaned over the rail from the catwalk.

The man jerked then wriggled out of the hole. His expression cleared when he looked up at Eli. "Mr. Kennebrae, sir." Soot streaked his large features and coated his bald head. "Just checking the fireboxes are still sound. I know it ain't a job for a foreman, but I figured I'd feel better if I looked them over myself." He rubbed his hands on his thighs.

"Gates"—Eli rolled his papers tighter—"I want you to see that a guard is installed at the shipyard gates. Nobody in or out who isn't a Kennebrae employee. There are plenty of shippers who'd give a considerable amount if they knew what we were doing here."

"Twenty-four hours?"

"Twenty-four hours a day until this ship slides off the ways."

❧

Josie followed Grandma Bess and Clarice into the next gallery. Sunlight streamed from high windows, bathing the room with natural light that picked out all the bright colors of the paintings on the walls.

"Look at this one. I love the way the mischief shines out of that little boy's eyes." Grandma lifted her lorgnette and peered at a painting of a boy and his dog.

Josie tilted her head to look down the long room and into the next. More paintings.

Clarice passed to the next frame but appeared not to see the arrangement of fruit and flowers portrayed there. She refused to talk to Josie about Geoffrey or her engagement, wandering the house like a ghost. Mama fretted over her lack of appetite, and Grandma Bess pursed her lips and lowered her brows whenever she encountered Clarice in the house. The outing had been Grandma's idea.

"Isn't it amazing? I had no idea there were so many women artists of this caliber." Grandma consulted her catalogue. "And wasn't it clever of the Duluth Women's Suffrage League to bring this exhibition here to raise money for the cause? I hear Melissa Kennebrae headed up the committee and arranged for the gallery space."

At the mention of the Kennebrae name, Clarice started out of her trance.

The now-familiar jab poked Josie's heart. It had happened so often this week, she wondered—if she could see her heart—whether it would look as bruised and battered as it felt.

"Just imagine, all these women striking out to make their mark in what has always been considered a man's field." Grandma's cane tapped on the shiny wooden floor as she made her way to the next painting. "And they've done so with grace and dignity. Two qualities to be admired in any woman."

Clarice nodded, her carriage becoming more erect. "I intend to be a woman of grace and dignity, too. 'Above all else, cultivate a gracious and courteous demeanor at all times.' And I intend to make Mama and Papa proud of me."

Josie grimaced and tugged at her gloves. Another quote from Mrs. Morris's book. Clarice was beginning to sound just like Mama. They practically ate that book for breakfast.

"Another quality I admire, though, is bravery. These women are brave."

"Brave? How scary is it to paint pictures of pears and puppies?" Josie shrugged and edged toward the door. She had no more interest or talent for painting than she had for singing. She wanted to get home to see if there was any word from Geoff about Eli's plans.

"On the contrary, child. These paintings took a particular brand of bravery. Bravery on the part of a woman to be who God made her to be. To use the talents He's given her for His glory and the betterment of mankind." Grandma shot Josie a pointed look. "It took a lot for these women to paint these fine pictures—confidence in their own abilities, a willingness to risk the condemnation of their male counterparts, and vulnerability to exhibit their work for the comments and criticism of the general public."

"You make it sound like a battle." Josie looked at the oil landscape in front her with new interest.

"It is a battle, dear, this struggle to be the women we were created to be. The tide is changing in America, but though the doors are opening for women, we must be careful how we charge through them. To rampage, to hurl ourselves against the male establishment, is to invite their scorn, to be treated as the hysterical females we're acting like." Grandma lowered herself to a bench and stacked her hands on her cane. The long ostrich feather decorating her hat wafted with her movements. "But my granddaughters"—she smiled at them—"are smarter than that. They have grace and dignity, as these women artists do. They will find ways to ensure men see them for the treasures they are, women of intelligence, ability, and sense, with God-given talents to be exercised and appreciated."

Josie mulled over her words as they walked the remaining galleries. If she could paint like these ladies or sing or sew. . .or do anything as well as these ladies, maybe she'd be brave, too.

"And how are your mathematical studies coming along now that you've outgrown Clement's instruction?" Grandma peered through her eyeglasses at a seascape, her back to Josie.

"Fine."

"Have you ever considered what God wants you to do with your skills?"

"What can I do with them? Papa forbids higher education." Josie stared at a herd of fat cows in a meadow. "Without a degree, no one will take me seriously. And women in mathematics are more rare than quiet when Giselle's around."

"Nonsense, child. Have you heard nothing I've said? God didn't make a mistake when He gave you that brain, and He expects you to use it." Grandma huffed in impatience. "Come along. All this walking has made me tired, and we don't want to miss the last tram down the hill."

Josie followed after her, confused and somehow dissatisfied with herself and the afternoon. Would Grandma consider a little clandestine mathematical consulting work to be using her talents wisely?

Chapter 6

Eli shoved a box of books out of the way with his foot and sagged into the new leather chair, allowing the smell of the upholstery to surround him. Why had he let Jonathan talk him into moving his office into the Kennebrae Building? Sure, it was closer to the shipyard, but was the upheaval worth it? Though he admitted to a small thrust of satisfaction seeing his name in gold letters on a door at Kennebrae Shipping, he hardly felt as if he deserved it—yet.

Eli hated change almost as much as he hated the time it took away from his plans for the *Bethany*. He really should see that everything was organized in here before delving into the designs again, but the drafting table pulled at him, beckoning him to get a new idea on paper before he lost it. Ignoring the books, papers, and boxes on the floor, Eli headed to his charts to jot the idea down. It would only take a minute or two, and he could get back to clearing away this mess and have his office organized by noon.

A knock startled him out of his concentration, and he glanced at the wall clock by the door, surprised that more than three hours had passed.

Geoff opened the door and stepped in, weaving around the clutter. "Looks like the aftermath of Bull Run in here." The lawyer picked up a wooden ship model poking out of a carton. "McKay said you'd be tinkering at the drafting table instead of tidying up. Guess he knows you pretty well. I got the impression he was itching to get in here and put things to rights." He set the model on the mantel and stepped back, clunking into a pile of books.

Eli rubbed the side of his head and yawned, relaxing his jaw after such a long period of intense concentration. He rolled his shoulders and flexed the fingers of his writing hand. "Sometimes I lose track of time. I'll get it shipshape. Anyway, having visited your office, I know firsthand you're not the tidiest lawyer in town."

Geoff grinned and picked up a book, scanned the spine, and replaced it. "Is that any way to treat a man who comes bearing gifts?"

"Gifts? Well, in that case, your office is impeccable. I wouldn't change a thing." Eli shifted a rolled-up rug off a chair and beckoned Geoff to sit. "What gift?"

The chair creaked like a new saddle. "You are in need of a mathematician, I believe?"

Eli's heart thumped. "You've found someone?"

"I found someone." He laced his fingers across his vest and stuck his feet out to the cold hearth. "Professor Zechariah Josephson."

"A math professor? Perfect. When can I meet him, show him the plans?"

Geoff studied the tips of his shoes. "We–ell," he drew the word out, "that might be a problem. You see, Professor Josephson is a recluse, preferring to work alone in his study. He doesn't entertain visitors and rarely leaves his house. He's interested in your project, but all correspondence would have to take place through me to preserve his privacy."

Refusal hovered on Eli's lips. "How can we work together if we can't even go over the plans face-to-face? And where did you find this fellow anyway? Do you trust him? Is he any good at what he does?"

Geoff coughed and cleared his throat, then stared at his fingertips. "He's a friend of a friend, and I've seen some of his work. Complicated stuff—flow dynamics, load equations, stuff like that. Way over my head, but he's confident he can help you. But remaining at arm's length is unconditional. He won't have his privacy invaded. You write out in detail what it is you're trying to accomplish, give me the notes and a copy of your drawings, and I'll deliver them to Professor Josephson. When the calculations are ready, I'll bring them to you."

Impossible. Design a ship with a partner he'd never met? And yet, secrecy was of utmost importance. Who better than a recluse who never left his house? Eli spent a second wondering what Grandfather and Jonathan would say then thrust that line of thought aside. It was his project, his design. He could choose whomever he wanted to work on it. After all, it had cost him a pretty penny to achieve—engagement to a woman he barely knew.

"All right, we'll try it. It will take me a couple days to get some notes together. Is the professor local? Will it take much time to get the plans to him?"

Again Geoff contemplated his shoes. "I can have it to him in under an hour from the time you give them to me."

Eli sat back. "That will make it easier, though I'm surprised I haven't heard of this Professor Josephson. Has he done much work in the area of ship design?" Doubts trickled into his mind.

"Why don't you just try him out? If the project doesn't go like you'd hoped, you can always call things off."

Too much was riding on this to call it off. The respect of his grandfather and his brothers, the chance to do what he'd always dreamed of doing, the chance to earn this spacious office he'd been given just because his name was Kennebrae. No, he wouldn't call it off.

The signal on the desk buzzed.

Eli levered himself out of his chair and flipped the switch to the new intercom system Grandfather had installed the previous winter. "Yes?"

"Mr. Kennebrae, there's a Mr. Fox here to see you."

Eli sighed and put his palm on the back of his neck. "Send him to the boardroom. I'll meet him there."

"Gervase Fox?" Geoff rose.

"Yes. That man is everywhere. He pops up like a gopher every time I turn around. Come with me to see what he wants."

They entered the boardroom through the private entrance from the Kennebrae office suite to find Gervase standing with his hands clasped below a life-sized oil painting of Abraham Kennebrae in his prime—before his stroke. Abraham stood tall and straight in the picture, his black eyes seeming alive and full of fire, his broad shoulders and strong hands indicative of the power of his mind and will. The portrait had long intimidated Eli, and when he found himself in this room, he usually maneuvered to sit where he couldn't see it.

Fox turned and smiled. The sight of so many teeth gave Eli the willies, and he braced himself for the man's aggressive handshake. "Eli, thank you for meeting with me."

Eli noted the use of his first name with irony. They weren't on a first-name basis, but he decided to play along. "Gervase, what brings you down here?" The Duluth offices of Keystone Steel and Shipping were in a less prestigious part of town than the Kennebrae offices.

"You, son. I want to discuss the repair and refit on the *Bethany*. I'm interested in those modifications, and I'm willing to pay top dollar for them. Not only that, but I'm offering you a job as my ship designer. And I'm willing to pay top dollar for you as well." He named a sum that caused Eli's head to reel.

Geoff sucked in a gasp, and when Eli darted a look at his lawyer, Geoff's face took a moment to return to its usual politely interested expression.

"That's a lot of money, Gervase, and I do appreciate the offer, but I'm afraid I couldn't possibly leave Kennebrae Shipping." Eli leaned against the back of one of the tall chairs flanking the table, trying to appear more relaxed than he felt.

"Don't be a fool. You won't get that much a year from anyplace else, and you're low man on the totem pole around here. Jonathan will inherit, and where will you be? Noah's set, marrying money like he did. But you, you're engaged to a woman who is one of a gaggle of females. Whatever her father settles on her at her marriage is likely to be all you get. He's got a fleet of girls to launch, and a lot of dowries to pay. Zahn's rich, but he isn't that rich. I'm offering you a sizeable sum for your ideas and a great deal more for your services." Gervase's eyes glittered much like Abraham's in the portrait over his head. "Tell him, Fordham. Tell him what a fair offer I'm making."

Geoff's brows had come down, and red climbed his cheeks. His hands shook slightly.

Eli's heart warmed to see Geoff so angry on his behalf. "Geoff doesn't have to say anything. I can make up my own mind. You've got a lot of nerve thinking you can buy me like you buy a trainload of wheat or a shipload of ore. I'm not for sale, Mr. *Fox*." He trod hard upon the name, emphasizing his desire to distance himself from the odious little man. "Geoff, would you be so kind as to show Mr. Fox out then come back to my office for those plans. I'd like to get them delivered as soon as possible."

Gervase's face smoothed out, but his eyes hardened. "I hope you don't regret your decision, young man. Keystone Steel and Shipping *will* be the biggest company on the lakes, and Kennebrae Shipping will be trying to keep up. Your grandfather and brothers have stood in my way long enough." He turned on his heel and strode out, slamming the door so hard behind him, the frosted-glass pane vibrated in his wake.

&c;

Josie followed Grandma Bess into the pew at the Kennebraes' church, feeling acutely the gap where Clarice should be sitting. Clarice sat in the row before them at Mama's insistence. Right beside Eli, her fiancé. Mama insisted they all attend here this morning. Didn't want to miss a single congratulation, no doubt.

Organ music swelled out as people found their seats. Normally, Josie would've taken in all the details of the sanctuary, it being her first time at this church, but she was so miserable sitting so close to Eli and having him out of her reach, she couldn't muster the curiosity.

Josie leaned forward slightly and saw Antoinette elbow Giselle. Mama quelled them both, and Josie sat back. All of them were attired in rose dresses with ivory lace trim. Antoinette and Giselle wore ivory pinafores, but aside from that, all four girls looked identical. Josie thumbed through the songbook and wished she had coppery red hair or dusky olive skin or eyes black as an Ojibwe, something, *anything*, to be different, to stand out from her sisters and be noticed as more than just one of the Zahn girls.

The reverend took his place in the pulpit and motioned for the congregation to stand and join in the first hymn.

Eli stood and angled his body to share a hymnal with Clarice. Clarice held herself rigid, keeping space between them at all times. If it had been Josie, she'd have inched as close as she dared, just to be near him, to feel the warmth of his arm pressed to hers, perhaps to let their fingers touch.

Grandma Bess tugged Josie's sleeve. She started and realized the song had ended and everyone else had resumed their seats. Red-hot embarrassment scuttled up her cheeks, and she plopped into the pew.

"Our text for today is found in the Psalms, chapter 139 and verse 16. 'Thine eyes did see my substance, yet being unperfect; and in thy book all my members were written, which in continuance were fashioned, when as yet there was none of them.' David knew that God had planned his existence long before David ever drew his first breath. Jesse, David's father, had many sons—strong, brave, handsome sons. Seven of them passed before Samuel, and yet God didn't choose any of them to be king. He chose David, whom He had equipped specifically for kingship before David was even born."

Josie's attention wandered from contemplating Eli's broad shoulders to center on the reverend. Poor David. Seven brothers. Three sisters were bad enough.

The preacher expounded on how unique David was within his own large family, and how God had given him special abilities.

And he wasn't afraid to use them. Not against bears, lions, or giants of the Philistines. Josie ran her thumbnail along the edge of her open Bible in her lap. *He wasn't afraid to be the man God made him to be.* Visions of the paintings from the exhibition floated in her mind. All those women who used their talents. Grandma's admiration for them. Josie's own desire to study higher mathematics and use her talents and gifts. David didn't let anyone keep him from using his gifts. Resolve began to harden in her.

The service ended before Josie was ready, before she'd pursued to the end all her thoughts on the passage. When the reverend voiced the final prayer, Josie added her own to it.

God, I know You made me just the way I am, and You gave me a love of mathematics. Help me to put aside my feelings for Eli and concentrate on being the woman you made me to be. Help me to use my talents for Your glory, like David did. Amen.

She stood to sing the doxology, more peaceful in spirit than she could remember being in a long time. Though her heart squeezed in a vise of longing tinged with regret, she kept her eyes focused on the pulpit. Eli would have to cease to matter to her. She couldn't be a serious mathematician and be mooning over her sister's fiancé at the same time. She'd just have to put him out of her mind.

"Eli, you will join us for dinner? You and your grandfather?" Mama made the request sound like a command.

Josie's peace cracked like lake ice during the spring thaw. This was going to be harder than she thought.

Clarice shot an imploring glance over Josie's shoulder. Josie turned to see Geoffrey, his hands fisted at his sides. Apprehension twisted her middle. Having all of them in such close proximity reminded her of the subterfuge they'd entered into. Her conscience protested. Here she stood in the house of God, deceiving everyone around her in one form or another.

Dinner would be a nightmare.

Chapter 7

A s it turned out, Sunday dinner differed little from any other. A messenger had arrived at the church as they were exiting, whispering to Mr. Kennebrae and departing.

"You'll have to excuse us, Mrs. Zahn." Mr. Kennebrae motioned for his carriage to be brought up. "It seems my grandchild has chosen to make his appearance nearly a month early. We must get back to Kennebrae House to await his arrival."

Eli had assisted his grandfather into the coach and departed with hardly a backward glance.

When the family trooped home, Clarice went straight to bed with a headache. Mama fussed and flitted, and mid-afternoon sent Josie up with a cup of tea to check on Clarice.

Josie tapped on the door and entered. Though the pulled shades shrouded the room in darkness, she walked confidently. The furnishings exactly matched those in Josie's own room; in this aspect, too, Mama expected them to be identical. The only marked difference was the desk. Clarice's desktop was bare, not a pencil, not a book, not so much as a box of stationery. Josie couldn't remember the last time she'd seen the entire top of her own desk. "Mama sent up some chamomile. How's your head?" She directed the comments to the lump under the covers.

The bundle shifted, and Clarice's face appeared in the gloom. "The head's fine."

Josie set the tea tray on the dressing table and sank onto the bed. "Useful things, headaches." She laced her fingers around the post at the foot of the bed and leaned back. "Keeps you from having to do all sorts of things."

"Humph. If it would keep me from having to marry Eli Kennebrae, I'd come down with a migraine for the rest of my adult life."

Josie pursed her lips. "I've come to a decision today. You want to hear what it is? It might take your mind off things for a while."

Clarice scooched up to rest against the mounds of lacy pillows. Her knees bent up to form a slope of bedspread. "Nothing will take my mind off things, but go ahead. I can see you're dying to tell me."

"I'm going to be the woman God made me to be." Josie couldn't keep the triumph out of her voice.

"Congratulations." Clarice looped her arms around her shins and rested her chin on her knees. She gave Josie a dubious look.

"No, seriously. I've decided to be like those painters we saw this week. I'm going to go to college and study mathematics."

Clarice rolled her eyes and shook her head. "Don't be silly. You can't go to college. Papa would have a fit, not to mention the absolute earthquake Mama would cause. And where will you get the money? Papa won't pay your tuition. 'Women have no business studying beyond what is necessary for running a household and raising children,'" Clarice intoned, deepening her voice in a fairly good imitation of Papa.

"I don't care. I'll find a way. Didn't you listen this morning? The reverend said we needed to use our talents like David did. God-given ability should be used for God's glory."

Clarice ran her tongue over her upper teeth and thought for a moment. "God also says obey your parents."

Josie flopped backward on the bed, wincing as her hairpins poked the back of her head. "What if your parents are wrong? Sometimes doing the right thing means you have to go against other people's ideas of what is right. David did what was right, even when his brothers didn't like it. He faced down a giant who was defying God. David knew what he had to do, and he did it in spite of opposition." She scowled at the canopy. "Mama and Papa can try to fit me into their mold of a 'proper young lady,' but I don't have to let them succeed."

Clarice wrapped her arms tighter around her legs and stared at the little bump her toes formed under the covers. "I wish I had your courage, Josie."

∽

Matthew Abraham Kennebrae arrived less than an hour after Eli and Grandfather made it home from church. The doctor, packing his bag, smiled and shook his head. "Mighty quick labor for a first child."

Grandfather wheeled his chair close to Melissa's side and peered at the swaddled bundle in her arms. "You're sure he's healthy? And Melissa, too? He's on the early side by a few weeks."

"Sound as a dollar. Though I can't say the same for Jonathan." The doctor looked over the rims of his glasses to where Jonathan lay sprawled in a chair. "His missus did well, and she'll be back on her feet in no time. It's the husbands who can't stand up under the strain."

Melissa motioned for Eli to step close. "Here, you should hold him. Everyone else has had a turn."

Eli backed up a step. "No, no. He's too little. I wouldn't want to break him." His mouth went dry at the very thought.

"He's a Kennebrae. They don't break so easily." Melissa bent a loving look on the squeaking, grunting infant. Her eyes glowed in a way that made Eli's chest feel full and empty at the same time. He found himself stepping forward and accepting his nephew into his arms.

It was like holding air. The baby regarded him solemnly with hazy-dark blue eyes. Eli's heart constricted for a moment. What would it be like to hold his own son? To cradle his heir and offspring and feel a tide of love and protectiveness crash over him? A whole little person in his arms. A miracle, right in front of his eyes.

"That's enough." The doctor took the baby and placed him in the crib beside the bed. "Mrs. Kennebrae needs her rest. She can't get it with you men in here."

Grandfather went to his bedroom to rest before dinner, while Eli headed to the parlor. He would spend the afternoon working on the sketches for the hatch mechanisms until dinner was ready. Jonathan followed, too keyed up to settle to anything.

An hour later, Eli wished he'd gone to the office. Jonathan wouldn't leave off talking, and becoming a new father seemed to make him an expert on marriage and family.

"You need to take this seriously. Ignoring the situation won't make it go away." Jonathan tossed the newspaper down on the footstool.

Eli put his pencil down and looked over his shoulder. "Who says I'm not taking it seriously?"

"I do. Every time I broach the subject, you skitter away like a bug on a stove lid. Marriage is serious business. It changes your whole life. Or at least it should. I bet you haven't spent more than five minutes considering the ramifications of marrying Clarice Zahn. How did Grandfather maneuver you into this engagement in the first place? What did he offer you?" As if he couldn't bear to be still another minute, Jonathan sprang up and paced the salon carpet. He clasped his hands together behind his back and lowered his chin.

Eli sighed and turned on his chair until he could rest his arm along the back. "That's between Grandfather and me, and who's to say it won't all work out fine? It sure did for you and for Noah."

Jonathan stopped and put his hands on his waist. "Your treatment of your fiancée is atrocious. You haven't spent more than an hour in her presence, and most of that time was in church. You have no idea if you'll be compatible. If I'd have treated Melissa in such a callous manner, our marriage would be a nightmare, and I'd have no one to blame but myself."

Eli shifted in his chair. "What do you expect from me? Grandfather arranged this marriage. It isn't as if I have to court the woman. And frankly, I get the distinct impression the lady would prefer me to keep my distance."

The fact chafed. Clarice had barely spoken to him this morning. When he'd offered his arm to see her out of church, she acted as if a timber rattler had slithered past her fingers. "I asked her if everything was all right, and she said, 'Fine.'"

Jonathan snorted. "If there's one thing I've learned from being married to Melissa, it's that when a woman says things are fine, it never means fine. If Melissa says she's fine, I'm usually in trouble. 'Fine' has a million meanings to a woman, and none of them match up to what it says in Webster's."

Eli tilted his head and cocked an eyebrow. "So what do you suggest I do?"

"Spend some time with Clarice. Figure out how she feels about the whole thing. Take her out; get to know her. She seems like a nice girl. And above all else, to save your sanity and the peace of your future marriage, find out what she means when she says, 'Fine.'"

The task of unraveling a woman's thought processes boggled Eli's mind. Why couldn't they be straightforward, like men? Eli knew where he was with a man. Like Gervase Fox. He got directly to the point. And Eli had been just as blunt in reply. No secrets, no hidden meanings, just straight shooting.

"They shouldn't make things so complicated." Eli stood and gathered up the papers he'd been working on. "I'm going to my room to work. I can't concentrate here."

Jonathan shook his head, eyeing Eli gravely. "Trust me, Eli. You're going to have to put some effort into this relationship before you take her as your wife. Your life and hers will be miserable if you don't."

⁓

Josie strolled down the canal pier, listening to the slap of waves against the pilings, wishing she could pull the pins from her upswept hair. A pleasant breeze teased the tendrils along her temples and nape. The high lace collar of her afternoon gown itched just below her jawline.

Clarice walked beside her, careful to shield her face from the sun with her parasol. All traces of her headache had disappeared the moment Josie suggested this excursion. "What time were you supposed to meet him?"

Gulls sailed and swooped overhead, squabbling and calling. Josie checked the watch pinned to her lapel. "He said six o'clock in his note. We're a few minutes early."

"Why did he want to meet you in the harbor? It isn't a very nice place. Why not in one of the parks?" Clarice sidestepped two gulls fighting over a piece of garbage. "It's so dirty down here." She tugged her lace gloves on more firmly.

Josie stopped to lean on the concrete wall. She loved the harbor, the sights, the smells, the sounds. Even on a late Sunday afternoon, Duluth Harbor hummed with energy. The lake surged with a life of its own, ever different, ever the same. She peered into the brownish-blue water of the canal.

A mama mallard bobbed on the waves, her clutch of ducklings like a small flotilla behind her, paddling furiously to keep up. Their tiny peeps made Josie smile. A brave mama indeed to take her babies out on the massive water, and yet they looked content enough.

"Geoffrey said he would explain when he got here." Josie wondered at the wisdom of bringing Clarice. She couldn't escape the fact that she was somehow abetting her sister in being unfaithful to Eli. But that was silly. Neither had sought the engagement they found themselves in. And what harm could come from Geoff and Clarice meeting in a public place like the harbor, especially with Josie in tow?

"There he is." Clarice's cheeks flushed, and her eyes took on a glow Josie had never seen before.

Geoff strode toward them, the breeze ruffling his hair, his long strides eating up the distance between them. He held a rolled-up bunch of papers clamped under his arm, and his hands were thrust deep into his pockets. When he arrived, he had eyes only for Clarice. His Adam's apple lurched, and Josie had the uncomfortable feeling that she was witnessing something deeply private.

Clarice's mouth trembled.

A shaft of sympathy arced through Josie. She knew what it was to be in love with someone out of her reach. Knowing she was intruding, Josie turned her back and contemplated the ducks again. *God, how did we wind up in this mess? They are so in love. How can it be wrong for them to be together? But what of Eli? What would he say if he knew?* She shoved aside her guilt and cleared her throat, turning around to face Geoff and Clarice.

Geoff seemed to realize for the first time that Josie was there. Faint ruddiness climbed his neck, and he touched the brim of his hat. "Hey there, Professor."

"Are those for me?" Josie motioned to the papers.

He took them out and handed them to her. "Schematics, supply lists, and here's an envelope with notes from Eli." A thick brown envelope appeared from inside his coat. "I picked them up on the way down here. Big uproar at Kennebrae House. Abraham's fit to burst his buttons. He has a great-grandson."

Was Eli as happy as his grandfather? As close as he seemed to his brothers, he must be happy for Jonathan and Melissa. Josie had to remind herself that she wasn't supposed to feel this glad. It wasn't as if she were part of the Kennebrae family. How deeply ingrained thoughts of Eli had become. This infatuation had to end. Eli was engaged to Clarice, and Josie had best get used to the idea. The wind fluttered the edges of the rolled-up papers, reminding her why she was here.

"Did Eli say when he expected a reply?" Josie turned and laid the plans on the wall, anxious to get her first peek at the design. She anchored the pages with her arms. It would just be the end if she let them drop into the water.

Geoff stepped close and looked at the drawings. "He said he put it all in the notes, just what he was looking for and what he needed help with. Are you sure you can do this?"

Josie glanced up, indignant.

Geoff's brow was wrinkled, and he ran his fingertips down his shirtfront. Clarice took his arm. "You don't need to worry, Geoff. Josie *dreams* in numbers."

Josie shot Clarice a grateful look and carefully rolled the pages up again. "I'll get to work on these as soon as I get home. How should I contact you when I'm done?"

Geoff dug again into his pocket and produced a card. "Send word to me at this address when you're ready, and we'll arrange a time to meet."

Josie scanned the card, plain white with bold black lettering, nodding. Now that she had the plans, she itched to get started. How she wished her relationship with Eli weren't so distant, having to go through someone else in order to share ideas and explore design possibilities. If only they could meet as equals, as peers in this project. . . But that was foolish. No powerful man like Eli would ever see her as a peer or respect her work and abilities enough to admit he needed her help. She glanced at her timepiece. "We'd best get back. Mama will be wondering where we've gotten to."

"Oh no, not yet." Clarice's eyes implored Josie. "Just a few more minutes, please?"

Clarice had never been so open with Josie, had never let Josie see her want something so desperately. Pity again swamped Josie at their tangled situation.

"Here, before you have to go, there's something I wanted you to see." Geoff handed Josie a pair of field glasses from his pocket. "If you look over there"—he pointed across the harbor beyond the ore docks—"you can see the Kennebrae Shipyard. The ship you're working on is the *Bethany*."

Josie smiled and took the glasses. "Here, hang on to these while I walk up the way for a better look."

Geoff took the plans and the envelope back, giving Josie a grateful smile. "Take your time."

Josie walked toward the bridge, and when she was out of earshot of the couple, she lifted the binoculars. The great hulk of the *Bethany* swung into her view. Scaffolding shrouded her in a maze of boards and poles. The cleft amidships showed bright with new welds and repairs, ropes swung in the wind, and the deck had been removed like the lid of a sardine can. All that remained of the ship that had sat icebound just outside the harbor last winter was the hull and pilothouse and the great smokestack. Behind the ship, the long, sloped roof of the shipyard building loomed, KENNEBRAE SHIPPING painted in high, white letters on a vertical sign at the peak.

Resolve and eagerness merged as Josie scanned the length of the ship. She could do this. She *would* do this, for herself and for Eli. Though he may be out of her reach forever, she could still be joined with him in this project. They'd be unknowing partners in fulfilling his plans.

She lowered the glasses and looked over her shoulder. Clarice and Geoffrey had their heads together. Josie sighed. She'd best get back there and act the chaperone. The last thing any of them wanted was someone wondering why Clarice, engaged to a Kennebrae, would be out walking alone with another man.

She headed their direction, and as she neared, she realized that someone else was on an intercepting vector with the couple. The short, rounded man looked familiar to her, but she couldn't place him from that distance. She raised the glasses and brought his face close in her vision.

Uneasiness quickened her pulse and her steps. Where had she seen him before? He looked determined and purposeful. "Here." Josie put out her hand for the ship plans when she was close enough to Geoff. "We need to go, now."

"So soon?" He handed her the papers and frowned. A page fluttered away.

"Quick, catch it!" Josie hurried up the sidewalk after the sheet. Just as she bent down for it a shoe came down hard, sticking the page to the ground.

"Lose something?"

She looked up into the short man's face.

He took her elbow and helped her upright, then bent to retrieve the sheet. He looked at it, then at her, calculation gleaming in his eyes.

She took the page and folded it, tucking it in with the others rolled under her arm.

Geoffrey stalked up and nodded curtly. "Fox, what brings you down to the canal on a Sunday afternoon?"

"Wish it was the same reason as you. Hello, ladies. I don't believe we've met." Mr. Fox tipped his hat.

"The Misses Zahn. But they were just leaving."

Josie took the hint, settled the papers in her arms, and took Clarice's elbow. "I'll contact you as soon as I can about these."

Chapter 8

This was a bad idea, and it had taken Eli an entire week since speaking with Jonathan about courting to come up with even this much. What had possessed him to invite Clarice to the circus of all things? He sat in the Zahn parlor, rotating his hat brim in his hands.

Geoffrey would have a good laugh when he heard about that. Eli frowned. No, Geoff probably wouldn't laugh about it. Geoff didn't seem to laugh about anything these days.

The clock on the table beside him chimed the quarter hour. What was keeping Clarice?

A movement caught his eye. The curtains in the doorway swayed, and a pair of bright-blue eyes peeked through the fringe edging. A black curl slipped off a shoulder, and a giggle erupted. More movement, scuffling, snickering, and two girls tumbled through the doorway onto the rug.

"You pushed me!" The smaller of the two scrambled up.

"Did not. You're just clumsy." The bigger girl stuck her tongue out at her little sister.

Eli said nothing. If there was anything that baffled him more than a woman, it was a little girl. The sisters seemed to suddenly remember his presence, for they lined up, shoulder to shoulder, and smoothed their aprons. They stared at him, the younger twisting one curl around her finger.

Mrs. Zahn sailed into the room.

Eli stood, grateful for an escape from the scrutiny.

"So sorry to keep you waiting, but it seems Clarice has succumbed to another of her sick headaches. She won't be able to accompany you on your outing." Her eyes had a hectic sheen, as if she were flustered but trying to hide it.

Relief rushed through his chest. Reprieve. "That's quite all right, madam. Please give her my regards." If he left now, he'd still have several hours to see to the laying of the first pieces of the loading system in the bottom of the hold. Not having to go to the circus felt more like shackles being dropped from his wrists.

"But I don't want to disappoint the girls. You see, Clarice promised them you'd take them in her stead." Mrs. Zahn cupped the back of the younger's head and pushed her forward a step. "They've talked of nothing else since breakfast. You will take them, won't you?"

He could have sworn the little girl's eyes filled with tears on command. How did she do that? The other one challenged him with her stare, unable to keep the excitement out of her eyes.

Before he could answer, Josie entered the room. She'd seemed levelheaded when he'd spoken to her at the wedding reception. When their eyes met, he couldn't seem to look away. What was it about her that intrigued him? The Zahn girls all looked cut from the same cloth, but something in her walk, in her expression, seemed so familiar to him and yet completely unknown.

He shrugged and forced himself to focus on what Mrs. Zahn was saying.

"They won't be any trouble. Josephine will go along and help you with them. And please, do accept my apologies for Clarice. She doesn't usually suffer from headaches."

Josie moistened her lips, and her right hand clasped the middle two fingers of her left hand and twisted them.

His attention was diverted by the littler one tugging on his coat sleeve. "You will take us, won't you? I want to see an elephant."

So Eli found himself in the center of a ruffled and beribboned tornado. High-pitched voices filled the airspace in the carriage; little bodies bounced on the seats, noticing everything. After less than three minutes, he gave up trying to follow the conversation and settled into his corner with crossed arms. How did he let himself get talked into this? His one goal of spending time with his intended had burst apart into this female cacophony. The closer they got to the circus tent, the more their excitement level grew.

Josie grabbed the smallest girl's waistband and pulled her back from where she tried to hang out the window. "Sit still, Giselle. You'll fall out on the road if you're not careful."

"But look at the flags. Look at the wagons."

Calliope music whistled and punctuated the air. Eli caught the scents of popcorn and sawdust and the musky smell of animals and canvas.

The Kennebrae coachman pulled the carriage up close to the big top and opened the door. Eli got out first to assist the girls. He needn't have bothered. They shot out like corks from a bottle, except for Josie. She took his hand and stepped down, not meeting his eyes. The wind blew a strand of hair across her cheek, and she hooked it back with her little finger, a gesture he remembered from the last time they'd spoken.

The barker beckoned them, and Antoinette grabbed his hand. "C'mon!" Her hair bounced as she wriggled and jumped.

He allowed himself to be led toward the open tent flap. "They sure are lively." He directed his comment over his shoulder to where Josie trailed behind. The little one had a tight grip on him, but he forced her to stop so he could dig in his pocket for enough change to buy four tickets. Josie stopped beside him, and he thought he caught a whiff of violets. "They seem to hop in all directions."

"You get used to it." She swallowed, and he found his attention centered on her delicate throat. "Thank you for taking us out today. I know you'd rather be with Clarice, and that Mama sort of cornered you into this. She can be quite forceful at times." A delicate flush brightened her cheeks, and her smoky lashes hid her eyes.

Would he? Would he rather be with Clarice? He had to admit no, not really. The little girls seemed eager for his company, where his fiancée avoided him to the point where it made her ill. And he found himself not reluctant to share Josie's company in particular. "Don't worry about it. You're never too old to see a circus."

They found seats on the hard benches, and Eli tried to maneuver them so he could sit by Josie, but he found himself between Antoinette and Giselle. Sharp elbows, enormous bows clipping him in the chin, and restless movement unsettled him. He looked over Giselle's head at Josie.

Her eyes moved, taking everything in. A band at the far end played a lively tune. "We've never been to the circus before." Her face, flushed with pleasure, attracted him.

"I'm glad you got to come then."

A man in a red-and-white-striped jacket and straw boater paused before their row. He carried a box suspended from his shoulders by wide straps. "Peanuts, popcorn, candy!"

Eli glanced down at Giselle, who had tucked her lips in and clasped her hands under her chin. It was the first time she'd sat still all day. Antoinette on his other side grinned at him with wide, hopeful eyes. With a chuckle and shrug, he dug into his breast pocket for his wallet. No sense going to the circus if you didn't eat some sweets.

Each girl selected her preference from the vendor. He noticed that Josie selected a striped bag of peppermint sticks, the least costly item offered. "Thank you, Mr. Kennebrae."

"Please, call me Eli, and it's my pleasure." And he found that it truly was. And that should bother him, shouldn't it? He had the distinct feeling that if Josie had been his fiancée and not the reluctant Clarice, he wouldn't mind the idea of matrimony in the least. His conscience jabbed him for his disloyal thoughts. But could a man be disloyal to a fiancée he'd neither sought nor wanted?

∞

Josie took another grip on her traitorous emotions. She shouldn't be enjoying this outing so much, not when she'd just finally decided to put Eli Kennebrae out of her mind and heart and pursue her mathematics. Not that it was the outing that caused her such turmoil. No, it was him.

The initial thrust of pleasure at seeing him again had subsided. In its wake, her heart beat fast against her ribs, her mouth went dry, and she couldn't seem to stop her eyes from straying in his direction every few seconds.

Poor Giselle. Josie had all but pushed her into the row before her so Josie wouldn't have to sit beside Eli. The little girl wriggled and gasped and talked nineteen to the dozen, masking Josie's emotional upheaval. At least she hoped it did.

"Balloons! Look at the balloons!" Giselle stood and pointed down where a white-faced clown with enormous checked pants walked past trailing a rainbow cloud of balloons.

Josie pressed her little sister's shoulder to get her to resume her seat. "Giselle, don't point. It's rude."

"But look at the funny man." She craned her neck and perched on the edge of the bench to follow him down the tent.

"Ladies and gentlemen, children of all ages!" The ringmaster bounded into the center ring, a bright light surrounding him and gleaming off his shiny high boots and tall hat.

Giselle's attention riveted on the red-coated man. Josie glanced out of the corner of her eye toward Eli. He appeared to be studying the poles and rigging overhead.

She allowed herself to be drawn into the spectacle, laughing at the clowns' antics, admiring the beautiful white horses and enormous elephants. The snarls of the tigers and lions made her skin prickle.

"And now, ladies and gentlemen, all the way from Budapest, I present to you the bravest, the most talented, the amazing Istvan Hrabowski!" The ringmaster made a sweeping gesture, and the spotlight shot upward to where a man stood on a tiny platform affixed to one of the tent poles. "Istvan, a magician of balance, a man who knows no fear, will dazzle you with his high-wire abilities! Thirty feet in the air, and no net should he fall. He risks death for your amusement."

Giselle pressed close to Josie. She pressed her lips against Josie's ear and whispered, "I'm scared. That man might fall."

Josie smoothed the girl's hair, not wanting to admit her own apprehension. She turned Giselle away from her and put her hands under the little girl's arms. "You can sit with me. And don't you worry. He's done this lots of times." At least she hoped he had.

Giselle snuggled close, hiding her eyes with her hands but peeking through her fingers. Josie suddenly realized that with Giselle in her lap, no one now sat between her and Eli.

He scooched along the bench toward her, his eyes clouded. "Is she all right?"

Josie nodded, touched by his concern. "It's a bit scary." She hugged Giselle close, taking comfort in the warm little body.

The performer, holding a long pole for balance, marched across the wire as casually as if he were walking down the street. The *rat-a-tat* of a drum accompanied him, echoing the beating of Josie's heart, intensifying her anxiety. Each trip he made across the taut cable, he added a level of difficulty. Each time he stepped safely onto the small platform, the band let out a flourish, and the man waved to the crowd, accepting their applause. Each time he started across with another apparatus, Josie sucked in her breath and held it.

When he started across with a chair in hand and placed it on the wire, she bit her lip, and Giselle tucked her head under Josie's chin. Eli slid a little closer, and somehow she found her hand clasped in his. Heat surged through her cheeks. Had she taken his hand, or had he taken hers?

He leaned close, his breath teasing her temple. "Don't be scared."

Josie forgot all about the man teetering dangerously overhead and concentrated on her heart teetering dangerously near to toppling over in her chest. This was wrong. Eli was Clarice's husband-to-be. No matter that he was only offering comfort, no matter that he hadn't shown the least inclination of affection for her, she shouldn't be holding his hand, and furthermore, she shouldn't be enjoying it so much. Her chest felt as if a dozen mice were scurrying around inside.

She didn't know who was more relieved when the Amazing Istvan navigated the wire for the last time, Giselle or herself. She disengaged her fingers from Eli's hand, already missing his touch but able to breathe easier after breaking contact. She couldn't look at him, instead lowering her chin to Giselle's shoulder so the little girl's head was between her and Eli.

The girls were much subdued on the ride home. Sated with sweets and popcorn, roasted peanuts and candy floss, they dragged into the carriage for the ride down the hill and across the canal. Josie kept Giselle in her lap and wasn't surprised when her two youngest sisters drifted into sleep. Antoinette's head rested against Eli's shoulder, and he smiled across the carriage at Josie.

She couldn't help responding to the warmth in his eyes. Her conscience elbowed her. He had been nothing but kind to them, a bachelor fettered with three girls on an outing. His handclasp had meant nothing more to him than if she had been Giselle. She should stop obsessing about it and try to remember he was her sister's fiancé.

Chapter 9

Y ou didn't even see her?" Grandfather pushed aside McKay's help and settled the lap robe across his thin legs himself. "I thought you had an outing planned."

Eli shrugged out of his jacket and draped it over the back of a chair. He yawned and loosened his tie. "I did, but she couldn't come. A headache, I believe." He had serious doubts about that headache.

"But you were gone all afternoon, and what's that smell?" Grandfather sniffed the air like a bird dog. "Is that popcorn?"

"Popcorn, peppermint, lemon drops, sawdust, and a dose of sarsaparilla. I spent the afternoon at the circus." He eased into the chair and rested his head against his jacket, breathing the scents in again. One scent lingered in his memory. Violets.

"The circus?"

"I tried to take Clarice but ended up taking her sisters instead."

McKay's normally impassive face twitched. He turned away and busied himself straightening things on Grandfather's desk. "Will that be all, sir?"

Grandfather waved the butler away. "Yes, yes, quit fussing. Go see if Melissa needs anything." He turned his attention back to Eli. "This is all your fault, you know."

"What's my fault?" Eli frowned and studied his fingernails.

"That things aren't progressing with Clarice. There's no reason why you two can't make a sensible, suitable match. I did my homework. Her family is respectable. She's even tempered and more than passably good-looking." Grandfather picked up the letter opener on his desk and rotated the point against his palm. "Radcliffe came by this morning and said he's not happy with how this engagement is going. He's concerned that you're not spending enough time with the girl. And I agree."

"What do you want me to do? I made the offer. She couldn't come. Or wouldn't come." He had to admit he wasn't used to women avoiding him. Though he hadn't ever courted before, he never assumed it would be so hard. How could he court a girl he couldn't get near?

"You're not doing anything to further this relationship. The circus? How childish is that? If you want to win this girl—and more importantly, win her father's approval again—you've got to do something romantic for her. Flowers,

303

candy, that sort of thing. When I courted your grandmother—God rest her soul—she expected flowers every time I visited. . .and the occasional drive in the country and sweets. And Jonathan brings Melissa roses for everything. You saw the bouquets after Matthew was born."

Flowers. He could do that. Get McKay to send a bunch or two. And the confectioner's shop delivered. "And that will get you off my back? I have work to do. She should understand that I can't be spending every waking minute trying to figure out what will make her happy." He rose, his muscles tight in annoyance. "I don't know why I have to court the girl anyway. We're already engaged, thanks to you. Seems we bypassed courting some time back."

The letter opener clattered to the desk. "You'll court the girl because it's the gentlemanly thing to do and because her father wishes it. Also because I wish it, and I'm footing the bride price by financing your shipbuilding schemes."

Eli bit back the hot retort burning his tongue. He couldn't afford to get Grandfather so riled he withdrew the money. "Any other suggestions?" If his lips got any stiffer, they might snap right off.

"It's high time you bought the engagement ring. Jewelry always works on a woman. Get her something you know she'll like, something big and sparkly that shows you spent some time and a considerable amount of cash. That will turn her head in your direction and mollify her mother at the same time."

"I don't know anything about jewelry shopping. And I've no clue what she would like." At the idea of walking into a jewelry store and picking out a ring, his heart quailed. It was too much to ask. "Couldn't she just go pick something out herself and charge it to my account?"

"You don't know a blessed thing about women."

"That's what I've tried to tell you. You're the one who backed me into this corner. If I had my way, I'd still be a happily oblivious bachelor who had nothing more complex to think about than what gauge steel to use for the new beams in the cargo hold of the *Bethany*. I couldn't begin to imagine what kind of engagement ring to buy for Clarice Zahn." Just saying the words made his skin crawl. All this was getting uncomfortably close to real and harder to push to the back of his mind. He wanted to concentrate on his ship, not on this stupid engagement.

"I raised you smarter than that. If you want to know what she likes, then ask her. Or better yet, ask her mother. But get it done." Grandfather rang the bell for McKay. "I can't do everything for you."

The butler entered so quickly, Eli suspected he had hovered in the hall. McKay shot him an inquiring glance, but Eli shrugged.

"He didn't want you. I did." Grandfather tugged on the wheels of his invalid chair. "I have to do everything around here. Send a note to Pearson's Jewelers that this stubborn grandson of mine will be in tomorrow afternoon to purchase an engagement ring. Tell them to have the best in the store ready for him and a private room for viewing."

"Tomorrow? I can't tomorrow. I'm meeting with my job foreman all afternoon."

"No, you're not. You're meeting with the jeweler. Find out what the girl likes, and get a ring on her hand as soon as possible."

❧

Josie hid in the library, trying to concentrate on mathematics and forget the happiness of being in Eli's presence all yesterday afternoon.

Clarice hadn't been the least bit interested in hearing about the circus, and it wasn't until much later last night she confessed that Geoffrey had met her in the garden while Josie was uptown. Her sister's eyes glowed, and she kept sighing and staring off into the distance. Her only response when Josie mentioned Eli was to brush aside the comment. "Don't worry about it. Geoffrey says he has a plan."

Josie didn't know what to do. On the one hand, her heart broke for Clarice, forced to marry one man when her heart clearly belonged to Geoffrey. But what about Eli? He didn't deserve such shoddy treatment from his fiancée. Why, if anyone found out about Geoffrey and Clarice's clandestine meeting, Clarice would be ruined, Geoffrey would be fired, and Eli would be humiliated. Geoffrey may have a plan, but it was only a delay tactic, keeping Eli focused on his ship. Eventually Mama would set a wedding date and expect Clarice to say her vows. What a mess. Josie had escaped to the library as soon as she could to try to get a hold on her emotions.

"Miss Josie, there's a gentleman here to see you." The housekeeper entered the library and handed Josie a calling card.

Her heart rocketed into high gear. Mr. Eli Kennebrae. "Are you sure this is for me? Isn't he here to see Clarice?" She casually turned over the paper she was working on in her lap, hiding the drawing.

"He asked for you." The spare, stern woman folded her weathered hands at the waist of her immaculate white apron. "Shall I tell him you're at home?"

Josie swung her feet down from the chair and straightened. "Show him to the parlor. I'll be there in a minute." Her mind raced. What could he want? She had to stand on tiptoe to see her reflection in the mirror over the desk. Traitorous color bloomed on her cheekbones. She smoothed her hair up into its loose bun and checked her dress was straight. Just before she left the library she tucked her books and papers away. It wouldn't do to leave them lying around where anyone could see them.

He stood near the front window, Mama's Boston fern almost touching his black pant leg. His hands clasped behind him, he didn't see her at first. She took a moment to notice how his brown hair swept back from his intelligent brow and how the strong column of his neck, suntanned and smooth, disappeared into his snowy collar.

Josie cleared her throat softly. His head came around, and she stared into his eyes. For a long moment, neither moved. All the warm feelings she'd been shoving down about him welled up and threatened to spill out of her gaze. She quickly lowered her eyelashes and schooled her features to be polite but distant. Why was it she could still feel the clasp of his fingers around hers? *Stop it. Concentrate or you'll say something stupid and embarrass yourself.*

"Josie." His smile brightened his face. "Thank you for seeing me. I have a tremendous favor to ask of you. Would you be so kind as to accompany me downtown this afternoon?"

He took her breath away. He was asking her? She tried to retrieve some air while her mind galloped as fast as her heart. What about Clarice? Was this proper? "Are you sure you don't want my sister?" Perhaps he had done what many people did and confused her for one of her siblings. There were a lot of Zahn girls.

His lips twitched. "I assure you I don't wish to see any other of your siblings. I have need of your expertise."

His words shot through her like a bolt. "My expertise?" Had Geoffrey spilled the beans about her math abilities?

"I find myself in the unfamiliar position of purchasing an engagement ring. I had hoped you would go to the jeweler's and assist me in choosing one your sister would like." He shook his head. "Grandfather suggested I ask your mother to help me, but I'd much prefer your aid. Surely you know your sister's tastes and could advise me."

Josie instantly knew the meaning of the word *bleak*. Was God testing her resolve?

At her hesitation, his gaze sharpened. "Have I stepped out of line? I suppose I assumed now would be all right. The jeweler is expecting me in about half an hour."

"No, not at all." Josie clamped down on her emotions and strove to be polite. "I'll just get my hat and gloves."

Josie practiced rigid self-control on the ride. She answered Eli politely when he commented about the weather and the ship lying at anchor just outside the harbor awaiting entrance to load tons of iron at the ore docks. She remembered to thank him again for taking her and her sisters to the circus.

He seemed to swallow up all the air in the carriage, though he sat across from her and didn't crowd her legs. "I hope it wasn't too stimulating for Giselle. I've never seen anyone sleep so soundly as she did on the ride home."

"She's talked of nothing else since." Josie smiled fondly, remembering how Giselle had clasped her hands round the bedpost and swung back and forth as she talked. "You made quite an impression on Giselle and Antoinette. I suspect both girls are nursing a bit of puppy love now." Not to mention herself and the silly infatuation she cherished for him that refused to die no matter how often she tried to strangle it.

He laughed. "Only Giselle and Antoinette? And here I thought I'd cast my net wider. And where did all those French names come from? Zahn's not French."

"No, Zahn is actually German." She grimaced. "The French names were Mama's idea, one that Papa regrets intensely. She thought it made us sound more aristocratic."

Eli shrugged in sympathy. "I'm told my mother insisted on Bible names for her sons. Jonathan and Noah are all right names, but Eli? Who wants to be named after a man who was such a dismal failure as a priest and as a father?"

"You shouldn't look at it that way. Look at his good qualities. He recognized the call of God on Samuel's life, and he raised Samuel right. Eli's a fine name." Josie didn't know why she felt the need to defend his name. It shouldn't matter to her if he liked his mother's choice or not.

The carriage rocked to a stop. Eli hopped out and helped her down before the coachman could. "Thank you for coming with me today. I confess I don't have the faintest idea what your sister might like."

Regret, jealousy, a bit of disgruntlement? Josie couldn't identify the emotions bouncing around inside her. This excursion would be so different if he were buying a ring for her. A hush descended the moment her foot touched the plush carpeting. Bright gaslights shone powerful beams down on display cases of dazzling jewels. Lighted alcoves of gleaming silver service and flatware marched down the walls of the shop.

"Mr. Kennebrae? I'm Marlow Pearson, the proprietor." A corpulent man with a jolly face came toward them. His quiet voice seemed in contrast to the smile he directed. Short arms barely reached across his middle, and his neck and several chins spilled out over the top of his collar. "And this is your young lady? Splendid."

Josie looked quickly at Eli's face then dropped her gaze to her hemline.

Eli shook the fat fingers offered to him and said, "This is Miss Zahn. She's come to help me choose just the right ring."

Josie looked up again. Why hadn't he bothered to correct the jeweler? And why did it feel nice to be considered his young lady?

"Right this way. I've laid out a selection for you, but if they don't suffice, let me know." Mr. Pearson's short legs rolled under his bulk, but his feet made no sound as he led them toward the back of the shop. A door that at first glance seemed part of the rich walnut paneling opened at his touch, revealing a small conference room.

"Please, have a seat." Mr. Pearson opened a heavy felt cloth and spread it on the gleaming tabletop. From a cart along the wall, he produced a tray of black velvet, studded with rings. "I'll just turn up the lights a bit, so you can see them better." He turned the key on the overhead lamp to increase the flame.

Eli held Josie's chair then sat beside her.

Josie couldn't take her eyes off those rings. Diamonds in every shape and arrangement, some big as gravel. Rubies, sapphires, emeralds, and more diamonds. They must be worth a king's ransom.

"See anything you like?" Eli leaned back as if he had no interest in the proceedings.

Pearson hovered, rubbing his fingertips with his thumbs. Probably already counting the profits to be made from her choice. So many rings to choose from. Not a single space on the tray remained empty. Having the proprietor looming like a gargoyle on a cornice didn't help. He seemed to sense her hesitation. "Let me get you some coffee or tea. It's a big decision, picking out a ring. Take your time."

As soon as the door closed silently behind the round little man, Josie turned to Eli. "These stones are huge. Are you sure?"

"You think she won't like one of them? Grandfather seemed to think the bigger the better when it came to precious stones."

"Clarice does like diamonds, and I know Mama would love for her to have a real showpiece to brag about."

"But you don't?" His attention focused on her face.

She shrugged. "This isn't about what I want. This is about Clarice." She wasn't sure if she said it to remind him or to remind herself.

"Well, suppose it were about what you wanted. What would you choose, and how would it differ from what Clarice would like?" He sat up and leaned on his crossed arms on the edge of the table.

She surveyed the engagement rings again. "I suppose I'd choose this one, if it were for me." An oval stone that shot rainbows of turquoise and magenta in tiny sparkles mingled with gold. An opal. The smallest, plainest ring in the collection.

His eyebrows shot up. "Not a diamond?" He seemed puzzled by her choice but not displeased.

"Diamonds always seem so cold to me. Opals seem alive. Look at how it shimmers in the light. At first glance, unimpressive, but when you get to know it, when you bother to take a closer look, the real beauty comes through. Diamonds all look alike. No two opals are ever the same."

Mr. Pearson elbowed the door open, holding a tray of coffee. When he saw her holding the opal ring, he set the tray down and held out his hand. "I see you found the ring I included to gauge size. That really isn't an engagement ring, certainly not one suitable for the bride of Eli Kennebrae."

Josie's fingers closed over the ring, reluctant to let it go. Eli took her hand and opened her chilly fingers. "Try it on. Might as well see what size would be best, right?"

Her mouth went dry as an attic floor. He slid the ring over her finger. She couldn't meet his eyes. The opal shimmered, a perfect fit. Her voice deserted her. Perhaps it was the enormous lump lodged in her throat.

"An excellent omen." Mr. Pearson beamed. "Now that we know the size, perhaps you'd like to try on one of the engagement rings."

Tears smarted Josie's eyes, and she had to force herself to remove the ring and concentrate on her real task for being there. When she could trust herself to speak, she swallowed hard and pointed to an emerald-cut diamond surrounded by smaller diamonds. "This one, I think. And the size is close enough."

At the broad smile that wreathed Mr. Pearson's face, she supposed her choice must've been among the most expensive rings on offer. She couldn't stand it anymore and pushed her chair away from the table. "I believe I'll wait out in the showroom."

Once in the serenity of the showroom, she paused beside a case of gold and silver watches to catch her breath. She hoped Clarice would like her choice. It wasn't Clarice's fault. And Mama would definitely approve of the ring.

A shop assistant watched her but didn't approach.

Eli and Mr. Pearson emerged from the back room, shook hands, and parted.

"Thank you, Mr. Kennebrae. A pleasure doing business with you. And don't forget, we have wedding rings and pearl necklaces as well. Pearls would make an excellent wedding gift for your bride."

Josie slipped out the door before she had to hear anymore.

Chapter 10

Eli pored over the calculations, his first installment from Professor Josephson. He had to admit the mathematics looked sound. Page after page of neat drawings in a legible hand. Suggestions for improvements to his original designs that stirred Eli's imagination and caused new ideas to mushroom in his mind.

"Sir?"

He looked up, tugging his mind away from his designs. His foreman stood in the doorway of the shack Eli had purloined at the shipyard for his on-site office. "Yes, Gates?"

"Sir, the steel that came in for the bulkhead supports..." Gates rubbed his hands along his sides and looked anywhere but at Eli.

Dread settled into his heart. What could go wrong now? One thing after another had delayed the project.

"The steel is four inches too long. We'll have to cut it down before we can install it."

Relief trickled through Eli's chest. "Too long is better than too short. How long will it take to trim it to fit?"

"A day at least."

"Our launch date is getting later and later. At this rate, the harbor will be iced in before we're finished."

"Yes, sir." Gates hovered, mangling his hat brim with his gnarled fingers. "And, sir?"

"What is it now?" Eli tucked his papers into his attaché case. He'd get no more work done here today.

"The men, sir. They've heard that Keystone Steel is hiring shipbuilders and paying a dollar a day more than Kennebrae's."

"A dollar more a day?"

Gates nodded and scratched the hair over his left ear. "A dollar more a day for general labor. Welders and crane operators get two dollars more per day."

Eli had the distinct feeling Gates wasn't finished. "And what about yard foremen? Is Gervase Fox looking for one of those, too?"

Gates studied the rafters of the lean-to. "Yes, sir, he is. One of his men met me on my way out of the shipyard last night. Said he could offer me double wages and a fifty-dollar bonus just for signing on with Keystone."

"How many have jumped ship so far?" Without workers, he'd never get this ship finished. How like Fox. Couldn't buy the plans, couldn't buy Eli, so he tried to buy Eli's workers.

"Nobody so far, but the men are talking. They sent me in here to negotiate for them."

A heavy weight pressed on Eli's shoulders. The last thing he needed was a workforce problem. But would Grandfather turn loose enough money to increase the payroll by that much? He'd have to risk it.

"Tell the men I'll match the offer from Keystone. And for you, too. But tell them I expect value for my money. This ship will be completed by the original deadline and according to the specifications I've laid out." Eli stared hard at Gates. "I'll expect you to handle the men. Do whatever it takes to keep them on task. At that kind of money, they should meet the deadlines I set for them."

Gates nodded, smiling. "I'll tell them, sir. They'll be glad to hear it."

Eli picked up his case and followed his foreman into the sunshine. He wished he thought Grandfather would be glad to hear it. At least the sun was shining. Four days of heavy rain and lightning had kept the crews off the refit. Iron clanked, sparks flew, and men shouted. The dank, muddy smell of the harbor mingled with the odor of smoke and oil.

Before he could leave the shipyard, three more small problems arose. It seemed for each step he made forward on the project, the details and irritants dragged him back five. If he wasn't dealing with personnel issues, it was supply or weather or finances. Were all projects as fraught with setbacks as this one?

The carriage ride to the shipping office barely gave him time to marshal his thoughts. He was still juggling papers and ideas as he mounted the marble steps to the second-floor conference room. He'd come to dread these weekly reports to Grandfather and Jonathan. If he had good news about the ship, they dogged him about his engagement. When he had some good news to report on that front—though he had to admit that hadn't happened often—they grilled him about progress on the *Bethany*.

They were waiting when he arrived five minutes late. He took his customary seat where he wouldn't have to look at Grandfather's portrait and he wouldn't have to look directly at Grandfather himself.

"Glad you could make it. Are you sure we're not imposing on your schedule?" Grandfather rapped the edge of the table.

Eli blew out his breath and reached for his papers. He could practically see the purse strings tightening.

Jonathan rolled a pencil between his palms, the soft clicking as it rolled over his wedding band rhythmic and somehow comforting. Jonathan had a way with Grandfather. Of course, he'd been the number-one grandson for years, and not just because he was the eldest but because he loved Kennebrae Shipping with a passion that rivaled Grandfather's. The fact that Jonathan's wife had produced an heir to the Kennebrae dynasty had further put him in Grandfather's good graces.

The meeting went far worse than Eli had imagined. Grandfather stormed at the delays, raged at the increase in wages, and scoffed at Eli's reasoning. Eli should've known better than to mention Professor Josephson.

"You've never met the man? You didn't review his credentials?" Grandfather smacked the arm of his chair. "Yet you're willing to hang the entire project on his so-called expertise. And not only this project but the reputation of Kennebrae Shipping."

Eli's temper raised its head. "Yes. Yes, I am. The calculations are sound, and your reputation is in no danger. The only smear on your good name would be if word got out that Gervase Fox had stolen your workforce through higher wages."

"Fox? Fox is the one behind this wage hike?"

"That's right. He offered substantial raises to any Kennebrae shipyard worker willing to leave us and go to work for him."

Grandfather's eyes glittered with an emotion Eli feared was hate. Certainly animosity. "We'll see about that. I'll authorize the wage increase, and I'll see about Fox."

"Now, don't go off half-cocked." Jonathan looked up from his notes. "You might not like Fox—I can't say that I do either—but don't let him goad you into doing something foolish because you can't separate business from personal feelings."

Grandfather's lips twitched, and he fingered the blanket in his lap. "Don't patronize me. I was dealing with varmints like Gervase Fox when you were still in short pants." He turned his attention back to Eli. "What else do you have to report?"

"That's all."

"That's all? What about Clarice? Did she like the ring?"

Rocking back in his chair, Eli winced. "I haven't given it to her yet."

"I have had it with your delays. Do I have to do everything? You get that ring on her finger before dinnertime, or you can kiss this project good-bye. In fact, I'll go along with you, just to make sure you do the thing up right. I'd like a word with Radcliffe anyway."

"Can't you trust me to get the job done by myself? I'm not a child, you know."

"There have been enough delays. I want this union signed and sealed and the Zahn lumber shipping contracts firmly in our pockets."

Eli winced at the mercenary gleam in Grandfather's eye.

Jonathan frowned at his papers. "You don't have to do this, Eli."

"Jonathan"—Grandfather held up his hand—"don't horn in here."

"I have to. Did you learn nothing from what you did to me and what you did to Noah? I can't stand by and let you shove Eli into a marriage he doesn't want to a girl he doesn't know, all for profit of a company that doesn't need the help. Kennebrae Shipping is bursting at the seams with orders and contracts. The Zahn lumber, though it would be nice, shouldn't be bought at the expense of Eli's freedom. I have a feeling you're more interested in keeping the contract away from Gervase Fox than you are about getting it for yourself."

"Your marriage and Noah's are the best things to ever happen to you boys, and you know it. Who's to say it won't be the same for Eli? I'm not a fool. Do you think I don't know my own grandsons? Did you think I didn't have these girls checked out thoroughly? I made wise choices for you all. It isn't my fault you both took the long way around to finding happiness. I intend for Eli to take a direct course. Get the ring on her finger, and get her to the altar. He'll thank me later."

"I can't tell you how enjoyable it is to be discussed as if I weren't sitting right here." Eli stared at his brother and grandfather, twisting his mouth wryly. "Jonathan, I appreciate the effort, but I have to see this through. As Grandfather's so proud of saying, once a Kennebrae gives his word, he follows through."

Grandfather almost purred in satisfaction on the way to the elevator.

Eli pushed Grandfather's chair through the lobby and toward the brass and glass front doors. When they were seated in Grandfather's carriage, Eli patted the ring in his pocket. In a long day of nothing going right, he hoped that this at least would be done to Grandfather's satisfaction. Eli certainly found no satisfaction in the idea, and from the skittish way Clarice behaved around him, he thought she might not either.

✍

Mama's wails could shatter glass. Josie sat in shock beside Grandma Bess, who flipped pages in the latest *Saturday Evening Post*, occasionally looking up to consider her daughter-in-law's hysterics.

Mama clutched her handkerchief and every so often picked up the piece of paper in her lap and scanned it again. "How could she do this to me? What will I tell Radcliffe? And you, Josephine, can explain to him just what your role in this catastrophe is. It's plain as a pineapple you had something to do with this." Mama waved the paper again.

The soft chime of the doorbell galvanized Josie. She rose, grateful for a valid reason to leave the room. Footsteps clattered on the upstairs hall, followed by a high-pitched little-girl giggle. Through the shirred curtain covering the oval of glass in the oak door, she could make out a man's shadow, tall with a hat.

She opened the door and froze stiff as an icicle.

Eli swept his hat from his head and smoothed his hair.

Josie opened her mouth but couldn't think of a thing to say.

Next to Eli on the porch, Abraham Kennebrae sat in his chair, his thin hands in his lap, his black suit and white shirt immaculate.

"Who is it, Josephine?" Mama seemed to have forgotten her manners completely, screeching the question from the front parlor.

Josie blinked, making sure she wasn't seeing things, then shrugged. "It's the Kennebraes," she called over her shoulder, still looking at Eli from the corner of her eye while she spoke.

Josie winced at the wail that followed. When she heard a soft thump, her heart tripled its pace. She rushed to the parlor, leaving their callers standing on the front porch. Mama had fainted.

Grandma Bess took control in the same calm manner in which she did everything.

Eli helped lift Mama onto the couch. Her head lolled back, and one arm hung over the side of the sofa and trailed the floor. He stepped back, eyebrows high, but asked no questions.

Josie tried to meld into the alcove beside the Boston fern.

Grandma dug in her enormous bag and produced a small vial of smelling salts. "Octavia, wake up. Pull yourself together, and stop giving in to these histrionics. You'd think the world had come crashing to an end." Grandma waved the little bottle under Mama's nose.

The pungent odor worked, for Mama's eyes shot open and she began to cough. Eli and Grandma helped her sit up. Mama clasped her chest, gasping for air, took one look at Eli, and wailed again.

"Madam, please." Abraham Kennebrae wheeled his chair closer. "Do we need to call a doctor? Or perhaps your husband? Is Radcliffe at home?"

Mention of Papa stopped Mama's cries like slamming a door. She snatched the handkerchief Grandma offered and dabbed her eyes and upper lip.

Eli stooped to pick up a piece of paper from the floor, and when Mama would've snatched it away, Grandma swatted her hand. "Let the young man read it. It concerns him more than you."

Eli scanned the page, but Mr. Kennebrae jabbed him in the side. "Read it aloud, boy."

> *"Dear Mama and Papa,*
>> *By now you know I've gone. I tried to stay, to do what you wished of me, but I just can't. You see, my heart belongs to another, and I could never be happy as Eli Kennebrae's bride. I do wish you'd have told me your plans before involving Mr. Kennebrae. He's a very nice man, but*

not for me. By the time you read this note, I will be married. I've eloped with my true love, Geoffrey Fordham. Please don't worry about me, and please tell Josie thanks for everything. Without her, I wouldn't have had the courage to do this.

Love,
Mrs. Geoffrey Fordham."

A hollow ache filled Josie for Eli. How did he keep his voice so calm, like he was reading about strangers instead of his fiancée and his good friend? She supposed Clarice couldn't resist the urge to sign her married name, but that had to hurt Eli. When she glanced over at him, his face merely looked thoughtful and detached.

His grandfather looked anything but disinterested. He snatched the paper from Eli's hand and read it himself. The spidery blue veins stood out on his hands, and his fingers shook, while a dull red crept up from his celluloid collar and spread to his cheeks. Josie thought Mama might faint again when his black, burning eyes bored into her.

Before he could say anything, Papa walked through the front doorway. He strolled into view through the parlor doorway, newspaper tucked under his arm, hat set at a jaunty angle. He tapped his walking stick a couple of times on the rug, then tossed it in the air and caught it before sliding it into the hall tree with a flourish. When he spied the crowd in the parlor, his eyebrows shot up. "Kennebrae, good to see you. Beautiful day out, isn't it? Stay for supper, won't you?"

Instead of answering, Mr. Kennebrae handed Papa Clarice's note. Josie held her breath. Papa's jovial expression vanished, as if someone had wiped a hand down his face. In its place, shock, disbelief, and anger cycled through. The last lingered. Josie expected a reaction like a boiler explosion, but Papa's words came out in a tight whisper. "Mother, go see to dinner. Abraham, Eli, Octavia, let us retire to my library to confer over this matter."

Mama walked as if she couldn't feel her feet on the carpet, lifting her legs high and coming down with more force than usual, and Father followed her.

Eli put his hands on the back of Mr. Kennebrae's chair. To Josie's surprise, a smile lifted the corners of Eli's mouth once he was out of sight of his grandfather. He caught her looking at him and shrugged.

Now what was she to make of that?

Chapter 11

Eli had to restrain himself from laughing out loud. No wonder Geoffrey had been so touchy about Eli's engagement to Clarice. He'd been in love with her all along. A condemned man escaping the hangman's noose couldn't have felt more elation than Eli did at that moment.

The scowl on Grandfather's features told him he'd better keep that elation to himself. He figured he could just about fry an egg on the top of Grandfather's head, the old man was so angry.

As soon as the library doors shut behind them, Grandfather started in. "Radcliffe, what's the meaning of this? My grandson comes over here in good faith to put a ring—a very expensive ring, mind you—on your daughter's finger, and what do we find? She's eloped!" He pounded the arm of his chair with one hand in a familiar gesture.

Zahn rocked back on his heels at this attack and glared at Abraham. "With *your* lawyer, I might add." He shifted his eyes to include Eli in his displeasure. "Did you put him up to it?"

"No, sir." Eli's lips twitched. "They did this all on their own. I had no idea Geoff had feelings for your daughter. If I had known, there's no way I would've gone along with this engagement. I don't poach on another man's preserve." He shoved his hands in his pockets and leaned against a bookcase.

Mrs. Zahn collapsed into a chair near the fireplace, her feet shooting out and kicking a pile of papers and books on the cold hearth. She seemed not to notice the mess she'd made, fanning herself with her handkerchief and staring into space. "What was she thinking? She'll be ruined, that's what. Running off to get married, and when she was engaged to another man." The lady hiccupped and blinked, choking on the words.

"When did you first notice she was gone?" Zahn fired the question at his wife. "Perhaps it isn't too late to fetch her back."

For a moment hope dawned on her rounded face. Then her shoulders slumped, and her eyelids fell. "I found the note this afternoon when I was getting ready to leave for Mrs. Grant's garden party. I don't know how I missed seeing it all day. Clarice wasn't at breakfast this morning, but you know how she is." Mrs. Zahn put her chin up defensively. "She rarely eats breakfast anyway, so I didn't miss her. I couldn't have known she'd do something like this. No one here has seen her since yesterday after the evening meal. She's probably been gone since last night."

Zahn paced the rug, his brows down like a thundercloud, his steps rigid.

Grandfather tugged on Eli's sleeve. "Well, don't just stand there like a lamppost. What are you going to do about this?"

"Me?" Eli shrugged. "I'm not going to do anything. I'm the wronged party here, remember?"

Zahn stopped mid-stride. Inspiration lifted his features from hard, etched lines to something resembling his expression when he first entered the house. "I've got it." His fingers snapped like a gunshot and brought Mrs. Zahn upright in her chair.

"What?" Grandfather hunched his shoulders and leaned forward.

"A Kennebrae-Zahn wedding." Zahn looked as if the ideas tumbling in his head were all falling into logical order. "Of course. Just because Clarice isn't here doesn't mean we can't go ahead with a wedding. There's the next one in line." He snapped his fingers again and looked to his wife.

"Josephine?"

"Yes, that's it." He turned to Eli. "You can marry Josephine."

Eli's thoughts boggled. The man couldn't even remember his daughter's name and here he was swapping one for another like a new tie or pair of gloves. "You're not serious."

"Of course I am." He seemed puzzled at the statement. "It's the perfect solution."

"No, it isn't." Eli shook his head. Had Zahn lost his wits?

Grandfather turned his chair. "Radcliffe, I'd like a few moments alone with my grandson, if you please."

Eli braced himself for whatever Grandfather would say. He took his hands out of his pockets and straightened away from the bookcase. Grandfather barely waited for the Zahns to leave before going on the attack. "This is all your fault."

"Excuse me?"

"If you'd put more of an effort into courting the girl, she wouldn't have eloped with Fordham. Who, by the way, will never work for Kennebrae's again."

Eli shrugged. "I think it took a lot of courage for Geoffrey to do this, and Clarice, too. Though I wish they would've come to me. I'd have released her from the engagement and given them my blessing."

"And lost yourself the *Bethany* in the process!" Grandfather's voice and color rose. "We had a deal."

Eli's anger charged forward to meet Grandfather's. "A deal I no longer want any part of. It's choked me for weeks. I'm not willing to exchange my freedom for a ship or money. I wanted to make my mark on Kennebrae

Shipping, but the cost is too great. You can keep the *Bethany*. I'll take my designs elsewhere. It isn't as if I haven't had other offers. You've manipulated me for long enough. Working for Fox couldn't be as bad as being stretched on the rack by you every day."

"You wouldn't leave."

"Watch me." Eli started for the door, intent on putting a lot of distance between him and his conniving grandsire. He was free, released from his obligations, and it felt great.

"Eli, please." The plea stopped him in his tracks. Grandfather sounded broken and defeated. "I want you to do this. . .for me." Grandfather picked up Clarice's letter from the corner of the desk and creased it with his thumbnail.

Frustration at his inability to just walk away from the old man made Eli's voice raspy. "Why? Why is it so important to you that I get married right now? Why can't you be happy that Jonathan and Noah are married and let me get on with my own life?"

"Because I gave my word."

"It doesn't matter now. Don't you see? *You* tried to keep your word. *I* tried to keep your word, but the girl has flown the coop. No one will blame you for not following through this time. It's impossible now that she's married. Zahn can't hold us to the bargain." Eli sank onto the window seat so that he was at eye level with Grandfather. "I'm sorry about the shipping contracts, but maybe you can still work something out with him."

"This isn't about Zahn. It never was." Grandfather scowled.

"Suppose you tell me then just what this *is* about."

Grandfather pinched the bridge of his nose and rested his elbows on the arms of his chair. He stared past Eli's shoulder for a long moment then breathed deeply, as if coming to a decision. "I promised your grandmother—God rest her soul—on her deathbed that I would see you boys all safely married to good girls before I died. I gave my word to her." He spoke the last phrase slowly, as if to emphasize just what it meant to him. "And I'm running out of time."

"You're not that old. You're going to live on for years yet. Look at how not even a stroke has slowed you down much. I plan to get married eventually. Why can't you wait until then?" Eli kept his hand on the doorknob, wary of another of Grandfather's traps.

"Time's always shorter than you think, and mine's dwindling fast." His words caused Eli to turn around. "The doc gave me the long face a year ago, said I'd best be making my final plans. That's why I've been after you boys to marry quickly. I promised your grandmother, and I aim to keep my word before it's too late."

"The long face?"

"It's something with my heart. The doc says I could go at any time."

"Your heart?" His mind refused to accept it. Life without his recalcitrant and calculating grandfather? Impossible.

"Help me, Eli. Help a Kennebrae keep his word to his own."

The noose Eli had so easily slipped out of only a short while before dropped over his head and tightened.

✑

Josie bolted up the stairs to change for dinner. The turmoil of this afternoon's events sent her thoughts tumbling.

Wild giggles emanated from her bedroom. She opened the door to see Giselle and Antoinette wearing her two best gowns and her widest-brimmed afternoon hats.

"Girls!"

They stopped pirouetting in front of the armoire mirror and looked up at her with wide blue eyes. Toni had tried to pin up her black tresses, and one long sausage curl escaped and bounced along her cheek.

"Hand it over." Josie held out her palm.

Giselle gave her the ivory fan she'd been fluttering under her chin and began to peel off the satin gloves.

"You, too." Josie waited for Toni.

The girls shed the dresses and necklaces, the hats and scarves.

"And put them away where you got them." Josie was inclined to indulge them. After all, what harm had they done? It brought back memories of a small Josie and Clarice invading Grandma Bess's bureau and trunk and trying on treasures.

The indulgence Josie felt evaporated the moment she saw her desk. "You little horrors, look what you've done!" An avalanche of papers and books had slid off the desk into a heap on the floor. Her carefully arranged drawings were under the desk, and the papers she'd intended to burn were mingled with the ones she needed to keep. "How many times do I have to tell you to keep your little paddies off my stuff?" She clapped her hands onto her hips and glared at her sisters.

Giselle's lower lip began to quiver, and water formed on her lashes. "Josie, we're sorry. We didn't mean to." The rose-colored satin and lace of Josie's best dress drooped off Giselle's narrow shoulders, and the skirts puddled around her on the floor.

Josie caved. "I'm sorry, girls. I know you didn't mean to, but you have to stay out of my things. If you'd have asked me, I'd have let you play dress-up. I have some very important papers in here that can't get messed up."

The tears released from Giselle's lower lashes and tracked down her pale cheeks. She sniffed and nodded, the ostrich feather on Josie's hat bobbing with the movement.

Toni shucked Josie's second-best dress and opened the armoire door. "We won't do it again, Josie. And we'll help you clean up."

"Good, because we're having guests for dinner, and I have to get ready."

With the help of her sisters, Josie got the mess cleaned up. "Here, Toni, these are the ones I'm done with. Put them in this envelope, and I'll throw them in the fire later." She held out the large brown envelope Geoffrey had sent, and Toni slid the much-scribbled pages and notes inside.

Josie hurriedly scrubbed her hands, scowling at an ink smear that wouldn't budge. Still, no one would be looking at her hands, not with the uproar Clarice's elopement had caused. With trepidation, she descended the stairs and entered the parlor.

Papa and Eli rose as she came in.

Mama popped up out of her chair and came toward Josie, smiles wreathing her face, her eyes suspiciously bright. "Here she is, and doesn't she look a picture?" Mama clasped Josie's hands, kissed the air beside her cheek, and whispered, "What took you so long?"

Josie glanced at Eli, who resumed his seat and stared at his hands. Worry lines wrinkled his forehead, and the relieved grin he'd worn the last time she saw him had vanished. Perhaps the reality of losing Clarice was beginning to set in. Josie's heart went out to him, and she wondered why he had agreed to stay to dinner. When they entered the dining room, he sat in the chair normally reserved for Clarice, and Josie took her customary spot in the next seat.

Grandma Bess's mouth looked pinched, as if she wanted to say something but refrained. And the way Mama avoided looking at Grandma made Josie wonder if verbal swords hadn't already been crossed. Mama kept the conversational ball bouncing, but only Papa and Mr. Kennebrae hit it back.

Josie could think of nothing but Clarice's defection and feared if she spoke she'd inadvertently draw attention to her absent sister. Eli's silence unnerved her, and she kept glancing at him, hoping for some sign of how he was dealing with all this. The dessert dishes couldn't be cleared fast enough to suit Josie.

Just when she thought she might gracefully escape—was, in fact, just pushing back her chair—Mama's voice stopped her. "Josephine, please sit. We have some news for you."

Papa cleared his throat and looked stern.

Anxiety clawed its way up Josie's rib cage and danced in her head. She looked from one face to the next, all staring at her, except Eli, who again contemplated the edge of the table.

Mr. Kennebrae, though somber, had a glitter in his eye that caused the hairs on Josie's arms to stand up. He couldn't contain a triumphant smile.

Papa cleared his throat again and rose, lifting his water glass. "Josephine..."

Uh-oh, this is serious. He remembered my name right off.

"We, your mother and I, have decided that, in light of Clarice disappointing us, you will take her place. The Kennebraes are amenable to this change. You will marry Eli."

Not a snatch of breathable air remained in the room. Josie blinked. That explained Mama's fake brightness and the mulish set to Grandma's jaw. It even explained Papa's determined look and Mr. Kennebrae's triumph. But what about Eli? She turned to him. He lifted his gaze to hers in a mute plea, though for what, she couldn't guess.

Indignation licked like fire through her. According to her father, any Zahn girl would do, and she was next in line. What about what she wanted? What about her promise to God to pursue her studies? What about being the woman God made her to be? Was all of it to be sucked away because she was needed to fill a quota in her father's schemes like another railcar of logs or unit of pine?

She straightened her back, hot words dancing on the tip of her tongue. They wouldn't coerce her like they had Clarice. And that was that.

Then Eli touched her hand, the merest whisper of a caress. She froze. He took a deep breath then gathered both her hands in his, turning in his chair to face her. "Josie, I'd hoped for some privacy to ask you, instead of having it announced like this."

She looked into his gentle eyes, drowning in his imploring gaze. What she saw there wasn't love, nor even affection, but a sort of calm desperation.

"But will you marry me?" His thumbs stroked the backs of her hands, warming the chilled shock from her fingers.

In spite of all she had meant to say, she found herself nodding, a wave of care for him crashing through her, extinguishing the fires of indignation to piles of steaming ash.

He kept hold of her hands in one of his while he reached into his pocket.

Papa and Mr. Kennebrae beamed. Papa raised his glass again. "This is wonderful. Abraham, later this week I'm hosting a picnic for all my workers as a thank-you for meeting a major contract deadline a month early. You and Eli should attend as my guests, and we'll announce the engagement then. If we get it all out in the open, hopefully things will all blow over then, and we can put this unpleasantness behind us."

Josie looked down at her left hand, noting the pale gray smudges where she hadn't been able to get all the ink off completely, trying to ignore the huge sparkling diamond Eli had put on her finger—the huge sparkling diamond she'd helped him pick out for Clarice. Evidently one Zahn girl was the same as another to Eli, too.

Chapter 12

For two long days, Josie tried to settle her mind and escape into her work. She sketched and erased, figured and reworked until her head ached, trying not to think about the matter of her engagement. Her eyes burned from lack of sleep and poring over ship plans.

Giselle bounced into Josie's room and wrinkled her nose. "Mama wants you downstairs, Josie. She's got a visitor."

"Is it Mrs. Jefferson?" Josie knew Giselle didn't like the florid Mrs. Jefferson, who pinched little girls' cheeks and talked too loudly.

"No, it's a fat man. With a yellow vest and shiny shoes. He's sitting in Papa's chair, and he has whiskers like a badger."

Mystified, Josie stood up. She checked her reflection in the mirror, combed her hair, and straightened her dress, brushing the wrinkles from her skirt. She hoped his visit wouldn't take long. Work was the only thing that took her mind off her engagement.

Mr. Fox scooted to the edge of his chair and stood when she entered the parlor. He waited until she drew near and held out her hand, as she knew Mama expected her to do. "How do you do?" He took her fingers in his beefy grip, lingering over his greeting.

When he finally let go, she resisted the urge to wipe her hand on her dress.

"Josephine, this is Mr. Fox. He's the owner of Keystone Steel and Shipping."

Fox waited until she was seated before speaking. "We've met briefly before. Miss Zahn, I hear congratulations are in order." He grinned, ingratiatingly, over his tea cup. "I'm sure you've made a sound match."

Mama beamed. "We're all very happy with the way things have worked out."

"Thank you, Mr. Fox." Josie kept her tone neutral. Something about the way this man looked at her unsettled her. What was he doing here in the middle of the workday? If he had business with Papa, why didn't he go to the sawmill office?

He set his cup down, the chair creaking as he leaned forward. "I understand you received quite a ring from young Kennebrae."

Josie clenched her fist and put her right hand over her left. But Mama gushed and twittered. "Oh my, yes. A beautiful ring, and large enough to gratify a girl's heart that her betrothed won't be stingy with her in the future. Do show it to him, Josephine."

She had no choice but to hold her hand out. Mama scowled at her, and she realized she was glaring at Fox. Schooling her features, she tried to appear the blushing bride. The entire charade irked her.

"Stunning. You're to be commended, Miss Zahn. When is the happy event?" Fox slid predatory eyes toward her hand. No doubt he saw everything in terms of acquisition and victory.

"We haven't set a date yet." Josie accepted a cup of tea from her mother but didn't drink. Her stomach roiled, something in her recoiling from Fox's calculating, insinuating gaze.

He leaned forward to pick up his cup from the low table before him. The china rattled, and he jumped back. "Oh, how careless of me." The cup rocked on its side in the saucer, tea covering the table and dripping to the floor. His pant leg had received a liberal splattering as well, and his fingers dripped. "I'm so sorry, Mrs. Zahn. Do you perhaps have a washroom where I could clean up?"

Mama, who had bounced out of her chair at the first clink of china, rang for the maid. "Show Mr. Fox to the facilities, please. And don't worry, Gervase, no harm done. I'll get another cup for you."

The moment the washroom door at the top of the stairs closed, Josie frowned at her mother. "Mama, I don't like that man. Did you have to talk to him about the engagement? About the ring?"

"Josephine Elizabeth Zahn"—Mama jerked her hand away and used the tray cloth to mop up the spilled tea—"don't take that tone with me. He's a respected businessman in this city, and he came to wish you well in your marriage. He moves in high circles in this town, and you will not antagonize him." Mama glared at Josie over her shoulder. "You'll be cordial to him and show some grace. I didn't spend every day of the last many years drilling manners into your head to have you embarrass me this way."

Josie bit her tongue and took the tray into the kitchen for the cook to reset.

Fox was gone a long time, and when he reappeared at the foot of the stairs, he slid his watch into his hand and refused Mama's offers of more tea and cakes. "It's been delightful, Mrs. Zahn, but I'm afraid I must fly. Businesses, as you well know, don't run themselves." He clasped Josie's limp hand and crushed her fingers in a hearty grip. "And, Miss Zahn, I wish you every happiness in your upcoming marriage." He bared his yellow teeth, flipped his hat onto his bushy gray hair, and departed, the door slamming briskly behind his rotund figure.

Josie breathed out a sigh of relief at his leaving and this time wiped her hand on her skirt. Obnoxious little man. He looked as if he were trying to figure out how to beat her at some game she didn't even know she was playing.

She returned to her room and sank onto her desk chair. "Giselle? Antoinette? Where are you little hoydens?" Her papers and books were strewn across the desk, as if someone had accidentally swept them to the floor and hastily piled them back up. She rose and headed to the nursery the little girls still shared. When were they going to learn to keep out of her things?

～

Josie crossed her arms at her waist and leaned against the slender bole of a young maple tree. Children ran, and women laughed. Men played horseshoes and talked, and wafting over the noise of happy picnickers was the smell of roasting chickens and mustard-laden potato salad. Flags and bunting flapped in the breeze, festooning the pavilion in gay colors. Brawny lumbermen cavorted like kids, nodding with broad smiles each time one of them passed her.

"Your father will be looking for you soon." Grandma Bess hitched her black bag higher on her arm. "The Kennebraes should be here in a little while."

"Are you sure he's looking for me? Or will any of his daughters do?" Josie rubbed the underside of her engagement ring with her thumb, twisting the big diamond in the sunlight.

"What kind of question is that?"

"I don't understand him. I don't understand so much right now." The need to talk to someone made the words pour from her throat. "How can he be so unfeeling to his own family and yet so generous to his workers? Half the time he doesn't even remember my name, but he'll throw a party that has his workers falling all over themselves to tell me what a wonderful boss he is."

Grandma tugged her arm and led her to a nearby park bench. "Your father can be as thick as two planks sometimes. I know. This picnic was my idea, actually. It would never occur to your father to do something like this."

"How did you talk him into it then?"

"I told him happy workers were productive workers."

"So you showed him how he would benefit from it, and he agreed to do something nice. That's just like him. Never do something for nothing." Josie tightened her lips in disapproval.

"You're too harsh on him. He isn't unkind, just a bit thoughtless. He needs a nudge in the right direction from time to time, that's all." Grandma dug in her bag for a magazine.

"Are all men like Papa?" Josie twisted her ring again, still unaccustomed to the weight of it on her hand. "Are they all just a bit thoughtless?"

"By 'all men' I assume you mean Eli?" Grandma folded the cover of the magazine back and scanned the table of contents.

Josie didn't answer, not sure what to say. Though she'd imagined herself engaged to Eli Kennebrae a thousand times in her girlish dreams, the reality had turned out much different. This ring was just the most prominent example of how wrong things were. She was everyone's second best.

"I think"—Grandma flipped another page—"that you should talk to Eli. You should get to know him and let him get to know you. You might both be surprised by what you find. And, Josie, you don't have to stand by and take this, not from your parents, not from Eli. If you're truly unsuited to wed, you should say so. But not before you give it a chance. From what I can tell, Eli Kennebrae is a bright, caring, good man. He's still a man, though, which means he's not a mind reader. If you want something from him, or you want him to know something, you're going to have to tell him."

"How do I tell him I want to pursue my studies in higher mathematics? How do I tell him that I despise this ring and everything it stands for? How do I tell him that just when I was sure I had things mapped out, that I had figured out just what God wanted me to do, my whole world got thrown into an uproar, with Eli Kennebrae right in the middle of it?"

Grandma chuckled, licked her finger, and turned a glossy page. "You have plenty of questions, that's plain. Have you prayed about any of them? How do you know what Eli's reaction to your gift for numbers will be if you never reveal that gift to him? Is it fair to harbor a grudge about that ring when Eli has no idea how you feel about it? And have you considered that marrying Eli might be what God had in store for you all along?"

Before Josie could answer, girlish squeals erupted in the pavilion. She rose, her mouth falling open.

Eli was wheeling Mr. Kennebrae's chair toward the pavilion, and at the same moment, Clarice and Geoffrey returned, hand in hand.

"Now might be a good time for you to go up there. Your mama might need you to spread a little oil on the water." Grandma stood and used her magazine as a sunshade. "The little girls look happy to see Clarice."

"Aren't you coming?" Josie didn't want to go up the slope alone.

"Plenty of drama up there without my adding to it. I'll wait here." She settled herself on the bench again and resumed reading.

When Josie reached the pavilion, the atmosphere of tension clogged her lungs like soot. Clarice lifted wide, imploring eyes to her. Papa's face resembled a November gale, cold and forbidding, while Mama sat in a wicker chair fanning herself, darting worried glances between her husband and her daughter with the occasional nasty look for her brand-new son-in-law.

Geoffrey stood behind Clarice with his hand protectively on her shoulder. His jaw muscles stood out and his legs were braced, as if to do battle.

Abraham Kennebrae's eyes drilled each person he looked at. Red flushed his hollow cheeks, and the breeze ruffled his white hair.

Beside him, Eli blew out a long breath. His eyes found Josie's.

The lid would blow off this tea kettle in a moment. Josie found herself moving forward, her mouth stretching in a smile she didn't feel. "Clarice, Geoffrey, welcome home." She embraced her sister's stiff shoulders and whispered, "Cheer up. It will all blow over." Josie turned to Geoffrey. "I've always wanted a brother. Welcome to the family, Geoffrey. I know Clarice will be very happy with you." She stood on tiptoe and kissed his rock-hard cheek. Josie walked over to Eli and slid her arm through his. "Things have worked out so well, Clarice. You got Geoffrey, and I got Eli." She gazed up into Eli's stunned eyes, begging him to catch on, to back her up.

Eli caught her meaning, for he stepped forward and held out his hand to Geoffrey. "Congratulations, Geoff." He smiled, shook his friend's hand, and cuffed him on the shoulder. "She's a great girl." He winked, then leaned down and kissed Clarice's rosy cheek. "I'd say my loss is your gain, but I don't think anybody lost here."

Josie could almost see the gears turning over in Mama's mind. Mama sat upright and stopped waving her handkerchief under her chin. All around them, the workers crowded, eyes watching, ears alert. Papa cleared his throat, unclenching his hands. Mama nudged him in the side.

Papa donned his making-the-best-of-things face. "As you can see, things have worked out for the best. Clarice, Geoffrey, welcome home." He motioned for the servers to begin dishing up the food for the gathered workers.

Though conscious of the uneasiness remaining, Josie blew out a breath she didn't realize she'd been holding.

Clarice clasped Josie's hand and lifted it to examine the diamond ring. "You're marrying Eli?" The words were hissed into Josie's ear.

She nodded. "Papa and Mr. Kennebrae still wanted the wedding, so Papa figured I'd do just as well."

"But what about your studies? I thought you were going to college."

The muddle of Josie's thoughts and feelings sloshed about in her chest. "I don't know what I'm going to do. I thought I had everything figured out, but now. . ." The little girls swarmed around Clarice, and Josie found herself once more beside Eli.

Abraham Kennebrae wrapped her wrist in one of his bony hands and gave her a squeeze. "You're a good girl, Josephine Zahn. I saw how you handled that situation. You'll make an excellent Kennebrae. You've got smarts and tact, just like my Genevieve had." The hand around her wrist tightened painfully. "What's *he* doing here?"

Josie followed his glare. Her scalp crinkled. Duluth wasn't such a small place that she should keep running into Gervase Fox.

Fox's eyes swept the assembly, stopping when they landed on the Kennebraes. He lost no time weaving his way through the picnic tables.

"Abraham, Eli, and Miss Zahn, you look even more fetching than you did yesterday." He bowed to Josie.

Eli wrapped his arm around Josie's waist and tucked her firmly into his side. "You've met?" His whisper brushed her temple, taking her breath away.

"He called on my mother yesterday." The warmth of Eli's embrace surrounded her. His side was rock hard, as was his arm around her. If she didn't know better, she'd think he was trying to protect her from something.

"Another successful Kennebrae wedding." Mr. Fox bowed and grinned at her. "Though this one might not sew up the shipping contracts quite as neatly as the previous two."

Abraham sucked in a breath. "What do you mean, Fox?"

"Just that I've been talking with Radcliffe Zahn. He sees no reason why he should tie himself down to exclusive contracts, not if someone else can do the job more efficiently."

"You bounder. How dare you come in here and try to steal business from me!" Mr. Kennebrae pounded his chair arm.

"Steal? It's not stealing. It's business. Zahn feels that the best shipper should haul his goods. If you have the best ship, you get the contract."

"We'll see about that." Abraham jerked his head at Eli. "Take me to Radcliffe."

Eli stood still a long moment, his arm remaining firmly around Josie.

Geoffrey, as if sensing the need for his presence, slipped alongside. "We'll all go, Mr. Kennebrae. I'm anxious to hear what Zahn has to say." He grasped the steering bar on the back of the chair.

Eli drew Josie with him as he fell into step with his lawyer.

∽

Eli's gut churned. Fox couldn't be trusted. He was wily and persuasive. Grandfather's plans looked to be going up in the smoke of Fox's schemes.

Zahn, when they drew near, shifted in his seat and poked his now-congealed potato salad with his fork.

"Zahn, what's this Fox is spewing? Are you going back on our agreement?"

Eli grimaced at Grandfather's direct approach. All the delicacy of a steam-powered ice breaker.

"Agreement? I'm not going back on anything, but business is business. Gervase tells me he can haul my lumber faster and in greater quantities than anyone on the lakes." Zahn put his fork down. "I can't pass up something like that, not if it's true."

Eli shot a glance at Fox, who rocked on his heels, a smug smile plastered on his face. He looked like a bear sucking on a fistful of honey. Josie's hand on Eli's arm gripped tight.

Grandfather looked ready to explode, his face growing red, his long, bony fingers gripping the arms of his chair hard enough to leave dents in the walnut.

Eli shook his head. "He's hornswoggled you, Mr. Zahn. Nothing on the lake will beat the *Bethany* when she's done. Not for speed, capacity, or loading time."

"Don't be so sure." Fox leered. "You're not the only one with new ideas in lumber shipping." Gervase leaned over the table and plucked an apple from the fruit bowl in the center. He polished it against his lapel then sank his teeth into it like a wolf on a rabbit's neck. "Why don't you put your ship to the test? That would settle things nicely."

Eli shook his head, refusing any kind of a wager, sensing a trap.

But Grandfather wasn't so cautious. "You're on. A race between your ship and the *Bethany*, winner gets the Zahn contract." He waggled his bushy eyebrows at Zahn, who looked bemused and interested. "Say, the first weekend in November? First ship to get to Two Harbors, load up, and return to Duluth wins the contract?"

The first weekend in November? They'd never be ready by then. Eli grabbed Grandfather's shoulder, but the old man shook him off.

"That all right with you, Zahn?" Fox checked, an eager gleam lighting his cold gray eyes.

Radcliffe nodded. "That sounds fair."

"Then we're agreed. But don't be sorry when you don't win. My ship's the fastest on the lake." Fox dug in his coat pocket for a fat cigar. He seemed to remember the ladies present, for he merely stuck it between his fingers and punctuated the air with it instead of lighting it.

Grandfather reacted as if he'd been stung. "I'm so sure the *Bethany* will win, that if she doesn't, you can have her."

Eli blinked, fear clawing up his spine. *No.* "Grandfather!" He swallowed, shocked at the old man's rash declaration. "You can't promise that."

"I can promise anything I want to. I'm still head of this family and head of Kennebrae Shipping."

Fox stuffed the cigar between his moist lips, a nasty smile climbing his face. "That'll do just fine, Abraham. I know your word is good. After all, how many times have you told me that once a Kennebrae makes a promise, he keeps it, no matter what?" He turned on his heel and left the shelter.

Unbearable pressure tightened around Eli's lungs and brain. A little less than a month to have all the conversions made to the *Bethany* and have her seaworthy enough to beat Gervase Fox's fastest ship.

Josie slipped her hand into his, her eyes watching the departing figure. She seemed to sense the enormity of what had just happened. If the *Bethany* lost, the pride of the Kennebrae fleet would go to Fox. Fox would win what he couldn't buy. Grandfather had fallen neatly into his trap.

The afternoon passed, though Eli was barely conscious of anything beyond his own scrambled thoughts. The ride home to Kennebrae House seemed hours long. Eli blew out a long breath.

Grandfather alternately fumed and fretted over the way Fox had suckered him into the race.

"Well, can we do it?" Grandfather poked Eli in the side.

"Now's a fine time to be asking me that."

"Stop being facetious and answer my question." His black eyes burned hot with a demand that Eli come through for him with the answer he wanted to hear.

"I hope so. I'll try."

"You'll try? Don't you understand the pressure we're under?" As usual, Grandfather's worry came out in a verbal assault against those around him. Eli was fed up to the back teeth.

"Understand? You're the one who doesn't understand. You walked right into this buzz saw. And you're dragging me with you. I'm the only one who really understands what you've done. And gambling! You know better. Kennebraes have never wagered before, especially not for something so stupid as a lumber contract. We may very well lose this ship and our reputation, and why? Because you couldn't resist rising to Fox's bait. He laid his trap, and *wham*! You jumped right into it."

The carriage driver slowed and looked back over his shoulder.

Eli realized he was shouting. Shame licked his cheeks. He struggled with himself and modulated his voice. "I'm doing the best I can, and so are the men. The ship will be ready. How she'll fare against Fox's ship is anybody's guess."

"That's not good enough. We have to win."

Eli took a healthy grip on his temper. He could do nothing at the moment. But as soon as he got home, he'd get to work on a new schedule. Grandfather would have to turn loose more cash to pay the workers overtime.

Chapter 13

Josie sat up and punched her pillow into a tighter wad. Her nightgown tangled about her knees, and she trod back the covers. The faint familiar blast of a steamship whistle traveled over the water from the harbor. Rolling to her side, she stared at the pale square of moonlight streaming through the window and tracking slowly across the floor.

From the stairwell, the clock chimed twice. "Lord, why can't I make my mind slow down? Seems the harder I try to get to sleep, the more awake I become."

Grandma Bess had told Josie once that being unable to sleep was a great opportunity to flex one's prayer muscles and talk to God. "God never sleeps, and quite often if I'm wide awake at night, He's got something He wants to say to me, or there's something He's waiting to hear me say."

Josie sat up, wrapped her arms around her updrawn legs, and put her chin on her knees. Her braid fell over her shoulder. "I'm in a muddle, Lord, though I guess You know that better than anyone." Her engagement ring glittered in the faint starshine. "All my feelings are in a muddle, too. I don't know what I want. I don't know what *You* want. I thought I wanted to marry Eli, but then he was engaged to Clarice. I tried so hard to kill my feelings for him, to focus on my mathematics. I thought You wanted me to pursue my studies and forget about Eli Kennebrae."

She sighed and slid out of bed to walk to the window. Drawing the curtain aside, she studied the gaudy diamond on her left hand. "This ring screams out everything that's wrong with my engagement. I'm Eli's second best. The next one in line. Any Zahn girl would do as far as my father is concerned. Am I wrong to want more? To want Eli to love me for myself? To love me the way I know I could love him?"

A shaft of honesty drove through her mind. *Could* love Eli? She *did* love Eli. With everything in her. She knew it as surely as she knew her own name. She stood at the window for a long time. Finally, after coming to terms with her feelings for Eli, peace filled her. She would go through with the marriage, and she would have enough love for both of them. Half a loaf was better than none, wasn't it? And by marrying him, she would honor her parents.

She twisted the ring on her finger. And she would stop despising this hunk of jewelry. It wasn't her choice, but instead of thinking of how much she disliked it, she would think of the giver instead.

Refreshed in mind, she decided to peruse the hatch cover drawings once more before trying to sleep. The original design had bothered her from the start. There had to be a better, more secure way to fasten the hatches.

She lit her lamp and drew the blueprints from the bedside table. Careful not to step on the spot beside her desk that creaked, she dug in a bottom drawer and pulled out the parcel that had arrived for her from her tutor just that day. Those hatches had plagued her since she first saw Eli's original design, and feeling uncertain of her abilities in this area, she'd written to Mr. Clement for his guidance. How she missed her bald-headed, bespectacled tutor and friend. If anyone could help her with the ship design, he could.

She opened the package and took out two books and a note. Josie settled into bed and unfolded the paper, a wave of affection and loneliness sweeping over her as she read his familiar, perfect handwriting.

My dear Josie,

I'm very pleased you've found a way to apply all that knowledge you worked so hard to gain under my tutelage. None of my students here in Detroit matches you for intellect, and I find myself bored with them.

Here are two books I thought might help you with the questions you posed regarding the hatch design. Maybe you should back up and consider it from another angle. If you still need help with it, I can pose the problem to the shipbuilders here, but you led me to believe the work was highly confidential.

Which reminds me, I had an inquiry last week about you and the work you might be doing in Duluth. He refused to tell me for whom he worked, which made me suspicious. He seemed more interested in confirming that you were my student and that your abilities were more reliable than just what you are working on at the moment. I sent the fellow away with a flea in his ear. But if someone knows enough to be asking me about you, I'd be careful. The shipbuilding industry can be quite cutthroat.

Sincerely,
K. Clement

Cutthroat. With the race looming ahead of her, with Eli's reputation as a shipbuilder on the line, as well as the fate of the *Bethany*, cutthroat just about described things. And who would ask after her from her former tutor? Should she tell Geoffrey about it? Or was it Geoffrey himself, checking up on her work?

She thrust those thoughts to the back of her mind and forced herself to concentrate. She paged through one of the books Mr. Clement had sent, scratched notes on a tablet, and chewed the end of her pencil. How could she improve this design to not only make it watertight—a must—but also ensure it would work with the cranes on the loading dock? Eli's initial design would make it simple to remove the hatches to keep them out of the way for loading, but the hinges he'd designed for easy use wouldn't hold against the strain of a severe storm. . .or even a moderate one.

She set the first book aside and picked up the second. Railroad design? A paper marker jutted from the middle of the book, and she opened to that page. A diagram of the rod and pin design for coupling railroad cars. Similar to Eli's design. She frowned. Why had Clement sent a book on railroads? She checked his note once more.

Maybe you should back up and consider it from another angle.

She flipped to the next page. Like a photographer's flash the answer to the problem of how to safely seal the hatches scorched her mind. That was it! A knuckle coupler.

Josie scribbled out a few notes, double-checked her calculations, and flopped back against the pillows. That was it. The idea would take a little polishing, but how simple. She'd have to write to Mr. Clement in the morning.

Pride of accomplishment and happy anticipation of what Eli would say drew her from the bed. She twirled on the patterned rug, her nightgown flaring out, catching the moonlight. Her braid whipped around as she danced a jig.

Then her face fell; her feet became still. She wouldn't get to hear what Eli would say when he was presented with the solution to the last major obstacle to construction. Geoffrey would. Geoffrey would take her papers and ideas and present them to Eli as coming from Professor Josephson.

Yet another barrier to her happiness. When she'd conceived the professor, she never imagined she would marry Eli. Now the secret stood between them like a seawall. Her decision to marry Eli would mean forever keeping the professor's identity a secret. Forever hiding from her husband her mathematical abilities.

With her feelings more jumbled than ever, she slid under the covers. She'd have to get word to Geoffrey as soon as possible.

～

Eli strode along the deep-carpeted hallway of the top floor of Kennebrae Shipping. He carried a folder of drawings and figures, tapping his thigh as he walked. The correspondence from Professor Josephson had started the day off right.

A smile tugged at Eli's lips, and his mind raced with all the things he needed to get done now that the final drawings were in his hand. The solution had turned out to be so simple he didn't know why he hadn't seen it himself. The oppression and desperation that weighed him down ever since Grandfather had argued with Fox at the picnic lifted like lake fog in a stiff breeze.

He just needed to get through one more meeting with Grandfather, one more look at the budget for the modifications, one more discussion of plans and workforce and security. And for the first time in weeks, he didn't dread the meeting. His goal was within reach. He would be able to look Grandfather in the eye, present him with the finished *Bethany*, and take his place with his brothers as an asset to Kennebrae Shipping. He would be needed and appreciated and a true Kennebrae.

The conference room sat empty. Grandfather must be running late.

Eli started toward his customary seat then stopped himself. No, this time he would sit where he could see the painting, look the titan in the eyes, and smile. Maybe his own painting would hang somewhere in this room someday. And now that he had accomplished his goal, or nearly so, he felt he had earned his place.

He spread his papers out on the table, organizing them into categories for discussion—financing, supplies, workers, timetables. If things went well, they could be through the particulars and Eli could be back down at the shipyard before lunch.

The door opened, and Grandfather wheeled in.

Eli took in the paper-white skin, the slight tremble of the left hand. Concern gripped his heart. . .and dread. How much longer would Grandfather be with them?

"Tell me you've made some progress." The old man's voice pierced the silence, as strong and commanding as ever.

"Professor Josephson came through with the final plans for the hatch covers, and we should be able to manufacture and install them in less than two weeks." Eli slid the drawings across the table.

"Two weeks? The race is in two weeks!" Grandfather snatched up the papers. He scanned the pages, shuffling through them quickly. "You'll have to move quicker than that. And have you met this professor yet? Are you sure you can trust him? Don't underestimate Fox. He's sneaky. He'd stoop to anything to win this race."

Eli bit back a sigh and forced his voice to sound cheerful. "No, Grandfather, I haven't met the professor, and yes, I trust him. He hasn't steered us wrong yet. And you may not like Fox, but be careful what you say about him. You don't want a nasty slander lawsuit on your hands."

"Don't tell me what to do. Find out who this professor is. For all we know, he's a spy for Fox. We can't be too careful. He'll do anything to win."

Eli refrained from telling Grandfather to stop telling *him* what to do. "Josephson doesn't want any contact. He's a recluse; I told you that. I thought you'd be happy with the progress, not picking and poking and looking for something to complain about."

Grandfather perused the rest of the papers, marking his initials against the spending chits.

Eli breathed a sigh of relief when the papers were returned to the folder. He pushed back his chair and glanced up at the portrait, giving the painting a wink.

"Don't leave just yet." Grandfather motioned him back to his seat. "I want your assurance you'll track down this professor character and have him thoroughly checked out. Something about this situation isn't ringing true. I have a bad feeling."

Eli stared at the folder before him. "I'm not saying the situation isn't a bit odd, but who am I to look a gift horse in the mouth? Josephson is saving my bacon with these drawings and calculations. Without his help, I never would've made it this far. And don't forget, if you hadn't been drawn into this ridiculous race, I wouldn't be under such pressure to finish the ship in two weeks."

"I know it." Grandfather shoved his chair back from the table and lifted his shaky hand to smooth his hair. "My temper and my tongue get the better of me from time to time. I should know better, but there it is. I jumped in, and I'll move heaven and earth to win now."

Eli shook his head. "Fox knew just how to provoke you. But with these final plans, we're almost home free." He itched to leave, to get started on the last modifications.

"You'll think I'm a silly old man, getting us into this trouble. But I've never held back, never been afraid to leap first and figure out the details later. And when I give my word, I keep it. I guess that's why Zahn's behavior galls me so. I know we never signed a formal contract with the marriage, but he led me to believe a union between our families would cement a union between our companies. I was more angry at his waffling in front of Fox than I was about Fox's outrageous statements and horning in at the picnic. I thought I knew Zahn's character better. I'm beginning to think forcing you into marriage with one of his girls might've been a mistake."

Eli gripped the arms of the chair, the brass studs marching down the leather making indentions in his fingers. "What about your promise to Grandmother? Your heart condition?" His mouth went dry.

Grandfather shrugged and stared at the fireplace at the end of the room, not meeting Eli's eyes. "Well, maybe I put it stronger than necessary. Your grandmother wanted you married to good girls, that's true."

Eli's arms trembled. "And what about your heart condition?"

That infuriating shrug again. "I saw a specialist, and he said it might not be quite as serious as I led you to believe."

Eli shot out of his chair, knocking his folder of papers across the glossy surface in a fan of pages. "You mean to tell me you lied about dying?"

"Not lied. . .exactly." Grandfather made tamping down motions with his hands. "Just maybe exaggerated the seriousness of the situation. I knew nothing else would budge you. You looked like a man holding a governor's pardon when you found out Clarice had eloped. I didn't intend to give up so easy."

"Exaggerated." Eli leaned close, bracing his hands on the table. "Do you or do you not have a heart ailment?"

Grandfather glared at Eli. "That's not important. What's important is your winning this race."

Eli ground his teeth. "And did you or did you not promise Grandmother that you would find us all brides before you died?"

"I surely did. And I aim to see that promise through, if I have to drag you to the altar." He glared at Eli. "Enough of this talk. I want you to find this professor, fix the hatches on the *Bethany*, and win that race." Abraham Kennebrae, stubborn and unrepentant, never backed down. Eli tapped together his papers and left before he did or said something he'd regret.

Chapter 14

Eli twirled his walking stick and glanced up at a sky so blue it hurt the eyes. A ton weight had fallen from his shoulders like an enormous, land-bound ship sliding off the ways and splashing into the lake with the last of Josephson's calculations. The hatch idea was brilliant.

And he had to admit a bit of relief since finding out the previous day that his grandfather wasn't in imminent danger of dying. Heart ailment. The old man would outlive them all on sheer force of will.

The pressure to finish the job still surrounded him, and the race loomed large before him, but in spite of those things, he found himself whistling as he sauntered up the Zahns' walkway. At last he felt he had time to give in to the thoughts that had plagued him for many days.

Thoughts of Josie Zahn.

He couldn't even say why he was here, for he had more than enough things to keep him busy at the shipyard, but after fighting the urge all morning, he finally gave in. He had to see her.

He twisted the bell on the center of the door, listening to the buzzing ring muffled on the other side. Perhaps he should've brought flowers. Or candy. Girls liked those kinds of things. He shrugged. Next time.

The curtain in the window darkened, and the door flew open. Giselle stared up at him for a moment, and then her face split in a smile to match his own. "Oh, Mr. Kennebrae, have you come to take us on another outing?" She stepped back and held the door wide.

"Sorry, not today, sweetheart. Today I've come to see Josie. Is she in?" He stepped inside and removed his hat.

Antoinette bounced down the stairs and stopped at the landing.

Grandma Bess looked up from her chair in the parlor, letting her magazine drop into her lap.

Antoinette grabbed the rounded balustrade and shouted upstairs over her shoulder. "Josie, somebody to see you!"

Giselle giggled and took Eli's hand, swinging it while grinning at him. "It's your beau!"

Eli chuckled and didn't know where to look. Little-girl eyes were everywhere.

"Giselle, enough of your nonsense." Grandma Bess levered herself up with her cane. "Take his things, and get back to your needlework. Your mother will expect to see some progress on that sampler before she gets home." She swatted the little girl's behind as Giselle scooted past her. "Good afternoon, Mr. Kennebrae. Very nice to see you again. Won't you come in and sit down? No doubt Josie heard someone's"—she sent a pointed glance up to Antoinette—"unladylike bellowing informing her of your arrival. She'll be down directly."

Eli, now without his hat or walking stick, didn't know what to do with his hands. He hoped Josie wouldn't be long.

Giselle stared at him over the top of a square of cloth, poking a needle in and out in a pattern he couldn't discern.

He sat opposite her, on a camelback sofa, uncomfortable in this decidedly feminine room. Ferns hung from the ceiling and flowed out of white urns. Bric-a-brac covered every surface—pictures in frames, shells, figurines. Oils and watercolors covered the walls. Overhead a chandelier, unlit at midday, hung from a plaster medallion of whorls, loops, and vines.

"I'm sorry Octavia isn't here to greet you. She's gone over to Clarice's new home to help her settle in. Things here have been in a complete uproar since the elopement." The old woman didn't seem to care that she was crashing about on a topic people had been studiously avoiding bringing up to Eli. "How are things at the shipyard?" Grandma Bess picked up her magazine. "Your grandfather sure landed you in the soup, didn't he? Old men can be so silly sometimes. Everything's a competition. Anyone could see Gervase Fox was baiting Abraham, and like a tethered bear, Abraham snarled back. And you're the one who has to pay for it." She turned a page. "Abraham always was half-genius, half-foolish."

Eli, taken aback at her forthright speech, cast about for something to say that wouldn't be disloyal to Grandfather.

She smiled at him, her eyes nearly buried in wrinkles. "I can tell I've surprised you, saying what I think. But I'm an old woman, and I've earned the right. I don't have time for shilly-shallying, and most people, when they get over the shock, find it refreshing. I've known your grandfather for twenty-five years or more. Knew your grandmother, too. Genevieve and I were great friends once upon a time. Salt of the earth, that woman, and loved your grandfather something fierce. I always felt a bit sorry for her, though, loving him like she did, and him so busy with his empire. He never seemed to get around to loving her back."

Eli frowned. "You don't think he loved her?"

"I think he did, in his own way, and it was only after she passed on that he realized how much he'd lost. He spent his time traveling and putting business before family. And he missed all he could've shared with Genevieve if he would've stayed home and cherished her for the treasure she was." She slapped the magazine closed and stuffed it into a black bag at her feet. "You'd be wise to learn from his example, Eli. No woman wants to come second in her husband's affection, be it to another woman, a business, or just his own pride and ambition."

"I think I understand what you mean." He laced his fingers together, leaning forward and putting his elbows on his knees.

"I hope you do. This marriage business isn't one to be taken lightly, and it isn't something that should be decided for you by someone else. My son and your grandfather think that anyone, provided he or she is of similar faith and social status, should be able to have an amiable marriage. But people aren't that tidy. You take Josie now. Josie's a girl in a thousand, and if you take the time to get to know her, you'll find she's of the caliber of your grandmother. Steel true, blade straight. And brighter than anyone around here gives her credit for. But that won't do you any good if you only take her at face value. Take the time to dig deeper, find out what kind of girl she really is."

The way she looked at Eli, sizing him up like he was a nailhead and she was holding a hammer, made him want to squirm. Josie chose that minute to enter, and he bolted out of his seat. "Hello."

She had her hair coiled up on the back of her head in a thick, shiny braid. He wondered what it would look like all loose and flowing around her shoulders. The thought made him swallow hard. Only a husband would be privileged to see a woman with her hair down. When she stepped near, the smell of violets surrounded him, taking him back to his childhood. Grandmother had grown African violets by the dozens in her conservatory—tiny pink, purple, and white blossoms that appeared to float above velvet-green heart-shaped leaves.

"Hello." She watched him, a reserved expression on her face but pleasant enough.

For a long moment he studied her then realized he was staring like an idiot. "Hello."

A smile teased her lips. "You already said that."

What was the matter with him? He'd never had trouble talking to her before. "I, uh, I came to see you." He felt Giselle's and Grandma Bess's eyes staring at him, but none affected him like Josie's, deep blue, nearly purple.

Grandma Bess snorted. "Why don't you two go out to the garden? It's more private there."

Eli shot her a grateful glance and offered his arm to Josie.

She took it, tilting her head to look up at him. "Would you like to see Mama's roses?"

The lake breeze cleared his head a bit. They walked down the flagstone path between rioting beds of flowers. Lilac bushes, long bereft of flowers, outlined the boundaries of the garden. Arches of climbing roses spanned the paths, nodding in the sunshine, sending showers of petals like pink snow to the grass.

"They're Mama's pride and joy. She tends them so carefully. Each fall she prunes them and covers them with straw and weighs them down with newspaper and stones. The climate is so harsh here, but she manages to keep them alive and thriving."

He didn't care about roses or gardening, but he found himself enjoying listening to her talk. She led him to a bench that overlooked the lake. The slap and scrape of the waves against the rocky shore provided a familiar background noise.

She settled in, smoothing her skirts and crossing her ankles in a purely feminine way. Her hands were so small, the diamond on her finger hung like an enormous drop of dew. Something about that ring disquieted him. Though he enjoyed the idea of being engaged to her, that ring didn't look quite right.

He did have something that she'd like better. But how to give it to her? The opal ring in its velvet box burned a hole in his pocket. His heart swelled a bit at the thought of having just the right gift, something he knew would make her happy. He gave himself a mental pat on the back for stopping off at the jeweler's on the way over to pick it up for her.

"How are things coming at the shipyard?"

He tore his gaze away from her hands. "Good now. I've solved the last major hurdle. Well, not me, exactly. Another engineer I've been working with. He came up with an absolutely ingenious design for the loading hatches. That problem has stumped us for weeks now."

She moistened her lips and looked up at the house on the slight slope above them. "And you'll be ready for the race?"

"Yes, and I just got word that Noah and Annie will be returning from their honeymoon soon. I can't tell you how relieved I am that Noah will be at the wheel of the *Bethany* for the race. Though he doesn't know about it all yet." Eli hoped Grandfather would be the one to break the news to Noah that the fate of his beloved ship was on the line. Noah, easygoing and gentle until pushed too far, just might blow his boiler when he found out how rash Grandfather had been. "I didn't come to talk about my ship, though, or the race."

"You didn't?"

"No, I'd like to talk about more pleasant things." He ventured to take her hand, thrilling when her fingers curled around his. "I think there are things about you that I don't know, but I'd very much like to. Things have been so snarled up between us, so cluttered with other people's wants and wishes, we've barely had time to get to know each other."

She chewed her lower lip lightly, her lashes hiding her eyes.

How could he break down this reserve of hers? When he had taken her to the circus, she had seemed so open and friendly, but ever since their engagement, it was as if a wall had grown up between them. "I suppose it isn't fair to ask you to reveal your secrets without being willing to share my own. I'll tell you one."

He ignored a thrust of vulnerability. "Ever since I was a little boy, I've dreamed of doing something big, something so important that my grandfather and my brothers would be amazed. I've always felt like the least important Kennebrae. Grandfather has an iron will and a Midas touch. Jonathan is a whiz at business and handling people. Noah is one of the youngest captains on the Great Lakes. . .and one of the best. And what have I done? Nothing. . .yet. The success of the *Bethany* means more than just winning this race. It means I'll have made my mark on the family business and on cargo shipping forever. I will have contributed to Kennebrae Shipping in a way that no other Kennebrae could have."

"Have your brothers made you feel unimportant? Has your grandfather said he feels you don't contribute?" Her delicate black brows arched.

"Not in so many words. It's just something I feel. Something I have to do for my own sake as much as the business's." He'd laid bare a part of his heart he'd hardly even acknowledged existed. He needed something in return from her to make it seem worthwhile. "What about you? Surely you have some dream or desire, something you've always wanted." As much as he needed her answer, he needed something to distract him from the thought running through his head continually since she walked into the parlor.

What would it be like to kiss her?

∽

Josie blinked. Did a dream you'd laid aside count?

The warmth of his palm pressing against hers distracted her. His hand tightened on hers. "You're hesitating. I'm sorry. I've pried too much. It was forward of me to ask you to reveal a secret." He looked so forlorn and alone, her heart wanted to cry.

"No, it isn't that." She returned the pressure of his grip. "It's just that it's hard to put into words the things I want."

His eyes glowed, and a smile brightened his expression. "I suppose you want what most women want. A home, a family."

It pained her how little he really knew her. Not that she didn't want a home and a family, but what about everything else she wanted? She had a calling, something she was compelled to do.

She studied their locked hands. Josie Kennebrae. Mrs. Eli Kennebrae. Heat shot up her cheeks, and her breath caught in her throat. Part of her thrilled at the idea, and part of her quailed.

When she married him, she would be obeying her parents, but would she also be disobeying God? She'd promised God she would be the woman He made her to be, that she would use her gifts for His glory. How could she do that if she married? No husband would allow his wife to be an engineer. "Would you like to know what I really want?"

"Tell me." He pressed her fingers, making the cold diamond band bite into her finger, reminding her of who he had bought it for.

"I want to be treated like an individual instead of one of many. I'm tired of being known as one of the Zahn girls. When people look at me, I want them to see me. I want. . ."

"When you marry me, you won't be a Zahn girl anymore. You'll be a Kennebrae." His voice sounded deep and rumbly, and his eyes bored into hers.

She jerked when his hand came up and touched her cheek. She swallowed, her mouth dry.

"Josie?" He leaned close. His eyes asked permission just before his lips came down on hers.

It was more wondrous and breathtaking than she'd even imagined. His arms came around her and drew her to him. The warmth of his lips seared through her. Her hand came up and touched the faint roughness of his cheek. Love for him coursed over her. If only she could stay here in his arms forever, loving and beloved.

Cold reality dashed over her, freezing her like an icy wave. She might love him, but he didn't love her. He didn't even know her. She was just the next Zahn girl in line. Her hands came up and thrust against his chest, breaking the kiss.

He rocked back, blinking.

"I can't do this. I can't. I thought I could." Tears sprang to her eyes and tumbled down her cheeks. "I'm so sorry." She wrenched the ring from her finger and pressed it into his palm. "This will never work. I should have known it the moment you put this ring on my finger, but I didn't want to believe it. I'm sorry." Knowing she'd made a fool of herself, tasting the bitterness of dashed hopes, she stumbled to her feet and ran to the house.

A last look over her shoulder showed Eli standing beside the garden bench, a bewildered expression on his face.

Chapter 15

Josie threw herself across her bed, sobs wracking her body. She cried from a place deep inside her heart, a place so secret she hadn't even known it existed. "God, I'm so sorry. Please help me."

She was barely aware of the mattress sinking down and someone smoothing her hair until Grandma Bess spoke. "There, there, child. It can't be that bad."

Josie pushed herself up and flung herself into Grandma's waiting arms. For long moments she cried, unable to stop, unable to catch her breath. When at last the tears were spent, she pulled back from Grandma's comforting embrace. Hiccups jerked her with every breath.

"All done?" Grandma leaned over the side of the bed and dug in her ever-present bag. "Here." She pressed a comfortingly large handkerchief into Josie's trembling hands. "Mop up a bit, and we'll talk."

Josie sniffed and wiped her tears. "There's—" *Hiccup*. "There's nothing to talk about."

Grandma leveled an "oh really" look at her. "Then you're just wailing for the fun of it?"

Josie knew she'd have to tell Grandma something or she'd never let it rest. And suddenly, the chance to come clean, to confess everything and have her ragged feelings soothed, seemed too good to pass up. "I gave Eli back his ring." Her heart tore afresh, and another cascade of tears gushed down her cheeks.

"Oh? You aren't going to marry him then?"

She shook her head, balling up the handkerchief. "I can't."

"Did he say or do something horrible to you?" The placid expression on Grandma's face told Josie she wasn't particularly worried about Josie's answer.

"Of course not. His behavior was impeccable." His kiss lingered on her lips, a memory she would treasure forever.

"Then you discovered something about him that makes him unsuitable as a husband?"

"No. He would be a perfect husband." So far, Grandma's soothing left a little to be desired.

"Then you've decided he is unlovable."

"Stop it. I love him, and you know it or you wouldn't keep after me this way."

Grandma sighed and got up from the side of the bed. She settled herself in the rocking chair in the corner and placed her bag on her lap. "Let me get this straight. He has impeccable manners, is perfectly suitable as a husband, and you love him, yet you aren't going to marry him."

"That's right. I can't."

"Why not? It's plain as a porcupine you're made for one another."

"I can't marry him because he doesn't return my love. He doesn't even know the real me. I'll always be just the next Zahn girl on the list." Bitterness laced her words.

"What nonsense is this? The next Zahn girl on the list?"

"Clarice was his first choice, but she eloped. And I was next in line. Like we're interchangeable parts. One is as good as another. Just like Papa. He can't remember our names half the time."

"Josephine Zahn, I thought you had more sense. People think an old woman doesn't notice things, but that's not true. I see more than people give me credit for. Clarice was no more his first choice than he was hers. And I saw how Eli acted around Clarice, and I've seen how he acts around you. Believe me, he knows the difference. As for your father, I suspect his forgetfulness regarding you girls is put on. He pretends with you. It's a game. Mark my words, young lady, Eli Kennebrae is in love with you. Even *he* might not know how much."

Josie hardly dared hope Grandma spoke the truth. Did he love her? Reality dragged her shoulders down. "But even if he does love me, I can't marry him. I'd be disobeying God."

Grandma blinked. "Disobeying God?"

Josie nodded. A strand of hair came loose out of her braid and clung to her damp cheek. "I've loved Eli for a long time. Right after Eli and Clarice became engaged, I promised God that instead of hankering after Eli I would be the woman He made me to be. I promised Him I would pursue His calling on my life to be an engineer. Then Clarice eloped and Eli proposed, and in a weak moment I accepted. I turned my back on my promise to God."

The way Grandma closed her eyes and moved her lips made Josie think she might be praying for patience. "Girl, you do get things in a snarl, don't you? How will marrying Eli keep you from being the woman God meant you to be? You think it is an either-or situation? And just because you promised something to God doesn't mean that was His will for you in the first place."

"But what about my abilities? If I marry Eli, I can't be an engineer. Men don't want wives who have careers. Geoffrey made that plain to me. That's why—" She broke off.

"That's why what? And what does Geoffrey have to do with anything?"

Josie twisted the soggy handkerchief, staring at her hands. Hot embarrassment flowed over her. "Eli has been corresponding with an engineer through Geoffrey. Someone who has been helping him with the designs for the *Bethany*." Her voice sounded small and faraway in her ears, like Giselle's when she was caught in some mischief. "I knew I could do the work, but I knew no man would take me seriously because I'm a girl. So I made up an identity, a Professor Josephson, to work with Eli. All communication is run through Geoffrey. Eli thinks the professor is a recluse and a hermit. But"—she swallowed hard against the lump in her throat—"the professor is me."

A sigh as deep as Lake Superior came from Grandma's chest. "So you've done exactly what you promised God you wouldn't do. You've hidden your light under a bushel, to pull a verse out of context. You're not being the woman God made you to be, too scared to stand up and say you are a fine engineer. No wonder you can't see which way God wants you to go. You've been lying, both to Eli and to Him. If you harbor sin in your heart—sin you know and do nothing about—God isn't likely to answer your prayers."

Grandma's words, though said with love and gentle correction, still hit Josie like knife blades. "What should I do?"

"I think you know the answer to that, at least the first thing."

A giant hand of guilt pressed against Josie's chest. She nodded, unable to speak. She needed to confess her sin. Then, and only then, could she begin to hope God would show her what to do about Eli.

"As for what to do after that, I think you know that, too. You need to tell Eli the truth. You've sold him short. By lying to him and assuming he would scorn your engineering efforts, you haven't given him a chance to handle things well. I think you're underestimating Eli. And God. You've been so busy trying to figure everything out, to engineer what you thought was the right solution, you've eliminated the need for faith and trust. You haven't trusted God with your future, and you haven't trusted Eli with your abilities."

Grandma rose from the rocker, crossed the room, and sat beside Josie again, putting her comforting arms around Josie's shoulders and hugging her close. "You are so like me. Do you know how often I've let something that should be my greatest strength become my greatest weakness? God gave you the ability to design, to calculate, to figure. And applied to shipbuilding or architecture or mathematics, it's a fine gift. But when you start trying to engineer circumstances and people, design and force God's plan to be revealed to you, or construct your future the way you want it to be instead of the way God has for you, you run into trouble."

Josie leaned her head against her grandmother's soft shoulder, breathing in the smell of lemon verbena toilette water and talcum powder. "Do you think it is too late for Eli and me?"

"Give the young man a chance. You might be surprised."

∾

Eli jammed his walking stick into the holder in the hall tree and smacked his hat onto a peg. The carpet on the stairs muffled his forceful footsteps in a totally unsatisfactory way. If he lived to be a thousand he would never understand women. One moment things were going well—laughing, talking, sharing deep secrets—and the next, *wham*! He was left alone in the garden holding a ring.

The feel of her in his arms, the rush of exultation when his lips met hers, the way her violet scent wrapped around him—all of it galled him. He'd been a fool to think she would accept his advances. And he blamed his grandfather as much as anyone. Grandfather had pushed him into the first engagement, held out promises to him. Then, when things looked like they were falling apart, he guilted Eli into another engagement with false claims of a bad heart. And Eli had allowed it like some dumb sheep.

He reached his bedroom and slammed the door. A sheaf of papers slid off a chair onto the floor. "If there was a prize for being a chump, I'd win, hands down."

"Is there a prize for being a chump?"

Eli spun toward the fireplace.

His brother Noah unfolded his long frame from the wing-back chair.

"Noah!"

"Hello, little brother."

Eli found himself in a bear hug that shoved the air from his chest. "Little brother, nothing," he gasped when Noah released him. "We're twins."

Noah cuffed him on the shoulder, his bearded face split in a wide grin. "But I was born first. Those few precious minutes make all the difference. But what's this about you being a chump?"

Eli shrugged. "Nothing out of the ordinary these days." He took Noah's measure. "Marriage agrees with you. You look. . .content."

Noah dropped back into his chair and stretched out his legs, lacing his fingers across his lean middle. "You're looking at a happy man. I highly recommend marital bliss, Eli. I understand you've jumped into the matrimonial pool, too."

"Humph. I thought I had, but apparently the pool is dry. The lady has rebuffed my advances, refused my suit, and given me back my ring. Though I'd just as soon you didn't tell Grandfather yet. I'll tell him later myself." He dug in his pocket and produced the offending bit of gold and gemstones. "And you know what she said? She should've known it wouldn't work the moment I put this ring on her finger." He tossed the ring to his brother.

Noah caught the ring and studied it, then glanced up at Eli, his eyes twinkling. "Well, that doesn't sound too promising. What are you going to do about it?"

"Do? What can I do? You can't argue with a returned ring. Just when I thought things were going well, she hands me the mitt and runs away. Women are a mystery well beyond my ability to solve."

"Now you sound like you're ready to get married. The moment you figure out that you'll never figure them out, you've got them figured out." Noah held up the diamonds to sparkle in the sunshine from the window.

"Make sense, will you? It's not funny." He snatched the ring back and stuffed it in his pocket.

Noah's grin faded, and his eyes narrowed. "Say, you sound really hurt. Don't tell me you've fallen for this girl?"

Eli tried to bear up under Noah's scrutiny, his mind scrambling for an answer. He didn't have to search far. He knew his heart. He knew how he felt about Josie, how he'd felt about her from the moment he saw her at the wedding reception. "Well, what if I have? Maybe I'm no different than you and Jonathan. You both fell in love with the women Grandfather chose for you."

Noah leaned forward and tapped Eli on the side of the knee. "Hey, there's nothing wrong with it. In fact, it's wonderful. Like I said, marriage is the best thing that ever happened to me."

"You're forgetting the lady turned me down."

"I'll give you a little hint, Eli. Sometimes women say one thing and mean another."

"Why do they do that? It's like they expect you to read their minds. But if she didn't mean she wanted to end the engagement, what did she mean?"

"If you think this girl is worth it, little brother, then you should find out. That is, if you love her."

Eli sighed and raked his fingers through his hair. "I love her, and it's driving me crazy."

Chapter 16

Eli stalked across the sidewalk and entered the restaurant. Business. That's what he needed. He needed to focus on business and put matters of the heart aside for now. He crossed the dining room, weaving between tables, catching snippets of conversation as he headed toward the back corner.

Noon at The Black Horse, and every businessman on Minnesota Point could be found here. More deals were done over steak at The Black Horse than in the boardrooms of Duluth. The sound of cutlery and commerce flowed.

Geoffrey waved to him. At least his lawyer was on time.

Eli took his seat and ignored the menu. "Geoff, I want to know who the professor is and no more of your slippery evasions." If he couldn't solve one problem, he'd solve another. "Grandfather insists on meeting the man, and I want to issue an invitation for him to accompany us on the race. The designing engineers deserve to be in the pilothouse." He snapped open his napkin and spread it across his lap.

"Now, Eli, you know I can't do that. Why don't you just trust me when I say he can't and won't come?" Geoff's face disappeared behind his menu.

"There's something fishy about this whole situation. Where'd you meet this man anyway? If he never sees anyone, then why will he see you? And how did you just happen to pull an engineer out of your pocket at the precise moment I needed one? It isn't you, is it? Put that menu down so I can look you in the eye."

A waiter hovered, and Eli clenched his fists at the delay.

They placed their orders, and Geoffrey lifted his water glass. "No"—he took a long swallow—"it isn't me. I wouldn't know the first thing about ship design."

"Then who is it? One of the college dons? I've checked. There is no Josephson on faculty at the college. In fact, there's no Josephson that I can find anywhere in town."

"You've been looking?" Geoff's eyebrows rose.

"Of course I have, and so has Grandfather. And you know how thorough his investigations can be. But so far they've turned up nothing." Eli placed his palms flat on the table. "Geoff, why are you lying to me? And don't deny it. I know you are. There's something wrong about all of this. Josephson either doesn't exist or that isn't his real name."

Geoff looked at the ceiling. "If I could tell you, I would, but I'm not at liberty to say."

"That's convenient." Eli knew he was overreacting, but the sting of Josie's refusal and the frustration of knowing he'd have to face his grandfather with it goaded him on. "I took your elopement in stride, knowing it was for the best, and I even took your part when Grandfather wanted to fire you. And how do you repay me? By hiding behind your lawyer talk." He thumped the table, surprised at his own vehemence. "Tell me where to find Professor Josephson."

A hand whacked him on the shoulder. "Kennebrae, how are things?"

He looked up into the badgerish face of Gervase Fox. Every muscle in his jaw tightened. "Just fine."

"I couldn't help but overhear. You're looking for Professor Josephson?" The look in Fox's eye made Eli instantly wary.

"That's right. Do you know him?" Surely not.

"Of course I do, my boy. And so do you." A nasty grin split Fox's whiskers.

"Enough, Mr. Fox." Geoffrey put down his fork. "Stop with your jests. You don't know anything about this situation, and it is boorish of you to insinuate otherwise."

A flush climbed above Fox's beard. "Young man, I'm not jesting. Not only do I know the identity of Professor Josephson, but I've been in contact with said engineer. You should know. You're the one who introduced us, though I don't suppose you meant to at the time. I will say bumping into you two down at the canal was fortuitous for me. I was able to put two and two together and do a little investigating, and *presto!*"

As much as it galled him, Eli had to know. "Then tell me where to find him. He's done some collaborative work for me, and I wish to meet him face-to-face."

A laugh shook Fox's belly. "My dear boy, there is no Professor Josephson, at least not the academic you seem to think. Your assistant engineer is none other than your own fiancée, Josephine Zahn." Billows of raucous laughter nearly choked Gervase. "I can't believe you didn't know. Your lawyer knew, that's for certain. Look at him. He looks like he's swallowed a wasp."

Incredulity stunned Eli speechless. He looked from the beet-red, guffawing Fox to Geoffrey's stricken face and knew Fox spoke the truth. Josie? An engineer?

When Fox regained his breath, he crossed his arms and leaned on the back of a vacant chair at their table. "I have to say, the 'professor's' designs are quite revolutionary. And they're good, too. Just to be sure of her ability, I had her teacher tracked down at his new employment in Detroit. Though my investigator couldn't get much out of the man, his students are known for their engineering abilities, and I've found no reason why Josephine should be any different. Her drawings are quite amazing. She's been quite good to work with." He wiped his eyes. "And your trying so hard to keep me out of your shipyard so I wouldn't see them, when I've had the information all the while."

Eli found his voice. "Josie's Professor Josephson? She's been giving you my ship plans all along?" His heart squeezed in a giant vise.

"Of course. Why do you think I was so quick to entice your grandfather into this match race? I never would've taken the chance otherwise, not if you truly had a secret design that might best me." Fox stood upright and hooked his thumbs in his vest pockets.

She'd lied to him. Lied to him and betrayed him. Everything he thought about her, everything he thought she stood for, that he thought she might feel for him, that he felt for her, underwent a radical change.

"Don't take it too hard, boy. You've just had a taste of the cutthroat world of business. You'll get used to it." Fox clapped him on the shoulder, but Eli barely felt it.

"I think you'd better leave." Geoff stood up and stepped forward. "You've said far too much."

"And you haven't said enough. If I found out my lawyer was lying to me the way you lie to the Kennebraes, he'd not only be unemployed, but I'd run him right out of town." Fox dug in his pocket for a cigar. "The only way to win in business is to look out for yourself. You can't be afraid to get your hands dirty. You'll both learn, though, some lessons come harder than others." He struck a match with his thumbnail and disappeared behind a puffing cloud of cigar smoke.

"Get out." Eli stood up. "You've had your fun; now leave." His gut muscles clenched so hard his body shook. He wanted to bury his fist in Fox's smug face, drive that cigar down his throat.

Fox barked with laughter. "Fine. I'll go. Give my regards to Josie." He waved his cigar and strode through the dining room, head back, still laughing.

Eli eased into his chair. Every eye in the place was on him, and the diners had heard at least part of the exchange with Fox. The only sound was the door closing behind Fox's retreating form.

Geoff looked across at him, his eyes clouded.

Slowly conversations picked up, forks scraped against china, and men turned their attention away from Eli's table.

"It's true, isn't it?"

Geoff nodded.

"Why?" One flat word, a single question that both asked for an explanation and accused his friend for his duplicity.

"Eli, it isn't as bad as you think." Geoff spread his hands in a placating gesture.

"I don't want any of your lawyer talk. I want the straight truth, not that I'll be able to trust it coming from you." A thrust of satisfaction charged through Eli when Geoff winced and dropped his gaze. "Why would you do this to me? Why would Josie?"

"At first we did it to stall. But after, we were both in so deep, and it seemed to be working, so we kept it up."

"Stall? Stall what?"

"Just hear me out." Geoff straightened his spine. "You were going to marry my girl, and I was desperate to find a way to stall your marriage and get her out of there. I knew you weren't keen on the situation, and you only wanted to work on the *Bethany*. I figured if I could keep your attention on your work, I'd have time to find a solution that would free Clarice. I knew you needed an engineer, and Clarice and Josie assured me Josie could do the work. But since she's a girl, she didn't think you'd listen to her ideas. So we dreamed up Professor Josephson." His eyes telegraphed his misery, but he didn't look away. "This is all my fault. Don't blame Josie."

"Don't blame her? After she's been duping me? And not only that, but giving my ideas to Fox? To *Fox* of all people?" Eli wasn't sure which hurt the worst, betrayal by his friend, his fiancée, or his foe. No, that wasn't true. Josie's betrayal hurt the worst.

"You can't believe anything Fox says." Geoff pushed back his nearly full plate and put his elbows on the table.

"Unlike you and Josie, who are models of truthfulness?" Sarcasm soaked his tone. "How else would he know her identity? Why else would he be so cocksure he would win the race?"

Geoffrey rammed his fingers into his hair. "I don't know how he knew. He's slippery. But Josie wouldn't have shared the information with him. She knew how sensitive it was. She knew how much it meant to you. How much it meant to her."

"If she knew and told him anyway, that makes it worse."

"Go talk to her. Find out how this happened."

"Forget it." Eli's heart went hard as a chunk of ice. She'd handed back her ring because she knew she'd betrayed him and she couldn't stomach it. "If Fox has implemented the same designs as the *Bethany*, then the race will be closer than I thought. I have more than enough work to do without confronting Josie with her duplicity." He stood and scooted his chair under the table.

For a long moment he looked down on the man he had thought was his best friend. "I don't know what I'll tell Grandfather. If I tell him the truth, he'll have you cleaning out your office in the Kennebrae Building before supper. I don't think you meant me any harm with your lying, but it's harmed me all the same. Just stay away from me from now on."

Chapter 17

But how did Fox find out?" Despair clawed up Josie's throat.

Geoff stood before her, mangling his hat brim. "I don't know. He mentioned meeting us together near the canal, and he said he'd had you checked out, sent an investigator to your tutor. Fox knew it all. He claimed you've been feeding him information all along, that he knows all the designs and modifications to the *Bethany*, and he's sure he can win the race. Threw it right into Eli's face."

"That's impossible. The designs have never left my room unless they were in your possession. Every time you brought me new plans, I took them right up to my desk." Josie sank onto the garden bench, the same bench where only two days before Eli had held her in his arms. "What did Eli say?"

"He walked out like he was in a trance. I went back to the office, but he wasn't in the Kennebrae Building. I don't know where he is. I decided I'd better head over here in case he'd come to confront you about things."

"Did he fire you?" Guilt at landing Geoffrey in so much trouble swamped her.

"No, but as good as. When Abraham finds out what we've been up to, he'll sack me for sure."

Josie blinked back tears and twisted her fingers. "Grandma Bess was right. She says a lie that goes on only gets more and more complicated until the liar is tied up in her own web. I'm so sorry, Geoff. I never should've drawn you into this."

"Don't take all the blame for yourself. I had a major hand in this." Geoff paced the flagstone path. "That still doesn't explain how Fox knew. If you didn't tell him, and I certainly didn't, then how would he get his hands on the plans? What about a servant? Could a maid have slipped him the information?"

"No, we don't have an upstairs maid for the bedrooms. Mama thinks we girls should care for our own rooms the way she had to."

"Are any of the plans missing?"

"No, that's just it. I've got them all. When I'm done with the papers, I either give them to you or I burn them in the stove."

Something tickled the back of Josie's mind, and she stopped speaking to focus on it. Something about Fox and her room. . . She shook her head. Grasping at straws. "What do you think Eli will do?"

Geoff stopped pacing and fixed his gaze on her face. "Clarice says you're

351

in love with Eli. That you've loved him for a long time. Is that true?"

Josie closed her eyes against the wave of pain and loss that crashed over her. Unable to speak around the lump in her throat, she could only nod. When she composed herself, she whispered, "It doesn't matter now. He won't even talk to me. He'll never be mine. I broke the engagement two days ago. And he'd never take me back, not believing I betrayed him."

Geoff sank down on the bench beside her and put his arm around her in a brotherly hug. "I'm so sorry, Josie. But don't give up yet. We'll think of something."

ℒ

"I'm not surprised she broke the engagement. The last shred of her conscience must've goaded her into it. Couldn't face marrying you when she'd lied." Grandfather edged his chair farther into Eli's shipyard workroom.

"I don't want to talk about it." Eli spread a map on the table. "Noah, now that you've been over the ship, what do you think of her?"

Noah leaned against the wall, arms crossed, one ankle over the other. "I'd hardly recognize her if her name weren't painted on the stern. You've done a remarkable job with the repairs."

"And I think you'll find she handles well, too. I wish we had time to give her a thorough shakedown before the race, but we'll just have time to get her launched and fueled before next week. The hatches will be done in a few more days. Those gaskets were harder to fashion than I anticipated."

"Don't you ignore me, young man." Grandfather poked Eli in the side. "I came down here to talk about Josie, so start talking."

"She broke the engagement. That's all there is to say. Now leave it. I'm busy." He pointed to the map. "Noah, you'll load here at the Zahn number two dock in Two Harbors. The cranes are being erected up there right now to lower the units into the hold. I've had to reinforce the pilings to accommodate the extra weight." He leafed through the large papers on the desk and withdrew the plan for the loading system. "No more shoving one board at a time into the hold. You can be loaded in under four hours. I guarantee it."

Noah gave a low whistle of appreciation. "Four hours to load a lumber ship. It's unheard of."

"We have to assume Fox has this plan. He's taken over Zahn's number one dock, and from what I can tell, he's making much the same adjustments over there to crane load." Eli ground his teeth.

"I'm sorry about that." Noah shook his head. "It's a shame your girl let you down like that."

Grandfather snorted. "Thick as thieves, Fox and those Zahns. You made a lucky escape, boy. Radcliffe turned on me over the shipping contracts, and that girl betrayed you to our rival."

Eli slammed his pencil down with a slap. "I said I'm through talking about this. If you'd minded your own business instead of trying to shove me into an engagement I never wanted in the first place *and* if you'd have kept your mouth shut when Fox showed up at that picnic, I wouldn't be in this mess. As usual, you leap first and think later. Now, unless you want to back out of this race and just hand the *Bethany* over to Fox right now, I suggest you leave me alone to finish the repairs." He turned to his brother. "I'll be back when the room is a little less crowded."

The entire shack shuddered when he slammed the door, but he didn't care. Grandfather could stew in his own juice. From now on, Eli was his own man. He'd do his best to win this race, for his brothers' sakes and Kennebrae Shipping, but after that, he was finished.

Good shipbuilders were needed back East. If he couldn't get hired on somewhere, he'd start his own company. And he'd stay away from women, lawyers, and interfering old men.

Chapter 18

Josie braced herself against the concrete pier wall, leaning out over the canal. People pushed and shoved, trying to find good spots from which to see the race. In the background, the Duluth City Band played a lively tune. Bunting and flags flapped in the gusting wind.

She glanced up at the swollen, tumbling clouds that looked ready to burst with rain at any moment. What should've been a glorious day hovered, anxious and out of sorts, much like Josie herself.

Whitecaps and chop slapped against the pier side, sucking and slurping as if trying to climb over each other to get onshore. She pulled her coat tight.

"Is it time?" Giselle tugged on Josie's hand. "When will the boats come?"

"I told you, wait for the whistle. The ships will pull out of their docks and head right through the canal. You won't miss a thing."

Josie put her hand on Toni's shoulder and tugged her back. "The race will be irrelevant to you if you plunge into that cold water. And Mama will have a fit."

Toni rolled her eyes but kept her heels on the ground.

Giselle yanked on Josie's sleeve. "I wish we could ride on the boat like Papa. Why'd he go on Mr. Fox's boat? I thought he would ride with Eli. That's where I'd go. I like Eli better. Mr. Fox thinks little girls are stupid. But he's the one who is stupid." She stuck out her tongue and crossed her eyes. "He couldn't even find the washroom when he was at our house, even though I told him where it was. He went right into your room instead. Stupid man."

Josie grabbed Giselle by the shoulders. "Mr. Fox was in my room? You saw him? When?"

The little girl blinked, her lower lip quivering. "I didn't do anything wrong. I promise."

Josie loosened her grip. "It's all right, Giselle. You're not in trouble. But you're sure you saw Mr. Fox in my room?"

The little girl's black curls bounced when she nodded. "He was in there a long time. That's why I thought he was stupid. He should've known right off that wasn't the washroom."

Josie's lips pressed tight in vindication. Fox *had* gone into her room and stolen the plans. Her shoulders sagged. Little good it would do her, though. If Eli wouldn't listen to her, he wasn't likely to listen to Giselle.

A whistle blast pierced the air, quickly swallowed by the shouts around her. The race was on!

Josie pressed her middle against the seawall and leaned out as far as she dared, trying to see past the heads and shoulders of others doing the same. Her hands pressed the concrete, her palms stinging.

The *Keystone Vulpine* appeared first, riding high, the water churning to foam in her wake. Almost in her shadow, the *Bethany* nosed forward. The *Vulpine* would make it out of Duluth Harbor first. The ship passed before them, stack belching smoke, cutting through the green blue water with ease. High above the crowd, deckhands lined the rail.

"There's Papa! Look, Josie, it's Papa!" Giselle hopped, clapping and waving by turns.

Radcliffe Zahn stood in the pilothouse doorway, the lapels of his great-coat fluttering.

Josie tore her gaze away, disappointment at her father's actions coursing through her. That he would treat his agreement with the Kennebraes so cavalierly, aligning himself with their rival while still expecting them to honor the engagement between the families, shamed her. His claim that it was "just business" and she "wouldn't understand" didn't cut much ice with Josie. The way a person conducted business revealed character. She hoped he would be as cavalier when she told him of the broken engagement.

She swallowed. She hadn't conducted her business very well. What did that say about her character?

The *Vulpine*'s midship glided past. Josie concentrated on the hull. A converted ore carrier just like the *Bethany*. She knew the hold would contain the same storage and loading apparatus as Eli had designed. The interior bracing, the hull dimensions, all of it stolen by Fox. She closed her eyes and could see in her mind the final drawings—every line, every curve, every calculation clear. When she opened her eyes, the stern of the *Vulpine* slid past.

But something was different. Josie concentrated on the aft hatch cover, the ship's propulsion shortening her angle of view. The housing around the hatch looked odd. The shadow line seemed off somehow. A wide-brimmed hat blocked her vision.

Josie stepped back from the crowd lining the waterway and grabbed Giselle's and Toni's hands. She shouldered her way up the pier toward the open lake. A wild elbow dislodged her hat, but she ignored it and moved on, trying to get a better look at the departing ship.

A man caught her by the arm. "Whoa there, miss, what's your hurry?" A pair of field glasses swung from a strap around his neck.

"Please, sir, might I borrow those?" She released Toni's hand. "Stay right by me."

He smiled, clearly bemused, and took off his hat to remove the glasses.

She snatched them and pressed them to her eyes. The *Vulpine*'s stern leaped close in her vision. The ship quartered slightly, but even that angle presented her enough of a view to know she hadn't been wrong.

Fox's ship was a bomb waiting to go off. The hinges fastening the hatches to the deck were the same ones Eli had originally intended to use. If Fox had used the drawings from her desk the day he had visited the house, then those hinges were under-engineered. They'd facilitate the loading, but in bad weather, with the tremendous strain of water crashing over the deck, they'd let go.

The *Bethany* plunged through the Duluth Canal, her steel bulk obliterating the *Vulpine* from view. Josie swung the glasses upward and trained them on the pilothouse. Dark silhouettes moved in the little room. A face appeared in the window. A lump formed in her throat when she made out Eli's features. Then he was gone, the *Bethany* taking him out onto the lake.

Abraham Kennebrae. He was the only one with the clout to call a halt to the race before it was too late. But where in this throng could she find him?

The Kennebrae Building. She pressed the glasses back into the stranger's hand, flashed him a smile, and snaked through the crowd, dragging her sisters along in her wake. Thanks to the Duluth papers, the race had brought throngs of people down to the canal. By the time she reached the steps of the Kennebrae Shipping headquarters, she was out of breath. The comparative quiet of the lobby wrapped around her.

"May I help you, miss?" A sour-faced man behind a counter fixed her with a fishy eye, and his mouth pinched tight at sight of her little sisters gaping at the ornate interior of the office building. "There are no public facilities here. You'll have to go up the street."

"I came to see Mr. Abraham Kennebrae. Is he here?" Josie squared her shoulders and took a step forward.

"The offices are closed to business." His narrow nostrils twitched.

"If he is here, I must see him." She smoothed her wild hair, knowing it must look as if she'd combed it with a broom.

The watchdog stepped out from behind his oak and marble barricade. "Miss, I'm going to have to ask you to leave. Mr. Kennebrae doesn't have time for casual callers. Reporters have been trying to gain access all day."

"I'm not a reporter." Josie's eyes widened. "Please, you've got to let me see him."

"Dawkins? Is there a problem?" Jonathan Kennebrae came down the staircase. His stern expression blew frost over Josie's hopes. "What can I do for you?"

"I need to see Mr. Kennebrae right away."

Jonathan's eyes looked her up and down. "He won't welcome you. He's very angry about what you did, giving Eli's designs to Fox." He crossed his arms.

"But I didn't! And I can prove it. Please, I have to see him. He's the only one who can help me." She clasped his arm, pleading with him.

He blew out a breath and shook his head, and for a moment Josie feared he wouldn't help her. Finally, he shrugged. "Come along then."

Dawkins retreated, head bowed.

Josie just avoided sending a triumphant glance his way as she took Jonathan's arm and allowed him to lead her upstairs. She looked back over her shoulder to make sure Giselle and Toni followed.

Jonathan escorted them through a door at the end of a long hallway.

Once inside Abraham Kennebrae's sanctum, the words clogged in her throat. He perched in his chair like a bird of prey, the sweeping views of the lake spreading before him. In the distance, the ships receded, steaming north to Two Harbors. Lightning split the sky, and the windows rattled with the crack of thunder that followed. As if the sound had burst the bottom of the clouds open, rain spattered the glass then sluiced down in a blurry sheet.

"Josephine." He turned hawk eyes toward them, so intense under lowered white brows her courage nearly deserted her. "Have you come to crow? Selling us out to Gervase Fox. Do you have any idea what you've done to Eli? What you've done to Kennebrae Shipping?" Though Jonathan made tamping down motions with his hands, Abraham stormed on. "You Zahns are turning out to be a rum lot."

"Mr. Kennebrae. . ." Her voice sounded small in the cavernous room. But she forged on, seeing again her father's profile on the deck of the *Vulpine*. Panic clawed her insides, forcing the words out though she wanted to flee his accusations. "Mr. Kennebrae, you have to stop this race."

He blinked and sat back.

She rushed on. "Fox's ship is unsafe. The hatches won't stand up to the strain, especially in a storm. I know you think I betrayed Eli, but I didn't. Mr. Fox stole the plans of the *Bethany* from my room." She turned to Giselle and drew the little girl forward. "Tell him what you told me about Mr. Fox."

Giselle took one look at Abraham and clamped her mouth shut. She gripped Josie's hand and lowered her chin, looking at the old man through her lashes.

"Please, Giselle, it's important."

"No, he's mean. He talked mean to you, Josie."

"I'll tell." Toni stepped forward, her hands on her hips. "That sneaky Mr. Fox came to our house pretending to be nice to Mama. But he wasn't really nice. He said he needed to use the washroom, but he didn't. He snuck into Josie's room and was in there a long, long time. That's where Josie keeps all her papers and drawings, all the stuff from helping Eli build his ship. And I think it's rotten of you to say Josie sold you out to Mr. Fox. She doesn't even like him. She'd never do anything to hurt Eli. She loves Eli."

Heat raced up Josie's cheeks.

Abraham looked up at her then returned his gaze to Toni. "She does, does she? And what makes you say that?"

"She's worked so hard on his plans. And she gets all dreamy after he visits, and I saw her kiss him in our garden. She wouldn't kiss him if she didn't love him."

Josie's humiliation was complete. If only she could evaporate right then.

Abraham fixed her with another sharp look. "That makes excellent sense, young lady. Now, tell me again about Mr. Fox."

Toni's hands came off her hips at his softened tone, and she edged forward, reciting once more how Mr. Fox had gone into Josie's room and looked through the papers on her desk.

"Josie, is there a problem with Fox's ship?" Jonathan cocked his head to the side.

"He took the plans from my room before I figured out the solution to the hatch flaw that had been plaguing Eli from the first. Fox has used the previous design, and it won't hold in rough seas. It might not give way during the race, but if any water comes over the bow, at best the hatches will leak, at worst they'll give way altogether."

She snatched a piece of paper off the desk and hastily sketched a few lines. "This is the old design. Unless he changed the specifications, they'll never hold. And here"—she scratched a rough outline—"is the new design. It's based upon a railroad coupling design, and it's much stronger. The rubber gasket paired with the new hatch closure will ensure a watertight seal."

Abraham, holding Toni's hand now, shook his head. "That's Fox's worry. Serves him right for stealing the plans in the first place."

"But Papa's on that ship." Giselle spoke up at last. "Is it going to sink?"

Jonathan knelt beside the little girl. "No, honey. Don't you worry. They'll be fine." He looked over her shoulder to his grandfather. "We'll see that your papa is safe. Won't we, Grandfather?"

Abraham scowled then motioned to the girls. "Why don't you girls check in the bottom drawer of my desk? There's a box in there. You can have whatever you like. Your sister and I are going to go out. Jonathan?" Abraham jerked his head toward the door. "Get someone to stay with the little girls, and then come downstairs."

Josie followed Mr. Kennebrae down the hall, his chair making no noise on the carpet. They entered a small elevator, and the old man pulled the lever for the first floor. "The ships are too far from shore to contact and stop. We'll have to see if we can intercept them while they're loading at Two Harbors." He shot out of the elevator across the lobby.

"By ship? Do you have a launch that can make it there so quickly?" Josie trotted after him.

"Not by ship. We'll go by motorcar up the Vermillion Trail." He snapped his fingers, and the watchdog by the door jerked to attention. "Get the car. . . and hurry."

Chapter 19

The ride up the North Shore was an adventure Josie would not soon forget. Exponentially more hair-raising than the gondola ride across the Duluth Channel. She bounced and bucked on the seat as scrub trees, rocks, and brief glimpses of the lake flashed by.

The driver, trench-coated and leather-gloved, took his employer at his word and kept the vehicle—a brand-new Oldsmobile—rocketing along the road. Rain poured down, and the wind howled off the water.

Several times on the journey, Jonathan turned to check on her from the front seat. Each time she tried to raise a smile and nod.

When the sturdy red brick lighthouse at Two Harbors rose before them and they bumped along the street toward the docks, Josie wanted to cry with relief. Both the *Vulpine* and the *Bethany* sat at the docks while two steam cranes loaded their gaping holds.

The car stopped at the end of the dock, and Josie shot out, not waiting for the Kennebraes.

The *Vulpine* sat closest to her, a group of men clustered around the crane. Fox strutted between the piles of lumber, pointing and directing traffic. Papa stood to one side, clutching an umbrella and observing the loading.

As she approached him, she looked over the side, fighting a bit of dizziness as a bundle swung from the end of the crane and into the hold far below. "Papa, I have to speak with you."

He gaped at her as if she had appeared out of the air. "What are you doing here, girl? And how'd you get here?"

"Papa, please, there isn't time. We need to stop the race and get the *Vulpine* home safely. Stop the loading. The more she's loaded, the worse the problem will become. She'll ride lower in the water and increase the likelihood that waves will break over the deck."

"Stop talking nonsense, Josephine. I know you fancy yourself some kind of engineer." He rolled his eyes. "It's my fault for letting your grandmother fill your head with nonsense. But you've no business butting in here. Fox has things well in hand. He'll win this race without too much trouble. We were in well ahead of the *Bethany*, and the loading's almost finished."

"It isn't nonsense, Papa. Please listen to me." She tugged at his arm, feeling as young as Giselle. "The ship isn't sound."

Abraham Kennebrae rolled near them, Jonathan right behind. "Listen to her, Radcliffe. We have to stop the race. Where's Fox?"

Fox rounded a stack of white pine. "I should've known you'd show up here. You've all but lost the race, Kennebrae. I'll be loaded and out of here in less than an hour."

"Mr. Fox, I know you stole the plans from my room." Josie clutched her coat closed at her throat and braced herself against the strong wind. "But you stole them too early. The hatch design you used won't hold in this weather. Especially when you're loading her so heavily. She'll have almost no freeboard if you fill her holds."

Fox ignored her words and sneered at Abraham. "Do you think I'm a fool? This is just another effort on your part to get me to lose this race. It won't work. I'm going to win, and the *Bethany* will belong to me."

No amount of arguing would change his mind, and Josie's father stood firm no matter how she pled with him.

"Let's go see Eli." Abraham pointed up the dock to the *Bethany*. "At the very least he should know to watch out."

The moment Josie dreaded now stared her in the face. She followed the Kennebraes down the dock, head down into the wind. Rain pounded across the dock and shocked her with its chill.

"Grandfather?" Eli spun on his heel when Abraham called out to him. "Jonathan? How did you get here?"

"Never mind that. Let's get out of this rain. We need to talk." Abraham rolled his chair toward the gangplank of the *Bethany*, and Jonathan grabbed the bar along the back to keep him from rolling off the side.

Eli turned to follow then froze. "Josie?" The incredulity and accusation in his eyes made her wish she'd never come.

∽

Why had she come? To gloat? To see for herself how the *Vulpine* fared against the *Bethany*? Eli had every confidence that Noah would best the *Vulpine* captain with a loaded boat in high seas. If Josie had come to lord it over him, she would be sorely disappointed.

Wind-whipped rain plastered her uncovered hair. She implored him with her eyes, her look slicing through him.

He quelled the rush of caring that rose over him. He knew a desire to shelter her from the elements, to take her into his arms. But she had betrayed him. Deceived him. His guard must remain firmly in place. "What do you want?" He kept his voice as cold as the rain.

"Eli, please, I know you're angry with me, but I had to come see Fox."

He turned away from her, the pain of her betrayal too great. From her own mouth she admitted coming to see Fox? "He's over there. Why come down here?" He pulled the collar of his oilskin higher. "No doubt he'll welcome you with open arms."

She shoved him hard enough to make him take a step to the side. "Stop being so thickheaded. I came because the *Vulpine* isn't seaworthy. It's the hatches."

He looked down into her face, streaked with rain and pinched with cold. A sodden lock of hair lay plastered to her pale cheek.

She grasped his forearm, her grip fierce. "Please, Eli, won't you listen? I know you think I betrayed you, and in a way, by lying about being Professor Josephson, I did. I'm sorry." She shook her head, remorse lining her brow. "But I didn't give your designs to Fox. He stole them. He got into my room and took the plans."

"No more lies, Josie." He disengaged her hand from his arm. "If you would lie about being an engineering professor, you'd lie about anything." A bitter taste coated his tongue and flowed down to flavor his heart.

Jonathan and Abraham appeared on the deck. A shout went up from a longshoreman near the crane.

Eli stepped back and pointed to the shore. "We're loaded. Go back to Duluth with Grandfather. I want to put this entire farce behind me."

"But, Eli, please. You have to listen to me. The *Vulpine*—"

Her pleading, and the fact that he felt himself weakening against it, irked him. "Don't talk to me about Fox or his ship. Just go."

Her shoulders drooped, and her chin went down. He couldn't be sure, but he thought a pair of tears mingled with the rain coursing down her cheeks.

His hands reached for her, but he stopped them in time. No, she wouldn't sway him with tears.

Jonathan pushed Grandfather's chair down the gangplank. Eli's oldest brother looked at Josie's defeated frame. His eyebrows shot down, and he glared at Eli. "Josie?"

She sniffed and shook her head, then turned and walked up the dock toward the shore.

Jonathan turned to Eli. "What did you do to her?"

Anger exploded in red bursts on the edge of Eli's vision. "What did I do to *her*?" He gestured in a wide arc. "Why is it that no one seems to care about what she did to me? She lied to me. She betrayed me, and she might've cost me this race."

Grandfather motioned for Jonathan to push his chair on. "Let's not waste time on this hardheaded goat. Get aboard, Eli, and get out of here. We've talked to Noah. He knows what to watch for, and *he* didn't doubt a word we said."

Eli didn't wait for them to leave. He stalked up the gangway and stormed into the pilothouse. The deck hands winched the last hatch cover into place and spun the wheels to tighten the gaskets. Josie's gaskets.

Noah settled into the tall captain's chair. The helmsman lounged against the front windows, waiting for the signal to move out. But it didn't come.

"What are you waiting for? Cast off the lines." Eli stuck his head back out the door to where the *Vulpine* was throwing off lines and preparing to leave the dock. "Hurry up. You're losing time."

Noah frowned at him, puzzlement clouding his eyes. "We're leaving second. Didn't you talk to Josie?"

"I talked to her all right. Not that it did her any good. She lied to me and sold me out. Nothing she can say will alter those facts. But we're going to win despite her betrayal. Now, cast off." Eli gripped the doorframe, every muscle tight.

Noah's eyes narrowed, appraising Eli. "What about those hatches? If we pull out ahead of them, we won't be able to keep an eye on them. I promised Grandfather and Jonathan we'd stick close in case Fox's crew needed help."

The *Vulpine*'s whistle sounded. She steamed by with the help of a tug, Fox's face grinning triumphantly from the pilothouse window, Radcliffe Zahn at his shoulder.

Panic seized Eli. "Hurry up! Cast off!" he yelled at the crewmen on the catwalk below the pilothouse. "Shove off!"

Noah rose and stood nose to nose with Eli. "Belay that order, helm. We'll wait until they clear the harbor. I'm the captain of this ship. You don't give orders to my crew."

"Then you do it. We're going to lose this race with your lying about. Don't you care that we might lose the *Bethany*? Don't you care that Fox will gloat and crow, that he and Josie will have duped us from start to finish?" Eli grabbed Noah's lapels. "She lied to me!" This truth scored him more deeply than anything else. Even losing the race wouldn't hurt as badly as losing his ability to trust Josie.

Noah gripped Eli's wrists. "Get ahold of yourself. Take a good look at that ship. Jonathan says Fox stole the plans for the *Bethany* from Josie's room, but he did it before she fixed the hatch problem. She's not seaworthy." He ripped Eli's hands from his coat. "We're going to follow them to make sure they get to port safely. In these seas and loaded like she is—" He broke off and returned to his seat. "Cast off the bowline."

The helmsman signaled to the dock, and the heavy ropes securing the ship fell away.

Noah dialed the chadburn to quarter speed, the familiar bell jangling through the room.

Eli pressed his hand against the window, staring after the *Vulpine*. He lifted the field glasses from the rack on the wall and brought the hatches near in his vision. Righteous indignation clogged his throat.

He turned the dial to sharpen the focus. The *Bethany* shuddered under his feet, shouldering away from the dock and thrusting forward through the chop of the bay. Pin hinges. The same pin hinges he'd wrestled with for weeks. The view began to shake, and he realized he was gripping the field glasses so hard his fingers trembled.

"All ahead full." Noah dialed the chadburn again.

The helmsman repeated the order with the obligatory "sir" tacked on the end.

"Did you see it?" The captain's question was directed at Eli.

"Yes, I saw it."

"Well?"

Eli returned the field glasses to the rack. Guilt raced up his arms and across his chest, pressing against him. All the accusations he'd hurled at Josie slammed through his head. "She was telling the truth."

"How do you know?" Noah's voice goaded Eli, taunting him, pushing him to admit things he didn't want to. "You said she lied to you."

Eli whirled around, his hands fisted, legs braced apart. "I know her. She would never put people in danger. She would never have given Fox that hatch closure design. She's the one who convinced me it was flawed in the first place."

"What about the professor bit?" Noah's eyes drilled Eli.

Eli made an impatient gesture. "That didn't bother me as much as the thought of her selling out to Fox. Imagine what it must be like to be a girl with those skills. Would you have taken her seriously if she'd come right out and admitted she wanted to be an engineer?"

Noah gave a low command to the helmsman then shook his head. "No. It never would've occurred to me that a woman could be so gifted. And that's no credit to me." He stroked his beard. "Melissa and Annie would have both our hides."

A smile quirked Eli's mouth in response. "I think Josie will fit in quite nicely with the Kennebrae brides, don't you?"

Noah quirked his eyebrow. "Little brother," he drawled out the jibe, "that particular ship has run aground. Your engagement needs a refit. Grandfather said they'd be waiting at Kennebrae House, and he'd make sure Josie was there."

∽

Eli bounded up the steps of Kennebrae House, shedding his coat and tossing it to McKay, not waiting for Noah or Radcliffe Zahn to climb out of the automobile.

"They're in the gallery, sir," McKay called after him. "Congratulations."

Eli waved a hand in acknowledgment and strode down the hall. When he entered the art gallery, he stopped at the sight of so many people in the room. The guests assembled applauded and clapped him on the back, shaking his hand.

"Well done, my boy." Grandfather edged forward in his chair.

"Thank you, sir. The *Bethany* is docked and unloaded."

"The messenger you sent from the dock told us you rescued the crew of the *Vulpine* before she went down. Heard Fox gave you a rough time. If he keeps it up, we'll sic Geoffrey on him and sue him for defamation."

A long buffet table stretched down the center of the room, with a splashing punch fountain, ice sculptures, and the best of the Kennebrae larder. People smiled and laughed, talking and eating, celebrating the Kennebrae victory.

Though this should've been the happiest moment of Eli's life, the pinnacle of his hopes and dreams for his design and his place in the Kennebrae family, he felt no joy. The past twenty hours, since Josie had walked away from him on the Two Harbors dock, had been the longest of his life. The rescue, the return trip, the unloading, a thousand-and-one details to see to, but nothing could crowd out the memory of her stricken expression when he'd rebuffed her and refused to listen.

Octavia Zahn rushed past him to cast herself into her husband's arms, clinging to him. Zahn bore it stoically, patting her shaking shoulder awkwardly, staring at the pipe organ, as if waiting for her to pull herself together. She did manage to gather herself but continued to dab at her eyes with a handkerchief and to hang on Zahn's arm. The little Zahn girls clustered around. But Josie wasn't among them.

Jonathan pressed a glass of punch into Eli's hand. "Well done, little brother. I'm proud of you."

Eli flicked a glance at his brother, nodding his thanks for the compliment, but continued to scan the room for the face he sought. His eyes rested on Melissa, her arms cradling Matthew, face serene. Noah, standing next to her, had Annie tucked into his side, his arm around her waist. The baby seemed fascinated with Noah's whiskers, staring round-eyed and somber into his uncle's face. Grandfather sat near the massive fireplace. Above him, a heavy gilt frame surrounded his favorite painting, an oil of the family yacht, the *Lady Genevieve*, skimming the waves of Lake Superior on a sun-drenched day.

"Nice job, Eli." Geoffrey slid through the crowd to shake Eli's hand. Clarice joined them, tucking her hand into Geoff's elbow. Geoff bent a smile down at her.

Eli's heart twisted with envy, wanting Josie so bad it made his chest ache. Though Grandfather had assured Noah she would be here waiting for their return, he hadn't spotted her in the crowd yet.

Jonathan nudged Eli. "Tell me about the rescue."

Eli shrugged. "The *Vulpine*'s hatches started taking on water, just like Josie said they would, and the bilge pumps couldn't keep up. About halfway to harbor, the forward hatch hinge pins broke loose. She listed hard, taking on water. Noah launched the lifeboat, and we rescued the crew. The *Vulpine* went down, and Fox is livid."

"He's got no one to blame but himself. Do you think she's salvageable?" Jonathan tasted his punch, made a face, and set it on a passing tray.

"If she didn't hit too hard on the lake floor, but it's pretty deep there," Eli answered absently, his chest churning. Where was she?

Then he saw her.

For a moment his heart stopped cold. . .then took up banging like pots in a ship's galley in a gale.

In the light of the electric lamps Grandfather had turned on to supplement the gaslight, her skin took on a porcelain delicacy. Her eyes looked enormous and sad. She stood a little apart, her attention decidedly away from where Eli stood. She twisted the middle fingers of her left hand with her right. And he saw the bare left ring finger.

Guilt stabbed him again. He thrust his punch cup into Jonathan's hand. "Hold this. I'll be right back." He took the stairs two at a time and jogged down the hallway to his room. The box sat right where he'd left it. He snatched it up and hurried back to the gallery on the first floor.

His heart beat fast when he spotted her again. He started toward her, but Grandfather's voice stopped him.

"Eli, come here. Speech!" The old man's voice rang out strong and imperious.

Heart trouble, my eye. He tried to ignore the call, skirting well-wishers, but the guests took up the chant. "Speech! Speech!"

Josie edged toward the door.

He needed to get to her before she left. Then he knew what he had to do.

༄

Josie again declined punch from the servant circulating. She couldn't eat or drink anything, not with the steel hawsers clamping around her middle.

Eli had ducked out of the party, after standing beside his brother and sipping punch like he hadn't a care in the world. She told herself she didn't care where he'd gone. He skidded into the room and looked from face to face as if searching for someone.

A sob surprised her, hiccupping out before she could squelch it. The room closed in, people and noise pressing against her until she couldn't stand it anymore. Solace and quiet were only a few steps away. She could slip out, and no one would notice.

A hand closed over her arm. "Where are you going, young lady?"

Grandma Bess. "I. . .I need some air." Josie stumbled over her words.

"You've got too much grit to turn tail and run now. Straighten up and show some backbone." Grandma Bess folded her arms, her ever-present valise banging against her waist.

How easy for Grandma to say, but just being in the same room with Eli and knowing he was lost to her forever was more than Josie could bear. What if they had met under other circumstances? What if she had told him the truth from the very beginning? What if he had believed her about Fox? What if, what if, what if?

The words pounded through her, leaving her aching and empty. When Eli responded to the calls for a speech, the lump in her throat grew so large she couldn't draw breath. *Lord, I can't do this. I know You've forgiven me, but having Eli doubt me. . . I just can't do this. Help me get out of here.*

Grandma Bess blocked the door.

"Ladies and gentlemen," Eli's voice cut through her like a hot knife, "no doubt you're expecting me to make some sort of eloquent speech praising myself and Kennebrae Shipping. But I'm not going to do that. Instead, I want to tell you about the person truly responsible for our victory." Eli stepped up on the hearth and scanned the crowd.

Josie couldn't help but stare at his handsome face, so earnest and alive.

"As you've no doubt heard, the *Keystone Vulpine* went down today in rough seas due to a design flaw. Though we at Kennebrae Shipping regret the loss of the ship and her cargo, we are grateful that no lives were lost. If I had had my own way, the *Bethany*, too, would've been built with these same design flaws, and the crews of two ships might have died today. Tragedy was averted due solely to the efforts of a brave young woman. Because she refused to bow to convention, refused to let stubborn men stand in her way, she corrected the flaw in my design and was brave enough to point it out when she noticed it on the *Vulpine*. If she hadn't exhibited such courage, the *Bethany* wouldn't have been in place to rescue her adversary's crew when they were in distress. Many lives would've been lost."

Josie blinked, her mouth going dry.

The guests looked at one another, puzzlement clear on their features.

"But that isn't what I most wanted to say about this remarkable young woman."

His eyes bored into hers across the room, compelling her to listen. She twisted her fingers harder, her knees quivering.

"This woman, beyond being the most capable engineer I've ever known, is beautiful, gentle, and caring. She has integrity and honor, and her loyalty knows no bounds. She's generous and forgiving." His gaze became warm, a smile playing about his mouth. "At least, I *hope* she's forgiving. You see"—he spread his hands in a gesture of appeal—"I've been an idiot where she's concerned. I didn't realize what a treasure I had until it slipped from my grasp. I treated her badly, and yet she didn't return hurt for hurt. She did the right thing when she broke our engagement."

Mama gasped, and Father pivoted to gape at her.

Josie wanted to sink through the floor. Did he have to announce their broken engagement before all of Duluth society?

But Eli wasn't finished yet. "I only hope she can forgive me yet again and accept the gift of my love. I'll never love another, for there's only one Josie." He stepped off the hearth and started toward her.

The crowd parted before him.

"When I asked you to marry me before, it was for all the wrong reasons. Now I'm asking you for the only right one. Forget about families; forget about contracts and ships and obligations. Put aside meddling grandfathers and blueprints and secret identities and all the things that have come between us, and know this. . .I love you, Josie Zahn. Will you marry me?"

Every head in the room swiveled to stare at her, but she couldn't take her eyes off Eli. Shock and disbelief welded her feet to the ground. Finally, Grandma Bess gave her a little push to get her started. Her legs shook with every step.

Eli met her halfway.

She stopped before him, staring up into his face, afraid to let go of the guard around her heart and believe his declaration. She didn't realize she was gripping her fingers tight until he eased them apart. The warmth of his touch penetrated her chill, and she looked down. The opal ring she'd so loved, that she'd dreamed of him putting on her hand, slipped onto her finger.

He cupped her face, his eyes imploring, full of love and remorse. "This ring comes with a couple of strings attached, you know."

"Strings?" The word came out a whisper, all she could muster under the circumstances.

He nodded. "Yeah. It comes with my heart. I'm useless without you. I love you, Josie. And I need to hear that you love me, too, and that you forgive me for being such an imbecile."

She blinked back tears that thickened her voice. "You're forgiven, Eli. I love you, too."

"Marry me?"

"Yes."

He folded her into his embrace, crushing her to him and bringing his lips down to hers.

All the hurt and misunderstanding, the uncertainty and guilt, washed away in the wonder of his love. She returned his embrace, giving and accepting love and forgiveness with her whole heart.

He raised his head but didn't release her as applause broke out around them.

Josie could barely breathe for the happiness welling up inside her.

Guests pressed forward to wish them well.

Eli kept his arm around her waist and, in a lull, pressed a kiss against her temple and whispered, "We'll sort everything out later, love."

A shiver raced up her spine, and she wondered if he would always affect her this way. "As long as you love me, there's nothing more that needs sorting out."

He squeezed her waist and kissed her again. His eyes took on a twinkle, and he inclined his head toward the fireplace.

Grandma Bess had taken a chair next to Mr. Kennebrae. Their white heads bent close together. "What do you suppose he's up to now?"

She giggled, happiness breaking over her again. "Plotting baby Matthew's engagement?"

Eli laughed. "We should turn the tables on him. I think your grandmother and my grandfather would make a nice couple, don't you?"

"Another Kennebrae-Zahn wedding? I think that's a wonderful idea."